MORSE'S
GREATEST
MYSTERY
&
SERVICE OF
ALL THE DEAD

Colin Dexter graduated from Cambridge University in 1953 and has lived in Oxford since 1966. His first novel, *Last Bus to Woodstock*, was published in 1975. There are now thirteen novels in the series, of which *The Remorseful Day* is, sadly, the last.

Colin Dexter has won many awards for his novels, including the CWA Silver Dagger twice, and the CWA Gold Dagger for *The Wench is Dead* and *The Way Through the Woods*. In 1997 he was presented with the CWA Diamond Dagger for outstanding services to crime literature, and in 2000 was awarded the OBE in the Queen's Birthday Honours List.

The Inspector Morse novels have, of course, been adapted for the small screen with huge success, by Carlton/Central Television, starring John Thaw and Kevin Whately.

MORSE'S GREATEST MYSTERY

&

SERVICE OF ALL THE DEAD

COLIN DEXTER

PAN BOOKS

Morse's Greatest Mystery first published 1993 by Macmillan as *Morse's Greatest Mystery and Other Stories*. First published by Pan Books 1994.
First published as *Morse's Greatest Mystery*
with the story 'As Good as Gold' and revisions and corrections by Pan Books 1995
Service of all the Dead first published 1979 by Macmillan.
First published by Pan Books 1996

This omnibus edition published 2004 by Pan Books
an imprint of Pan Macmillan Ltd
Pan Macmillan, 20 New Wharf Road, London N1 9RR
Basingstoke and Oxford
Associated companies throughout the world
www.panmacmillan.com

ISBN 0 330 43924 3

1 3 5 7 9 8 6 4 2

A CIP catalogue record for this book is available from
the British Library.

Photypeset by Intype, London Limited
Printed and bound in Great Britain by
Mackays of Chatham plc, Chatham Kent

MORSE'S GREATEST MYSTERY

FOR MY GRANDSONS
THOMAS AND JAMES

CONTENTS

AS GOOD AS GOLD

AS GOOD AS GOLD

> Whereby are given unto us exceeding great and precious
> promises: that by these ye might be partakers of the divine
> nature, having escaped the corruption that is in the world.
>
> (*2 Peter*, ch. 1, v. 4)

(i)

> *Admiring friend*: 'My, that's a beautiful baby you have there!'
> *Mother*: 'Oh, that's nothing – you should see his
> photograph.'
>
> (Anon)

Chief Superintendent Strange took back the snapshot of Grandson Number One (two years, three months) and lovingly looked at the lad once more.

'Super little chap. You can leave him with anybody. As good as gold.'

He poured a little more of the Macallan into each of the glasses.

Birthdays were becoming increasingly important for Strange as the years passed by – fewer and ever fewer of them left, alas. And he thought he was enjoying the little early-evening celebration with a few of his fellow senior officers.

Only two of them remaining now, though.

Quite predictably remaining, one of the two.

Musing nostalgically, Strange elaborated on memories of childhood.

'Huh! One of the first things I ever remember as a kid, that. This woman was looking after me when my ol' mum had to go out somewhere – and when she came back she asked her whether I'd been a good boy while she'd been away and she'd been looking after me – and she said she could leave me with her any time she liked because I'd been as good as gold. Those were the very words – "As good as gold".'

There was a short silence, before he resumed, briefly.

'I'm not boring you by any chance, Morse?'

The white head across the desk jerked quickly to the vertical and shook itself emphatically. Seven – or was it eight? – "she"s. With one or two "her"s thrown in for good measure? Yet in spite of the bewildering proliferation of those personal pronouns (feminine), Morse had found himself able to follow the story adequately, feeling gently amused as he pictured the (now) grossly overweight Superintendent as a podgy but obviously pious little cherub happily burbling to his baby-sitter.

All a bit nauseating, but . . .

'Certainly not, sir,' he said.

'You know the origin of the phrase, of course?'

Oh dear. Just a minute . . .

But Strange was already a furlong ahead of him.

'All to do with the Gold Standard, wasn't it? If you needed some gold – to buy something, say – well, it was going to be too heavy to cart around all the time – and there probably wasn't enough in the bank anyway. So they gave you a note instead – a bit o' paper promising to "pay the bearer" and all that sort of thing – and that bit o' paper was as *good* as gold. If you took that bit o' paper to the Bank of England or somewhere, you could bet your bottom dollar – well, not "dollar" perhaps – you know what I mean, though – you could get your gold-bar – if you really wanted it. You could have all the confidence in the *world* in that bit o' paper.'

Thank you, Mr Strange.

Clearly, in terms of frequency, the "bit o' paper" had usurped the personal pronouns (feminine). But Morse was apparently unconcerned, and nodded his head encouragingly as the bottle, now at a virtually horizontal level, hovered over his empty glass.

'You're not driving yourself home, Morse, I hope?'

'Certainly not, sir.'

'Little more for you, Crawford?'

Strange turned to the only other person there in the room, seated at the desk beside Morse.

'No more for me, thank you, sir. I shall have to get back to the office.'

'Still some work to do – this time of day?'

'Just a bit, sir.'

'Ah – the Muldoon business! Yes. Going all right?'

Detective Inspector Crawford looked rather less confident than Strange's putative bearer of the promissory bank-note.

'We're making progress, sir.'

'Good! Fine piece of work that, Crawford. Aggregation, accumulation of evidence – that's what it's all about, isn't it? I know we've got a few smart Alecs like Morse here who – you know, with all that top-of-the-head stuff . . . but real police work's just honest graft, isn't it? And I mean *honest*. We're winning back a lot of public support, that's for sure. We've taken a few knocks recently, course we have. Bad apples – one or two in every barrel; in every profession. Not here though! Not in our patch, eh, Morse?'

'Certainly not, sir.'

'Above suspicion – that's what *we've* got to be. Compromise on the slightest thing and you're on the slope, aren't you – on the slippery slope down to . . .'

5

Strange gulped back a last mouthful of Malt – clearly the name to be found at the bottom of the said slope temporarily eluding him. It was time to be off home. Almost.

'No, you can't afford to start on that.'

'Certainly not,' agreed Morse with conviction, happily unaware that he was becoming almost as repetitive as Strange.

'It's just like Caesar's wife, isn't it? "Caesar's wife must be above suspicion." You'll remember that, Morse. You were a Classics man.'

Morse nodded.

'What was her name?' asked Strange.

Oh dear. Just a minute . . .

Morse dredged his memory – unproductively. What *was* her name? She'd been accused (he remembered) of some extra-marital escapade, and Caesar had divorced her on the spot; not because he thought she was necessarily guilty, but because he couldn't afford to have a wife even suspected of double-dealing. Well, that's what *Caesar* said . . . Like as not he was probably just fed up with her; had some woman on the side himself . . . What *was* her name?

'Pomponia,' supplied Crawford.

Mentally Morse kicked himself. Of course it was.

'You all right, Morse?' Strange looked anxiously over his half spectacles, like a schoolmaster disappointed in a star pupil. 'Not had too much booze, have you?'

'Certainly not, sir.'

'You know,' Strange sat back expansively in his chair, fingers laced over his great paunch, 'you're a couple of good men, really. I know you may have cut a few corners here and there – by-passed a few procedures. Huh! But we've none of us ever lost sight of what it's really all about, have we? The

Police Force? Integrity, fairness . . . honesty . . .' – then, after a deep breath, an impressive heptasyllabic finale – 'incorruptibility.'

The Super had sounded fully sober now, and had spoken with a quiet, impressive dignity.

He rose to his feet.

And his fellow officers did the same.

In the corridor outside, as they walked away from Strange's office, Crawford was clearly agitated.

'Can I speak to you, Morse? It's very urgent.'

(ii)

'How did you get your wooden leg?'

Silas Wegg replied, (tartly to this personal inquiry), 'In an accident.'

(Charles Dickens, *Our Mutual Friend*)

Oxford Prison, closed permanently a few years earlier, had recently been re-opened as a temporary measure. And with nothing in life quite so permanent as the temporary, the prison officers now temporarily posted there were fairly confidently expecting a permanent sojourn in Oxford.

On the evening of Strange's birthday, a wretched man sat wretchedly on his bed in a cell on A-Wing. From what he had gathered so far, he feared that his own temporary accommodation there would very soon be exchanged for a far more permanent tenancy in one of Her Majesty's top-security prisons somewhere else in the UK.

The man's name was Kieran Dominic Muldoon.

The question at stake was not really one of innocence or

guilt, since there was universal consensus in favour of the latter. Even at the age of sixteen, Muldoon had been flirting with terrorism; and now, twenty years later, she had long been his permanent mistress.

That much was known.

It was now only a question of evidence – of sufficient evidence to shore up a case for a prosecuting counsel.

So far he'd been lucky, Muldoon knew that. Both in Belfast and in Birmingham, when he'd been detained, incriminatory links between people and places and plans had proved too difficult to substantiate; and the authorities had released him.

Had been compelled to release him.

This time, though, he'd surely been a bit *un*lucky?

He'd been conscious of that when they'd arrested him three days earlier from his Cowley Road bed-sit and taken him to St Aldate's Police Station in the City Centre, when with conspicuous confidence they'd straightaway charged him, and when the Magistrates' Court (immediately opposite) had granted a remand into custody without the slightest demur.

That, in turn, had been only a few hours after they'd discovered the explosive and the timers and the detonators out in the flat in Bannister Close on the Blackbird Leys Estate.

Jesus! What a mistake that had been to tell them he'd never been anywhere near the flat; didn't even know where the bloody block of flats *was*.

Why had they smiled at him?

Thinking back on things, he *had* felt uneasy that late afternoon a week ago when he'd gone along there – the *only* time he'd ever gone along there. He'd heard neither the clicks of any hidden camera nor the tell-tale whirr of a Camcorder; had seen no flashes; had spotted no suspicious unmarked van. No. It

must have been someone in one of the council houses opposite
– if they'd got some photographic evidence against him.

Because the police had got *something*.

So calm, this time. Especially that bugger Crawford.

So bloody cocky.

It couldn't be fingerprints, surely? As ever, the three of
them had been almost neurotically finicky on that score; and
the dozen or so cans of booze had been put into a black plastic
bag and duly consigned (Muldoon had no reason to doubt) to
one of the skips at the local Waste Reception Area.

But could they have been careless, and left something.

Because the police had got *something*.

Still, he'd kept his cool pretty well when they'd grilled him
on names, addresses, train-journeys, stolen cars, money-
transfers, weapons, explosives . . . For apart from a few
regular protestations of ignorance and innocence, he'd
answered little.

Or nothing.

It was at a somewhat lower level of anxiety that he worried
about the ransacking of his bed-sit. They must have found
them all by now.

The videos.

Ever since he could remember, Muldoon had been preoccupied with the female body, in which (as he well knew) he joined
the vast majority of the human race, masculine, and some
significant few of the human race, feminine. But in his own case
the preoccupation was extraordinarily obsessive and intense;
and intensifying as the years passed by – frequently satisfied
(oh, yes!) yet ever feeding, as it were, upon its own satiety.

Only thirteen, he had been, when the hard-eyed woman
had ushered him through into the darkened warmth of the

cinema where, as he groped for a seat, his young eyes had immediately been transfixed upon the luridly pornographic exploits projected on the screen there, his whole being jerked into an incredible joy . . .

Since he'd been in Oxford – three months now – he'd learned that the boss of the Bodleian Library was entitled to receive a copy of every single book published in the UK. And in his own darkly erotic fancies, Muldoon's idea of Heaven was easily conceived: to be appointed Curator of some Ethereal Emporium receiving a copy of every hard-porn video passed by some Celestial Film Censor as 'Suitable Only For Advanced Voyeurs', with crates of Irish whiskey and trays of stout and cartons of cigarettes stacked double-deep all round his penthouse walls . . .

Jesus!

How could he even begin to cope if they put him inside for five – ten – years? Longer?

Please, God – no!

He'd not started off wanting too desperately to change the world; indeed not too troubled, in those early days, even about changing the borders of a divided Ireland. Certainly never *positively* wanting to kill civilians . . . women and children.

But he had done so. Twice now.

Or his bombs had.

He rose from his bed, lit another cigarette, and with the aid of an elbow-crutch stomped miserably around the small cell.

Sixteen years ago the accident had been, in Newry – when he'd crashed a stolen car at 96.5 mph (according to police evidence). Somehow a piece of glass had cut a neat slice from the top of his left ear; and the paramedics had had little option but to leave his right leg behind in the concertina'ed Cortina.

All right, they'd given him an artificial leg; patiently taught him how to use it. But he'd always preferred the elbow-crutch; indoors, anyway. And no choice in the matter now, since the leg was back there in the bed-sit – in a cupboard – along with the videos.

Yes, they must have found them all by now.

And a few other things.

According to the solicitor fellow, they were still going through his room with a tooth-comb; still going through the flat in Bannister Close, too.

Jesus!

If they found him guilty – even on the possession of firearms and explosives charge . . .

Would he talk? Would he grass – if the police suggested some . . . some arrangement?

Course not!

He had a right to silence; he had a duty to silence.

Say nothing!

Let *them* do the talking.

He wouldn't.

Unless things became unbearable, perhaps . . .

Muldoon sat down on the side of his bed once more, conscious that just a tiny corner of his resolution was starting to crumble.

(iii)

You may not drive straight on a twisting lane.

(Russian proverb)

Twenty minutes later, Sergeant Lewis was still waiting patiently in the corridor outside the office of Detective

Inspector Crawford. He could hear the voices inside: Morse's, Crawford's, and a third – doubtless that of Detective Sergeant Wilkins; but the general drift of the conversation escaped him. Only when (at last!) the door partially opened did individual words become recognizable – and those, Morse's:

'No!' (*fortissimo*) 'No!' (*forte*) 'And if you take *my* advice, you'll have nothing to do with it yourself, either. There are better ways of doing things than that, believe me.' (*mezzo piano*) '*Cleverer* ways, too.'

Looking unusually perturbed, his pale cheeks flushed, Morse closed the door behind him; and the words 'Christ Almighty!' (*pianissimo*) escaped his lips before he was aware of Lewis's presence.

'What the 'ell are you doing here?'

'The Super rang me, sir. You told him I was running you back home.'

'So what?'

'Well, I *wasn't*, was I?'

'What's that got to do with Strange?'

'He was just checking up, that's all.'

'Suspicious bugger!'

'He didn't think you should be driving yourself.'

'You get off home. I'm fine.'

'You're not, sir. You know you're not.'

About to expostulate, suddenly Morse decided to capitulate.

'What was all that about, then?' asked Lewis, as they walked along the endless corridors towards the car-park.

*

12

(iv)

> Barring that natural expression of villainy which we all
> have, the man looked honest enough.
>
> (Mark Twain)

Behind them, in Crawford's office, Sergeant Wilkins gave vent to his exasperation:

'A stuffed *prick* – that's what *he's* getting!'

'That's unfair,' said Crawford quietly.

'But he doesn't seem to understand. We're not really *planting* evidence at all, are we? We've *got* the bloody evidence. It was all there.'

'*Was* all there,' agreed Crawford, dejectedly.

'How bloody unlucky can you get in life!'

Crawford was silent.

'You – you still going ahead with things, sir?'

'Look. I'll *never* let Muldoon off the hook now. I'll do *anything* to see that murderous sod behind bars!'

'Me, too. You know that.'

'It's just that I'd have been happier in my own mind if Morse had been with us. He worries me, you see. "Cleverer ways," he said . . .'

'Seems to me he's more worried about keeping his nose clean than seeing justice done.'

'Got a pension to worry about, hasn't he? He's finishing with us soon.'

A sudden thought struck Sergeant Wilkins:

'He won't . . . he wouldn't *say* anything about it, would he?'

13

'Morse? Oh, no.'

'Some people blab a bit – especially when they've had a drop too much to drink.'

'Not Morse. He's never had too much to drink, anyway – not as *he* sees things.'

'Not much help, though, is he?'

'No. And I'm disappointed about that, but . . .'

'But what, sir?'

Crawford took a deep breath. 'It's just that – well, I found it *moving*, what he said just now – you know, what he thought about what was valuable, what was important in life. The Super was saying exactly the same thing really, but . . . I dunno, compared with Morse he sounded sort of all big words and bull-shit—'

'Instead of all little words and horse-piss!'

'You've got him wrong, you know. He's a funny bugger, I agree. But there's a big streak of integrity somewhere in Morse.'

'Perhaps so. Perhaps I'm being very unfair.'

Crawford rose to his feet. 'Not *very* unfair – don't be too hard on yourself. Let's just say he's a stuffed shirt, shall we? That'd be a bit fairer than, er, than what *you* just called him.'

(v)

The colleague may be exceptionally thick-headed, like
Watson.

(Julian Symons, *Bloody Murder*)

The sole trouble with Malt Whisky, Morse maintained, was that it left one feeling rather thirsty; and he insisted that if

Lewis really wished to learn what had transpired in Crawford's office, it would have to be over a glass of beer.

Thus it was that, ten minutes after being driven from Kidlington Police HQ, Morse sat drinking a Lewis-purchased pint at the King's Arms in Banbury Road, and spelling out Crawford's unhappy dilemma . . .

Following information received, a flat in Bannister Close had been under police surveillance for several weeks. Patience had been rewarded, gradatim; and a dossier of interesting, suggestive, and potentially incriminating evidence had been accumulated.

At intermittent periods the flat, it was believed, served in three separate capacities: first, as a meeting-house for members of a terrorist cell (suspected of being responsible for the two recent bombing incidents in Oxford); second, as a storehouse for explosive and bomb-making equipment; third, as a safe-house for any other member of the group on the run from elsewhere in the UK.

For the police to rush in where hardened terrorists were so fearful of treading would have been to miss a golden opportunity of smashing an entire cell and of arresting its ringleaders. But, perforce, this softly-softly policy had been rescinded on the specific orders of the Home Office, following hot intelligence that a big step-up in terrorist activity was scheduled for mainland Britain in the spring. 'Damage limitation' – that was the buzz-phrase now. All very well waiting patiently to net some of the big fish – very laudable too! – but no longer justifiable in terms of potential civilian casualties.

Hence the slightly precipitate actions taken: first the

raiding of the flat, empty of people, yet full enough of explosive materials, bombing equipment, and fingerprints; second, the arrest of Kieran Dominic Muldoon, the only one of the shadowed terrorists who had established himself as 'of fixed address' in the City of Oxford.

Not the best of outcomes, certainly, since the other birds had by now abandoned their nests; as they would have done in any case, unless they had been cornered en bloc . . . or unless Kieran Muldoon could now be 'persuaded' in some way . . . bribed, cajoled, decoyed, lured, trapped – into betraying the whereabouts of his fellow fanatics . . . For example, there were two other properties being watched: one in Jericho; one out on the Botley Road.

There had been some *little* disappointment about the contents of Muldoon's own small living-quarters in the Cowley Road: a technical manual on bomb-making, though, and some dozens of addresses, code-names, telephone numbers: *almost* enough evidence there, and all duly impounded and documented and despatched for forensic tests and all the rest of it – and finally, of course, to be exhibited.

And – *and* – in addition to all this, two little solidly connecting links between Muldoon's bed-sit and Bannister Close.

Two little beauties!

The first, a can of Beamish stout, found under a sofa in the flat at Bannister Close, with Muldoon's fingerprints daubed all over it. The second, a photograph of Muldoon himself, climbing the outside iron staircase leading up to the balconied first floor there: an unequivocal, unambiguous photograph – both of the place, yes, and of the man – with the left side of his face in profile; and a splendid view of that unmistakable ear, a segment sliced so neatly from the top.

16

In addition the police had a taped interview with Muldoon, as well as a signed statement – the latter containing a firm denial of his ever having been at the Blackbird Leys Estate, let alone in Bannister Close.

Every procedure had been scrupulously followed from the start: a comprehensive register of exhibits had been typed out and checked; the key 'continuity' in the handling of these exhibits had been meticulously maintained; and the Exhibits Officer appointed was an experienced man, fully conversant with his specific responsibilities.

'Everything hunky-dory, Lewis. Except . . .'

'Don't tell me they've lost something?'

'Not "they"; "he".'

'The photo?'

'*And* the can!'

'Bloody hell! Who was he? Who *is* he?'

'Watson. Detective Constable Watson.'

'Poor chap!'

Morse grinned feebly. 'Perhaps he never *should* have been a detective – not with a name like that.'

'How did he come to lose—?'

'Ah! That's the good news, Lewis. He's not exactly lost them at all, so he says.'

'What's the bad news, then?'

'The bad news is he can't find them. Nor can half a dozen other people – who've been through everything umpteen times.'

Lewis, a man who swore very rarely, surprised his chief a second time:

'Bloody hell!'

'And Crawford, my colleague and *former* friend Crawford –

17

you'll never believe this! – is planning *to put them both back* on the Exhibits Register: the can and the photo.'

'How on earth does he think—?'

'That's where he thought I might come in.'

'Well, you can't really blame him too much, perhaps.'

Morse looked up in amazement, his blue eyes penetratingly fierce upon those of his subordinate. He spoke in a chilling hiss:

'What – did – you – say?'

Lewis sought to stand his ground: 'It's not – I mean, it's not as if he was *fabricating* the evidence, is it, sir?'

Morse exploded now, and several other customers turned round as they heard his furious rejoinder.

'What the hell *is* it, then – if it isn't fabrication? Come on, man! For Christ's sake tell me what *you* think it bloody well is!'

Lewis was badly taken aback. The blood had drained from his cheeks, and he could make no answer.

'*Facilis descensus Averno*,' mumbled Morse.

'Pardon, sir?'

'Forget it. And take me home!' Morse drained his beer and banged his glass down heavily on the table.

There was a supremely awkward silence between the two of them until the car pulled into Morse's parking-space outside his North Oxford flat. Then it was Lewis who spoke:

'Inspector Crawford,' he said slowly and quietly, 'was very kind to me when I first came to HQ – couple of years before I knew you. He's a good man. He wouldn't do *anything* that was basically unfair – I know that. So, if you will, sir, I want you to do me a big favour. I want you to go and see him, tell him that you told *me* about . . . things, and tell him that if I can do anything—'

18

But Morse cut him viciously short. 'Look, my son! Don't you start giving *me* bloody orders, all right?'

'I wasn't really—'

'*Shut up!* And if you don't forget all this bloody nonsense – now! – you stop being my sergeant, is that clear? And you won't be anybody else's bloody sergeant, either – not while I'm in the Force! You'll be queuing up for your dole money, like plenty of other poor sods. Is that understood?'

Morse got out of the car and slammed the door shut with an almighty bang.

(vi)

U-turn: a turn made by a vehicle reversing into the
direction of oncoming traffic, recommended only when
there appear no signs of oncoming traffic.

(*Small's Enlarged English Dictionary*, 12th edition)

Next morning, with extreme reluctance, with deep distaste – and with considerable embarrassment – Morse called into Crawford's office, and did his sergeant's bidding.

(vii)

Television is more interesting than people. If it were not,
we should have people standing in the corners of our rooms.

(Alan Coren, *The Times*)

He was being treated fairly well – better than he deserved or expected – Muldoon knew that. Even Crawford had been pretty reasonable: distanced, unsmiling, yes – but not *positively*

19

unpleasant. Told him about his rights: his right to receive a few visitors (he didn't want any of *them*!); to wear his own clothes; to have food brought in to him – if he could afford it, if he wanted it; to share in the recreational facilities provided, including TV and snooker . . .

So tight, the supervision though – oppressive, constricting supervision. How he longed to be *out* somewhere: out in the streets, out in a car, out in a pub – out anywhere.

Oh, Jesus!

With naked lust he looked at a photograph of a naked model taken in the sun, in the *Sun*, when the door of his cell was unlocked and Crawford (again!) came in.

It was all about those houses (again!) – those other houses the police had been watching: the Jericho house – the 'safe-house', as Muldoon had always known it; and that (much dodgier) semi-detached, semi-derelict little property out on the Botley Road. Why did Crawford keep going on about those bloody houses?

Why?

'You stayed in either of them, Muldoon?'

'No.'

'Never?'

'Never.'

'Any of your friends ever stayed there?'

'Stayed where?'

'Well, let's talk about Jericho first, shall we?'

'Where?'

'Jericho.'

'I thought Jericho was near Jerusalem.'

'What about Botley Road?'

'Which road?'

'You know, just down past the station.'

'You mean the bus station?'

'No. The railway station.'

'Never bin down there. Don't think so.'

'All right. So why not come out with us? Just to have a look, that's all.'

'No chance.'

'Might jog the memory, you never know.'

'No memory to jog, is there?'

'You *said* you'd never been to Blackbird Leys.'

'So?'

'We've got a photo of you there.'

'So you say.'

'Why not come out and have a quick look at these other places, that's all we ask?'

'No point, is there?'

Crawford half rose to his feet. 'Pity, you know. We could have made life that little bit easier for you, one way or another.'

'What's that s'posed to mean?'

'Look, Muldoon. We don't expect you to shop your mates. All I'm saying is this: if you agree to come out and make a couple o' statements – even if they're a load of rubbish . . .'

Muldoon not only looked puzzled; he *was* puzzled.

'What's it you're *after*? How the hell's it going to help you if—'

But Crawford, risen to his feet, now brusquely cut short Muldoon's protestations.

'No! You're right. It's not going to help much at all, is it? It was just that . . .'

'Yeah? Just *what*?' Muldoon leaned forward, interested in

21

spite of himself; and Crawford slowly sat down again on the hard, upright chair.

'Look, lad! Let me put my cards on the table. It's going to be bloody difficult for you to stay out of prison – this time. *I* know that – *you* know that. And shall I tell you something else? It's one helluva job – even for *me* – to get you out of this place, even for an hour or two; even to buy you a ride on one of the Tourist Buses. D'you know how many signatures I'd need for that – apart from the Governor's?'

Jesus!

Muldoon looked down at the floor as Crawford continued.

'There's only two ways we can give you any little outing. One's if you get transferred somewhere – up to Bullingdon Prison, say. Not very likely that, though, for a few weeks yet. And the other's if you'd agree to . . . But I'm wasting my breath. Pity though! As I say, we could have made it worth your while – *well* worth your while . . .'

Muldoon suddenly squared his mouth, and bared a set of ugly, deeply nicotined teeth.

'Come on! Spill it, Crawford. What's in it for *me*?'

'Not much. We couldn't afford to give you a season-ticket at the local knocking-shop, but . . .'

'But *what*?'

'Next best thing, perhaps?'

'Yeah? And what's that s'posed to mean?'

Crawford sighed. 'I can't make any marvellous promises – you know that. But if you agreed to keep your mouth shut – like *we* would . . .'

'Go on!'

'Well, what do you want? Fags? Booze? Money? Sex-videos? . . .'

Muldoon shook his head, albeit indecisively.

'OK. Well, that settles it, then.' Crawford rose quickly to his feet now, this time with a purposiveness heralding an imminent departure.

But Muldoon was on his feet too.

'When d'you reckon – when could this have bin? With the videos, say?'

Crawford shrugged indifferently. 'Tomorrow? Day after? Not quite sure, really. It's just that we got some pretty hot stuff in last week – from Denmark – and one or two of the lads thought they ought just to give it, you know, give it the once-over.'

'How long would they be? Watching that stuff?'

'Dunno, really. Couple of hours? Bit longer? Till the booze runs out? Some of 'em tell me they get a little bit bored – after a while. But I don't reckon they're going to get bored too quickly with this little lot.'

Muldoon sat silent for a while.

Muldoon sat silent for a considerable while.

Finally he breathed in deeply, held his breath – and exhaled, noisily.

Then he lit yet another cigarette.

And another little corner of his resolution was collapsing. Had collapsed.

'Tomorrow, you say?'

Phew!

Outside the re-locked room, Inspector Crawford also exhaled, though silently. And to Sergeant Wilkins, standing at the far end of the corridor, he gave a faint smile, and raised his right fist to shoulder-level, the thumb upstandingly proud like some *membrum virile* blessed with a joyous erection.

23

(viii)

The fastest recorded time for completing *The Times* crossword under test conditions is 3 minutes 45 seconds, by Mr Roy Dean, of Bromley, Kent.

(*The Guinness Book of Records*)

After returning from Inspector Crawford's room late that same afternoon, Sergeant Lewis found Morse seated at his desk, *The Times* in front of him, looking grim – and smoking a cigarette. It seemed to Lewis, in view of the tight-lipped taciturnity hitherto observed between the pair of them throughout the day, that it was the latter activity which afforded the more promising ice-breaker.

'I thought you'd given up, sir?'

'I have – many times. In fact I've given up smoking more often than anyone else in the history of the habit. By rights I should have a paragraph all to myself in *The Guinness Book of Records*.'

The tone of Morse's words was light enough, perhaps, but the underlying mood was sombre.

And Lewis, too, as he sat down, looked far from happy with himself.

'You told me off good and proper last night, didn't you, sir? *And* I deserved it. You were right. To be truthful, I wish I'd taken a bit more notice of you.'

'Why this sudden change of heart?'

'Well, it's getting . . . it's getting all a bit involved and underhand—'

'Dishonest.'

'Yes . . . and *messy*.'

24

The hard lines on Morse's face relaxed somewhat. 'You can hardly expect the sort of classical economy and purity of line you get when you're working with me! Crawford's a cretin – that's common knowledge, isn't it?'

'No he's not! It's just that – well, I don't honestly think he's *all that* bright.'

'Your judgement is reasserting itself, Sergeant.'

Lewis was silent.

'Come on. You know you're dying to tell me all about it.'

'I thought you didn't want anything to do with it.'

'How right you are!' snapped Morse bitterly.

He got up and took his mackintosh off its peg.

A persistent drizzle had stippled the window that looked out over the car-park – a window through which Lewis had so often seen Morse gazing as he grappled in his mind with the problems of a case.

Saw him so gazing now; but only for a few seconds, before he put on his mackintosh and walked to the door.

'Make sure you lock up! If there's some crook around prepared to pinch an empty can of Beamish, what the hell's he going to do with my Glenfiddich? Goo' night!'

The door slammed, and Morse was gone.

But Lewis heard no footsteps along the corridor; and twenty seconds later the door re-opened slowly, and Morse stepped back into his office.

'It *would* help, Lewis, wouldn't it, if you told me what's worrying you.'

'Yes,' replied Lewis simply.

'You should have told me earlier.'

'You looked, well, pretty grim, sir.'

'What? Oh, that! That was just *me* – not you. Six minutes –

to the second almost – with the crossword! Would have been just about the record – except for one clue: I couldn't do 14 across. *Still* can't do bloody 14 across.'

'Shall *I* have a look at it?'

'You? Fat lot o' use that'd be!'

Lewis looked down at the threadbare patch of off-white carpet on his own side of Morse's desk.

'If you *could* spare five minutes, sir – I'd feel a lot happier.'

Morse took off his mackintosh, replaced it on its peg, and resumed his seat in the black-leather armchair behind his desk.

(ix)

Now faith is the substance of things hoped for, the evidence
     of things not seen.

(*Hebrews*, ch. 11, v. 1)

As Morse now began to see, Crawford's scheme hardly matched the strategic genius of Napoleon at Austerlitz, or NASA in planning one of its moon missions . . .

At 20.30, an hour after lighting-up time, on Thursday, 31 March, Muldoon, handcuffed to a police officer, his head concealed from any inquisitive public or press intrusion beneath a grey prison blanket, would be taken from Oxford Prison in an unmarked police van. The outing had already been sanctioned (no problem) 'in pursuance of corroborative or associative evidence'. No one had ever understood this long-winded phrase, yet it had the merit of sounding most impressive.

The prisoner would be taken first to Jericho, then to Botley; shown over the two properties in question; and invited, on each occasion, to make a brief statement. This, in truth, in the interests of verisimilitude only. Yet (as Crawford maintained) there was always just the possibility that Muldoon *would* say something of value. Prisoners had grassed in the past; prisoners would grass in the future.

Thereafter things would become a little more complicated.

Muldoon would then be informed that the reward for his co-operation lay some ten miles away, along the A40, in a police-house in Witney. In fact, the van would be driven out from Botley on to the western Ring Road; and, after a suitably convincing 'ten-mile' detour, would land up in the Blackbird Leys Estate, on the eastern side of Oxford, beyond the Rover car-plant at Cowley.

At which point, Crawford's careful, albeit clumsy, planning would enter its critical phase.

The outward appearance of Bannister Close might well be fairly familiar to Muldoon. Although he had visited the flat only once (as it appeared) there was the real possibility that he might recognize some aspect of the block – its architectural style, its black-painted balcony, the colours of its doors and windows – even in semi-darkness. And no risks could be taken.

Therefore . . .

Muldoon, still handcuffed, would be dropped off at the *rear* of the block, where a main road ran behind the back of the properties. In the interests of public safety a five-foot fence of vertical wooden slats had been erected to separate this road from Bannister Close. But as in so many parts of the Estate, vandals had been at work here too, and several irregular gaps had been kicked through the fencing; and (Crawford had done his homework) there was a most convenient opening, two or three feet wide, in the stretch almost immediately behind Number 14.

Easy.

And since a fairly steep grassy slope led down from the fence to the concreted path running beside the rear entrance to the flats, it seemed wholly unlikely that a man with only one leg was going to be too deeply engrossed in his environment.

The flat originally raided was on the first floor, with access only via an external stairway, one at each end of the block. But by a stroke of good fortune, the flat beneath it, on the ground floor, was empty; had been empty for several months – the For Sale notice stuck into the scratty patch of weedy waste which passed itself off in the property's specification as 'a small front garden'. And it was to be in the living-room of *this* flat (Crawford had decreed) that the scene was to be set: off screen, and on screen, as it were.

One of Crawford's old colleagues, now a senior member of the Obscene Publications Squad – a man with the not inappropriate name of Cox – would be providing an outsize TV screen, together with a veritable feast of video-sex for the viewers. Only five viewers though: Cox himself, Crawford, Wilkins, Lewis – and Muldoon.

An inviting tray of Beamish stout would be available, and the four police officers would each nonchalantly help themselves from it, drinking straight from the cans – no glasses! And a man who had tasted no alcohol for a week – and an Irishman, to boot – would surely speedily succumb.

And if he didn't? Well, no real worry.

Quite a few props would be required to set the stage and –

wait for it! – behold now Crawford's *coup de grâce*! A ridiculously oversized furniture-van had been hired to convey a carpet, four chairs, a settee, a table, a large TV set . . .

Wait!

. . . and this van would *still* be parked outside the property when, after the final curtain, Muldoon would emerge – *through the front door*. And there, bang in front of him, instead of a potentially recognizable prospect, would stand the great pantechnicon, blocking anything and everything – particularly the council houses opposite.

And now – O Napoleon! – mark a stroke of rare genius. Not only would the van serve to bring the props; not only would it conceal the view over that unlovely neighbourhood; *it would also house the photographer*, who would once more capture Muldoon on film outside the very place of which earlier he had so vehemently denied all knowledge. This time, though, from much closer quarters – from behind a grille (removed) in the side of the van, with a camera loaded with 1000 ASA film, and positioned on a tripod to prevent any shake.

And that would be that. A whole *series* of shots this time. *And* (Crawford had averred) if DC Watson or some other incompetent idiot lost *those*, then good luck to Muldoon and his co-criminals! The police wouldn't deserve to catch, or the courts to convict them.

But that wouldn't happen again.

For Muldoon it would be back to Oxford. Back to prison. And very soon, if there were any justice in life, back to prison *for* life. For whatever the dishonesty of the scheme devised against him, Muldoon was a cruel and murderous bastard.

There could be no mistake on that score.

(x)

If I repent of anything, it is very likely to be my good
behaviour.

(Henry David Thoreau)

Such was Lewis's account – of Crawford's account – itself, in
turn, transmuted in Morse's mind to the heightened version
presented to the reader in the preceding paragraphs.

When it was finished, Morse looked almost as puzzled as
(apparently) the prisoner himself had looked earlier.

'Has Muldoon got any idea that things have gone missing?'

'Seems not, sir.'

'He must be suspicious, though – about being offered
something for nothing? It's surely very improbable, isn't it,
that he's going to spill any beans?'

'We *do* get informers, though. *And* they get paid.'

'Unusual currency – sex-videos.'

'Well, that's his particular taste, according to Crawford.
They found dozens of 'em in his room. Not natural, is it?'

'Not all that *un*-natural, would you say?'

'Have you *seen* some of these videos?'

'No, Lewis. Unlike you, I've lived a very sheltered life. I
have *tried* to get invited along to one of these porno-parties,
but everybody seems to think I'm above such things.'

'You wouldn't enjoy 'em, sir. They make you feel – well,
cheap, somehow.'

'Perhaps most of us *are* cheap.'

Lewis shook his head. 'And goodness knows what the
missus would say if she knew.'

'*Need* she know?'

'You'd understand better if you were married, sir.'

Morse was silent for a short while before continuing. 'I'll tell you one thing: I wish I could understand *Crawford* better. Why doesn't he do things a bit more *simply*?'

'What are you thinking of?'

'Well, if he's lost a beer-can, why doesn't he just give the fellow *another* beer-can – and then stick it in the exhibits locker?'

'I'm not sure. But I think he feels it'll salve his conscience a bit if it comes from Blackbird Leys, you know – not from the prison.'

'What's the difference? It's dishonest either way.'

'You'd have to ask Crawford that. I don't know.'

'And why not just *fiddle* the photo? I know a Spanish chap – name of McSevich—'

'Spanish? With a name like that?'

'Like you, Lewis, I am not privy to some of the greater mysteries in life. All I know is that this chap's a wizard with a camera. He can stick a ghost in the middle of a group-photograph – all that sort of fake stuff. He can probably let you have a snap of the Home Secretary outside a strip-club – in his jock-strap.'

'In the dark.'

Morse grinned. 'No problem.'

'That would be even *more* dishonest, though.'

'What? What are you talking about?'

'I think – I *think* I understand why Crawford's doing it this way.'

'You *do*? Well, tell me. Come on! Come on, Lewis! Try!'

Lewis took a deep breath. It was going to be difficult – but he would try.

'Look at it this way, sir. If I – let's say I was being unfaithful to the missus and going off somewhere with a lady-friend. Let's say I'd told the missus I was going by train – but I wasn't really going by train at all, because this lady-friend was going to pick me up in her car somewhere, all right?'

'Lewis, I look at you in a completely new light!'

'It's just that I'd rather have a taxi actually *take* me to the station, and get picked up *there* – rather than meet in St Giles' or somewhere. I know you wouldn't understand something like that, but . . .'

'But I do,' said Morse quietly. 'I know exactly what you mean.'

Lewis felt encouraged to add a gloss: 'It's as if Crawford's only prepared to be dishonest in an honest sort of way.'

Morse recited the couplet that had been going through his mind:

> 'Honour rooted in Dishonour stood,
> And Faith, unfaithful, kept him falsely true.'

'Who wrote that, sir?'

'Forget.'

Morse rose from his desk, a final thought striking him.

'You know, if your prisoner's going to be handcuffed all the while, it's bound to be a funny old photo, isn't it? Won't it give the game away?'

'No. He's only got one leg. And he couldn't scarper if he wanted to. Even *you* could catch him if he tried anything on, sir.'

'Thank you very much!'

Lewis too rose from his chair, reluctantly, unhappily – and made his decision.

'I'm going back to see Inspector Crawford. I'm not having anything to do with it. I'm letting him down, I know – after what I told him. But I – it's just not on. I can't do it. He'll have to find somebody else.'

Morse came round the desk and placed a hand on Lewis's shoulder.

'You get off home and see the missus. Leave all this to me. I'll go along and see Crawford myself. Have no fears!'

'You're sure, sir?'

'Absolutely. There'll be no trouble finding somebody to take your place.'

After Lewis had gone, Morse walked over to the window, and spent several minutes gazing out across the car-park.

(xi)

All men are tempted. There is no man that lives that can't
be broken down, provided it is the right temptation, put in
the right spot.

(Henry Ward Beecher, *Proverbs from a Plymouth Pulpit*)

When, after Muldoon, he had squeezed himself through the gap in the fencing, Morse stood beside his charge and unlocked the handcuffs – almost immediately to realize that the man with only one leg and an elbow-crutch was considerably more nimble than he in negotiating the grassy slope at the rear of the Bannister Close flats.

But Muldoon was patiently waiting for his escort, on the concreted path, when Morse finally effected his descent, the palm of his left hand ever reaching out for support to the side wall of a row of sheds in which the residents of the block doubtless stored bicycles, and old lawnmowers, and (inevitably) virtually empty pots of house-paint.

The ground here was liberally littered with crisp and cigarette packets and all the usual detritus of a run-down neighbourhood: a circumstance most grievous to Chief Inspector Morse. But the first part of the operation had been accomplished successfully, and sufficient light was thrown from the lace-curtained, white-painted windows there for Morse to see exactly where they were. Behind the kitchen window of Number 13, beside a carton of Persil washing-powder, was a 'Vote Conservative' poster, propped upside-down against a broken pane.

Morse had done his homework too.

'Sh!'

Morse raised a finger to his lips, then pointed across to the right – towards the far end of the flats. He spoke very quietly:

'Let me know if you hear a whistle. That'll be Sergeant Wilkins, giving us the all-clear.'

Muldoon nodded.

'Or if you hear anything else for that matter,' mumbled Morse, moving over to Muldoon's right.

For half a minute or so, the two men stood there side by side, unmoving, silent.

No noise.

Then, all of a sudden, to the left, at some point at the side of the sheds, there was the sound of a metal dust-bin lid, as if blown off its base in a gust of wind and now rumbling in a decelerating circle.

Muldoon whipped himself round immediately to face the

direction whence the rattle had originated, crouching down instinctively, and remaining frozen for several seconds – both he and Morse (the latter still facing the opposite way) experiencing a frisson of fear, though each for a different reason.

'Wha's tha'?' whispered Muldoon.

But Morse made no answer, and the night, beneath the darkly overcast sky, was wholly still once more.

No more noise at all, in fact; and if there had been a low whistle from the far end of the block, it was heard by neither escort nor prisoner.

Instead, Inspector Crawford now appeared at the double-fronted glass doors slightly further along; and first Muldoon, then Morse, stepped over the threshold into the living-room of Number 13 Bannister Close.

(xii)

High definition is the state of being well filled with data. A photograph is, visually, 'high definition'.

(Marshal McLuhan, *Understanding Media*)

Although he had lost his religious faith many years since, Morse still retained a sort of residual religiosity; and two days after the bizarre incidents just described, he was seated, in mid morning, in his North Oxford flat, listening with awesome reverence to the Fauré *Requiem* – when the door-bell rang.

'Can I come in, Morse?' Ill-at-ease, on the doorstep, stood Inspector Crawford.

'Look,' he began, seated a minute later opposite Morse in the lounge. 'I just want to thank you for your help, that's all. I know you didn't approve of what I did, but . . .'

'What's gone wrong?' asked Morse, reluctantly switching off the CD player.

Crawford shook his head sadly. '*Every* bloody thing – that's what! You remember that Beamish we had—'

'Much appreciated!'

'—it was a new thing of theirs. "Cask Pour", they call it.'

Morse knew all about such things: 'All the flavour from a can you'd normally expect from a barrel – that's the idea.'

'Yes, but *that* particular product only came on to the market on the 28th March – *last Monday* – you couldn't get it before then. Big launch on the telly, in the papers . . .'

'So . . . so the can with Muldoon's fingerprints on it . . . ?'

'Yes! Couldn't *possibly* have come from the flat at the time we raided it.'

'Will anybody notice, though?'

'Watson noticed.'

'Not PC Watson?'

'PC Watson!'

Morse raised his eyebrows. 'I see what you mean,' he said slowly. 'Not exactly an Einstein, is he?'

'And if *he* noticed it . . .'

'Ye-es.'

'All that palaver, Morse – and I go and act like a greenhorn.'

'Never mind. You've got your photographs.'

'No! They're no bloody good either!'

'Don't tell me your fellow forgot to put a film in the camera?'

'Oh no. He took some fine photos. Marvellously clear – too bloody clear. You see, Muldoon almost *never* ventured out and about with his elbow-crutch – I'd forgotten that. And the original photo we took showed him with an artificial leg. Course it bloody did!'

'Oh dear! Did, er, did Watson spot that as well?'

'He did.'

'You know, if that fellow could only stop losing things, he'd probably make "inspector".'

'He can have my job any time he likes!'

'Can't you just cut the bottom off the photos?' suggested Morse.

'Trouble is, I'd cut off the flat numbers as well if I did that – the way they've turned out; then they might just as well have been taken in Timbuktu as in Bannister Close.'

'I take your point,' said Morse.

'Anyway, I didn't come here to burden you with my troubles. As I say, I just wanted to thank you – in person. I didn't want to say anything over the blower – can't be too careful. So – if we can . . . if we can just, well, draw a veil over things? And I'm sorry I've been such a cretin.'

Morse got to his feet and stood in front of Crawford.

'Don't say that.' He spoke in a kindly fashion, oblivious (it appeared) that this was the self-same word he'd used so recently himself to describe his fellow officer. 'You could do with a drink.'

'I could do with *two*,' corrected Crawford.

Morse went to his drinks-cabinet and took out the Glenfiddich, at the same time switching on again, albeit softly, the 'In Paradisum' from the Fauré *Requiem*.

(xiii)

> I am a camera with its shutter open, quite passive,
> recording, not thinking.

> (Christopher Isherwood, *Goodbye to Berlin*)

Four days later, on Wednesday 6 April, an oblong buff envelope ('Please Do Not Bend') arrived by Registered Delivery at the Thames Valley Police HQ, addressed to Chief Inspector Morse.

Inside the envelope, together with two very glossy black-and-white photographs, was an invoice – and a letter:

Morse, old boy,

Sorry about the delay – Easter post and all that. Not bad, are they? Cheque please, as per invoice, asap. No extra fee charged for knocking over that bloody dust-bin! What will you think of next?

Pity I couldn't get the crutch in – he'd turned too far round. Interesting configuration of the left ear, though. I trust you'll approve of the 'topographically recognizable setting' (your specification). In fact the capsized Tory poster is a nice little prop, don't you reckon?

By the way, what the hell are they doing voting Tory down there?

Yours aye,

Manuel (McS)

PS Did I mention the cheque – asap?

Morse looked at the two photographs; and like the Almighty surveying one of his acts of Creation, he saw that they were good.

He reached for the phone and rang Inspector Crawford to tell him of his eleventh-hour reprieve – soon learning from Sergeant Wilkins that Crawford had just been called in to see Strange. He'd pass the message on, though.

(xiv)

Confessions are good for the soul but bad for the reputation.

(Thomas Robert Dewar)

When, half an hour later, Crawford came in, Morse reached into a drawer for the envelope. But it was Crawford, looking preternaturally pleased with himself, who immediately seized the initiative.

'I was just going to call *you*. You'll never guess what's happened.'

'Watson's unearthed his lost exhibits?'

'Better than that.'

'They've just appointed PC Watson Chief Constable?'

Crawford blurted it out: 'Muldoon! He's changed his plea – through his lawyer. He's pleading guilty as charged on all counts. *And* he's come clean on the Jericho and Botley places. *Very* interesting what he's told us about *them*. Complete change of heart, that's what he's had, Muldoon – with the, er, encouragement of some, you know – one or two little privileges.'

'Well done!' said Morse, quietly slipping the envelope back into its drawer.

'And *Strange*? He's over the moon.'

'Everybody'll be pleased.'

'Lucky though, wasn't I?' said Crawford reflectively.

'We all deserve a little bit of luck now and then,' said Morse.

After Crawford had gone, Morse once more took the photographs from their envelope, and looked at them briefly again – especially at that neatly sliced left ear – before slowly tearing them up and dropping the pieces into his waste-paper basket.

Then he wrote out a cheque, and addressed an envelope to Manuel McSevich, Esquire, The Studio, High St., Abingdon, Oxon. It seemed to Morse a quite disproportionate sum to pay; yet, perhaps, not totally exorbitant – considering the nature of the entertainment which that most unusual of evenings had provided.

(xv)

> If children grew up according to early indications, we
> should have nothing but geniuses.

> (Johann Wolfgang von Goethe)

Only very occasionally did Superintendent Strange patronize the canteen at HQ. But that lunchtime, as the solitary Morse sat at a corner table, his back to his colleagues, rather dejectedly sipping a bowl of luke-warm leek soup, he felt a hand on his shoulder.

'Can I join you?'

Morse nodded a supererogatory 'yes', as Strange unloaded from his tray a vast plateful of steak-and-kidney pie, two

40

bread rolls, and a substantial wodge of treacle-tart covered – nay smothered – with custard.

'You heard about Muldoon, Morse?'

'Inspector Crawford told me the good news.'

Strange rubbed his hands gleefully. 'Excellent, isn't it? Excellent! Not the slightest suspicion of any undue police pressure either – you know that!'

'So I understand, sir.'

'*Above* suspicion, eh? Like Caesar's wife.'

'Let's hope so.'

'*You* couldn't remember her name, could you?'

'No.'

'Crawford could, though.'

Morse nodded. Crawford was clearly the flavour of the month. So be it.

'You're not eating much?' queried Strange, forking another great gobbet of meat into his mouth.

'I'm not very hungry today.'

'It's a wonder you're not in the pub, then. You're usually *thirsty* enough.'

The reminder did little to lighten Morse's mood; and in sycophantic fashion he quickly sought to change the drift of the conversation.

'How's that little grandson of yours, sir?'

'Fine. Absolutely fine! Did I show you his latest photo?'

Morse nodded, hurriedly. 'Still behaving himself?'

For a few seconds, Strange looked slightly uneasy – before leaning over the almost empty plate of treacle-tart, a mischievous glint in his eye.

'To tell you the truth, Morse, his mother rang us only last

41

night. Seems she left him with a baby-sitter when she went to church for Easter-morning service. And d'you know what the little bugger did? He went and bit the bloody baby-sitter's hand!'

'Just a temporary lapse,' suggested Morse.

'Course it was! We can't be good *all* the time, can we? None of us can.'

Morse nodded slowly. 'No, sir. We all have the occasional moment when we're not – we're not particularly proud of ourselves.'

Strange appeared gratified by this latter sentiment; and after spooning up his last mouthful of custard he sat back, replete and relaxed. Taking out his wallet, he extracted, just as he had done a week earlier, the latest snapshot of Grandson Number One (two years, three months).

'Super little chap, Morse. You can leave him with anybody – well, *almost* anybody! As good as gold, almost.'

As if with mutual understanding, the two policemen looked at each other then.

And smiled.

MORSE'S
GREATEST MYSTERY

'Hallo!' growled Scrooge, in his accustomed voice as near as he could feign it. 'What do you mean by coming here at this time of day?'

(Dickens, *A Christmas Carol*)

He had knocked diffidently at Morse's North Oxford flat. Few had been invited into those book-lined, Wagner-haunted rooms: and even he – Sergeant Lewis – had never felt himself an over-welcome guest. Even at Christmas time. Not that it sounded much like the season of good-will as Morse waved Lewis inside and concluded his ill-tempered conversation with the bank manager.

'Look! If I keep a couple of hundred in my current account, that's *my* look-out. I'm not even asking for any interest on it. All I *am* asking is that you don't stick these bloody bank charges on when I go – what? once, twice a year? – into the red. It's not that I'm mean with money' – Lewis's eyebrows ascended a centimetre – 'but if you charge me again I want you to ring and tell me *why*!'

Morse banged down the receiver and sat silent.

'You don't sound as if you've caught much of the Christmas spirit,' ventured Lewis.

'I don't like Christmas – never have.'

'You staying in Oxford, sir?'

'I'm going to decorate.'

'What – decorate the Christmas cake?'

'Decorate the kitchen. I don't like Christmas cake – never did.'

'You sound more like Scrooge every minute, sir.'

'*And* I shall read a Dickens novel. I always do over Christmas. *Re*-read, rather.'

'If I were just *starting* on Dickens, which one—?'

'I'd put *Bleak House* first, *Little Dorrit* second—'

The phone rang and Morse's secretary at HQ informed him that he'd won a £50 gift-token in the Police Charity Raffle, and this time Morse cradled the receiver with considerably better grace.

'"Scrooge", did you say, Lewis? I'll have you know I bought five tickets – a quid apiece! – in that Charity Raffle.'

'I bought five tickets myself, sir.'

Morse smiled complacently. 'Let's be more charitable, Lewis! It's *supporting* these causes that's important, not *winning*.'

'I'll be in the car, sir,' said Lewis quietly. In truth, he was beginning to feel irritated. Morse's irascibility he could stomach; but he couldn't stick hearing much more about Morse's selfless generosity!

Morse's old Jaguar was in dock again ('Too mean to buy a new one!' his colleagues claimed) and it was Lewis's job that day to ferry the chief inspector around; doubtless, too (if things went to form) to treat him to the odd pint or two. Which indeed appeared a fair probability, since Morse had so managed things on that Tuesday morning that their arrival at the George would coincide with opening time. As they drove out past the railway station, Lewis told Morse what he'd managed to discover about the previous day's events . . .

The patrons of the George had amassed £400 in aid of the Littlemore Charity for Mentally Handicapped Children, and this splendid total was to be presented to the Charity's Secretary at the end of the week, with a photographer promised from *The Oxford Times* to record the grand occasion. Mrs Michaels, the landlady, had been dropped off at the bank in Carfax by her husband at about 10.30 a.m., and had there exchanged a motley assemblage of coins and notes for forty brand-new tenners. After this she had bought several items (including grapes for a daughter just admitted to hospital) before catching a minibus back home, where she had arrived just after midday. The money, in a long white envelope, was in her shopping bag, together with her morning's purchases. Her husband had not yet returned from the Cash and Carry Stores, and on re-entering the George via the saloon bar, Mrs Michaels had heard the telephone ringing. Thinking that it was probably the hospital (it was) she had dumped her bag on the bar counter and rushed to answer it. On her return, the envelope was gone.

At the time of the theft, there had been about thirty people in the saloon bar, including the regular OAPs, the usual cohort of pool-playing unemployables, and a pre-Christmas party from a local firm. And – yes! – from the very beginning Lewis had known that the chances of recovering the money were virtually nil. Even so, the three perfunctory interviews that Morse conducted appeared to Lewis to be sadly unsatisfactory.

After listening a while to the landlord's unilluminating testimony, Morse asked him why it had taken him so long to conduct his business at the Cash and Carry; and although the explanation given seemed perfectly adequate, Morse's dismissal of this first witness had seemed almost offensively abrupt. And no man could have been more quickly or more effectively antagonized than the temporary barman (on duty the previous morning) who refused to answer Morse's

47

brusque enquiry about the present state of his overdraft. What then of the attractive, auburn-haired Mrs Michaels? After a rather lop-sided smile had introduced Morse to her regular if slightly nicotine-stained teeth, that distressed lady had been unable to fight back her tears as she sought to explain to Morse why she'd insisted on some genuine notes for the publicity photographer instead of a phonily magnified cheque.

But wait! Something dramatic had just happened to Morse, Lewis could see that: as if the light had suddenly shined upon a man that hitherto had sat in darkness. He (Morse) now asked – amazingly! – whether by any chance the good lady possessed a pair of bright green, high-heeled leather shoes; and when she replied that, yes, she did, Morse smiled serenely, as though he had solved the secret of the universe, and promptly summoned into the lounge bar not only the three he'd just interviewed but all those now in the George who had been drinking there the previous morning.

As they waited, Morse asked for the serial numbers of the stolen notes, and Lewis passed over a scrap of paper on which some figures had been hastily scribbled in blotchy Biro. 'For Christ's sake, man!' hissed Morse. 'Didn't they teach you to write at school?'

Lewis breathed heavily, counted to five, and then painstakingly rewrote the numbers on a virginal piece of paper: 773741–773780. At which numbers Morse glanced cursorily before sticking the paper in his pocket, and proceeding to address the George's regulars.

He was *virtually* certain (he said) of who had stolen the money. What he was *absolutely* sure about was exactly where that money was *at that very moment*. He had the serial numbers of the notes – but that was of no importance whatsoever now. The thief might well have been tempted to spend the money earlier – but not any more! And why not? Because at this Christmas time that person *no longer had the power to resist his better self.*

In that bar, stilled now and silent as the grave itself, the faces of Morse's audience seemed mesmerized – and remained so as Morse gave his instructions that the notes should be replaced in their original envelope and returned (he cared not by what means) to Sergeant Lewis's office at Thames Valley Police HQ *within the next twenty-four hours.*

As they drove back, Lewis could restrain his curiosity no longer. 'You really *are* confident that—?'

'Of course!'

'I never seem to be able to put the clues together myself, sir.'

'Clues? What clues, Lewis? I didn't know we had any.'

'Well, those shoes, for example. How do they fit in?'

'Who said they fitted in anywhere? It's just that I used to know an auburn-haired beauty who had six – *six*, Lewis! – pairs of bright green shoes. They suited her, she said.'

'So . . . they've got nothing to do with the case at all?'

'Not so far as I know,' muttered Morse.

The next morning a white envelope was delivered to Lewis's office, though no one at reception could recall when or whence it had arrived. Lewis immediately rang Morse to congratulate him on the happy outcome of the case.

'There's just one thing, sir. I'd kept that scrappy bit of paper with the serial numbers on it, and these are brand-new notes all right – but they're not the same ones!'

'Really?' Morse sounded supremely unconcerned.

'You're not worried about it?'

'Good Lord, no! You just get that money back to ginger-knob at the George, and tell her to settle for a jumbo-cheque next time! Oh, and one other thing, Lewis. I'm on *leave*. So no interruptions from anybody – understand?'

'Yes, sir. And, er . . . Happy Christmas, sir!'

'And to you, old friend!' replied Morse quietly.

The bank manager rang just before lunch that same day. 'It's about the four hundred pounds you withdrew yesterday, Inspector. I did promise to ring about any further bank charges—'

'I explained to the girl,' protested Morse. 'I needed the money quickly.'

'Oh, it's perfectly all right. But you did say you'd call in this morning to transfer—'

'Tomorrow! I'm up a ladder with a paint brush at the moment.'

Morse put down the receiver and again sank back in the armchair with the crossword. But his mind was far away, and some of the words he himself had spoken kept echoing around his brain: something about one's better self . . . And he smiled, for he knew that this would be a Christmas he might enjoy almost as much as the children up at Littlemore, perhaps. He had solved so many mysteries in his life. Was he now, he wondered, beginning to glimpse the solution to the greatest mystery of them all?

EVANS TRIES
AN O-LEVEL

Dramatis Personae
The Secretary of the Examinations Board
The Governor of HM Prison, Oxford
James Evans, a prisoner
Mr Jackson, a prison officer
Mr Stephens, a prison officer
The Reverend S. McLeery, an invigilator
Detective Superintendent Carter
Detective Chief Inspector Bell

> The unexamined life is not worth living.
>
> (Plato)

It was in early March when the Secretary of the Examinations Board received the call from Oxford Prison.

'It's a slightly unusual request, Governor, but I don't see why we shouldn't try to help. Just the one fellow, you say?'

'That's it. Chap called Evans. Started night classes in O-level German last September. Says he's dead keen to get some sort of academic qualification.'

'Is he any good?'

'He was the only one in the class, so you can say he's had individual tuition all the time, really. Would have cost him a packet if he'd been outside.'

'We-ell, let's give him a chance, shall we?'

'That's jolly kind of you. What exactly's the procedure now?'

'Oh, don't worry about that. I'll be sending you all the forms and stuff. What's his name, you say? Evans?'

'James Roderick Evans.' It sounded rather grand.

'Just one thing, Governor. He's not a violent sort of fellow, is he? I don't want to know his criminal record or anything like that, but—'

'No. There's no record of violence. Quite a pleasant sort of chap, they tell me. Bit of a card, really. One of the stars at the Christmas concert. Imitations, you know the sort of thing: Mike Yarwood stuff. No, he's just a congenital kleptomaniac, that's all.' The Governor was tempted to add something else,

53

but he thought better of it. He'd look after *that* particular side of things himself.

'Presumably,' said the Secretary, 'you can arrange a room where—'

'No problem. He's in a cell on his own. If you've no objections, he can sit the exam in there.'

'That's fine.'

'And we could easily get one of the parsons from St Mary Mags to invigilate, if that's—'

'Fine, yes. They seem to have a helluva lot of parsons there, don't they?' The two men chuckled good-naturedly, and the Secretary had a final thought. 'At least there's one thing. You shouldn't have much trouble keeping him *incommunicado*, should you?'

The Governor chuckled politely once more, reiterated his thanks, and slowly cradled the phone.

Evans!

'Evans the Break' as the prison officers called him. Three times he'd escaped from prison, and but for the recent wave of unrest in the maximum-security establishments up north, he wouldn't now be gracing the Governor's premises in Oxford; and the Governor was going to make absolutely certain that he wouldn't be *dis*gracing them. Not that Evans was a *real* burden: just a persistent, nagging presence. He'd be all right in Oxford, though: the Governor would see to that – would see to it personally. And besides, there was just a possibility that Evans was genuinely interested in O-level German. Just a slight possibility. Just a very slight possibility.

*

At 8.30 p.m. on Monday 7 June, Evans's German teacher shook him by the hand in the heavily guarded Recreational Block, just across from D Wing.

'*Guten Glück*, Herr Evans.'

'Pardon?'

'I said, "Good luck". Good luck for tomorrow.'

'Oh. Thanks, er, I mean, er, *Danke schön*.'

'You haven't a cat in hell's chance of getting through, of course, but—'

'I may surprise everybody,' said Evans.

At 8.30 the following morning, Evans had a visitor. Two visitors, in fact. He tucked his grubby string-vest into his equally grubby trousers, and stood up from his bunk, smiling cheerfully. 'Mornin', Mr Jackson. This is indeed an honour.'

Jackson was the senior prison officer on D Wing, and he and Evans had already become warm enemies. At Jackson's side stood Officer Stephens, a burly, surly-looking man, only recently recruited to the profession.

Jackson nodded curtly. 'And how's our little Einstein this morning, then?'

'Wasn't 'e a mathematician, Mr Jackson?'

'He was a bloody Kraut,' snapped Jackson. Evans's quiet voice always riled him, and Evans's present insight into his own vast ignorance riled him even more.

'I think 'e was a Jew, Mr Jackson.'

'I don't give a monkey's fuck what he was, you scruffy sod.'

'Scruffy' was, perhaps, the right word. Evans's face was

COLIN DEXTER

unshaven, and he wore a filthy-looking red-and-white bobble hat upon his head. 'Give me a *chance*, Mr Jackson. I was just goin' to shave when you bust in.'

'Which reminds me.' Jackson turned his eyes on Stephens. 'Make sure you take his razor out of the cell when he's finished scraping that ugly mug of his. Clear? One of these days he'll do us all a favour and cut his bloody throat.'

For a few seconds Evans looked thoughtfully at the man standing ramrod straight in front of him, a string of Second World War medals proudly paraded over his left breast-pocket. 'Mr Jackson? Was it *you* who took me nail-scissors away?' Evans had always worried about his hands.

'*And* your nail-file, you poncy twit.'

'Look!' For a moment Evans's eyes smouldered danger-ously, but Jackson was ready for him.

'Orders of the Governor, Evans.' He leaned forward and leered, his voice dropping to a harsh, contemptuous whisper. 'You want to *complain*?'

Evans shrugged his shoulders lightly. The crisis was over.

'You've got half an hour to smarten yourself up, Evans – and take that bloody hat off!'

'Me 'at? Huh!' Evans put his right hand lovingly on top of the filthy woollen, and smiled sadly. 'D'you know, Mr Jackson, it's the only thing that's ever brought me any sort o' luck in life. Kind o' lucky charm, if you know what I mean. And today I thought – well, with me exam and all that . . .'

Buried somewhere in Jackson, beneath all the bluster and the bullshit, was a tiny core of compassion; and Evans knew it.

'Just this once, then, Shirley Temple.' (If there was one

thing that Jackson genuinely loathed about Evans it was his long, wavy hair.) 'And get bloody shaving!'

At 8.45 the same morning the Reverend Stuart McLeery left his bachelor flat in Broad Street and stepped out briskly towards Carfax. The weatherman reported temperatures considerably below the normal for early June, and a long black overcoat and a shallow-crowned clerical hat provided welcome protection from the steady drizzle which had set in half an hour earlier and which now spattered the thick lenses of his spectacles. In his right hand he was carrying a small brown suitcase, which contained all that he would need for his morning duties, including a sealed question-paper envelope, a yellow invigilation form, a special 'authentication' card from the Examinations Board, a paper-knife, a Bible (he was to speak to the Women's Guild that afternoon on the book of Ruth), and a current copy of *The Church Times*.

The two-hour examination was scheduled to start at 9.15 a.m.

Evans was lathering his face vigorously when Stephens brought in two small square tables, and set them opposite each other in the narrow space between the bunk on the one side and on the other the distempered stone wall, plastered at eye-level with a proud row of naked women, vast-breasted and voluptuous. Next, Stephens brought in two hard chairs, the slightly less battered of which he placed in front of the table which stood nearer the cell door.

57

Jackson put in a brief final appearance. 'Behave yourself, laddy!'

Evans turned and nodded.

'And these' – (Jackson pointed to the pin-ups) – 'off!'

Evans turned and nodded again. 'I was goin' to take 'em down anyway. A minister, isn't 'e? The chap comin' to sit in, I mean.'

'And how did you know that?' asked Jackson quietly.

'Well, I 'ad to sign some forms, didn't I? And I couldn't 'elp—'

'You sneaky little bastard.'

Evans drew the razor carefully down his left cheek, and left a neat swath in the white lather. 'Can I ask you something, Mr Jackson? Why did they 'ave to bug me bloody cell?' He nodded his head vaguely to a point above the door.

'Not a very neat job,' conceded Jackson.

'They're not – they don't honestly think I'm goin' to try to—'

'They're taking no chances, Evans. Nobody in his bloody senses would take any chances with *you*.'

'Who's goin' to listen in?'

'I'll tell you who's going to listen in, laddy. It's the Governor himself, see? He don't trust you a bloody inch – and nor do I. I'll be watching you like a bleedin' hawk, Evans, so keep your nose clean. Clear?' He walked towards the door. 'And while we're on the subject of your nose, Evans, it's about time you changed that filthy snot-rag dangling from your arse pocket. Clear?'

Evans nodded. He'd already thought of that, and Number Two Handkerchief was lying ready on the bunk – a neatly folded square of off-white linen.

'Just one more thing, Einstein.'

'Ya? Wha's 'at?'

'Good luck, old son.'

In the little lodge just inside the prison's main gates, the Reverend S. McLeery signed his name neatly in the visitors' book, and thence walked side by side with a silent prison officer across the exercise yard to D Wing, where he was greeted by Jackson. The Wing's heavy outer door was unlocked, and locked behind them, the heavy inner door the same, and McLeery was handed into Stephens's keeping.

'Get the razor?' murmured Jackson.

Stephens nodded.

'Well, keep your eyes skinned. Clear?'

Stephens nodded again; and McLeery, his feet clanging up the iron stairs, followed his new guide, and finally stood before a cell door, where Stephens opened the peep-hole and looked through.

'That's him, sir.'

Evans, facing the door, sat quietly at the farther of the two tables, his whole attention riveted to a textbook of elementary German grammar. Stephens took the key from its ring, and the cell lock sprang back with a thudded, metallic twang.

It was 9.10 a.m. when the Governor switched on the receiver. He had instructed Jackson to tell Evans of the temporary little precaution – that was only fair. (As if Evans wouldn't spot it!) But wasn't it all a bit theatrical? Schoolboyish, almost? How on earth was Evans going to try anything on today? If he was so anxious to make another break, why in heaven's name hadn't he tried it from the Recreational Block? Much easier. But he hadn't. And there he was now – sitting in a locked cell, all the prison officers on the alert, two more locked doors between his cell and the yard, and a yard with a wall as high as a haystack. Yes, Evans was as safe as houses . . .

Anyway, it wouldn't be any trouble at all to have the receiver turned on for the next couple of hours or so. It wasn't as if there was going to be anything to listen to, was it? Amongst other things, an invigilator's duty was to ensure that the strictest silence was observed. But . . . but still that little nagging doubt! Might Evans try to take advantage of McLeery? Get him to smuggle in a chisel or two, or a rope-ladder, or—

The Governor sat up sharply. It was all very well getting rid of any potential weapon that *Evans* could have used; but what about *McLeery*? What if, quite unwittingly, the innocent McLeery had brought in something himself? A jack-knife, perhaps? And what if Evans held him hostage with such a weapon? Sort of hi-jack-knifed him?

The Governor reached for the phone. It was 9.12 a.m.

The examinee and the invigilator had already been introduced by Stephens when Jackson came back and shouted to McLeery through the cell door. 'Can you come outside a minute, sir? You too, Stephens.'

Jackson quickly explained the Governor's worries, and McLeery patiently held out his arms at shoulder level whilst Jackson lightly frisked his clothes. 'Something hard here, sir.'

'Ma reading glasses,' replied McLeery, looking down at the spectacle case.

Jackson quickly reassured him, and bending down on the landing thumb-flicked the catches on the suitcase. He picked up each envelope in turn, carefully passed his palms along their surfaces – and seemed satisfied. He riffled cursorily through a few pages of Holy Writ, and vaguely shook *The Church Times*. All right, so far. But one of the objects in McLeery's suitcase was puzzling him sorely.

'Do you mind telling me why you've brought this, sir?' He held up a smallish semi-inflated rubber ring, such as a young child with a waist of about twelve inches might have struggled into. 'You thinking of going for a swim, sir?'

McLeery's hitherto amiable demeanour was slightly ruffled by this tasteless little pleasantry, and he answered Jackson somewhat sourly. 'If ye must know, I suffer from haemorrhoids, and when I'm sitting down for any length o' time—'

'Very sorry, sir. I didn't mean to, er . . .' The embarrassment was still reddening Jackson's cheeks when he found the paper-knife at the bottom of the case. 'I think I'd better keep this though, if you don't mind, that is, sir.'

It was 9.18 a.m. before the Governor heard their voices again, and it was clear that the examination was going to be more than a little late in getting under way.

McLeery: 'Ye've got a watch?'
Evans: 'Yes, sir.'
McLeery: 'I'll be telling ye when to start, and again when ye've five minutes left. A' right?'

	Silence.
McLeery:	'There's plenty more o' this writing paper should ye need it.'
	Silence.
McLeery:	'Now. Write the name of the paper, 021–1, in the top left-hand corner.'
	Silence.
McLeery:	'In the top right-hand corner write your index number – 313. And in the box just below that, write your centre number – 271. A' right?'
	Silence. 9.20 a.m.
McLeery:	'I'm now going to—'
Evans:	''E's not goin' to stay 'ere, is 'e?'
McLeery:	'I don't know about that. I—'
Stephens:	'Mr Jackson's given me strict instructions to—'
Evans:	''Ow the 'ell am I supposed to concentrate on me exam with a bleedin' screw breathin' down me neck? Christ! Sorry, sir, I didn't mean—'

The Governor reached for the phone. 'Jackson? Ah, good. Get Stephens out of that cell, will you? I think we're perhaps overdoing things.'

'As you wish, sir.'

The Governor heard the exchanges in the cell, heard the door clang to once more, and heard McLeery announce that the examination had begun at last.

It was 9.25 a.m.; and there was a great calm.

At 9.40 a.m. the Examinations Board rang through, and the Assistant Secretary with special responsibility for modern languages asked to speak to the Governor. The examination had already started, no doubt? Ah, a quarter of an hour ago. Yes. Well, there was a correction slip which some fool had forgotten to place in the examination package. Very brief. Could the Governor please . . . ?

'Yes, of course. I'll put you straight through to Mr Jackson in D Wing. Hold the line a minute.'

Was this the sort of thing the Governor had feared? Was the phone call a fake? Some signal? Some secret message . . . ? But he could check on that immediately. He dialled the number of the Examinations Board, but heard only the staccato bleeps of a line engaged. But then the line *was* engaged, wasn't it? Yes. Not very intelligent, that . . .

Two minutes later he heard some whispered communications in the cell, and then McLeery's broad Scots voice:

'Will ye please stop writing a wee while, Mr Evans, and listen carefully. Candidates offering German, 021–1, should note the following correction. "On page three, line fifteen, the fourth word should read *goldenen*, not *goldene*; and the whole phrase will therefore read *zum goldenen Löwen*, not *zum goldene Löwen*." I will repeat that . . .'

The Governor listened and smiled. He had taken German in the sixth form himself, and he remembered all about the agreements of adjectives. And so did McLeery, by the sound of things, for the minister's pronunciation was most impressive. But what about Evans? *He* probably didn't know what an adjective *was*.

The phone rang again. The Magistrates' Court. They needed a prison van and a couple of prison officers. Remand case. And within two minutes the Governor was wondering whether *that* could be a hoax. He told himself not to be so silly. His imagination was beginning to run riot.

Evans!

For the first quarter of an hour Stephens had dutifully peered through the peep-hole at intervals of one minute or so; and after that, every two minutes. At 10.45 a.m. he nipped off to the gents', and was in such a hurry to get back that he found he'd dribbled down his trousers. But everything was still all right as he looked through the peep-hole once more. It took four or five seconds – no more. What was the point? It was always more or less the same. Evans, his pen between his lips, sat staring straight in front of him towards the door, seeking – it seemed – some sorely needed inspiration from somewhere. And opposite him McLeery, seated slightly askew from the table now: his face in semi-profile; his hair (as Stephens had noticed earlier) amateurishly clipped pretty closely to the scalp; his eyes behind the pebble lenses peering short-sightedly at *The Church Times*; his right index finger hooked beneath the narrow clerical collar; and the fingers of the left hand, the nails meticulously manicured, slowly stroking the short black beard.

At 10.50 a.m. the receiver crackled to life and the Governor realized he'd almost forgotten Evans for a few minutes.

Evans: 'Please, sir!' (A whisper)

Evans: 'Please, sir!' (Louder)

Evans: 'Would you mind if I put a blanket round me shoulders, sir? It's a bit parky in 'ere, isn't it?'

	Silence.
Evans:	'There's one on me bunk 'ere, sir.'
McLeery:	'Be quick about it.'
	Silence.

At 10.51 a.m. Stephens was more than a little surprised to
see a grey regulation blanket draped round Evans's
shoulders, and he frowned slightly and looked at the examinee more closely. But Evans, the pen still between his teeth,
was staring just as vacantly as before. Blankly beneath a
blanket . . . Should Stephens report the slight irregularity?
Anything at all fishy, hadn't Jackson said? Mm. He looked
through the peep-hole once again, and even as he did so
Evans pulled the dirty blanket more closely to himself. Was
he planning a sudden batman leap to suffocate McLeery in
the blanket? Don't be daft! There was never any sun on this
side of the prison; no heating, either, during the summer
months, and it could get quite chilly in some of the cells.
Mm. Stephens decided to revert to his earlier every-minute
observation.

At 11.20 a.m. the receiver once more crackled across the
silence of the Governor's office, and McLeery informed Evans
that only five minutes remained. The examination was almost
over now, but something still gnawed away quietly in the
Governor's mind. He reached for the phone once more.

At 11.22 a.m. Jackson shouted along the corridor to
Stephens. The Governor wanted to speak with him – '*Hurry,*
man!' Stephens picked up the phone apprehensively and

listened to the rapidly spoken orders. Stephens himself was to accompany McLeery to the main prison gates. Understood? Stephens personally was to make absolutely sure that the door was locked on Evans after McLeery had left the cell. Understood?

Understood.

At 11.25 a.m. the Governor heard the final exchanges.

McLeery: 'Stop writing, please.'

Silence.

McLeery: 'Put your sheets in order and see they're correctly numbered.'

Silence.

Scraping of chairs and tables.

Evans: 'Thank you very much, sir.'

McLeery: 'A' right, was it?'

Evans: 'Not *too* bad.'

McLeery: 'Good . . . Mr Stephens!' (Very loud)

The Governor heard the door clang to for the last time. The examination was over.

'How did he get on, do you think?' asked Stephens as he walked beside McLeery to the main gates.

'Och. I canna think he's distinguished hissel, I'm afraid.' His Scots accent seemed broader than ever, and his long black overcoat, reaching almost to his knees, fostered the illusion that he had suddenly grown slimmer.

Stephens felt pleased that the Governor had asked *him*, and not Jackson, to see McLeery off the premises, and all in all the morning had gone pretty well. But something stopped him from making his way directly to the canteen for a belated cup of coffee. He wanted to take just one last look at Evans. It was like a programme he'd seen on TV – about a woman who could never *really* convince herself that she'd locked the front door when she'd gone to bed: often she'd got up twelve, fifteen, sometimes twenty times to check the bolts.

He re-entered D Wing, made his way along to Evans's cell, and opened the peep-hole once more. *Oh, no!* CHRIST, NO! There, sprawled back in Evans's chair was a man (for a semi-second Stephens thought it must be Evans), a grey regulation blanket slipping from his shoulders, the front of his closely cropped, irregularly tufted hair awash with fierce red blood which had dripped already through the small black beard, and was even now spreading horribly over the white clerical collar and down into the black clerical front.

Stephens shouted wildly for Jackson: and the words appeared to penetrate the curtain of blood that veiled McLeery's ears, for the minister's hand felt feebly for a handkerchief from his pocket, and held it to his bleeding head, the blood seeping slowly through the white linen. He gave a long low moan, and tried to speak. But his voice trailed away, and by the time Jackson had arrived and despatched Stephens to ring the police and the ambulance, the handkerchief was a sticky, squelchy wodge of cloth.

McLeery slowly raised himself, his face twisted tightly with pain. 'Dinna worry about the ambulance, man! I'm a' right . . . I'm a' right . . . Get the police! I know . . . I know where . . . he . . .' He closed his eyes and another drip of blood splashed like a huge red raindrop on the wooden floor. His hand felt along the table, found the German question paper, and grasped it tightly in his bloodstained hand. 'Get the Governor! I know . . . I know where Evans . . .'

Almost immediately sirens were sounding, prison officers barked orders, puzzled prisoners pushed their way along the corridors, doors were banged and bolted, and phones were ringing everywhere. And within a minute McLeery, with Jackson and Stephens supporting him on either side, his face now streaked and caked with drying blood, was greeted in the prison yard by the Governor, perplexed and grim.

'We must get you to hospital immediately. I just don't—'

'Ye've called the police?'

'Yes, yes. They're on their way. But—'

'I'm a' right. I'm a' right. Look! Look here!' Awkwardly he opened the German question paper and thrust it before the Governor's face. 'It's there! D'ye see what I *mean*?'

The Governor looked down and realized what McLeery was trying to tell him. A photocopied sheet had been carefully and cleverly superimposed over the last (originally blank) page of the question paper.

'Ye see what they've done, Governor. Ye see . . .' His voice trailed off again, as the Governor, dredging the layers of long-neglected learning, willed himself to translate the German text before him:

Sie sollen dem schon verabredeten Plan genau folgen. Der wichtige Zeitpunkt ist drei Minuten vor Ende des Examens . . . 'You must follow the plan already somethinged. The vital point in time is three minutes before the end of the examination but something something – something something . . . Don't hit

68

him too hard – remember, he's a minister! And don't overdo the Scots accent when . . .'

A fast-approaching siren wailed to its crescendo, the great doors of the prison yard were pushed back, and a white police car squealed to a jerky halt beside them.

Detective Superintendent Carter swung himself out of the passenger seat and saluted the Governor. 'What the hell's happening, sir?' And, turning to McLeery: 'Christ! Who's hit *him*?'

But McLeery cut across whatever explanation the Governor might have given. 'Elsfield Way, officer! I know where Evans . . .' He was breathing heavily, and leaned for support against the side of the car, where the imprint of his hand was left in tarnished crimson.

In bewilderment Carter looked to the Governor for guidance. 'What—?'

'Take him with you, if you think he'll be all right. He's the only one who seems to know what's happening.'

Carter opened the back door and helped McLeery inside; and within a few seconds the car leaped away in a spurt of gravel.

'Elsfield Way', McLeery had said; and there it was staring up at the Governor from the last few lines of the German text: 'From Elsfield Way drive to the Headington round-about, where . . .' Yes, of course. *The Examinations Board was in Elsfield Way*, and someone from the Board must have been involved in the escape plan from the very beginning: the question paper itself, the correction slip . . .

The Governor turned to Jackson and Stephens. 'I don't need to tell you what's happened, do I?' His voice sounded almost calm in its scathing contempt. 'And which one of you two morons was it who took Evans for a nice little walk to the main gates and waved him bye-bye?'

'It was me, sir,' stammered Stephens. 'Just like you told me, sir. I could have sworn—'

'What? Just like I told you, you say? What the hell—?'

'When you rang, sir, and told me to—'

'When was that?' The Governor's voice was a whiplash now.

'You know, sir. About twenty past eleven, just before—'

'You blithering idiot, man! It wasn't *me* who rang you. Don't you realize—' But what was the use? He *had* used the telephone at that time, but only to try (unsuccessfully, once more) to get through to the Examinations Board.

He shook his head in growing despair and turned on the senior prison officer. 'As for you, Jackson! How long have you been pretending you've got a brain, eh? Well, I'll tell you something, Jackson. Your skull's *empty*. Absolutely bloody empty!' It was Jackson who had spent two hours in Evans's cell the previous evening; and it was Jackson who had confidently reported that there was nothing hidden away there – nothing at all. And yet Evans had somehow managed to conceal not only a false beard, a pair of spectacles, a dog-collar and all the rest of his clerical paraphernalia, but also some sort of weapon with which he'd given McLeery such a terrible blow across the head. Aurrgh!

A prison van backed alongside, but the Governor made no immediate move. He looked down again at the last line of the German: '. . . to the Headington roundabout, where you go straight over and make your way to ... to Neugraben.' 'Neugraben'? Where on earth—? 'New' something. 'Newgrave'? Never heard of it. There was a 'Wargrave', somewhere near Reading, but ... No, it was probably a code word, or— And then it hit him. Newbury! God, yes! Newbury was a pretty big sort of place but—

He rapped out his orders to the driver. 'St Aldates Police Station, and step on it! Take Jackson and Stephens here, and when you get there ask for Bell. Chief Inspector Bell. Got that?'

He leaped the stairs to his office three at a time, got Bell on the phone immediately, and put the facts before him.

'We'll get him, sir,' said Bell. 'We'll get him, with a bit o' luck.'

The Governor sat back, and lit a cigarette. Ye gods! What a beautifully laid plan it had all been! What a clever sod Evans was! Careless leaving that question paper behind; but then, they all made their mistakes somewhere along the line. Well, *almost* all of them. That's why they were doing their porridge, and that's why very very shortly Mr clever-clever Evans would be back inside doing *his* once more.

The phone on his desk erupted in a strident burst, and Superintendent Carter informed him that McLeery had spotted Evans driving off along Elsfield Way; they'd got the number of the car all right and had given chase immediately, but had lost him at the Headington roundabout; he must have doubled back into the city.

'No,' said the Governor quietly. 'No, he's on his way to Newbury.' He explained his reasons for believing so, and left it at that. It was a police job now – not his. He was just another good-for-a-giggle, gullible governor, that was all.

'By the way, Carter. I hope you managed to get McLeery to hospital all right?'

'Yes. He's in the Radcliffe now. Really groggy, he was, when we got to the Examination offices, and they rang for the ambulance from there.'

The Governor rang the Radcliffe a few minutes later and asked for the accident department.

'McLeery, you say?'

'Yes. He's a parson.'

'I don't think there's anyone—'

'Yes, there is. You'll find one of your ambulances picked him up from Elsfield Way about—'

'Oh, *that*. Yes, we sent an ambulance all right, but when we got there, the fellow had gone. No one seemed to know where he was. Just vanished! Not a sign—'

But the Governor was no longer listening, and the truth seemed to hit him with an almost physical impact somewhere in the back of his neck.

A quarter of an hour later they found the Reverend S. McLeery, securely bound and gagged, in his study in Broad Street. He'd been there, he said, since 8.15 a.m., when two men had called and . . .

Enquiries in Newbury throughout the afternoon produced nothing. Nothing at all. And by tea-time everyone in the prison knew what had happened. It had not been Evans,

72

impersonating McLeery, who had walked *out*; it had been Evans, impersonating McLeery, who had stayed *in*.

The fish and chips were delicious, and after a gentle stroll round the centre of Chipping Norton, Evans decided to return to the hotel and have an early night. A smart new hat concealed the wreckage of his closely cropped hair, and he kept it on as he walked up to the reception desk of the Golden Lion. It would take a good while for his hair to regain its former glories – but what the hell did *that* matter. He was *out* again, wasn't he? A bit of bad luck, that, when Jackson had pinched his scissors, for it had meant a long and tricky operation with his only razor blade the previous night. Ah! But he'd had his good luck, too. Just think! If Jackson had made him take his bobble hat off! Phew! That really *had* been a close call. Still, old Jackson wasn't such a bad fellow . . . One of the worst things – funny, really! – had been the beard. He'd always been allergic to sticking plaster, and even now his chin was irritatingly sore and red.

The receptionist wasn't the same girl who'd booked him in, but the change was definitely for the better. A real honey, this one. As he collected his key, he gave her his sexiest smile, told her he wouldn't be bothering with breakfast, ordered the *Daily Express*, and asked for an early-morning call at 6.45 a.m. Tomorrow was going to be another busy day.

He whistled softly to himself as he walked up the broad stairs . . . He'd sort of liked the idea of being dressed up as a minister – dog-collar and everything. Yes, it had been a jolly good idea for 'McLeery' to wear *two* black fronts, *two* collars. But that top collar! Phew! It had kept on slipping off the back stud; and there'd been that one panicky moment when 'McLeery' had only just got his hand up to his neck in time to stop the collars springing apart before Stephens ... Ah! They'd got *that* little problem worked out all right, though: a pen stuck in the mouth whenever the evil eye had appeared at the peep-hole. Easy! But all that fiddling about under the blanket with the black front and the stud at the back of the collar – that had been far more difficult than they'd ever bargained for ... Everything else had gone beautifully smoothly, though. In the car he'd found everything they'd promised him: soap and water, clothes, the map – yes, the *map*, of course. The Ordnance Survey Map of Oxfordshire ... He'd got some good friends; some very clever friends. Christ, ah!

He unlocked his bedroom door and closed it quietly behind him – and then stood frozen to the spot, like a man who has just caught a glimpse of the Gorgon.

Sitting on the narrow bed was the very last man in the world that Evans had expected – or wanted – to see.

'It's not worth trying anything,' said the Governor quietly, as Evans's eyes darted desperately around the room. 'I've got men all round the place.' (Well, there were only *two*, really: but Evans needn't know that.) He let the words sink in. 'Women, too. Didn't you think the blonde girl in reception was rather sweet?'

Evans was visibly shaken. He sat down slowly in the only chair the small room could offer, and held his head between his hands. For several minutes there was utter silence.

Finally, he spoke. 'It was that bloody correction slip, I s'pose.'

'We-ell' (the Governor failed to mask the deep satisfaction

74

in his voice) 'there *are* a few people who know a little German.'

Slowly, very slowly, Evans relaxed. He was beaten – and he knew it. He sat up at last, and managed to smile ruefully. 'You know, it wasn't *really* a mistake. You see, we 'adn't been able to fix up any 'otel, but we could've worked that some other way. No. The really important thing was for the phone to ring just before the exam finished – to get the screws out of the way for a coupla minutes. So we 'ad to know exactly when the exam *started*, didn't we?'

'And, like a fool, I presented you with that little piece of information on a plate.'

'Well, *somebody* did. So, you see, sir, that correction slip killed two little birds with a single stone, didn't it? The name of the 'otel for *me*, and the exact time the exam started for, er, for, er . . .'

The Governor nodded. 'It's a pretty common word, though, "Löwe". It's on the beer labels for a start.'

'Good job it *is* pretty common, sir, or I'd never 'ave known where to come to, would I?'

'Nice name, though: *zum goldenen Löwen.*'

''Ow did you know which Golden Lion it was? There's 'undreds of 'em.'

'Same as you, Evans. Index number 313; Centre number 271. Remember? Six figures? And if you take an Ordnance Survey Map for Oxfordshire, you find that the six-figure reference 313/271 lands you bang in the middle of Chipping Norton.'

'Yea, you're right. Huh! We'd 'oped you'd bugger off to Newbury.'

'We did.'

'Well, that's something, I s'pose.'

'That question paper, Evans. Could you really understand all that German? I could hardly—'

'Nah! Course I couldn't. I knew *roughly* what it was all about, but we just 'oped it'd throw a few spanners in the works – you know, sort of muddle everybody a bit.'

The Governor stood up. 'Tell me one thing before we go. How on earth did you get all that blood to pour over your head?'

Evans suddenly looked a little happier. '*Clever*, sir. Very clever, that was – 'ow to get a couple o' pints of blood into a cell, eh? When there's none there to start off with, and when, er, and when the "invigilator", shall we say, gets searched before 'e comes in. Yes, sir. You can well ask about that, and I dunno if I ought to tell you. After all, I might want to use that particular—'

'Anything to do with a little rubber ring for piles, perhaps?'

Evans grinned feebly. 'Clever, though, wasn't it?'

'Must have been a tricky job sticking a couple of pints—'

'Nah! You've got it wrong, sir. No problem about *that*.'

'No?'

'Nah! It's the *clotting*, you see. That's the big trouble. We got the blood easy enough. Pig's blood, it was – from the slaughter'ouse in Kidlington. But to stop it clotting you've got to mix yer actual blood' (Evans took a breath) 'with one tenth of its own volume of 3.8 per cent trisodium citrate! Didn't know that, did you, sir?'

The Governor shook his head in a token of reluctant admiration. 'We learn something new every day, they tell me. Come on, m'lad.'

Evans made no show of resistance, and side by side the two men walked slowly down the stairs.

'Tell me, Evans. How did you manage to plan all this business? You've had no visitors – I've seen to that. You've had no letters—'

'I've got lots of friends, though.'

'What's that supposed to mean?'

'Me German teacher, for a start.'

'You mean—? But he was from the Technical College.'

'*Was* 'e?' Evans was almost enjoying it all now. 'Ever check up on 'im, sir?'

'God Almighty! There's far more going on than I—'

'Always will be, sir.'

'Everything ready?' asked the Governor as they stood by the reception desk.

'The van's out the front, sir,' said the pretty blonde receptionist. Evans winked at her; and she winked back at him. It almost made his day.

A silent prison officer handcuffed the recaptured Evans, and together the two men clambered awkwardly into the back seat of the prison van.

'See you soon, Evans.' It was almost as if the Governor were saying farewell to an old friend after a cocktail party.

'Cheerio, sir. I, er, I was just wonderin'. I know your German's pretty good, sir, but do you know any more o' these modern languages?'

'Not very well. Why?'

Evans settled himself comfortably on the back seat, and

grinned happily. 'Nothin', really. I just 'appened to notice that you've got some O-level Italian classes comin' up next September, that's all.'

'Perhaps you won't be with us next September, Evans.'

James Roderick Evans appeared to ponder the Governor's words deeply. 'No. P'r'aps I won't,' he said.

As the prison van turned right from Chipping Norton on to the Oxford road, the hitherto silent prison officer unlocked the handcuffs and leaned forward towards the driver. 'For Christ's sake get a *move* on! It won't take 'em long to find out—'

'Where do ye suggest we make for?' asked the driver, in a broad Scots accent.

'What about Newbury?' suggested Evans.

DEAD AS A DODO

'Why,' said the Dodo, 'the best way to explain it is to do it.' (And as you might like to try the thing yourself, some winter day, I will tell you how the Dodo managed it.)

(Lewis Carroll, *Alice in Wonderland*)

It was more from necessity than from kindliness, just after 5 p.m. on a rain-soaked evening in early February 1990, that Chief Inspector Morse of the Thames Valley Police leaned over and opened the Jaguar's near-side door. One of his neighbours from the North Oxford bachelor flats was standing at the bus stop, was getting very wet – and was staring hard at him.

'Most kind!' said Philip Wise, inserting his kyphotic self into the passenger seat.

Morse grunted a vague acknowledgement as the car made a few further slow yards up the Banbury Road in the red-tail-lighted queue, his wipers clearing short-lived swaths across the screen. Only three-quarters of a mile to go, but at this time of day twenty minutes would be par for the progressively paralytic crawl to the flats. Never an easy conversationalist himself – indeed, known occasionally to lapse into total aphasia when driving a car – Morse was glad that Wise was doing all the talking. 'Something quite extraordinary's happened to me,' said the man in the dripping mackintosh.

In retrospect, Morse was aware that he'd listened, at least initially, with no more than polite passivity. But listen he had done.

*

Philip Wise had gone up to Exeter College, Oxford, in October 1938; and in due course his linguistic abilities (particularly in German) had ensured for him, when war broke out a year later, a cushy little job in an Intelligence Unit housed on the outskirts of Bicester. For two years he had lived there in a disagreeable and draughty Nissen-hut; and when the chance came of his taking digs back in Oxford, he'd jumped at it. Thus it was that in October 1941 he had moved into Crozier Road, a sunless thoroughfare just off the west of St Giles'; and it was there that he'd first met Miss Dodo Whitaker ('Only the one "t", Inspector') who had a tiny top-floor bedsitter immediately above his own room in the grimy four-storey property that stood at number 14.

Why on earth she'd been saddled with a name like 'Dodo', he'd never discovered – nor enquired; but she was certainly a considerably livelier specimen than the defunct *Didus ineptus* of Mauritius. Although physically hardly warranting any second glance, especially in the wartime 'Utility' boiler-suit she almost invariably wore, she had the inestimable merit of being interesting. And sometimes, over half a glass of mild beer in the ill-lit bar at the rear of the Bird and Baby, her wonted nervousness would disappear, and in her rather deep, husky voice she would talk with knowledge, volubility, and wit, about the class-structure, about the progress of the war – and about music. Yes, above all about music. The pair of them had joined the Record Library, thereafter spending a few candle-lit evenings together in Dodo's room listening to everything from Vivaldi to Wagner. On one occasion, Wise had almost been on the verge of telling her of the Platonic-plus pleasure he was beginning to experience in her company.

82

Almost.

Dodo had a brother called Ambrose who now and then managed to get a weekend leave-pass and come to stay with Dodo, usually (though quite unofficially) sleeping on the floor of her single room. Almost immediately, Philip Wise and Ambrose Whitaker became firm friends, spending (somewhat to Dodo's annoyance) rather too many hours together drinking whisky – a commodity plentiful enough, if over-priced, in the Bird and Baby, but a rare one in the wilds of Bodmin, where Ambrose, with two stripes on each arm, spent his days initiating recruits into the mysteries of antiquated artillery pieces. He was a winsome, albeit somewhat raffish, sort of fellow whose attraction to alcohol apparently eclipsed even his love of music (Dodo spoke of Ambrose, amongst other things, as a virtuoso on the piano). Those weekends had flashed by, with Wise far too soon finding himself walking across Gloucester Green to see his friend off at the Great Western station late on Sunday afternoons.

Brother and sister – what an engaging couple they were!

Rich, too – at least their parents were.

Dodo, in particular, made no secret of her parents' extremely comfortable lifestyle, which Wise himself had once (and only once) experienced at first hand, when Dodo had suggested – on his having to spend a week in Bristol in February 1942 – that he stayed with them; had even loaned him a key to the family mansion in case they were out when he arrived. Wise had already known that Dodo's parents lived in Bristol, since he'd noticed the post-mark on the letter (doubtless from Mummy) that lay each week on the undusted mahogany table in the small entrance hall of number 14 – her name in the address, incidentally, always prefixed by the letter 'A'. Alice? Angela? Anne? Audrey? – Wise had never been told and, again, had never enquired. But that little fact was something else he'd known earlier, too, since he was with her when, with a practised flourish of those slim and sinewy fingers, she'd signed her membership card at the Record Library. As for the parents, they turned out to be a straight-laced, tight-faced pair who remained frigidly reserved towards their guest throughout his short stay, and who appeared less than effusively appreciative of Dodo – and almost embarrassingly dismissive of Ambrose. Oddly, Wise had not found a single fond memento of their talented offspring in the Whitakers' gauntly luxurious villa, and not a single family photograph to grace the daily-dusted mantelpieces.

It was three weeks after his return from this ill-starred visit that Dodo left Oxford, her wartime work (something 'hush-hush', it was understood) necessitating a move to Chelten-ham. Only about forty miles away – and she'd keep in touch, she said.

But she hadn't.

'Forty-eight years ago, this was, Inspector. Forty-eight! I was twenty-three myself, and she must have been about the same. Year or two older, perhaps – I'm not sure. You see, I never even asked her how old she was. Pretty spineless specimen, wasn't I?'

In the darkness, Morse nodded his silent assent, and the Jaguar finally turned into the Residents Only parking area.

Wise contrived to keep talking as the two men dashed through the rain to the entrance hall. 'I'd be glad to give you a cup of tea . . . or something . . . You see, I haven't really told you anything yet.'

As they sat opposite each other in the living area, Wise passed across a white, six-page booklet containing details of **A Service of Thanksgiving for the Life of AMBROSE WHITAKER, MA (Cantab.), FRAM 1917–1989**, and Morse glanced cursorily at the contents: music; hymn; lesson; music; address; prayers; hymn; music; blessing; music; more music. Observing only that if he ever had a voice in his own funeral arrangements he would join Whitaker in choosing the 'In Paradisum' from the Fauré *Requiem*, Morse handed the leaflet back.

'The thing is this,' continued Wise. 'I saw an obituary in *The Times* in December, and I was sure it was the same man I'd known in the war. Quite apart from the pretty unusual Christian name, as well as the *very* unusual spelling of the surname, everything else fitted, too: born in Bristol, prodigy on the piano – everything! And I just couldn't help thinking back and wondering whether *she* was still alive – Dodo, that is. Anyway, a fortnight ago I read about this Memorial Service in Holborn, and I decided to go up and pay my last respects to an old friend – and perhaps . . .'

'Find some plump-bosomed old spinster—'

'Yes!'

'Did you find her?' asked Morse quietly.

Wise shook his head. 'There were an awful lot of important people from the musical world – I hadn't realized what a name Ambrose had made for himself. I got to the church early and stayed outside for a good while watching the people going in, including – pretty obvious who she was – Ambrose's wife, who drew up in a chauffeur-driven Rolls – registration AW 1! But I didn't see the woman I was looking for – and she wasn't in the church, either. I'd have spotted her straight-away if she had been. She was smallish, stockily built – just like her mother. And there was something else. She had a nasty little red scar – well, a nasty *big* scar really – just across the left-hand side of her jaw: a bicycle accident when she was a youngster, I think. She was awfully conscious of it and always used a lot of face-powder to try to cover it up a bit. But it was still pretty noticeable, I'm afraid. Well, to cut a long story a bit shorter, I went up to Ambrose's wife after the service and told her I'd known her husband in the war and said how sorry I was and all the rest of it. She was pleasant enough, but she seemed a bit strained, and there were other people waiting to have a word with her. So I didn't say much more except to mention that I'd known her husband's sister as well.' Wise paused a second or two before continuing.

'Do you know what happened then, Inspector? Ambrose's wife pointed to a grey-haired woman in a black dress standing with her back to us, a woman very much the same height and build as Dodo had been. "This gentleman here says he used to know you, Agnes . . ."

'Agnes!

'But I didn't hear any more – I just didn't know what to do – or say. You see, the woman in black turned round and faced me, *and she wasn't Dodo Whitaker.*'

*

It was Morse who broke the silence which followed. 'Ambrose only had the one sister?'

Wise nodded, a wry, defeated smile upon his face. 'Yes – Agnes. He never did have a sister named "Dodo"!'

Again the two men were silent.

'Well?' asked Wise, finally.

It had always appeared to Morse an undeniable fact that coincidence plays a far greater role in human affairs than is generally acknowledged. And here was yet another instance of it – it must be! Wise's tale was interesting enough – assuredly so: but it wasn't much of a *problem*, surely? Ostentatiously he drained his whisky, gratefully witnessed the replenishment, and then pronounced judgement: 'There were two Ambrose Whitakers, both musical men, and both from Bristol, and the one you knew wasn't the one who died.'

'You think not?' The half-smile on Wise's face made Morse rather uncomfortably aware that a slightly more intelligent analysis had been expected of him.

'You don't think,' suggested Morse weakly, 'that Agnes might have had some plastic surgery or something?'

'No, no. It's just that there are far too many coincidences for *me* to swallow. *Everything* fitted – down to the last detail. For example, Dodo told me that she and Ambrose once got a bit morbid about the possibility of his being killed in the war and how he'd told her that he'd settle for a couple of bits of music when they buried him: the "In Paradisum"—'

'Lovely choice!' interjected Morse. 'I saw that in the Service.'

'—and the adagio from the Mozart Clarinet Concerto—'

'Ah yes! K662.'

'K622.'

'Oh!'

Morse knew that he wasn't scoring many points; knew, too, that Wise was perfectly correct in believing that the coincidences were getting way out of hand. But he had no time at all to develop the quite extraordinary possibility that suddenly leaped into his brain; because Wise himself was clearly most anxious to propound his own equally astonishing conclusions.

'What would you say, Inspector, if I told you that Dodo wasn't Ambrose Whitaker's sister at all – *she was his wife.*'

Morse's face registered a degree of genuine surprise, but he allowed Wise to continue without interruption.

'It would account for quite a few things, don't you think? For example, it always seemed a bit odd to me that when Ambrose got any leave he invariably came all the way from Cornwall here to Oxford – via *Bristol*, at that! – just to see his *sister*. You'd think he'd have called in on his parents once in a while, wouldn't you? They were much nearer than Dodo was; and well worth keeping the right side of, surely? But it wouldn't be surprising if he took every opportunity of coming all the way to Oxford to see his *wife*, would it? And that would certainly tie up with him sleeping in her room. You know, with all that family money he could have taken a suite in The Randolph if he'd wanted. Yet instead of that, he slept – or so he said – on Dodo's *floor*. Then again, it would probably account for the fact that she never once let me touch her physically – not even hold hands. She was fond of me, though – I know she was . . .'

Momentarily Wise stopped, nodding slowly to himself. 'For some reason the Whitakers must have disapproved of

Ambrose's marriage and wanted as little as possible to do with his wartime bride – hence their cool reception of me, Inspector! There may have been talk of disinheriting him – I don't know. I don't *know* anything, of course. But I suspect she was probably pregnant underneath that boiler-suit of hers, and as her time drew nearer she just *had* to leave Oxford. Then? Your guess is as good as mine: she died – she was killed in an air-raid – she got divorced – anything. Ambrose remarried, and the woman I met at the Memorial Service was his *second* wife.'

'Mm.' Morse was looking decidedly dubious. 'But if this Dodo girl *was* his wife, and if his parents couldn't stand the sight or sound of her, why on earth did they write to her every week? And why did she think she had the right to invite *you* down to Bristol? To *have* a key, even – let alone to give *you* one.' Morse shook his head slowly. 'She must have been pretty sure she could take their good-will for granted, I reckon.'

'You think they *were* her parents, then,' said Wise flatly.

'I'm sure of it,' said Morse.

Wise shook his head in exasperation. 'What the hell *is* the explanation, then?'

'Oh, I don't think there's much doubt about that,' said Morse. But he spoke these words to himself, and not to Wise. And very soon afterwards, seeing little prospect of any further replenishment, he took his leave – with the promise that he would give the problem 'a little consideration'.

The following Monday morning, Morse stood beside the Traffic Comptroller at Kidlington Police HQ and watched as

'AW 1' was keyed into the Car Registration computer. Immediately, the VDU spelled out the information that the car was still registered under the name of Mr A. Whitaker, 6 West View Crescent, Bournemouth; and noting the address Morse walked thoughtfully back to his ground-floor office. After ringing Directory Inquiries, and getting the Bournemouth telephone number, he was soon speaking to Mrs Whitaker herself, who in turn was soon promising to do exactly as Morse had requested.

Then Morse rang the War Office.

Ten days later, Philip Wise returned from a week's holiday in Spain to find a long note from Morse.

P. W.

I've discovered a few more facts, but some of what follows may possibly be pure fiction. As you know, records galore got destroyed in the last war, affording limitless opportunity for people to cover up their traces by means of others' identity-cards and so on, especially after a period of chaos and carnage when nobody knew who was who or which corpse was which.

After Dunkirk, for instance.

Gunner (as he then was) Whitaker was the only man of thirty on board who survived, quite miraculously, when the Edna (a flat-bottomed barge registered in Felixstowe) was blown out of the water by a German dive-bomber on May 30th, 1940. He was picked up, with only a pair of waterlogged pants and a wrist-watch to call his own, by the naval sloop Artemis, and was landed at Dover, along with tens of thousands of other soldiers from almost every regiment in the land. (My own imaginative faculties now come wholly into play.) In due course, he was put on a train and sent to a temporary rehabilitation camp – as it happened, the one here in Oxford up on Headington Hill.

The fact that he was in a state of profound shock, with his nerves half-shot to pieces, is probably sufficient to account for his walking out of this camp (quite literally) after only one night under canvas, and hitch-hiking down to Bristol. But he didn't walk out alone. He took a friend with him, a man from the same regiment; and they both quite deliberately got out of the camp before either could be re-documented and re-posted. This second man had only a mother and sister as close family, who were both killed in one of the very first air-raids on Plymouth; and for some (doubtless considerable) sum of money, donated by the protective Whitaker parents, this man agreed to leave on permanent record the official War Office version of his fate after Dunkirk – 'Missing presumed killed' – and for the rest of the war to assume the name and role of Ambrose Whitaker. In short, my guess is that the man who came up from Bodmin to see Dodo <u>was not Ambrose Whitaker at all</u>.

Your own guess about things fitted some of the facts well enough; but those facts also fit into a totally different pattern. Just consider some of them again. First, there was the weekly letter from Bristol, from parents who seemingly didn't even want to acknowledge their daughter and who hid all the family photos when you stayed with them. Odd! Then, take this daughter of theirs, Dodo. No great shakes physically, and only just up to attracting an impressionable young man after he'd had a few pints (please don't think me unfair!) in a dim pub-lounge or a candle-lit bedroom – yet she decided to hide whatever charms she'd got under a baggy boiler-suit. Decidedly odd! What else did you tell me about her? She was nervy; she had a deepish voice; she wore too much face-powder; she knew a great deal about the war ... (You've guessed the truth by now, I'm sure.) Her Christian name began with 'A', and you saw her sign her name that way at the Record Library – with the sinewy fingers of an executant musician. But that *wasn't* odd, was it? Her name *did* begin with 'A', and Ambrose Whitaker, as we know, was himself a fine pianist. And so it wasn't only the scar on her jaw she was anxious to conceal with those layers of face-powder – it was the stubble of a beard that grew there every day. Because Dodo Whitaker was a man! And not just any tuppeny-ha'penny old man, either: he was Ambrose Whitaker.

Two points remain to be cleared up. First, why was it necessary for Ambrose Whitaker to pose as a woman? Second, what was the relationship between Ambrose and the artillery corporal from Bodmin? On the first point, it's clear that if he wanted to avoid any further wartime traumas Ambrose couldn't stay in Bristol, where he was far too well known. Even if he moved to a place where he wasn't known, it wouldn't have been completely safe to move as a man; because suspicious questions were always going to be asked in wartime about a young fellow who looked as if he might well be dodging the column. So he took out a double insurance on his deception – for him a desperately needed deception – not only by moving to Oxford, but also by dressing and living as a woman. On the second point, we don't perhaps need to probe too deeply into the reasons why the sensitive and effeminate Ambrose was happy to take every opportunity of spending his nights with (forgive me!) the rather crude, whisky-swilling opportunist you got to know in the war. Such speculation is always a little distasteful, and I will say no more about it.

I rang Ambrose's widow, asking for a wartime photograph of her husband, and I gave her your address, telling her you are an archivist working for the Imperial War Museum. You should hear from her soon; and when you do you'll be as near as anyone is ever likely to be to knowing the truth about this curious affair.

E. M.

It was two days later that a still-pyjamaed Wise took delivery of a stiff white envelope, in which he found a brief note, together with a photograph of a young man in army uniform – a photograph in which no attempt had been made to turn the left-hand side of the sitter's face away from the honesty of the camera lens, or to retouch the line of a cruel scar that stretched across the face's lower jaw. And as Philip Wise looked down at the photograph he saw staring back at him the familiar, faithless eyes of Dodo Whitaker.

AT THE LULU-BAR
MOTEL

'I am sorry I have not learnt to play at cards. It is very useful in life.'

(Samuel Johnson, as reported by Boswell in
Tour to the Hebrides)

I shall never be able to forget what Louis said – chiefly, no doubt, because he said it so often, a cynical smile slowly softening that calculating old mouth of his: 'People are so gullible!' – that's what he kept on saying, our Louis. And I've used those selfsame words a thousand times myself – used them again last night to this fat-walleted coach-load of mine as they debussed at the Lulu-Bar Motel before tucking their starched napkins over their legs and starting into one of Louis' five-star four-coursers, with all the wines and a final slim liqueur. Yes, people are so gullible ... Not *quite* all of them (make no mistake!) – and please don't misunderstand me. This particular manifestation of our human frailty is of only marginal concern to me personally, since occasionally I cut a thinnish slice of that great cake for myself – as I did just before I unloaded those matching sets of leather cases and hulked them round the motel corridors.

But let's get the chronology correct. All that hulking around comes right after we've pulled into the motel where – as always – I turn to all the good people (the black briefcase tight under my right arm) and tell them we're here, folks; here for the first-night stop on a wunnerful tour, which every single one o' you is goin' to enjoy real great. From tomorrow – and I'm real sorry about this, folks – you won't have me personally lookin' after you any more; but that's how the operation operates. I'm just the first-leg man myself, and someone else'll have the real privilege of drivin' you out on the second leg post-breakfast. Tonight itself, though, I'll be hangin' around the cocktail bar (got that?), and if you've any problems about . . . well, about *anything*, you just come along and talk to me, and we'll sort things out real easy. One thing, folks. Just one small friendly word o' counsel to you all. There's one or two guys around these parts who are about as quick an' as slick an' as smooth as a well-soaped ferret. Now, the last thing I'd ever try to do is stop you enjoyin' your vaycaytions, and maybe one or two of you could fancy your chances with a deck o' cards against the deadliest dealer from here to Detroit. But . . . well, as I say, just a friendly word o' counsel, folks. Which is this: *some people are so gullible!* – and I just wouldn't like it if any o' you – well, as I say, I just wouldn't like it.

That's the way I usually dress it up, and not a bad little dressing up at that, as I think you'll agree. 'OK' (do I hear you say?) 'if some of them want to transfer their savings to someone else's account – so what? You can't live other folks' lives for them, now can you? You did your best, Danny boy. So forget it!' Which all makes good logical sense, as I know. But they still worry me a little – all those warm-hearted, clean-living folk, because – well, simply because they're so gullible. And if you don't relish reading about such pleasant folk who plop like juicy pears into the pockets of sharp-fingered charlatans – well, you're not going to like this story. You're not going to like it one little bit.

Most of them were in their sixties or early seventies (no children on the Luxi-Coach Package Tours), and as they filed past the old driving cushion they slipped me a few bucks each and thanked me for a real nice way to start a vaycaytion.

After that it took a couple of hours to hump all that baggage around the rooms, and it was half-past eight before I got down to some of Lucy's chicken curry. Lucy? She's a honey of a girl – the sort of big-breasted blonde that most of my fellow sinners would willingly seek to seduce and, to be honest with you . . . But let me return to the theme.

The cocktail bar is a flashily furnished, polychrome affair, with deep, full-patterned carpet, orange imitation-leather seats and soft wall-lighting in a low, pink glow; and by about half-past nine the place was beginning to fill up nicely. Quite a few of them I recognized from the coach: but there were others. Oh yes, there were a few others . . .

He wasn't a big fellow – five-six, five-seven – and he wore a loud check suit just like they used to do on the movies. When I walked in he was standing by the bar, a deck of cards shuttling magically from hand to hand. 'Fancy a game, folks? Lukey's the name.' He was pleasant enough, I suppose, in an ugly sort of way; and with his white teeth glinting in a broad-mouthed smile, you could almost stop disliking him. Sometimes.

It was just before ten when he got his first bite – a stocky, middle-aged fellow who looked as if he could take pretty good care of himself, thank you. So. So, I watched them idly as they sat opposite each other at one of the smooth-topped central tables, and it wasn't long before a few others began watching, too. It was a bit of interest – a bit of an incident. And it wasn't *their* money at stake.

Now Lukey loved one game above all others, and I'll have to bare its bones a bit if you're going to follow the story. (Be patient, please: we're running along quite nicely now.) First, it's a dollar stake in the kitty, all right? Then two cards are dealt to each of the players, the court cards counting ten, the ace eleven, and all the other cards living up to their marked face-value. Thus it follows, as day follows night and as luck follows Luke, that the gods are grinning at you if you pick up a ten and an ace – for that is vingt-et-un, my friends, whether you reckon by Fahrenheit or Centigrade, and twenty-one's the best they come. And so long as you remember not to break that twenty-one-mile speed-limit, you can buy as many more cards as you like and . . . but I don't think you're going to have much trouble in following things.

It was the speed with which hand followed hand that surprised all the on-lookers, since our challenger ('Call me Bart') was clearly no stranger to the Lukesberry rules and five or six hands were through every minute. Slap! A dollar bill in the kitty. Slap! A dollar bill on top. Flick, flick; flick, flick; buy; stick; bust. Dollar, dollar; flick, flick; quicker, ever quicker. Soon I'm standing behind Barty and I can see his cards. He picks up a ten, and a four; and without mulling it over for a micro-second he says, 'Stick.' Then Lukey turns over a seven, and an eight – and then he flicks over another card for himself: a Jack. Over the top! And Barty pockets yet another kitty; and it's back to that dollar-dollar, flick-flicking again. And when Bart wins again, Luke asks him nicely if he'd like to deal. But Bart declines the kind offer. 'No,' he says. 'I'm on a nice li'l winnin' streak here, pal, so just you keep on dealing them pretty li'l beauties same as before – that's all I ask.'

So Lukey goes on doing just that; and by all that's supersonic what a sharp our Lukey is! I reckon you'd need more than a slow-motion replay to appreciate that prestissimo prestidigitation of his. You could watch those fingers with the eagle eye of old Cortes – and yet whether he was flicking the cards from the top or the middle or the bottom, I swear no one could ever tell. In spite of all this, though, Barty-boy is still advancing his winnings. Now he picks up a seven, and a four; and he decides to buy another card for ten dollars. So Lukey covers the ten dollars from his own fat roll, deals Barty a nine – and things are looking mighty good. Then Luke turns over his own pair (why he bothers, I can't really say, for he knows them all along): a six, and a nine, they are – and things look pretty bad. He turns over another card from the deck – an eight. And once more he's out of his dug-out and over the top.

'My luck'll change soon,' says Luke.

'Not with me, it won't,' says Bart, picking up the twenty-two dollars from the kitty.

'You quitting, you mean?'

'I'm quitting,' says Bart.

'You've played before, I reckon.'

'Yep.'

'You always quit when you're winning?'

'Yep.'

Luke says nothing for a few seconds. He just picks up the deck and looks at it sourly, as if something somewhere in the universe has gone mildly askew. Then he calls on the power of the poets and he quotes the only lines he's ever learned:

'Barty,' he says,

'"If you can make one heap of all your winnings
And risk it on one turn of pitch and toss . . ."'

Remember that? What about it? You've taken seventy-odd dollars off o' me, and I'm just suggestin' that if you put 'em

101

in the middle – and if I cover 'em . . . What do you say? One hand, that's all.'

The audience was about thirty strong now, and as many were urging Barty *on* as were urging him *off*. And they were all pretty committed, too – one way or the other. One of them in particular . . .

I'd seen him earlier at the bar, and a quaint little fellow he was, too. By the look of him he was in his mid- or late-seventies, no more than four-ten, four-eleven, in his built-up shoes. His face was deeply tanned and just as deeply lined, and he wore a blazer gaudily striped in red and royal blue. Underneath the blazer pocket, tastelessly yet lovingly picked out in purple cotton, was the legend: Virgil K. Perkins Jnr. Which made you wonder whether Virgil K. Perkins Snr was still somewhere in circulation – although a further glance at his senile son seemed to settle that particular question in the negative. Well, it's this old-timer who tries pretty hard to get Barty to pocket his dollars and call it a night. And for a little while it seemed that Barty was going to listen. But no. He's tempted – and he falls.

'Okey doke,' says Barty. 'One more hand it is.'

It was Luke now who seemed to look mildly uneasy as he covered the seventy-odd dollars and squared up the deck. From other parts of the room the crowd was rolling up in force again: forty, fifty of them now, watching in silence as Luke dealt the cards. Barty let his pair of cards lie on the table a few seconds and his hands seemed half full of the shakes as he picked them up. A ten; and a six. Sixteen. And for the first time that evening he hesitated, as he fell to figuring out the odds. Then he said, 'Stick'; but it took him twice to say it because the first 'stick' got sort of stuck in his larynx. So it was Lukey's turn now, and he slowly turned over a six – and then a nine. Fifteen. And Luke frowned a long time at his fifteen and his right hand toyed with the next card on the top of the deck, quarter turning it, half turning it, almost turning it – and then putting it back.

'Fifteen,' he said.

'*Sixteen*,' says Barty, and his voice was vibrant as he grabbed the pile of notes in the middle.

Then he was gone.

The on-lookers were beginning to drift away as Luke sat still in his seat, the cards still shuttling endlessly from one large palm to the other. It was the old boy who spoke to him first.

'You deserve a drink, sir!' he says. 'Virgil K. Perkins Junior's the name, and this is my li'l wife, Minny.'

'We're from Omaha,' says Minny dutifully.

And so Virgil gets Luke a rye whiskey, and they start talking.

'You a card player yourself, Mr Perkins?'

'Me? No, sir,' says Virgil. 'Me and the li'l wife here' (Minny was four or five inches the taller) 'were just startin' on a vaycaytion together, sir. We're from Omaha, just like she says.'

But the provenance of these proud citizens seemed of no great importance to Luke. 'A few quick hands, Mr Perkins?'

'No,' says Virgil, with a quiet smile.

'Look, Mr Perkins! I don't care – I just don't *care* – whether it's winnin' or losin', and that's the truth. Now if we just—'

'No!' says Virgil.

'You musta heard of beginner's luck?'

'*No!*' says Virgil.

'You're from Omaha, then?' says Luke, turning all pleasant-like to Minny . . .

I left them there, walked over to the bar, and bought an orange juice from Lucy, who sometimes comes through to serve about ten o'clock. She's wearing a lowly cut blouse, and a highly cute hair-style. But she says nothing to me; just winks – unsmilingly.

Sure enough, when I returned to the table, there was Virgil K. Perkins 'just tryin' a few hands', as he put it; and I don't really need to drag you through all the details, do I? It's all going to end up exactly as you expect . . . but perhaps I'd better put it down, if only for the record; and I'll make it all as brief as I can.

From the start it followed the usual pattern: a dollar up; a dollar down. Nice and easy, take it gently; and soon the little fellow was beaming broadly, and picking up his cards with accelerating eagerness. But, of course, the balance was slowly swinging against him: twenty dollars down; thirty; forty . . .

'Lucky little run for me,' says Luke with a disarming smile, as if for two dimes he'd shovel all his winnings across the table and ease that ever-tightening look round Virgil's mouth. It was all getting just a little obvious, too, and surely someone soon would notice those nimble fingers that forever flicked those eights and nines when only fours and fives could save old Virgil's day. And someone did.

'Why don't you let the old fella deal once in a while?' asks one.

'Yeah, why not?' asks another.

'You wanna deal, pop?' concedes Luke.

But Virgil shakes his white head. 'I've had enough,' he says. 'I shouldn't really—'

'Come on,' says Minny gently.

'He can deal. Sure he can, if he wants to,' says Luke.

'He can't deal off the bottom, though!'

Luke was on his feet in a flash, looking round the room. 'Who said that?' he asked, and his voice was tight and mean. All conversation had stopped, and no one was prepared to own up. Least of all me – who'd said it.

'Well,' said Luke, as he resumed his seat, 'that does it, pop! If I'm bein' accused of cheatin' by some lily-livered coward who won't repeat such villainous vilification – then we'll have to settle the question as a matter of honour, I reckon. *You* deal, pop!'

The old man hesitated – but not for too long. 'Honour' was one of those big words with a capital letter, and wasn't a thing you could shove around too lightly. So he picked up the cards and he shuffled them, boxing and botching the whole business with an awkwardness almost unmatched in the annals of card-play. But somehow he managed to square the deck – and he dealt.

'I'll buy one,' says Luke, slipping a ten-dollar bill into the middle.

Virgil slowly covers the stake, and then pushes over a card.

'Stick,' says Luke.

Taking from his blazer pocket an inordinately large handkerchief, the old man mops his brow and turns his own cards over: a queen; and – an ace!

Luke merely shrugs his shoulders and pushes the kitty across. 'That's the way to do it, pop! Just you keep dealing yourself a few hands like that and—'

'No!' cries Minny, who'd been bleating her forebodings intermittently from the very beginning.

But Virgil lays a gentle hand on her shoulder. 'Don't be cross with me, old girl. And don't *worry*! I'm just a-goin' to deal myself one more li'l hand and . . .'

And another, and another, and another. And the gods were not smiling on the little man from Omaha: not the slightest sign of the meanest grin. Was it merely a matter of saving Face? Of preserving Honour? No, sir! It seemed just plain desperation as the old boy chased his losses round and round that smooth-topped table, with Minny sitting there beside him, her eyes tightly closed as if she was pinning the remnants of her hopes in the power of silent prayer. (I hitched the briefcase tighter under my right arm as I caught sight of Lucy behind the crowd, her eyes holding mine – again unsmilingly.)

By half-past ten Virgil K. Perkins Jnr had lost one thousand dollars, and he sat there crumpled up inside his chair. It wasn't as if he was short of friends, for the large audience had been behind him all along, just willing the old fellow to win. And it wasn't as if anyone could blame our nimble-fingered Lukey any more, for it was Virgil himself who had long since been dealing out his own disasters.

Not any longer, though. He pushed the deck slowly across the table and stood up. 'I'm sorry, old girl,' he says to Minny, and his voice is all choked up. 'It was your money as much as mine . . .'

But Luke was leaning across and he put his mighty palm on the old boy's skinny wrist. And he speaks quietly. 'Look, pop! You've just lost yourself a thousand bucks, right? So I want you to listen to me carefully because I'm gonna tell you how we can put all that to rights again. Now, we'll just have one more hand—'

'NO!' (The little old lady's voice was loud and shrill this time.) 'He *won't*! He won't lay down another dollar, d'you hear me? He's just – he's just a poor old fool, can't you see that? He's just a gullible, poor old—' But the rest of her words were strangled in her throat, and Virgil sat down again and put his arm round her shoulder as she began to weep silently.

'Don't you *want* to get all your money back?' Luke's voice is quiet again, but everyone can hear his words.

'Don't listen to him!' shouts one.

'Call it a day, sir!' shouts another.

Says Luke, turning to all of them: 'Old pop, here, he's got one helluva sight more spunk in him than the rest o' you put together! And, what's more, not a single man jack o' you knows the proposition I'm proposin'. Well?' (Luke looks around real bold.) 'Well? *Do* you?'

It was all silence again now, as Luke looks across to Virgil and formulates his offer. 'Look, pop. I've been mighty lucky tonight, as I think you might agree. So, I'm going to give you the sort o' chance you'll never have again. And this is what we'll do. We'll have just one last hand and we'll take two points off my score. Got that? I pick up eighteen – we call it sixteen. And just the same whatever score it is. What do you say, pop?'

But old Virgil – he shakes his head. 'You're a good sport, Luke, but—'

'Let's make it *three* off then,' says Luke earnestly. 'I pick up twenty – we call it seventeen. OK? Look, pop!' (He leans across and grips the wrist again.) 'Nobody's *ever* gonna make you any better offer than that. *Nobody*. You know something?

107

It's virtually *certain* you're gonna get all that lovely money right back into that wallet o' yours, now, isn't it?'

It was tempting. Ye gods, it was tempting! And it was soon clear that the audience was thinking it was pretty tempting, too, with a good many of them revising their former estimate of things.

'What d'you say?' asks Luke.

'No,' says Virgil. 'It's not just me – it's Minny here. I've made enough of a fool of myself for one night, haven't I, old girl?'

Then Minny looked at him, straight on, like. A surprising change had come over her tear-stained face, and her blue eyes blazed with a sudden surge of almost joyous challenge. 'You take him on, Virgil!' she says, with a quiet, proud authority.

But Virgil still sat there dejected and indecisive. His hands ran across that shock of wavy white hair, and for a minute or two he pondered to himself. Then he decided. He took most of the remaining notes from his wallet, and counted them with lingering affection before stacking them neatly in the centre of the table. 'Do you wanna count 'em, Luke?' he says. And it was as if the tide had suddenly turned; as if the old man sensed the smell of victory in his nostrils.

For a few seconds now it seemed to be Luke who was nervy and hesitant, the brashness momentarily draining from him. But the offer had been taken up, and the fifty or sixty onlookers were in no mood to let him forget it. He slowly counted out his own bills, and placed them on the top of Virgil's.

Two thousand dollars – on one hand.

Luke has already picked up the deck, and now he's shuffling the spots with his usual, casual expertise.

'Why are *you* dealin'?'

Luke looks up, and stares me hard in the eye. 'Was that *you* just spoke, mister?'

I nod. 'Yep. It was me. And I wanna know why it is you think you got some goddam right to deal them cards – because you don't deal 'em straight, brother. You flick 'em off the top and you flick 'em off the bottom and for all I know you flick 'em—'

'I'll see you outside, mister, as soon as—'

'You'll do no such thing,' I replies quietly. 'I just ain't goin' to be outside no more tonight again – least of all for you, brother.'

He looked mighty dangerous then – but I just didn't care. The skin along his knuckles was growing white as he slowly got to his feet and moved his chair backwards. And then, just as slowly, he sat himself down again – and he surprises everybody. He pushes the deck over the table and he says: 'He's right, pop. *You* deal!'

Somehow old pop's shaking hands managed to shuffle the cards into some sort of shape; and when a couple of cards fall to the floor, it's me who bends down and hands them back to him.

'Cut,' says pop.

So Luke cuts – about halfway down the deck (though knowing Lukey I should think it was *exactly* halfway down). Miraculously, it seems, old Virgil's hands had gotten themselves rid of any shakes, and he deals the cards out firm and fine: one for Luke, one for himself; another for Luke, and

109

another for himself. For a few moments each man left them lying there on the top of the table. Then Luke picks up his own – first the one, and then the other.

'Stick!' he says, and his voice is a bit hoarse.

Every eye in the room was now on Virgil as he turned over his first card – a seven; then the second card – a ten. Seventeen! And all you've got to do, my friends, is to add on three – and that's a handsome little twenty, and the whole room was mumbling and murmuring in approval.

Every eye now switches to Luke, and in the sudden tense silence the cards are slowly turned: first a king, and then – ye gods! – an ace! And as Lukey smiles down at that beautiful twenty-oner the audience groaned like they always do when its favourite show-jumper knocks the top off the last fence.

And where, my friends, do we go from there? Well, I'll tell you. It was Lucy who started it all immediately Luke had left. She pushed her way through the on-lookers and plunged her hand deep down between those glorious breasts of hers to clutch her evening's tips.

'Mr Perkins, isn't it? I know it isn't all that much; but – but if it'll help, please take it.' About seven or eight dollars, it was, no more – but, believe me, it bore its fruit two-hundred-fold. It was me who was next. I'd taken about thirty-five dollars on the coach and (once more hitching the old briefcase higher under my arm) I fished it all out of my ·back pocket and placed it a-top of Lucy's crumpled offerings.

'Mr Perkins,' I said sombrely. 'You should've been on *my* coach, old friend.' That's all I said.

As for Virgil, he said nothing. He just sat back all crumpled up like before, with Minny sobbing silently beside him. I reckon he looked as if he couldn't trust himself to say a single word. But it didn't matter. All the audience was sad and sullenly sympathetic – and, as I said, they'd had their fill of Louis' vintage wines. And I've got to hand it to them. Twenty dollars; another twenty dollars; a fifty; a few tens; another twenty; another fifty – I watched them all as these clean-living, God-fearing folk forked something from their careful savings. And I reckon there wasn't a single man-jack of them who didn't make his mark upon that ever-mounting pile. But still Virgil said nothing. When finally he stumbled his way to the exit, holding Minny in one hand and a very fat pile of other people's dollars in the other, he turned round as if he was going to say something to all his very good friends. But still the words wouldn't come, it seemed; and he turned once more and left the cocktail bar.

I woke late the next morning, and only then because Luke was leaning over me, gently shaking me by the shoulder.

'Louis says he wants to see you at half-past ten.'

I lifted my left arm and focused on the wrist-watch: already five to ten.

'You all right, Danny?' Luke was standing by the door now (he must have had a key for that!) and for some reason he didn't look mightily happy.

'Sure, sure!'

'Half-past, then,' repeated Luke, and closed the door behind him.

I still felt very tired, and I was conscious that the back of my head was aching – and that's unusual for me. Nothing to drink the night before – well, only the odd orange juice that Lucy had . . . orange juice . . . ? I fell to wondering slightly,

111

and turned to look at the other side of the bed, where the sheet was neatly turned down in a white hypotenuse. Lucy had gone – doubtless gone early; but then Lucy was always sensible and careful about such things . . .

I saw my face frowning as I stood in front of the shaving-mirror; and I was still frowning when I took the suit off the hanger in the wardrobe and noticed that the briefcase was gone. But I'd have been frowning even more if the briefcase *hadn't* gone; and as I dressed, my head was clearing nicely. I picked up the two thick sealed envelopes that had nestled all night under my pillow, put them, one each, into the pockets of my overcoat, and felt happy enough when I knocked on the door of Louis' private suite and walked straight in. It was ten thirty-two.

There were the usual six chairs round the oblong table, and four of them were taken already: there was Luke, and there was Barty; then there was Minny; and at the head of the table, Louis himself – a Louis still, doubtless, no more than four-ten, four-eleven in his built-up shoes, but minus that garishly striped blazer now; minus, too, that shock of silvery hair which the previous evening had covered that large, bald dome of his.

'You're late,' he says, but not unpleasantly. 'Sit down, Danny.' So I sat down, feeling like a little boy in the first grade. (But I usually feel like that with Louis.)

'You seen Lucy?' asks Minny, as Barty pours me a drop of Irish.

'Lucy? No – have you tried her room?'

But no one seemed much willing to answer that one, and we waited for a few minutes in silence before Louis spoke again.

'Danny,' he says, 'you'll remember that when we brought you into our latest li'l operation a few months back I figured we'd go for about a quarter of a million before we launched out on a new one?'

I nodded.

'Well, we're near enough there now as makes no odds – a fact perhaps you may yourself be not completely unaware of? After all, Danny, it was one o' your jobs to take my li'l Lucy down to the bank on Mondays, now wasn't it? And I reckon you've got a pretty clear idea of how things are.'

I nodded again, and kept on looking him straight in the eyes.

'Well, it was never no secret from any of us – was it? – that I'd be transferrin' this li'l investment o' mine over to Luke and Bartholomew here as soon as they – well, as soon as they showed me they was worthy.'

I was nodding slowly all the time now; but he'd left something out. 'Lucy was goin' to be in it, too,' I said.

'You're very fond of my Lucy, aren't you?' says Minny quietly.

'Yep. I'm very fond of her, Minny.' And that was the truth.

'It's not bin difficult for any of us to see that, old girl, now has it?' Louis turned to Minny and patted her affectionately on the arm. Then he focuses on me again. 'You needn't have no worries about my li'l daughter, Danny. No worries at all! Did it never occur to you to wonder just why I christened this latest li'l investment o' mine as the "Lulu-Bar Motel"?'

For a few seconds I must have looked a little puzzled, but my head was clearing nicely with the whiskey, and I suddenly saw what he meant. Yes! What a deep old devil our Louis was! The *Lu*-cy, *Lu*-ke, *Bar*-tholomew Motel . . .

But Louis was still speaking: 'I only asked you down this mornin', Danny, because I was hopin' to wind it all up here and now – and to let you know how much I've bin aware o' your own li'l contribution. But – well, it's all tied up in a way with Lucy, isn't it? And I reckon' (he looked at Luke and Bart) 'I reckon we'd better call another li'l meeting tonight? About eight? All right?'

It seemed all right to all of us, and I got up to go.

'You off to town, Danny?' asks Louis, eyeing the overcoat.

'Yep.' That's all I said. Then I left them there and caught the bus to the station.

I'd always noticed it before: whenever I'd felt a bit guilty about anything it was as if I sensed that other people somehow seemed to *know*. But that's behind us now. And, anyway, it had been Lucy's idea originally – not mine. She'd needed me, of course, for devising the cheque and forging Louis' signature – for though I'm about as ham-fisted with a deck of cards as an arthritic octopus, I got my own particular specialism. Yes, sir! And Lucy trusted me, too, because I'd been carrying all that lovely money – 240,000 dollars of it! – all neatly stacked in five-hundred bills, all neatly enveloped and neatly sealed – why, I'd been carrying it all around with me in the old briefcase for two whole days! And Lucy – Lucy, my love! – we shall soon be meeting at the ticket barrier on number one platform – and then be drifting off together quietly in the twilight . . .

At a quarter to twelve I was there – standing in my overcoat and waiting happily. (Lucy had never been early in her life.) I lit another cigarette; then another. By twelve forty-five I was beginning to worry a little; by one forty-five I was beginning to worry a lot; and by two forty-five I was beginning to guess at the truth. Yet still I waited – waited and waited and waited. And, in a sense, I suppose, I've been waiting for Lucy ever since . . .

It was when the big hand on the station clock came round to four that I finally called it a day and walked over to look at the Departure Board. I found a train that was due for New York in forty-five minutes, and I thought that that had better be that. I walked into the buffet and sat down with a coffee. So? So, here was yet another of life's illusions lying shattered in the dust, and yet . . . Poor, poor, lovely Lucy! I nearly allowed myself a saddened little smile as I thought of her opening up those two big envelopes in the briefcase – and finding there those 480 pieces of crisp, new paper, each exactly the size of a 500-dollar bill. She must have thought I was pretty – well, pretty gullible, I suppose, when we'd both agreed that *she* should take away the briefcase . . .

A single to New York would cost about fifty or sixty dollars, I reckoned; and as I joined what seemed to be the shorter queue at the ticket office I took the bulky envelope from the right-hand pocket of the overcoat, opened it – and stood there stunned and gorgonized. Inside were about 240 pieces of crisp, new paper, each exactly the size of a 500-dollar bill; and my hands were trembling as I stood away from the queue and opened the other envelope. Exactly the same. Well, no – not *exactly* the same. On the top piece of blank paper there were three lines of writing in Louis' unmistakably minuscule hand:

I did my best to tell you Danny boy but you never did really understand that filosofy of mine now did you? It's just what I kept on telling you all along. People . . .

By now, though, I reckon you'll know those last few words that Louis wrote.

I walked back across to the buffet and ordered another coffee, counting up what I had in my pockets: just ten dollars and forty cents; and I fell to wondering where it was I went from here. Perhaps . . . perhaps there were one or two things in my favour. At least I could spell 'philosophy'; and then there was always the pretty big certainty (just as Louis said so often) that somewhere soon I'd find a few nice, kindly, gullible folk.

But as I glance around at the faces of my fellow men and women in the station buffet now, they all look very mean, and very hard.

NEIGHBOURHOOD WATCH

Sed quis custodiet ipsos custodes?

(But what about the vigilantes? Who's going to watch after *them*?)

(Juvenal, *Satires*)

'We must never make the criminal the *hero*, though!' proclaimed Marcus Price, Fellow of All Souls, as he drained his beer and put down his glass with the gesture of a man announcing to the company that *he'd* bought the previous round himself and whose turn, pray, was it now.

'What about old Raffles, though? Gentleman-burglar and all that. Remember him?'

The speaker was another Oxford don, Denis Stockman, an authority (*the* authority) on the Grand Duchy of Lithuania in the fifteenth century.

'Stole the Crown Jewels or something,' Stockman continued, 'then took 'em back when he found out what they were. No chivalry like that these days, eh, Morse?'

'Oh no,' mumbled Morse.

Oh dear! But Morse had only himself to blame. He'd meant to nip into the King's Arms just briefly that Wednesday lunchtime; and for a start things had looked promising. The one other customer was a very attractive thirty-odd-year-old brunette with sludgy green eyes. She had smiled momentarily as he'd sat down a few feet from her – before turning her attention back to *The Times* crossword puzzle, in which even as he took his first draught she wrote another word, with her left hand, the middle fingernail marked with a broad, white lateral line, as if she might have trapped it in a door.

Yes, only himself to blame . . .

Almost as soon as they'd spotted him there they'd pounced. *How* long is it? Mind if we *join* you? What are you *drinking*? Morse should, of course, have pleaded urgency in some criminal pursuit. But he didn't. The prospect of a further pint gladdened his heart, and he heard himself saying, 'Best Bitter.'

It was the fourth member of the quartet who now volunteered to get in the second round of drinks – a small, bald-headed man with a beer-belly and an NHS hearing-aid in his right ear. Morse had met him once or twice before and recalled that he'd been a refugee from pre-war Germany who now lived (very near Morse, wasn't it?) in a large North Oxford property reputedly stuffed with eminently collectable furniture and ornaments. Yes! Dr Eric Ullman – that was his name! A bachelor – like Morse.

'Good health, gentlemen!' Ullman's diction was precise, pedantic almost, as he raised his glass and toasted his two university acquaintances – and the chief inspector. 'And please forgive me perhaps if I tell you something – well, something that may surprise you a little?'

If any of the three pairs of eyebrows raised themselves, it was by little more than a millimetre.

'You're wrong, I think,' began Ullman, 'about there being no honour among thieves these days. Please let me explain. Last Friday I went to see *Così fan Tutte* at the Apollo Theatre here in Oxford. The Welsh National were doing it – doing it this week too, as you'll know. I got home at about a quarter past eleven, and most foolishly I didn't bother to put my car away in the garage. Next morning, when I looked out of the window? The drive was completely empty. The car was gone!'

'Metro, wasn't it?' asked Price.

Ullman nodded. 'I've had it for nine years.'

Stockman coughed slightly. 'Was it *worth* pinching, Eric?'

'It was worth a lot to me,' said Ullman simply.

Price grinned. 'Three hundred quid – in part exchange? No more.'

'You didn't *hear* anything?' asked Morse.

'No. And shall I tell you something else? They'd even closed the gates behind them.'

'Probably *pushed* it out of the drive,' suggested Morse. 'Saves any noise. And you're only a couple of hundred yards from the Ring Road . . .'

'I suppose so.'

'Did you ring us? Ring the police?'

'Straightaway. It would probably turn up in three or four days, they said. Out on one of the estates – minus wheels, minus radio, minus anything detachable – panels kicked in – windows smashed . . .'

'Bloody *mind*-less, isn't it!' Price shook his head vehemently. 'I know what I'd give some of these young sods – and it *wouldn't* be a few gentle hours of community service!'

'Just – just a minute.' Ullman raised his right hand, and the others were silent again. 'You see, they *didn't* find it out in East Oxford. Oh no. Three days went by, and then on Monday – last Monday – I was invited out to dinner at The Randolph. And when I got back, about eleven or so, there – there in the drive . . .'

Ullman was telling his little tale well, and three pairs of eyes now betrayed an unexpected interest.

'. . . completely undamaged – in fact looking *very* spick-and-span. And under the windscreen wiper – this!'

From his breast-pocket he took out a letter, a letter written in a small, neat, upright script, with no address, no date, no salutation, no valediction; a letter which each of Ullman's immediate audience now read in turn:

Sorry about the inconvenience – very sorry indeed. I just had to have a car and your's was there. Its had a shampoo and I filled the petrol tank – unleaded, like it says in the handbook. Your little car saved my bacon, that's the truth, and I'm grateful. Please then do me the honour of accepting the enclosed ticket. I know you enjoy opera. I wasn't sure what performance to choose but Wagner is king for me, and in my opinion Die Valkurie is the greatest thing he ever wrote. Enjoy your evening, and thanks again.

Morse was the last to read the letter, his face betraying some slight puzzlement – as Ullman produced a ticket for the following Friday's performance.

£40!

Phew!

'Is it genuine?' queried Stockman.

' "Ring-side" seat, if you see what I mean,' replied Ullman.

Morse smiled gently at the little man's pleasantry as he held the ticket up to the light and pretended to be checking a possible irregularity of watermark.

'Genuine enough, I reckon,' he said, wishing dearly that the ticket was his own.

Beer glasses were empty again now, and Morse decided that it was either him or Stockman for the next round.

Let it be Stockman!

The back bar was a popular venue – ill-designed, intimate, awkward – and was now almost full this mid-lunchtime as Morse excused his premature departure and carefully squeezed his way past the woman to his right. Apparently she had been paying more attention to Ullman than to her crossword puzzle, for as far as Morse could see she had made very little, if any, progress.

And indeed Morse was right. Like most of the other customers there she had been very interested in Ullman's tale; interested in one or two other things as well. Had anyone apart from herself, for example, noticed that Morse (inadvertently?) had forgotten to hand back to Ullman the letter from the car thief? Had anyone apart from herself observed the conspiratorial exchange of glances between the two of them – between the man the others called Morse and Ullman himself? 'Conspiratorial'? No, that was too strong a word for it, perhaps. But something *like* that had been there. She could have sworn it.

Interesting!

There was something else too. After Morse had left, the little man's eyes had caught hers – almost as if she might have been a vague acquaintance. Not that she was: she'd never seen him in her life before. But she thought there'd been something almost . . . sinister about his look. 'Sinister'? Yes, that *wasn't* too strong a word for it. It was as if he knew something about her that she hardly knew herself.

Morse sauntered around Blackwell's for half an hour before walking over to the bus stop in Cornmarket. On the ride back to Kidlington he read the letter twice more, reflecting yet again on the bizarre coincidence that a car thief – a car thief! – should share his own highly idiosyncratic view about the greatest opera ever composed . . . Reflecting also on just those two (forgivable?) lapses in English grammar; and on that one (wholly unforgivable!) lapse which still puzzled Morse sorely as he walked up the incline to Police HQ.

'Nice, er, lunch, sir?' Lewis broke off his typing and looked down at his wrist-watch.

'Shut up and listen! Chap has his car pinched – OK? Few days later it's returned, in better nick than when it was pinched – with a note saying very sorry but I had to have a car and to make up for all the trouble here's an expensive ticket for the opera. You with me?'

Lewis nodded.

'So this chap goes along to the opera and when he gets back home—'

'He finds he's been burgled,' said Lewis flatly.

'You been sleeping in the knife-box?'

'No. Heard of it before, sir. There was a case like that a few weeks ago out in High Wycombe – so one of the lads was saying.'

'Oh!'

'Sorry to disappoint you, sir.'

'You think many other people have heard of it?'

'Doubt it. Not the sort of thing you want broadcasting, is it? I mean, you'd probably get lots of copy-cat crimes. For a start anyway.'

'Mm.'

'Clever though.'

124

'Bloody clever!'

'Why did you mention it, sir?'

Morse grinned. 'What are you doing on Friday evening?'

'Not sure. The wife's got a Tupperware party, I think, but—'

'Would you be glad to get away?'

It was Lewis's turn to grin. 'What time do you want me?'

It was at one minute past seven, from the front seats of a white Self Hire van, that the pair of them saw the man leave his property and walk briskly away.

'You're a *very* clever bugger to think of this, you know, Millie!'

'Don't count your chickens – not yet.'

'No – plenty o' time.'

'Three and a half hours – Christ!'

'More'n two football matches.'

'You're a philistine, Charlie!'

'What me? Don't be daft. Wagner's me greatest passion in life, didna tell yer?'

It was from their unmarked car that Morse and Lewis observed Ullman leave on foot. With a new alarm system fitted, and with a stout Krooklok fixed between steering-wheel and clutch, the Metro was now safely housed in the bolted garage. Clearly Ullman was taking no further risks; and in any case, buses were fairly frequent down the Banbury Road – down to the City Centre – down to the Apollo Theatre.

At half-past eight, Lewis ventured his first criticism:

'What time do you say this thing started?'

'Give 'em a *chance*, Lewis! They've got till midnight, near as dammit.'

'But we've already been here—'

'Ssshhh!' hissed Morse as a strong-bodied woman walked up the gravel drive to Ullman's front door, looked around with some interest – before pushing what appeared to be a free newspaper into the letter-box; then retracing her steps, and closing the gate to the drive behind her.

'Exciting little incident, wouldn't you say, sir?' asked Lewis wearily.

But Morse refused to rise to the bait.

At ten minutes past nine, a man opened the drive gate, closed it behind him, and walked up to the front door, where he looked over his shoulder for a good many seconds as if almost expecting to see someone, before extracting the newspaper from the letter-box, finding a key, and entering the house.

Dr Eric Ullman.

Morse was still shaking his head a quarter of an hour later when Lewis came back from the bar at the Dew Drop in Summertown with a pint of Best Bitter, and half a glass of Beamish.

'He might just have got fed up with it, sir? Not everybody's cup o' tea – Wagner.'

'It's *his* cup o' tea though: that's the whole point. No, there's something very wrong somewhere, I'm sure of it,

Lewis. They must've *known* he'd come back early . . . They must have got wind of it somehow.'

'Perhaps Dr Ullman guessed – well, what *you* guessed, sir?'

'Ye-es! Do you know, I think you may be right.' Morse took out the letter yet again. 'You see, whoever wrote this says he's a great Wagner fan, agreed?'

'Like you.'

'Like me, yes. But I don't believe him. Look!' Morse jabbed a forefinger at two words in the letter: 'Die Valkurie'.

Lewis looked appropriately vague. 'All German to me, sir.'

Morse tried to smile. 'Oh no, Lewis! That, if I may say so, is precisely the point. It *isn't* German! If you spend your life with anything – if you read about it – if you think about it – if you play it time and time again—'

'Like you.'

'Like me, yes.'

'I'm still not—'

'He can't even *spell* the bloody word!'

'We all make the occasional spelling mistake—'

'What? Three spelling mistakes in one word? *Three?* Come off it! He spells it with a "V" instead of a "W"; he sticks a spurious "i" in before the "e"; and he misses the umlaut off the "u"—'

'The what, sir?'

Morse peeled the back off a beer-mat and wrote out the correct spelling of the opera: 'Die Walküre'.

'Ullman's a German though, isn't he?' asked Lewis slowly.

'German origin, yes.'

'So why . . . why didn't *he* notice, well – what you noticed?'

'I'm beginning to think he did, Lewis. I'm beginning to think he did.'

'But you still felt pretty certain that Dr Ullman was going to be burgled tonight?'

'If I'd felt all *that* certain, I'd have had a few heavies round the corner in a police van.'

'Well, at least he's still got all that valuable furniture of his – that's one good thing.'

'That's one way of looking at it.'

'You got anything valuable in the furniture line yourself, sir?'

'Me? Oh, just the one piece, that's all. The family heirloom – nest of tables – Chippendale – 1756. What about you?'

'Just the big mahogany wardrobe – Utility – 1942. We've been trying to give it away this last year but nobody seems to appreciate the quality.'

Lewis drove the two of them back up to North Oxford, where on Morse's instruction they stopped for a brief while outside Ullman's residence once again. And even as they watched, the small portly figure of Eric Ullman passed across the uncurtained window of the lighted front room.

'If he's been burgled tonight, I'm a Dutchman,' volunteered Lewis.

But Lewis was no Dutchman, Morse knew that. 'You get off home, Lewis. I'll walk from here.'

'You sure, sir? It must be all of three hundred yards.'

'Less of the sarcasm, Sergeant!'

'Night, sir.'

*

Morse had put out his two Co-op semi-skimmed milk tokens, and was pouring himself a touch of the malt – when he suddenly knew that something was terribly wrong. Why hadn't he spotted the short note on the kitchen table immediately?

> Sorry about the inconvenience – very sorry indeed. It was the only thing you'd got worth pinching though and I'm hoping I'll get a good price.

That was all.

Morse bounded up the stairs, where on the landing he surveyed the empty square of unhoovered carpet upon which, until so very recently, had stood the one *objet d'art* that had been passed down from one generation of the Morse clan to the next – the family heirloom – the nest of tables – Chippendale – 1756.

It was Sergeant Dixon on night duty. 'Thank goodness you've rung, sir. We've been trying to get you but your phone's not been answering—'

'I've been *out*, man! You don't *mind*, do you?'

'Course not. It's just that you've had burglars, I'm afraid—'

'That's exactly what I'm ringing to tell you!'

'No need to worry though, sir. They didn't pinch anything. We've caught 'em – the pair of 'em.'

'You've done *what*?'

'You see this fellow rang us and said there was somebody in your flat, but when our boys got there they'd scarpered.

129

This fellow'd got the number though – white Self Hire van – and we stopped it out on the A40 near Wheatley. Just a few old tables in the back – don't think they could've taken anything of yours, sir. They must have got wind of us somehow, I reckon.'

'Who *was* this fellow?'

'A Dr Ullman, sir – lives quite near you, so he said.'

Morse was shaking his head yet again as he put down the phone. Everything – almost everything – was becoming clear at long last. The same thought must have struck the two of them, both himself and Ullman, in the King's Arms that lunchtime; the same strange thought that far from being a gesture of courtesy and gratitude, the letter and the opera ticket were merely the appropriate stages in a subtle strategy of deception.

Yes!

And Morse's thinking had gone one step further.

And Ullman's thinking had gone *two* steps further.

Morse locked his front door very carefully behind him and walked out into the night.

'A wee drop of the malt, Chief Inspector?'

'Excellent!'

'I was hardly expecting you *tonight*.'

'Did you ever think of joining the police force, Doctor?'

'I'm not tall enough.'

'You were always a move or so ahead of me!'

'Ah! But to be honest with you I *did* have one little

advantage over you. I've got a pair of wrens nesting in the front garden, you see, and I was watching them through the field-glasses recently when I noticed a woman, at the bus stop just outside; and I could see that *she* was watching something too – watching the house, the drive, the garage . . . Then two days later I saw her again, and I looked at her *very* closely through the field-glasses and I could see she was copying something down in a red notebook, writing with her left hand – and I noticed that she had a white scar on the nail of her middle finger, as if she'd trapped it in a door. And then I saw her *again*, didn't I . . .?'

Ullman smiled, and as he did so his features momentarily took on an almost sinister appearance.

'And you felt pretty certain that it was *me* who was going to get burgled tonight,' said Morse slowly.

'It seemed logical, yes. After all, if you were watching *my* property, you couldn't be watching your own as well, now could you?'

'You took a huge risk though.'

'You think so?' The little man appeared puzzled.

'Well, if they burgled *you*, while you were round at my place watching *me* . . .'

'Oh no. I've finished taking risks, you see. The private detective I hired to keep a look-out here was the very best in the business, so they told me: black belt at judo, Lord knows what else.'

'He must have been pretty good – we certainly didn't spot him.'

'*Her*, Chief Inspector. She said she'd probably do her "free-newspaper-delivery" routine—'

'Bloody 'ell!' mumbled Morse to himself.

'—and I told her she could pack it in for the night just after I'd rung the police – just before I got back here – about nine o'clock.'

'Ten past nine, to be accurate – that's when we spotted you.'

'Er' – Ullman coughed modestly and drained his malt – 'if we're to be accurate, Chief Inspector, shouldn't it be when *we* spotted *you*?'

For the last time that day Morse shook his head. Then draining his own glass and making his farewell, slowly he walked the three hundred yards back home.

A CASE OF
MIS-IDENTITY

His friend and foil, the stolid Watson with whom he
shares rooms in Baker Street, attends Holmes throughout
most of his adventures

(*The Oxford Companion to English Literature*)

Long as had been my acquaintance with Sherlock Holmes, I
had seldom heard him refer to his early life; and the
only knowledge I ever gleaned of his family history sprang
from the rare visits of his famous brother, Mycroft. On
such occasions, our visitor invariably addressed me with
courtesy, but also (let me be honest!) with some little
condescension. He was – this much I knew – by some
seven years the senior in age to my great friend, and was
a founder member of the Diogenes Club, that peculiar
institution whose members are ever forbidden to converse
with one another. Physically, Mycroft was stouter than
his brother (I put the matter in as kindly a manner as
possible); but the single most striking feature about him
was the piercing intelligence of his eyes – greyish eyes
which appeared to see beyond the range of normal mortals.
Holmes himself had commented upon this last point: 'My
dear Watson, you have recorded – and I am flattered by
it – something of my own powers of observation and deduction. Know, however, that Mycroft has a degree of observation somewhat the equal of my own; and as for deduction,
he has a brain that is unrivalled – *virtually* unrivalled – in the
northern hemisphere. You may be relieved, however, to learn
that he is a trifle lazy, and quite decidedly somnolent – and
that his executant ability on the violin is immeasurably
inferior to my own.'

(Was there, I occasionally wondered, just the hint of competitive envy between those two unprecedented intellects?)

I had just called at 221B Baker Street on a fog-laden November afternoon in 188–, after taking part in some research at St Thomas's Hospital into suppurative tonsilitis (I had earlier acquainted Holmes with the particulars). Mycroft was staying with Holmes for a few days, and as I entered that well-known sitting room I caught the tail-end of the brothers' conversation.

'Possibly, Sherlock – possibly. But it is the *detail*, is it not? Give me all the evidence and it is just possible that I could match your own analyses from my corner armchair. But to be required to rush hither and thither, to find and examine witnesses, to lie along the carpet with a lens held firmly to my failing sight . . . No! It is not my *métier*.'

During this time Holmes himself had been standing before the window, gazing down into the neutral-tinted London street. And looking over his shoulder I could see that on the pavement opposite there stood an attractive young woman draped in a heavy fur coat. She had clearly just arrived, and. every few seconds was looking up to Holmes's window in hesitant fashion, her fingers fidgeting with the buttons of her gloves. On a sudden she crossed the street, and Mrs Hudson was soon ushering in our latest client.

After handing her coat to Holmes, the young lady sat nervously on the edge of the nearest armchair, and announced herself as Miss Charlotte van Allen. Mycroft nodded briefly at the newcomer, before reverting to a monograph on polyphonic plainchant; whilst Holmes himself made observation of the lady in that abstracted yet intense manner which was wholly peculiar to him.

'Do you not find,' began Holmes, 'that with your short sight it is a little difficult to engage in so much type-writing?'

Surprise, apprehension, appreciation, showed by turns upon her face, succeeded in all by a winsome smile as she appeared to acknowledge Holmes's quite extraordinary powers.

'Perhaps you will also tell me,' continued he, 'why it is that you came from home in such a great hurry?'

For a few seconds, Miss van Allen sat shaking her head with incredulity; then, as Holmes sat staring towards the ceiling, she began her remarkable narrative.

'Yes, I did bang out of the house, because it made me very angry to see the way my father, Mr Wyndham, took the whole business – refusing even to countenance the idea of going to the police, and quite certainly ruling out any recourse to yourself, Mr Holmes! He just kept repeating – and I *do* see his point – that no real harm has been done . . . although he can have no idea of the misery I have had to endure.'

'Your father?' queried Holmes quietly. 'Perhaps you refer to your step-father, since the names are different?'

'Yes,' she confessed, 'my step-father. I don't know why I keep referring to him as "father" – especially since he is but five years older than myself.'

'Your mother – she is still living?'

'Oh, yes! Though I will not pretend I was over-pleased when she remarried so soon after my father's death – and then to a man almost seventeen years younger than herself. Father – my real father, that is – had a plumbing business in the Tottenham Court Road, and Mother carried on the company after he died, until she married Mr Wyndham. I think he considered such things a little beneath his new wife, especially with his being in a rather superior position as a traveller in French wines. Whatever the case, though, he made Mother sell out.'

'Did you yourself derive any income from the sale of your father's business?'

'No. But I do have £100 annual income in my own right; as well as the extra I make from my typing. If I may say so, Mr Holmes, you might be surprised how many of the local businesses – including Cook and Marchant – ask me to work for them a few hours each week. You see' (she looked at us with a shy, endearing diffidence) 'I'm quite good at *that* in life, if nothing else.'

'You must then have some profitable government stock—?' began Holmes.

She smiled again. 'New Zealand, at four and a half per cent.'

'Please forgive me, Miss van Allen, but could not a single lady get by very nicely these days on – let us say, fifty pounds per annum?'

'Oh, certainly! And I myself live comfortably on but ten shillings per week, which is only half of that amount. You see, I never touch a single penny of my inheritance. Since I live at home, I cannot bear the thought of being a burden to my parents, and we have reached an arrangement whereby Mr Wyndham himself is empowered to draw my interest each quarter for as long as I remain in that household.'

Holmes nodded. 'Why have you come to see me?' he asked bluntly.

A flush stole over Miss van Allen's face and she plucked nervously at a small handkerchief drawn from her bag as she stated her errand with earnest simplicity. 'I would give everything I have to know what has become of Mr Horatio Darvill. There! Now you have it.'

'Please, could you perhaps begin at the beginning?' encouraged Holmes gently.

'Whilst my father was alive, sir, we always received tickets for the gas-fitters' ball. And after he died, the tickets were sent to my mother. But neither Mother nor I ever thought of going, because it was made plain to us that Mr Wyndham did not approve. He believed that the class of folk invited to such gatherings was inferior; and furthermore he asserted that neither of us – without considerable extra expenditure – had anything fit to wear. But believe me, Mr Holmes, I myself had the purple plush that I had never so much as taken from the drawer!'

It was after a decent interval that Holmes observed quietly: 'But you *did* go to the ball?'

'Yes. In the finish, we both went – Mother and I – when my step-father had been called away to France.'

'And it was there that you met Mr Horatio Darvill?'

'Yes! And – do you know? – he called the very next morning. And several times after that, whilst my step-father was in France, we walked out together.'

'Mr Wyndham must have been annoyed once he learned what had occurred?'

Miss van Allen hung her pretty head. 'Most annoyed, I'm afraid, for it became immediately clear that he did not approve of Mr Darvill.'

'Why do you think that was so?'

'I am fairly sure he thought Mr Darvill was interested only in my inheritance.'

'Did Mr Darvill not attempt to keep seeing you – in spite of these difficulties?'

'Oh yes! I thought, though, it would be wiser for us to stop seeing each other for a while. But he did write – every single day. And always, in the mornings, I used to receive the letters myself so that no one else should know.'

'Were you engaged to this gentleman?'

'Yes! For there was no problem about his supporting me. He was a cashier in a firm in Leadenhall Street—'

'Ah! Which office was that?' I interposed, for that particular area is known to me well, and I hoped that I might perhaps be of some assistance in the current investigation. Yet the look on Holmes's face was one of some annoyance, and I sank further into my chair as the interview progressed.

'I never did know exactly which firm it was,' admitted Miss van Allen.

'But where did he live?' persisted Holmes.

'He told me that he usually slept in a flat on the firm's premises.'

'You must yourself have written to this man, to whom you had agreed to become engaged?'

She nodded. 'To the Leadenhall Street Post Office, where I left my letters *poste restante*. Horatio – Mr Darvill – said that if I wrote to him at his work address, he'd never get to see my envelopes first, and the young clerks there would be sure to tease him about things.'

It was at this point that I was suddenly conscious of certain stertorous noises from Mycroft's corner – a wholly reprehensible lapse into poor manners, as it appeared to me.

'What else can you tell me about Mr Darvill?' asked Holmes quickly.

'He was very shy. He always preferred to walk out with me in the evening than in the daylight. "Retiring", perhaps, is the best word to describe him – even his voice. He'd had the quinsy as a young man, and was still having treatment for it. But the disability had left him with a weak larynx, and a sort of whispering fashion of speaking. His eyesight, too, was rather feeble – just as mine is – and he always wore tinted spectacles to protect his eyes against the glare of any bright light.'

Holmes nodded his understanding; and I began to sense a note of suppressed excitement in his voice.

'What next?'

'He called at the house the very evening on which Mr Wyndham next departed for France, and he proposed that we should marry before my step-father returned. He was convinced that this would be our only chance; and he was so dreadfully in earnest that he made me swear, with my hand upon both Testaments, that whatever happened I would always be true and faithful to him.'

'Your mother was aware of what was taking place?'

'Oh, *yes*. And she approved so much. In a strange way, she was even fonder of my fiancé than I was myself, and she agreed that our only chance was to arrange a secret marriage.'

'The wedding was to be in church?'

'Last Friday, at St Saviour's, near King's Cross; and we were to go on to a wedding-breakfast afterwards at the St Pancras Hotel. Horatio called a hansom for us, and put Mother and me into it before stepping himself into a four-wheeler which happened to be in the street. Mother and I got to St Saviour's first – it was only a few minutes' distance away. But when the four-wheeler drove up and we waited for him to step out – he never did, Mr Holmes! And when the cabman got down from the box and looked inside the carriage – *it was empty.*'

'You have neither seen nor heard of Mr Darvill since?'

'Nothing,' she whispered.

'You had planned a honeymoon, I suppose?'

'We had planned,' said Miss van Allen, biting her lip and scarce managing her reply, 'a fortnight's stay at the Royal Gleneagles in Inverness, and we were to have caught the lunchtime express from King's Cross.'

'It seems to me,' said Holmes, with some feeling, 'that you have been most shamefully treated, dear lady.'

But Miss van Allen would hear nothing against her loved one, and protested spiritedly: 'Oh, no, sir! He was far too good and kind to treat me so.'

'Your own opinion, then,' said Holmes, 'is that some unforeseen accident or catastrophe has occurred?'

She nodded her agreement. 'And I think he must have had some premonition that very morning of possible danger, because he begged me then, once again, to remain true to him – whatever happened.'

'You have no idea what that danger may have been?'

'None.'

'How did your mother take this sudden disappearance?'

'She was naturally awfully worried at first. But then she became more and more angry; and she made me promise never to speak to her of the matter again.'

'And your step-father?'

'He seemed – it was strange, really – rather more sympathetic than Mother. At least he was willing to discuss it.'

142

'And what was his opinion?'

'He agreed that some accident must have happened. As he said, Mr Darvill could have no possible interest in bringing me to the very doors of St Saviour's – and then in deserting me there. If he had borrowed money – or if some of my money had already been settled on him – then there might have been some reason behind such a cruel action. But he was absolutely independent about money, and he would never even look at a sixpence of mine if we went on a visit. Oh, Mr Holmes! It is driving me half-mad to think of—' But the rest of the sentence was lost as the young lady sobbed quietly into her handkerchief.

When she had recovered her composure, Holmes rose from his chair, promising that he would consider the baffling facts she had put before him. 'But if I could offer you one piece of advice,' he added, as he held the lady's coat for her, 'it is that you allow Mr Horatio Darvill to vanish as completely from your memory as he vanished from his wedding-carriage.'

'Then you think that I shall not see him again?'

'I fear not. But please leave things in my hands. Now! I wish you to send me a most accurate physical description of Mr Darvill, as well as any of his letters which you feel you can spare.'

'We can at least expedite things a little in those two respects,' replied she in business-like fashion, 'for I advertised for him in last Monday's *Chronicle*.' And promptly reaching into her handbag, she produced a newspaper cutting which she gave to Holmes, together with some other sheets. 'And here, too, are four of his letters which I happen to have with me. Will they be sufficient?'

Holmes looked quickly at the letters, and nodded. 'You say you never had Mr Darvill's address?'

'Never.'

'Your step-father's place of business, please?'

'He travels for Cook and Marchant, the great Burgundy importers, of Fenchurch Street.'

'Thank you.'

After she had left Holmes sat brooding for several minutes, his fingertips still pressed together. 'An interesting case,' he observed finally. 'Did you not find it so, Watson?'

'You appeared to read a good deal which was quite invisible to me,' I confessed.

'Not invisible, Watson. Rather, let us say – unnoticed. And that in spite of my repeated attempts to impress upon you the importance of sleeves, of thumb-nails, of boot-laces, and the rest. Now, tell me, what did you immediately gather from the young woman's appearance? Describe it to me.'

Conscious of Mycroft's presence, I sought to recall my closest impressions of our recent visitor.

'Well, she had, beneath her fur, a dress of rich brown, somewhat darker than the coffee colour, with a little black plush at the neck and at the sleeves – you mentioned sleeves, Holmes? Her gloves were dove-grey in colour, and were worn through at the right forefinger. Her black boots, I was not able, from where I sat, to observe in any detail, yet I would suggest that she takes either the size four-and-a-half or five. She wore small pendant earrings, almost certainly of imitation gold, and the small handkerchief into which the poor lady sobbed so charmingly had a neat darn in the monogrammed corner. In general, she had the air of a reasonably well-to-do young woman who has not quite escaped from the slightly vulgar inheritance of a father who was – let us be honest about it, Holmes! – a plumber.'

A snort from the chair beside which Holmes had so casually thrown Miss van Allen's fur coat served to remind us that the recumbent Mycroft had now reawakened, and that perhaps my own description had, in some respect, occasioned his disapproval. But he made no spoken comment, and soon resumed his former posture.

"Pon my word, Watson,' said Holmes, 'you are coming along splendidly – is he not, Mycroft? It is true, of course, that your description misses almost everything of real importance. But the method! You have hit upon the *method*, Watson. Let us take, for example, the plush you mention on the sleeves. Now, plush is a most wonderfully helpful material for showing traces; and the double line above the wrist, where the type-writist presses against the table, was beautifully defined. As for the short-sightedness, that was mere child's play. The dent-marks of a *pince-nez* at either side of the lady's nostrils – you did not observe it? Elementary, my dear Watson! And then the boots. You really *must* practise the art of being positioned where all the evidence is clearly visible. If you wish to observe nothing at all, like brother Mycroft, then you will seek out the furthest corner of a room where even the vaguest examination of the client will be obscured by the furniture, by a fur coat, by whatever. But reverting to the lady's boots, I observed that although they were very like each other in colour and style, they were in fact *odd* boots; the one on the right foot having a slightly decorated toe-cap, and the one on the left being of a comparatively plain design.

Furthermore, the right one was fastened only at the three lower buttons out of the five; the left one only at the first, third, and fifth. Now the deduction we may reasonably draw from such evidence is that the young lady left home in an unconscionable hurry. You agree?'

'Amazing, Holmes!'

'As for the glove worn at the forefinger—'

'You would be better advised,' suddenly interposed the deeper voice of Mycroft, 'to concentrate upon the missing person.'

May it have been a flash of annoyance that showed itself in Holmes's eyes? If so, it was gone immediately. 'You are quite right, Mycroft! Come now, Watson, read to us the paragraph from *The Chronicle*.'

I held the printed slip to the light and began: 'Missing on the 14th November 188–. A gentleman named Mr Horatio Darvill: about 5 feet 8 inches in height; fairly firmly built; sallow complexion; black hair, just a little bald in the centre; bushy black side-whiskers and moustache; tinted spectacles; slight infirmity of speech. When last seen, was dressed in—'

'But I think,' interrupted Holmes, 'he may by now have changed his wedding vestments, Watson?'

'Oh, certainly, Holmes.'

There being nothing, it seemed, of further value in the newspaper description, Holmes turned his attention to the letters, passing them to me after studying them himself with minute concentration.

'Well?' he asked.

Apart from the fact that the letters had been typed, I could find in them nothing of interest, and I laid them down on the coffee-table in front of the somnolent Mycroft.

'Well?' persisted Holmes.

'I assume you refer to the fact that the letters are type-written.'

'Already you are neglecting your newly acquired knowledge of the *method*, Watson. Quite apart from the one you mention, there are three further points of immediate interest and importance. First, the letters are very short; second, apart from the vague "Leadenhall Street" superscription, there is no precise address stated at any point; third, it is not only the body of the letter which has been typed, but the signature, too. Observe here, Watson – and here! – that neat little "Horatio Darvill" typed at the bottom of each of our four exhibits. And it will not have escaped you, I think, how conclusive that last point might be?'

'Conclusive, Holmes? In what way?'

'My dear fellow, is it possible for you not to see how strongly it bears upon our present investigations?'

'*Homo circumbendibus* – that's what you are, Sherlock!' (It was Mycroft once more.) 'Do you not appreciate that your client would prefer some positive action to any further proofs of your cerebral superiority?'

It is pleasing to report here that this attempt of Mycroft to provoke the most distinguished criminologist of the century proved largely ineffectual, and Holmes permitted himself a fraternal smile as his brother slowly bestirred his frame.

'You are right, Mycroft,' he rejoined lightly. 'And I shall immediately compose two letters: one to Messrs Cook and Marchant; the other to Mr Wyndham, asking that gentleman to meet us here at six o'clock tomorrow evening.'

Already I was aware of the easy and confident demeanour with which Holmes was tackling the singular mystery which confronted us all. But for the moment my attention was diverted by a small but most curious incident.

'It is just as well, Sherlock,' said Mycroft (who appeared now to be almost fully awakened), 'that you do not propose to write three letters.'

Seldom (let me admit it) have I seen my friend so perplexed: 'A *third* letter?'

'Indeed. But such a letter could have no certain destination, since it apparently slipped your memory to ask the young lady her present address, and the letters she entrusted to you appear, as I survey them, to be lacking their outer envelopes.'

Momentarily Holmes looked less than amused by this light-hearted intervention. 'You are more observant today than I thought, Mycroft, for the evidence of eye and ear had led me to entertain the suspicion that you were sleeping soundly during my recent conversation with Miss van Allen. But as regards her address, you are right.' And even as he spoke I noted the twinkle of mischievous intelligence in his eyes. 'Yet it would not be too difficult perhaps to *deduce* the young lady's address, Mycroft? On such a foul day as this it is dangerous and ill-advised for a lady to travel the streets if she has a perfectly acceptable and comfortable alternative such as the Underground; and since it was precisely 3.14 p.m. when Miss van Allen first appeared beneath my window, I would hazard the guess that she had caught the Metropolitan-line train which passes through Baker Street at 3.12 p.m. on its journey to Hammersmith. We may consider two further clues, also. The lady's boots, ill-assorted as they were, bore little evidence of the mud and mire of our London streets; and we may infer from this that her own home is perhaps as adjacent to an Underground station as is our own. More significant, however, is the fact, as we all observed, that Miss van Allen wore a dress of linen – a fabric which, though it is long-lasting and pleasing to wear, is one which has the disadvantage of creasing most easily. Now the skirt of the dress had been most recently ironed, and the slight creases in it must have resulted from her journey – to see me. And – I put this forward as conjecture, Mycroft – probably no more than three or four stops on the Underground had been involved. If we remember, too, the "few minutes" her wedding-carriage took from her home to St Saviour's, I think, perhaps . . . perhaps . . .' Holmes drew a street-map towards him, and surveyed his chosen area with his magnification-glass.

'I shall plump,' he said directly, 'for Cowcross Street myself – that shabbily genteel little thoroughfare which links Farringdon Road with St John Street.'

'Very impressive!' said Mycroft, anticipating my own admiration. 'And would you place her on the north or the south side of that thoroughfare, Sherlock?'

But before Holmes could reply to this small pleasantry, Mrs Hudson entered with a slip of paper which she handed to Holmes. 'The young lady says she forgot to give you her address, sir, and she's written it down for you.'

Holmes glanced quickly at the address and a glint of pride gleamed in his eyes. 'The answer to your question, Mycroft, is the south side – for it is an even-numbered house, and if I remember correctly the numbering of houses in that part of London invariably begins at the east end of the street with the odd numbers on the right-hand side walking westwards.'

'And the number is perhaps in the middle or late thirties?' suggested Mycroft. 'Thirty-six, perhaps? Or more likely thirty-eight?'

Holmes himself handed over the paper to us and we read:

Miss Charlotte van Allen
38, Cowcross Street

I was daily accustomed to exhibitions of the most extraordinary deductive logic employed by Sherlock Holmes, but I had begun at this point to suspect, in his brother Mycroft, the existence of some quite paranormal mental processes. It was only some half an hour later, when Holmes himself had strolled out for tobacco, that Mycroft, observing my continued astonishment, spoke quietly in my ear.

'If you keep your lips sealed, Dr Watson, I will tell you a small secret – albeit a very simple one. The good lady's coat was thrown rather carelessly, as you noticed, over the back of a chair; and on the inside of the lining was sewn a tape with her name and address clearly printed on it. Alas, however, my eyes are now not so keen as they were in my youth, and sixes and eights, as you know, are readily susceptible of confusion.'

I have never been accused, I trust, of undue levity, but I could not help laughing heartily at this coup on Mycroft's part, and I assured him that his brother should never hear the truth of it from me.

'Sherlock?' said Mycroft, raising his mighty eyebrows. 'He saw through my little joke immediately.'

*

It was not until past six o'clock the following evening that I returned to Baker Street after (it is not an irrelevant matter) a day of deep interest at St Thomas's Hospital.

'Well, have you solved the mystery yet?' I asked, as I entered the sitting room.

Holmes I found curled up in his armchair, smoking his oily clay pipe, and discussing medieval madrigals with Mycroft.

'Yes, Watson, I believe—'

But hardly were the words from his mouth when we heard a heavy footfall in the passage and a sharp rap on the door.

'This will be the girl's step-father,' said Holmes. 'He has written to say he would be here at a quarter after six. Come in!'

The man who entered was a sturdy, middle-sized fellow, about thirty years of age, clean-shaven, sallow-skinned, with a pair of most penetrating eyes. He placed his shiny top-hat on the sideboard, and with an insinuating bow sidled down into the nearest chair.

'I am assuming,' said Holmes, 'that you are Mr James Wyndham and' (holding up a type-written sheet) 'that this is the letter you wrote to me?'

'I am that person, sir, and the letter is mine. It was against my expressed wish, as you may know, that Miss van Allen contacted you in this matter. But she is an excitable young lady, and my wife and I will be happy to forgive her for such an impulsive action. Yet I must ask you to have nothing more to do with what is, unfortunately, a not uncommon misfortune. It is clear what took place, and I think it highly unlikely, sir, that even you will find so much as a single trace of Mr Darvill.'

'On the contrary,' replied Holmes quietly, 'I have reason to believe that I have already discovered the whereabouts of that gentleman.'

Mr Wyndham gave a violent start, and dropped his gloves. 'I am delighted to hear it,' he said in a strained voice.

'It is a most curious fact,' continued Holmes, 'that a typewriter has just as much individuality as does handwriting. Even when completely new, no two machines are exactly alike; and as they get older, some characters wear on this side and some on that. Now in this letter of yours, Mr Wyndham, you will note that in every instance there is some slight slurring in the eye of the "e"; and a most easily detectable defect in the tail of the "t".'

'All our office correspondence,' interrupted our visitor, 'is typed on the same machine, and I can fully understand why it has become a little worn.'

'But I have four other letters here,' resumed Holmes, in a slow and menacing tone, 'which purport to come from Mr Horatio Darvill. And in each of these, also, the "e"s are slurred, and the "t"s un-tailed.'

Mr Wyndham was out of his chair instantly and had snatched up his hat. 'I can waste no more of my valuable time with such trivialities, Mr Holmes. If you can catch the man who so shamefully treated Miss van Allen, then catch him! I wish you well – and ask you to let me know the outcome. But I have no interest whatsoever in your fantastical notions.'

Already, however, Holmes had stepped across the room and turned the key in the door. 'Certainly I will tell you how I caught Mr Darvill, if you will but resume your chair.'

'What?' shouted Wyndham, his face white, his small eyes darting about him like those of a rat in a trap. Yet finally he sat down and glared aggressively around, as Holmes continued his analysis.

'It was as selfish and as heartless a trick as ever I encountered. The man married a woman much older than himself, largely for her money. In addition, he enjoyed the interest on the not inconsiderable sum of the step-daughter's money, for as long as that daughter lived with them. The loss of such extra monies would have made a significant difference to the lifestyle adopted by the newly married pair. Now the daughter herself was an amiable, warm-hearted girl, and was possessed of considerable physical attractions; and with the added advantage of a personal income, it became clear that under normal circumstances she would not remain single for very long. So he – the man of whom I speak – decided to deny her the company and friendship of her contemporaries by keeping her at home. But she – and who shall blame her? – grew restive under such an unnatural regimen, and firmly announced her intention to attend a local ball. So what did her step-father do? With the connivance of his wife, he conceived a cowardly plan. He disguised himself cleverly: he covered those sharp eyes with dully tinted spectacles; he masked that clean-shaven face with bushy side-whiskers; he sank that clear voice of his into the strained whisper of one suffering from the quinsy. And then, feeling himself doubly secure because of the young lady's short sight, he appeared *himself* at the ball, in the guise of one Horatio Darvill, and there he wooed the fair Miss van Allen for his own – thereafter taking the further precaution of always arranging his assignations by candlelight.'

(I heard a deep groan which at the time I assumed to have come from our visitor, but which, upon reflection, I am inclined to think originated from Mycroft's corner.)

'Miss van Allen had fallen for her new beau; and no suspicion of deception ever entered her pretty head. She was flattered by the attention she was receiving, and the effect was heightened by the admiration of her mother for the man. An "engagement" was agreed, and the deception perpetuated. But the pretended journeys abroad were becoming more difficult to sustain, and things had to be brought to a head quickly, although in such a *dramatic* way as to leave a permanent impression upon the young girl's mind. Hence the vows of fidelity sworn on the Testaments; hence the dark hints repeated on the very morning of the proposed marriage that something sinister might be afoot. James Wyndham, you see, wished his step-daughter to be so morally bound to her fictitious suitor that for a decade, at least, she would sit and wilt in Cowcross Street, and continue paying her regular interest directly into the account of her guardian: the same blackguard of a guardian who had brought her to the doors of St Saviour's and then, himself, conveniently disappeared by the age-old ruse of stepping in at one side of a four-wheeler – and out at the other.'

Rising to his feet, Wyndham fought hard to control his outrage. 'I wish you to know that it is you, sir, who is violating the law of this land – and not me! As long as you keep that door locked, and thereby hold me in this room against my will, you lay yourself open—'

'The law,' interrupted Holmes, suddenly unlocking and throwing open the door, 'may not for the moment be empowered to touch you. Yet never, surely, was there a man who deserved punishment more. In fact . . . since my hunting-crop is close at hand—' Holmes took two swift strides across the room; but it was too late. We heard a wild clatter of steps down the stairs as Wyndham departed, and then had the satisfaction of watching him flee pell-mell down Baker Street.

'That cold-blooded scoundrel will end on the gallows, mark my words!' growled Holmes.

'Even now, though, I cannot follow all the steps in your reasoning, Holmes,' I remarked.

'It is this way,' replied Holmes. 'The only person who profited financially from the vanishing-trick – was the step-father. Then, the fact that the two men, Wyndham and Darvill, were never actually seen *together*, was most suggestive. As were the tinted spectacles, the husky voice, the bushy whiskers – all of these latter, Watson, hinting strongly at disguise. Again, the type-written signature betokened one thing only – that the man's handwriting was so familiar to Miss van Allen that she might easily recognize even a small sample of it. Isolated facts? Yes! But all of them leading to the same inevitable conclusion – as even my slumbering sibling might agree?'

But there was no sound from the Mycroft corner.

'You were able to verify your conclusion?' I asked.

Holmes nodded briskly. 'We know the firm for which Wyndham worked, and we had a full description of Darvill. I therefore eliminated from that description everything which could be the result of deliberate disguise—'

'Which means that you have *not* verified your conclusion!' Mycroft's sudden interjection caused us both to turn sharply towards him.

'There will always,' rejoined Holmes, 'be a need and a place for informed conjecture—'

'*Inspired* conjecture, Holmes,' I interposed.

'Phooey!' snorted Mycroft. 'You are talking of nothing but wild *guesswork*, Sherlock. And it is my opinion that in this case your guesswork is grotesquely askew.'

I can only report that never have I seen Holmes so taken aback; and he sat in silence as Mycroft raised his bulk from the chair and now stood beside the fireplace.

'Your deductive logic needs no plaudits from me, Sherlock, and like Dr Watson I admire your desperate hypothesis. But unless there is some firm evidence which you have thus far concealed from us . . . ?'

Holmes did not break his silence.

'Well,' stated Mycroft, 'I will indulge in a little guesswork of my own, and tell you that the gentleman who just stormed out of this room is as innocent as Watson here!'

'He certainly did not *act* like an innocent man,' I protested, looking in vain to Holmes for some support, as Mycroft continued.

'The reasons you adduce for your suspicions are perfectly sound in most respects, and yet – I must speak with honesty, Sherlock! – I found myself sorely disappointed with your reading – or rather complete misreading – of the case. You are, I believe, wholly correct in your central thesis that there is no such person as Horatio Darvill.' (How the blood was tingling in my veins as Mycroft spoke these words!) 'But when the unfortunate Mr Wyndham, who has just rushed one way up Baker Street, rushes back down it the other with a writ for defamation of character – as I fear he will! – then you will be compelled to think, to analyse, and to act, with a little more care and circumspection.'

Holmes leaned forward, the sensitive nostrils of that aquiline nose a little distended. But still he made no comment.

'For example, Sherlock, two specific pieces of information vouchsafed to us by the attractive Miss van Allen herself have been strongly discounted, if not wholly ignored, in your analysis.' (I noticed Holmes's eyebrows rising quizzically.) 'First, the fact that Mr Wyndham was older than Miss van Allen *only by some five years*. Second, the fact that Miss van Allen is so competent and speedy a performer on the typewriter that she works, on a free-lance basis, for several firms in the vicinity of her home, including Messrs Cook and Marchant. Furthermore, you make the astonishing claim that Miss van Allen was totally deceived by the disguise of Mr Darvill. Indeed, you would have her not only blind, but semi-senile into the bargain! Now it is perfectly true that the lady's eyesight is far from perfect – *glaucopia Athenica*, would you not diagnose, Dr Watson? – but it is quite ludicrous to believe that she would fail to recognize the person with whom she was living. And it is wholly dishonest of you to assert that the assignations were always held by candlelight, since on at least two occasions, the morning after the first meeting – the *morning*, Sherlock! – and the morning of the planned wedding ceremony, Miss van Allen had ample opportunity of studying the physical features of Darvill in the broadest of daylight.'

'You seem to me to be taking an unconscionably long time in putting forward your own hypothesis,' snapped Holmes, somewhat testily.

'You are right,' admitted the other. 'Let me beat about the

bush no longer! You have never felt emotion akin to love for any woman, Sherlock – not even for the Adler woman – and you are therefore deprived of the advantages of those who like myself are able to understand both the workings of the male and also the female mind. Five years her superior in age – her step-father; *only five years*. Now one of the sadnesses of womankind is their tendency to age more quickly and less gracefully than men; and one of the truths about mankind in general is that if you put one of each sex, of roughly similar age, in reasonable proximity . . . And if one of them is the fair Miss van Allen – then you are inviting a packet of trouble. Yet such is what took place in the Wyndham ménage. Mrs Wyndham was seventeen years older than her young husband; and perhaps as time went by some signs and tokens of this disproportionate difference in their ages began to manifest themselves. At the same time, it may be assumed that Wyndham himself could not help being attracted – however much at first he sought to resist the temptation – by the very winsome and vivacious young girl who was his step-daughter. It would almost certainly have been Wyndham himself who introduced Miss van Allen to the part-time duties she undertook for Cook and Marchant – where the two of them were frequently thrown together, away from the restraints of wife and home, and with a result which it is not at all difficult to guess. Certain it is, in my own view, that Wyndham sought to transfer his affections from the mother to the daughter; and in due course it was the daughter who decided that whatever her own affections might be in the matter she must in all honour leave her mother and step-father. Hence the great anxiety to get out to dances and parties and the like – activities which Wyndham objected to for the obvious reason that he wished to have Miss van Allen as close by himself for as long as he possibly could. Now you, Sherlock, assume that this objection arose as a result of the interest accruing from the New Zealand securities – and you are *guessing*, are you not? Is it not just possible that Wyndham has money of his own – find out, brother! – and that what he craves for is not some petty addition to his wealth, but the love of a young woman with whom he has fallen rather hopelessly in love? You see, she took *him* in, just as she took *you* in, Sherlock – for you swallowed everything that calculating little soul reported.'

'Really, this is outrageous!' I objected – but Holmes held up his hand, and bid me hear his brother out.

'What is clear, is that at some point when Wyndham was in France – and why did you not verify those dates spent abroad? I am sure Cook and Marchant would have provided them just as quickly as it furnished the wretched man's description. But as I was saying, with Wyndham in France, mother and daughter found themselves in a little *tête-à-tête* one evening, during the course of which a whole basketful of dirty linen was laid bare, with the daughter bitterly disillusioned about the behaviour of her step-father, and the mother hurt and angry about her husband's infidelity. So, together, the pair of them devised a plan. Now, we both agree on one thing at least, Sherlock! There appears to be no evidence whatsoever for the independent existence of Horatio Darvill except for what we have heard from Miss van Allen's lips. Rightly, you drew our attention to the fact that the two men were never seen together. But, alas, having appreciated the *importance* of that clue, you completely misconceived its *significance*. *You* decided that there is no Darvill – because he

159

is Wyndham. *I have to tell you that there is no Darvill – because he is the pure fabrication of the minds of Mrs Wyndham and her daughter.*'

Holmes was staring with some consternation at a pattern in the carpet, as Mycroft rounded off his extravagant and completely baseless conjectures.

'Letters were written – and incidentally I myself would have been far more cautious about those "e"s and "t"s: twin faults, as it happens, of my very own machine! But, as I say, letters were written – *but by Miss van Allen herself*; a wedding was arranged; a story concocted of a non-existent carriage into which there climbed a non-existent groom – and that was the end of the charade. Now, it was you, Sherlock, who rightly asked the key question: *cui bono?* And you concluded that the real beneficiary was Wyndham. But exactly the contrary is the case! It was the mother and daughter who intended to be the beneficiaries, for they hoped to rid themselves of the rather wearisome Mr Wyndham – but not before he had been compelled, by moral and social pressures, to make some handsome money-settlement upon the pair of them – especially perhaps upon the young girl who, as Dr Watson here points out, could well have done with some decent earrings and a new handkerchief. And the *social* pressure I mention, Sherlock, was designed – carefully and cleverly designed – to come from *you*. A cock-and-bull story is told to you by some wide-eyed young thing, a story so bestrewn with clues at almost every point that even Lestrade – given a week or two! – would probably have come up with a diagnosis identical with your own. And why do you think she came to you, and not to Lestrade, say? Because "Mr Sherlock Holmes is the greatest investigator the world has ever known" – and his judgements are second only to the Almighty's in their infallibility. For if you, Sherlock, believed Wyndham to be guilty – then Wyndham *was* guilty in the eyes of the whole world – the whole world except for one, that is.'

'Except for two,' I added quietly.

Mycroft Holmes turned his full attention towards me for the first time, as though I had virtually been excluded from his previous audience. But I allowed him no opportunity of seeking the meaning of my words, as I addressed him forthwith.

'I asked Holmes a question when he presented his own analysis, sir. I will ask you the same: have you in any way verified your hypothesis? And if so, how?'

'The answer, Dr Watson, to the first part of your question is, in large measure, "yes". Mr Wyndham, in fact, has quite enough money to be in no way embarrassed by the withdrawal of Miss van Allen's comparatively minor contribution. As for the second part . . .' Mycroft hesitated awhile. 'I am not sure what my brother has told you of the various offices I hold under the British Crown—'

It was Holmes who intervened – and impatiently so. 'Yes, yes, Mycroft! Let us all concede immediately that the, shall we say, "unofficial" sources to which you are privy have completely invalidated my own reconstruction of the case. So be it! Yet I would wish, if you allow, to make one or two observations upon your own rather fanciful interpretation of events? It is, of course, with full justice that you accuse me of having no first-hand knowledge of what are called "the matters of the heart". Furthermore, you rightly draw attention to the difficulties Mr Wyndham would have experienced in deceiving his step-daughter. Yet how you under-rate the power of disguise! And how, incidentally, you *over*-rate the intelligence of Lestrade! Even Dr Watson, I would suggest, has a brain considerably superior—'

For not a second longer could I restrain myself. 'Gentlemen!' I cried. 'You are both – *both* of you! – most tragically wrong.'

The two brothers stared at me as though I had taken leave of my senses.

'I think you should seek to explain yourself, Watson,' said Holmes sharply.

'A man,' I began, 'was proposing to go to Scotland for a fortnight with his newly married wife, and he had drawn out one hundred pounds in cash – no less! – from the Oxford Street branch of the Royal National Bank on the eve of his wedding. The man, however, was abducted after entering a four-wheeler on the very morning of his wedding-day, was brutally assaulted, and then robbed of all his money and personal effects – thereafter being dumped, virtually for dead, in a deserted alley in Stepney. Quite by chance he was discovered later that same evening, and taken to the White-chapel Hospital. But it was only after several days that the man slowly began to recover his senses, and some patches of his memory – and also, gentlemen, his *voice*. For, you see, it was partly because the man was suffering so badly from what we medical men term suppurative tonsilitis – the quinsy, as it is commonly known – that he was transferred to St Thomas's where, as you know, Holmes, I am at present engaged in some research on that very subject, and where my own professional opinion was sought only this morning. Whilst reading through the man's hospital notes, I could see that the only clue to his identity was a tag on an item of his underclothing carrying the initials "H. D.". You can imagine my excitement—'

'Humphry Davey, perhaps,' muttered Mycroft flippantly.

'Oh no!' I replied, with a smile. 'I persisted patiently with the poor man, and finally he was able to communicate to me the name of his bank. After that, if I may say so, Holmes, it was almost child's play to verify *my* hypothesis. I visited the bank, where I learned about the withdrawal of money for the honeymoon, and the manager himself accompanied me back to St Thomas's where he was able to view the patient and to provide quite unequivocal proof as to his identity. I have to inform you, therefore, that not only does Mr Horatio Darvill exist, gentlemen, he is at this precise moment lying in a private ward on the second floor of St Thomas's Hospital!'

For some little while a silence fell upon the room. Then I saw Holmes, who these last few minutes had been standing by the window, give a little start. 'Oh, no!' he groaned. And looking over his shoulder I saw, dimly beneath the fog-beshrouded lamplight, an animated Mr Wyndham talking to a legal-looking gentleman who stood beside him.

Snatching up his cape, Holmes made hurriedly for the door. 'Please tell Mr Wyndham, if you will, Watson, that I have already written a letter to him containing a complete recantation of my earlier charges, and offering him my profound apologies. For the present, I am leaving – by the back door.'

He was gone. And when, a minute later, Mrs Hudson announced that two angry-looking gentlemen had called asking to see Mr Holmes, I noticed Mycroft seemingly asleep once more in his corner armchair, a monograph on polyphonic plainchant open on his knee, and a smile of vague amusement on his large, intelligent face.

'Show the gentlemen in, please, Mrs Hudson!' I said – in such peremptory fashion that for a moment or two that good lady stared at me, almost as if she had mistaken my voice for that of Sherlock Holmes himself.

THE
INSIDE STORY

PART ONE

Dido attempted to raise her heavy eyes again,
but failed; and the deep wound gurgled in her breast.

(Virgil, *Aeneid IV, 688–9*)

'Get a *move* on!'

'I'll get there as fast as I can, sir – I always do.'

'And what's *that* supposed to mean?'

Lewis turned left at Carfax, down into the High, and then over Magdalen Bridge, car siren wailing, before driving past the Asian grocers' shops and the Indian restaurants in the Cowley Road.

'I mean,' replied Lewis finally, 'that here we are with another murder, and you'll get there, won't you? You always do.'

'Nearly always,' conceded Morse.

'And *I* won't. I've got a second-class mind—'

'Don't underrate yourself, Lewis! Let others do it for you.'

Lewis grunted humourlessly. 'I'm like a second-class stamp, and well you know it.'

'But second-class stamps usually get there in the end.'

'Exactly. Just take a dickens of a lot longer—'

'Slow down!'

Morse had been consulting an Oxford street plan, and now jabbed a finger to his right.

167

'That's it, Lewis: Jowett Place. What number did you say?'

'Probably where those two police cars are parked, sir.'

Morse grinned weakly. 'Maintain that level of deductive brilliance, Lewis, and we'll be through this case before the pubs are open.'

It was 8.50 on the dull, intermittently drizzly morning of Monday, 15 February, 1993.

The Oxford City Police had contacted Kidlington CID an hour or so earlier after receiving a 999 call from one Paul Bayley, first-floor tenant of the narrow, two-storey property that stood at 14 Jowett Place. Bayley, an erstwhile History graduate from Magdalen College, Oxford, had found himself out of milk that morning – had walked downstairs – knocked on the door of the woman tenant directly below him, Ms Sheila Poster – had found the door unlocked – and there . . .

Or so he said.

Morse looked down at the fully dressed woman lying just inside the ground-floor living room, the left arm extended, the pleasingly manicured fingernails straining, it appeared, to reach the door. Beneath and in front of the body was a distressingly copious pool of dully matted blood; and although the weapon had been removed it was possible even for such a non-medical man as Morse to unjumble the simple truth that the woman had most probably been stabbed through the heart. Longish dark curls framed the pale face – from which the large brown eyes now stared, for ever fixedly, at a threadbare square of the lime-green carpet.

'Lovely looking girl,' said Lewis quietly.

Morse averted his eyes from the terrible sight, glanced

168

across to the curtained window, then stepped outside the room into the narrow hallway, where Dr Laura Hobson, the police pathologist, stood in subdued conference with a scene-of-crime officer.

'She's all yours,' said Morse, in a tone suggesting that the abdication of responsibility for the body was something of a relief. As indeed it was, for Morse had always recoiled from the sight of violent death.

'Funny name – "Poster"!' volunteered Lewis as the two detectives stepped up the narrow stairs of number 14.

'Is it?' asked Morse, his voice betraying no real interest in the matter.

Bayley was sitting beside a police constable in his untidy living room – a large-buttocked, lank-haired, yet handsome sort of fellow, in his late twenties perhaps; unshaven, pony-tailed, with a small earring in his left ear. To whom, predictably, Morse took an instant and intense dislike.

He had been out drinking (Bayley claimed) throughout most of the previous evening, not leaving the King's Arms in Broad Street until closing time. After which he'd gone back to a friend's flat to continue the celebrations, and in fact had slept there – before returning to Jowett Place at about a quarter past seven that morning. The rest he'd already told the police, OK?

As he gave his evidence, Bayley's hands were nervously opening and closing the Penguin translation of Virgil's *Aeneid*, and Morse noted (again with distaste) the lines of ingrained dirt beneath the fingernails.

'You slept with a woman last night?'

Bayley nodded, eyes downcast.

'We shall have to know her name – my sergeant here will have to check with her. You understand that?'

Again Bayley nodded. 'I suppose so, yes.'

'You didn't leave her at all?'

'Went to the loo coupla times.'

'You in the habit of sleeping around?'

'I wouldn't put it like that, no.'

'Ever sleep with – with the woman downstairs?'

'Sheila? No, never.'

'Ever ask her?'

'Once.'

'And?'

'She said if we were going to have a relationship it would have to be cerebral – not conjugal.'

'Quite a way with words she had, then?'

'You could say that.'

'When did you last speak to her?'

'Week or so ago? We were talking – *she* was talking – about epic poetry. She . . . lent me this . . . this book. I was going to give it back to her . . . today.'

Lewis looked away in some embarrassment as a curtain of tears now covered Bayley's eyes; but for a while longer Morse himself continued to stare cynically at the young man seated opposite him.

Downstairs, in the second of the two rooms which (along with the kitchen) were offered for rent at 14 Jowett Place, Morse contemplated the double bed in which, presumably, the murdered tenant had usually slumbered overnight. Two fluffy pillows concealed a full-length, bottle-green night-dress, which Morse now fingered lightly before turning back the William-Morris-patterned duvet and examining the undersheet.

'No sign of any recent nocturnal emissions, sir.'

'You have a genteel way of putting things,' said Morse.

The room was sparsely furnished, sparely ornamented – with a large mahogany wardrobe taking up most of the space left by the bed. On the bedside table stood a lamp; an alarm clock; a box containing half a dozen items of cheap jewellery; and a single book: *Reflections on Inspiration and Creativity*, by Diogenes Small (Macmillan, £14.99).

Picking up the latter, Morse opened its pages at the point where a blue leather bookmarker ('Greetings from Erzincan') had been placed – and then with no obvious enthusiasm read aloud the few sentences which had been highlighted in the text with a yellow felt-tipped pen:

Obviously our writer will draw upon character and incident taken from personal experience. Inevitably so. Laudibly so. Yet always it is those *fictional* addenda which will effect the true alchemy; which will elevate our earth-bound artist, and send him forth high-floating on the wings of freedom and creativity.

'Bloody 'ell!'

'Pardon, sir?'

'Can't even spell,' muttered Morse, as Lewis picked up the bookmarker.

'Where's Erzincan?'

'Dunno. When I was at school we had to do one of the three "G"s: Greek, German, or Geography.'

'And you didn't do Geography . . .'

But a silent Morse was standing now at the window (curtains drawn back) which looked out on to a patch of leaf-carpeted lawn at the rear of the house. Strangely, something had stirred deep down in his mind, like the opening chords of *Das Rheingold*; chords that for the moment, though, remained below his audial range.

Lewis opened the wardrobe doors, exposing a modest collection of dresses and coats hanging from the rail; and half a dozen pairs of cheap shoes stowed neatly along the bottom.

Overhead they heard the creaking of floorboards as some-one – must be Bayley? – paced continuously to and fro. And Morse's eyes rose slowly to the ceiling.

But he said nothing.

Neither the bedroom nor the kitchen had yielded anything of significant interest; and Morse was anxious to hear Dr Hobson's verdict, however tentative, when half an hour later she emerged from the murder-room.

'Sharp knife by the look of things – second attempt – probably entering from above. Bled an awful lot – as you saw . . . still, most of us would – with the knife-blade through the heart. Shouldn't be too difficult to be fairly precise about the time – I'll be having a closer look, of course – but I'd guess, say, eight to ten hours ago? No longer, I don't think. Eleven o'clock, twelve o'clock last night?'

'After the pubs had closed.'

'*She* hadn't been drinking, Inspector.'

'Oh!'

Morse placed his hand lightly on the young pathologist's shoulder and thanked her. Her eyes looked interesting – and interested. Sometimes Morse thought he could fall in love with Laura Hobson; and sometimes he thought he couldn't.

It was almost midday before Morse gave the order for the body to be removed. The scene-of-crime personnel had finished their work, and a thick, transparent sheeting had now been laid across the carpet. Lewis, with two DCs, had long since been despatched to cover the preliminary tasks: to check Bayley's alibi, to question the neighbours, and to discover whatever they could of Sheila Poster's past. And Morse himself now stood alone, and gazed around the room in which Sheila Poster had been murdered.

Almost immediately, however, it was apparent that little was likely to be found. The eight drawers of the modern desk which stood against the inside wall were completely empty; with the almost inevitable conclusion to be drawn that the murderer had systematically emptied the contents of each, as well as whatever had stood on the desk-top, into . . . well, into something – black plastic bag, say? And then disappeared into the night; in gloves, like as not, for Morse had learned that no extraneous prints had been discovered – only those left almost everywhere by the murdered tenant. The surfaces of the desk, the shelving, the furniture, the window – all had been dutifully daubed and dusted with fingerprint powder; but it seemed highly improbable that such a methodical murderer had left behind any easily legible signature.

No handbag, either; no documents of any sort; nothing.

Or was there?

Above the desk, hanging by a cord from the picture-rail,

was a plywood board, some thirty inches square, on which ten items were fixed by multicoloured drawing-pins: five Medici reproductions of well-known paintings (including two Pre-Raphaelites); a manuscript facsimile of Keats's 'Ode to a Nightingale'; a postcard showing the death-mask of Tutankhamun; a photograph of a kingfisher, a large fish balanced in its mouth, perched on a 'No Fishing' sign; a printed invitation to a St Hilda's Old Girls' evening in March 1993; and a leaflet announcing a crime short-story competition organized by Oxfordshire County Libraries: 'First prize £1,000 – Judges Julian Symons and H.R.F. Keating – Final date 10 April 1993'.

Huh! Still seven weeks to go. But there'd now be no entry from Sheila Poster, would there, Morse?

He methodically unpinned each of the cards and turned them over. Four were blank – obviously purchased for decorative purposes. But two had brief messages written on them. On the Egyptian card, in what Morse took to be a masculine hand, were the words: 'Cairo's bloody hot but wish you were here – B.' And on the back of Collins's 'Convent Thoughts', in what Morse took to be a feminine hand: 'On a weekend retreat! I knew I wouldn't miss men. But I do!! Susan.'

On each side of the boarded-up fireplace were five bookshelves, their contents systematically stacked in order: Austen novels, top left, Wordsworth poems, bottom right. Housman's *Collected Poems* suddenly caught Morse's eye, and he extracted his old hero, the book falling open immediately at 'Last Poems' XXVI, where a postcard (another one) had been inserted: the front showing a photograph of streets in

San Jose (so it said) and, on the back, a couplet written out
in black Biro:

> And wide apart lie we, my love,
> And seas between the twain.
>
> (7.v.92)

Morse smiled to himself, for the poem from which the lines
were taken had been part of his own mental furniture for
many moons.

Yet so very soon the smile had become a frown. He'd seen
that same handwriting only a few seconds since, surely? He
unpinned the postcard from Cairo again; and, yes, the
handwriting was more than a reasonable match.

So what?

So what, Morse? Yet for many seconds his eyes were as
still as the eyes that stared from the mask of Tutankhamun.

Lewis came briskly into the room twenty minutes later,
promptly reading from his note-book:

'Sheila Emily Poster; second-class honours degree in English from St Hilda's 1990; aged twenty-five – comes from
Bristol; Dad died in 'eighty-four – Hodgkin's disease; Mum
in a special home there – Alzheimer's; only child; worked for
a while with the University Geology Department in the
reference section; here in this property almost ten months –
£490 a month; £207 in the Building Society; £69.40 in her
current account at Lloyds.'

'You can get interest on current accounts these days, did
you know that, Lewis?'

'Useful thing for you to know, sir.'

'You've been quick.'

'Easy! Bursar of St Hilda's, DSS, Lloyds Bank – no problems. Murder does help sometimes, doesn't it?'

A sudden splash of rain hatched the front window and Morse stared out at the melancholy day:

'I know not if it rains, my love,
    In the land where you do lie . . .'

'Pardon, sir?'

But Morse seemed not to hear. 'There's all this stuff here, Lewis . . .' Morse pointed vaguely to the piles of magazines lying around. 'You'd better have a look through.'

'Can't we get somebody else—'

'No!' thundered Morse. 'I need help – *your* help, Lewis. For Chrissake get on with it!'

Far from any annoyance, Lewis felt a secret contentment. In only one respect was he unequivocally in a class of his own as a police officer, he knew that: for there was only one person with whom the curmudgeonly Morse could ever work with any kind of equanimity – and that was himself, Lewis.

He now settled therefore with his accustomed measure of commitment to the fourth-grade clerical chore of sorting through the piles of women's magazines, fashion journals, brochures, circulars, and the like, that were stacked on the floor-space in the two alcoves of the living room.

He was still working when just over an hour later Morse returned from his lunchtime ration of calories, taken entirely in liquid form.

'Found anything?'

Lewis shook his head. 'One or two amusing bits, though.'

'Well? Let's share the joke. Life's grim enough.'

Lewis looked back into one of the piles, found a copy of the *Oxford Gazette* (May 1992), and read from the back page:

CLEANER REQUIRED

Three mornings per week
Hourly rate negotiable
Graduate preferred

Morse was unimpressed. 'We're all of us overqualified in Oxford.'

'Not *all* of us.'

'How long will you be?'

'Another half-hour or so.'

'I'll leave you then.'

'What'll you be doing, sir?'

'I'll still be thinking. See you back at HQ.'

Morse walked out again, down Cowley Road to the Plain; over Magdalen Bridge, along the High, and then up Catte Street to the Broad; and was standing, undecided for a few seconds, in front of Blackwell's book shop and the narrow frontage of the adjoining White Horse ('Open All Day') – when the idea suddenly struck him.

He caught a taxi from St Giles' out to Kidlington. Not to Police HQ though, but to 45 Blenheim Close, the address given on the leaflet advertising the Oxfordshire short-story competition.

'You're a bit premature, really,' suggested Rex De Lincto, the short, fat, balding, slightly deaf Chairman of the Oxford Book Association. 'There's still about a couple of months to go and we'll only receive most of the entries in the last week or so.'

'You've had *some* already, though?'

'Nine.'

De Lincto walked over to a cabinet, took out a handwritten list of names, and passed it across.

1   IAN BRADLEY
2   EMMA SKIPPER
3   VALERIE WARD
4   JIM MORWOOD
5   CHRISTINA COLLINS
6   UNA BROSHOLA
7   ELISSA THORPE
8   RICHARD ELVES
9   MARY ANN COTTON

Morse scanned the list, his attention soon focusing on the last name.

'Odd,' he mumbled.

'Pardon?'

'Mary Ann Cotton. Same name as that of a woman hanged in Durham jail in the 1880s.'

'So?'

'And look at *her*!' Morse's finger pointed to number five, Christina Collins. 'She got herself murdered up on the canal in Staffordshire somewhere. Surely!'

'I'm not quite with you, Inspector.'

'Do you get phoney names sometimes?'

'Well, you can't tell, really, can you? I mean, if you say you're Donald Duck—'

Morse nodded. 'You *are* Donald Duck.'

'You'd perhaps use a *nom de plume* if you were an established author . . .'

'But this competition's only for first-timers, isn't it?'

'You've been reading the small print, Inspector.'

'But how do you know who they are if they've won?'

'We don't sometimes. Not for a start. But every entrant sends an address.'

'I see.'

Morse looked again at the list, and suddenly the blood was running cold in his veins. The clues, or some of them, were beginning to lock together in his mind: the short-story leaflet; the advice of Diogenes Small, that guru of creative writing; the book that young Bayley had borrowed . . . the translation of Virgil's *Aeneid*, in which Dido, the queen of Carthage, had fallen in love with Aeneas and then stabbed herself in her despair . . . Dido . . . known also by an alternative name – Elissa!

Morse took out a pencil and lightly made twelve oblique strokes through each letter of ELISSA THORPE, in what seemed to De Lincto a wholly random order; but an order which in Morse's mind spelled out in sequence the letters of the name SHEILA POSTER.

179

Morse rose to his feet and looked across at the cabinet. 'You'd better let me have story number seven, if you will, sir.'

'Of course. And if I may say so, you've made a very good choice, Inspector.'

Only one message was awaiting Morse when he returned to his office at HQ: Dr Hobson had called to say that Sheila Poster was about twelve weeks pregnant. But Morse paid scant attention to this new information, for there was something he had to do immediately.

He therefore sat back comfortably in the old black-leather armchair.

And read a story.

PART TWO

Yet always it is those *fictional* addenda which will effect the true alchemy.

(Diogenes Small, *Reflections on Inspiration and Creativity*)

The story (printed verbatim here) which Morse now began to read was cleanly typed and carefully presented.

I'd seen the advert in the Gazette.

She was going to be a woman who walked silent and unsmiling through any door held open for her; a woman who would speak in a loud voice over the counter at a bank; a woman conscious of her congenital superiority over her fellow beings.

In short she was going to be a North Oxford lady.

And she was — a double-barrelled one.

I was gratified though surprised that my carefully worded application had been considered and I caught the bus in good time.

At 10.30 a.m. to the minute I walked along the flagged path that bisected the weedless front lawn and knocked at the door of The Grange in Squitchey Lane.

A quarter of an hour later, after a last mouthful of some bitter-tasting coffee, I'd landed the job.

How?

I wasn't sure, not then. But when she asked me if I'd enjoyed the coffee, I said I preferred a cup of instant, and she'd smiled thinly.

'That's what my husband says.'

I hoped my voice showed an appropriate interest.

'Your husband?'

'He's abroad. The Americans are picking his brains.' She stood up.

'Do you know why I've offered you the job?'

It was a bit risky but I said it: 'No one else applied?'

'I'm not surprised you have a degree. You're quite bright really.'

'Thank you.'

'You need the money, I suppose?'

I lowered my eyes to the deep Wilton and nodded.

'Goodbye,' she said.

I left her standing momentarily there at the front door – slim, elegantly dressed, and young – well, comparatively young.

And, yes, I ought to admit it, uncommonly attractive.

The tasks allotted to me could only just be squeezed into the nine hours a week I spent at The Grange.

But £36 was £36.

And that was a <u>bonus</u>.

Can you guess what I'm saying? Not yet?

You will.

Two parts of the house I was forbidden to enter: the

master bedroom (remember that bedroom!) and the master's study — the latter by the look of it a large converted bedroom on the upstairs floor whose door was firmly closed.

Firmly locked, as I soon discovered.

There was no such embargo on the mistress's study — a fairly recent addition at the rear of the house in the form of a semi-conservatory, its shelves, surfaces and floor all crammed with books and littered with loose papers and typescripts. And dozens of house-plants fighting for a little Lebensraum.

I was invariably fascinated with the place as I carefully (too carefully) watered the plants, replaced the books in alphabetical order, shuffled untidy piles into tidy piles, and carefully (too carefully) hoovered the carpeted floor and dusted around.

I love charging around with a duster. It's one of the only jobs I do where I can actually see a result.

And I like seeing a result . . .

There was only one thing wrong with that room.

The cat.

I hate all cats but especially this cat, which occasionally looked at me in a mysterious knowing aristocratic potentially ferocious manner.

Like his mistress.

A small two-way cat-flap had been cut into the door leading from the conservatory to the rear garden through which the frequently filthy-pawed 'Boswell' (huh!) would make his exits and his entrances.

Ah, but bless you, Boswell!

*

I felt confident that Mrs Spencer-Gilbey could not have taken up my single reference since from the beginning she called me 'Virginia' without the slightest hint of suspicion.

For my part, I called her 'ma'am', to rhyme with 'jam'. It was five syllables shorter than any more formal address, and I think the royal connotation was somewhat pleasing to her.

Early on the Wednesday morning of my third week the amateurish tack-tack-tack of the typewriter in the conservatory stopped and my employer came through into the downstairs lounge to inform me she had to go out for two hours.

It was at that point I made my first bold move.

I took a leather-bound volume from the bookshelf beside me and blew a miniature dust-storm along the golden channel at the top of its pages.

'Would you like me to give the books a wipe with a duster?'

For a few seconds I thought I saw in those cold grey eyes of hers something very close to hatred.

'If you can put them all back exactly as you found them.'

'I'll try, ma'am.'

'Don't try. Do it!'

It was going to be a big job.

Bookshelves lined three whole sides of the room, and at mid-morning I had a coffee-break in the kitchen.

Outside by the garden shed I saw the steatopygous odd-job man who appeared intermittently —

usually when I was leaving — to fix a few things as I supposed.

I held my coffee-cup up to the window and my eyes asked him if he'd care to join me.

His eyes replied yes and I saw he was younger than I had thought.

More handsome too.

I asked him how well he knew her ladyship but he merely shrugged.

'She's writing a book, did you know?' I asked.

'Really?'

He took a swallow of his coffee and I saw that his hands though grubby enough were not those of a manual labourer.

'On Sir Thomas Wyatt,' I continued. 'I had a look when I was hoovering.'

'Really?'

If his vocabulary seemed rather limited, his eyes ranged over me more widely, and he smiled in a curiously fascinating way.

'I don't suppose you know much about Sir Thomas Wyatt?'

He shrugged again. 'Not much. But if you're going to tell me he died in 1542, you'll be wasting your time, won't you?'

Jesus!

He smiled again, this time at my discomfiture; then leaned forward and kissed me fully on the lips.

'Are you on the pill?'

'It's all right. You see, I'm pregnant,' I replied.

*

185

Afterwards we dared to have a cigarette together. It was the first I'd smoked for six months and it tasted foul. Stupid!

His lighter was out of fuel and I used one of the extra-long Bryant & May matches kept in the kitchen for various purposes.

For various purposes . . .

I'd almost finished the second wall of bookshelves when milady came back.

Just after I had turned round to acknowledge her presence a single sheet of paper fluttered to the floor.

Quickly I bent down to pick it up but she was immediately beside me, snatching it from my hand.

It was only a brief note and its contents could be read almost at a glance:

> Darling J
> Please do try to keep these few lines
> somewhere as a memento of my love

The message had been typed on cheap thin paper with the signatory's name written in light-blue Biro — 'Marie', the 'i' completed in girlish fashion with a largish ring instead of the usual dot.

But Mrs S-G said nothing, and half an hour later I was on my way home — unobtrusively as ever.

I had advertised to no one the fact that I was working as a part-time charwoman and I took care to be seen by as few people as possible.

There were reasons for this. You will see.

*

The following Monday I asked Mrs S-G if I could vary my time slightly and start half an hour earlier.

'Do you <u>have</u> to?' Her voice was contemptuous of the request.

'It's just that if I caught the earlier bus—'

'Oh, don't <u>explain</u>, for heaven's sake! Do you <u>have</u> to? — that's all I asked.'

I said I did, and it was agreed that I should henceforth begin at 8.30 a.m.

On Friday of that same week the postman called at 8.50 a.m., and three letters seemed to slither through the front door: a communication from British Telecom; a letter addressed to Mrs S-G, marked 'Strictly Private'; and a letter for Mr S-G, the name and address written in light-blue Biro, the 'i' of 'Squitchey' completed in girlish fashion with a largish ring instead of the usual dot.

Even as I picked up the letters I knew that my employer was just behind me.

'Thank you. I'll take them.'

Her manner was offensively brusque. But I made no demur and continued wiping the skirting boards around the entrance hall.

'I'm sorry,' I said (it was the following Wednesday), 'but I shan't be able to come on Friday.'

'Oh?'

'You see I've got to go to the ante-natal clinic ...'

'Don't <u>explain</u>, for heaven's sake. I thought I'd told you that before.'

'You did, yes.'

She said no more.

Nor did I.

The phone was seldom used at The Grange but that morning I heard her ring up someone from the conservatory.

I stood close to the door and tried hard to listen but the only part of the proceedings I caught was 'Saturday night . . .'

My appointment at the hospital was for 10.30 a.m. but an emergency put the morning's programme back by about an hour.

During the wait I read a few articles from various magazines, including an interview with an old gardener now aged one hundred who claimed that for getting rid of dandelions there was nothing quite so effective as arsenic, a small quantity of which he always kept in his garden shed.

Was it at this point I began to think of getting rid of Mrs S-G? Along with the dandelions?

I suppose I'd already pondered the problems likely to face unmarried mums. Problems so often caused by married dads.

What really irks me more than anything, though, is all that sickening spiel they come up with. You know, about not wanting anyone to get hurt. Above all not wanting the little wife to get hurt.

Hypocrites!

*

It was my turn for receiving letters on the Thursday of the following week. Two of them.

The first was from the hospital. I was fine. The baby was fine. I felt almost happy.

The second was from the father of my child, with the postmark 'Los Angeles'.

Here's the bit I want you to read:

Haven't you heard of women's equal rights and responsibilities, you stupid girl? Yes, of course there's such a thing as a condom. OK! And there's also such a thing as the pill! What did you think you were playing at? But that's all water under the bridge. Abortion's the only answer. I'll foot the bill on condition there's a complete break between us. Things can't go on like this. I land at Heathrow at lunchtime on Saturday 13th, so we can meet next Sunday. Let's say the usual — twelve noon in the back room of the Bird and Baby. Please be there — for both our sakes.

How nice and cosy that would be!
And I would be there, perhaps.
Yes, there was a chance that I would be there.

The following day, Friday, was to be my last in employment as a cleaning lady, and that morning I put the finishing touches to my plan.

Originally I had intended to kill only Mrs S-G. But my terms of reference had now widened.

That same afternoon I acted in an uncharacteristically careless way. I wrote a letter to my former employer:

189

Dear Mrs S-G

I was grateful to you for employing me but I
shall not be coming to work for you again.

My circumstances have changed significantly
in the past few days.

I am sure you will not have any difficulty in
finding a replacement.

> Yours
> Virginia

It <u>would</u> have been tit-for-tat in the resig-
nation—dismissal stakes. But I didn't post the letter
that day.

Nor the next.

Mrs S-G however had clearly been better stocked
with first-class stamps and her letter lay on the hall-
mat the following morning, Saturday 13th, with mine
still propped up against the Kellogg's packet on the
kitchen table.

Dear Marie Lawson,

Oh yes I do know your real name and I made no
attempt to take up your bogus reference. At first I
thought you were quite bright and I told you so.
But in truth you must be as stupid as you
obviously consider <u>me</u> to be. I was curious about
why you'd applied and it amused me to offer you
the job. So I watched you. And all the time you
thought you were watching <u>me</u>! You see my
husband told me all about your affair although I
didn't know you were pregnant. Nor, as it
happens, do I believe you <u>are</u>. The charades with

the note and the letter were prettily performed yet really quite unnecessary. I steamed open the letter as no doubt you wished me to in what (I have to assume) was your futile plan for bringing matters out into the open. I made a photocopy of the letter and forwarded your pathetic plea to America. I think the real reason for my writing — apart from giving you the sack — is to thank you for those two pieces of evidence you provided. I am informed by my lawyer that they will significantly expedite the divorce proceedings I shall be bringing against my husband. After that I expect my own life to turn into happier paths, and I trust that if I later remarry I shall be more fortunate with my second husband than I was with the man who amused himself with a whole host of harlots besides yourself.

V. Spencer-Gilbey (Mrs)

Stupid.
Both of them had called me stupid.

On that same Saturday night — or rather in the early hours of the Sunday morning — I waited with great patience for the light to be switched off in the master bedroom. (You remember it?)

If they were not in the same bed at least they were in the same bedroom, since I had seen the two figures silhouetted several times behind the curtains.

I further waited one whole hour, to the minute, before moving soundlessly along the side of the house

COLIN DEXTER

and then into the rear garden where I stooped down beside the conservatory door.

Good old Boswell! (Remember him?) I almost hoped he'd decided to sleep out in the open that night.

I struck one of the extra-large Bryant & May matches. (Remember them?) And shielding the flame I pushed my hand slowly through the cat-flap.

Behind the glass-panelled door I could see the loose sheets of paper (so carefully stacked) catching light almost immediately.

No more than ten seconds later I felt rather than heard the sudden 'whoosh' of some powerful updraught as a tongue of flame licked viciously at the items (so carefully stacked) beside the conservatory door.

The colour of the blaze reminded me so very much of Boswell's eyes.

I departed swiftly via the front path before turning round fifty or so yards down the road.

The window of the master bedroom was still in darkness. But at the rear of the house I had the impression that although it was still only 2.15 a.m. the rosy-fingered dawn was beginning to break already.

It was big news.

Headlined in Monday's edition of The Oxford Mail, for example, I read:

TWO DIE IN NORTH OXFORD INFERNO
It seems unlikely that the burned-out shell of

the listed thatch-and-timber property in
Squitchey Lane (picture p.2) will provide too
many clues to the cause of the fire. The blaze
spread with such rapid intensity that ...

My eyes skipped on to the next paragraph:

The remains of two bodies, charred beyond all
chance of recognition, have been recovered
from a first-floor bedroom and it is feared that
these are the bodies of Mr J. Spencer-Gilbey
and of his wife Valerie. Mr Spencer-Gilbey had
just returned from America where ...

But I wasn't really interested about where.
So I turned to look at the picture on page two.
It hadn't after all seemed worthwhile to turn up at
the Bird and Baby the previous day. So I hadn't gone.
You can see why.
The fire was still big (bigger) news in the Tuesday
evening's edition of The Oxford Mail:

BLAZE MYSTERY DEEPENS
The Oxford City Police were amazed to receive
a call late yesterday evening from Heathrow.
The caller was Mr John Spencer-Gilbey who,
it had been assumed, had perished with his
wife in the fire which completely destroyed
their home in Squitchey Lane, Oxford, in the
early hours of Sunday morning.
    Mr Spencer-Gilbey had been expected back
in England on Saturday from a lecture tour in
America. However it now appears that indus-

trial action by air-traffic controllers on the western seaboard of America had effected the cancellation of the original flight, and Mr Spencer-Gilbey told the police that he had earlier rung his wife to inform her of the rescheduling of his return to England.

A police spokesman told our reporter that several aspects of the situation were quite extraordinarily puzzling and that further enquiries were being pursued. The police appeal to anyone who might have been in or near Squitchey Lane in the late evening of Saturday 13th or the early morning of Sunday 14th to come forward to try to assist in these enquiries. Please ring (0865) 266000.

'... he had earlier rung his wife ...'

Yes.

And he had also rung me.

For a start I was tempted to 'come forward' myself — over the phone and anonymously — with a tentative (hah!) suggestion about the identity of that second fire-victim.

God rot his lecherous soul!

But I shan't make that call.

One call I shall quite certainly make though. Once the dust, once the ashes have started to settle.

You see, I think that a meeting between the two of us could possibly be of some value after all. Don't you?

And even as I write I almost hear the words that I shall use:

'John? Sunday? The usual? Twelve noon in the back room of the Bird and Baby? Please be there!'

Yes, John, please be there – for both our sakes . . .

PART THREE

They flee from me, that sometime did me seek
With naked foot, stalking in my chamber.

(Sir Thomas Wyatt, *Remembrance*)

Lewis came into Morse's office just before four o'clock that afternoon.

'Not much to report, sir. There's a card on the noticeboard there – looks as if it might be from a boyfriend.'

'I saw it.'

'And there's this – I reckon it's probably in the same handwriting.'

Lewis handed over a postcard showing a caparisoned camel standing in front of a Tashkent mosque. On the back Morse read the brief message: 'Travelling C 250 K E.'

'What's that all about, do you think, sir?'

Morse shook his head: 'Dunno. Probably the number of the aeroplane or the flight number or . . . something. Where did you find it, anyway?'

'There was an atlas there and I was looking up that place – you know, Erzincan. The postcard was stuck in there. You know, like a sort of marker.'

'Oh.'

'Don't you want to know where Erzincan is?'

'No. I looked it up when I got back here.'

196

'Oh.'

With a glint of triumph in his eyes, Morse now picked up the pink folder containing the Sheila Poster story and quickly explained its provenance.

'I want you to read this.'

'What, *now*, sir?'

'Did you think I meant on your summer holidays?'

'I'm a slow reader, you know that.'

'So am I.'

'You want me to read it *here*?'

'No. I've got things to be getting on with here. Go and have a sandwich. And take your time. Enough clues there to fill a crossword puzzle.'

After Lewis had gone, Morse looked at his watch and started on *The Times* crossword.

When, eleven minutes later, he filled in the four blanks left, in – E – S – I – , he knew he should have been quicker in solving that final clue: 'Gerry-built semi is beginning to collapse in such an upheaval' (7).

Not bad, though.

A further hour passed before Lewis returned from the canteen and sat down opposite his chief.

'Lot's o' clues, you're right, sir. Probably made everything up, though, didn't she?'

'Not *everything*, not by a long chalk – not according to Diogenes Small.'

'According to who, sir?'

'To *whom*, Lewis – please!'

'Sorry, sir. I'm getting better about spelling, though. She made *one* mistake herself, didn't she?'

'Don't *you* start making things up!' Morse passed a handwritten list across the desk. 'You just rope in Dixon and Palmer – and, well, we can get through this little lot in no time at all.'

Lewis nodded: 'Have the case sewn up before the pubs close.'

For the first time that day there appeared a genuine smile on Morse's face. 'And these are only the obvious clues. You'll probably yourself have noticed a good many clues that've escaped *my* notice.'

'*Temporarily* escaped,' muttered Lewis, as he looked down at Morse's notes:

- Names (road, house, people): all phoney, like as not?
- Gazette: same ad you found? check
- Mr X (potential father): an academic surely? lecture tour of USA?
- Boswell: owners of this strange orange-eyed breed? check with the Cat Society
- Publishers (OUP etc): any recent work known/ commissioned on Sir T W?
- Ante-natal clinics: check – esp. JR2
- Bird and Baby: check, with photograph

'We should come up with *something*, I agree, sir. But it's going to take quite a while.'

'You think so?'

'Well, I mean, for a start, *is* there such a thing as the Cat Society?'

'That's what you're going to check *up* on, Lewis!'

'Seven lots of things to check up on, though.'

'Six!' Morse rose from his armchair, smiling happily once again. 'I'll check up on that last bit myself.'

'But where are you going to get a photo from?'

'Good point,' conceded Morse, allowing, in his mind, that occasionally it was perfectly acceptable to end a sentence with a preposition.

At 10.15 p.m. Lewis rang Morse's home number, but received no reply. Was the great man still immersed in his self-imposed assignment – with or without a photograph?

In fact Morse was at that moment still sitting in the murder-room at 14 Jowett Place.

His mind had earlier informed him that he had *missed* something there; and at 8.15 p.m. he had re-entered the property, assuring the PC guarding the front door that he wouldn't be all that long.

But nothing had clicked in that sad room. And the over-beered Morse had sat in the sole armchair there and fallen asleep – finally awakening half an hour after midnight, and feeling as rough (as they say) as a bear's backside.

The following morning Lewis reported on his failures, Dixon's failures, Palmer's failures; and Morse reported on his own failures.

'You know this *house* business?' volunteered a rather subdued Lewis. 'She's very specific about it, isn't she? Listed building, thatched, timbered, conservatory at the back – couldn't we try the Council, some of the up-market estate-agents . . .'

'Waste o' time, I reckon.'

'So? What do we do next?'

COLIN DEXTER

'Perhaps we ought to look at things from the, er, the motivation angle.'

'Doesn't sound much like *you*, sir.'

No, it wasn't much like him – Morse knew that. He loved to have some juicy facts in front of him; and he'd never cared to peer too deeply down into the abyss of human consciousness. Yet there now seemed no alternative but to erect *some* sort of psychological scaffolding around Sheila Poster's hopes and fears, her motives and mistakes . . . And only then to look in turn once more through each of the windows; once more to ask what the murdered woman was trying to tell everyone – trying to tell *herself* – in the story she had written.

Morse sought to put his inchoate thoughts into words whilst Sergeant Lewis sat opposite and listened. Dubiously.

'Let's assume she's had a fairly permanent job in the past – well, we know she has – but she's been made redundant – she's got hardly any money – everything she owns is just that bit cheap – she meets some fellow – falls for him – he's married – but he promises to take her where the lemon trees bloom – she believes him – she carelessly gets herself pregnant – by chance she finds an advert his *wife* has put in the local rag – she goes to work there – she's curious about the wife – jealous about her – she wants the whole situation out in the open – things turn sour though – lover-boy has second thoughts – he jilts her – the wife gives her the sack into the bargain – and our girl is soon nourishing a hatred for *both* of them – she wants to *destroy* both of them – but she can't really bring herself to destroy the father of her child – so in her story she changes things a bit – and sticks the wife in bed with a lover of her own – because then her *own* lover, Sheila's lover, will still be around, still alive – so there'll always be the chance of her winning him back – but he's bored with her – there's some academic preferment in the offing perhaps – he wants to get rid of her for good – he's prepared to play the faithful husband again – but Sheila won't play ball – she threatens to expose him – and when he goes to see her she becomes hysterical – he sees red – he sees all the colours of the rainbow – including orange, Lewis – because he knows she *can* ruin everything – *will* ruin everything – and then he knifes her . . .'

'*Who* knifes her?' asked Lewis quietly.

Morse shook his head. 'I haven't the faintest idea. I know what, though. I know I'm *missing* something!'

For a few moments the look on Morse's face was potentially belligerent – like that of Boswell in the story; and Lewis felt diffident about asking the favour.

Yet his wife had insisted that he did.

'I hope you won't mind, sir, but if I could take a couple of hours off this lunchtime? The wife—'

Morse's eyebrows rose. 'Doesn't she know you're in the middle of a murder enquiry? What's she want you to do? Take her a bag of spuds home?'

Lewis hesitated: 'It's just that, well, there's this great big crack that's appeared overnight in the kitchen wall and the wife's worried stiff that if we don't—'

'Bit of subsidence, you reckon?' (The pedantic Morse gave the stress to the first of the three syllables.)

'More like an earthquake, sir.'

For several seconds Morse sat utterly immobile in his chair, as if petrified before the sight of the Gorgon. And for the same several seconds Lewis wondered if his chief had suffered some facial paralysis.

Then Morse's lips slowly parted in a beatific smile. 'Lewis, my old friend, you've done it again! You've-gone-and-done-it-once-again! I think I see it. Yes, I think I see *all* of it!'

The happily bewildered Lewis sat back to learn the nature of his latest involuntary feat; but any enlightenment would have to wait awhile – that much was clear.

'Don't you let that missus of yours down!' beamed Morse. 'She's one in a million, remember that! Get off and sort things out with the surveyor or something—'

'Or the demolition squad.'

'—and get back here' (Morse looked at his watch) 'two o'clock, say?'

'You're sure—?'

'Absolutely. I've got a few important things to do here. And, er, just ask Dixon to come in, will you? *And* Palmer, if he's there?'

Lewis's euphoria was dissipating rapidly; but he had no opportunity to remonstrate, for Morse had already dialled a number and was asking if he was through to the Atlas Department of the Oxford University Press.

Sergeant Lewis returned to Kidlington HQ just before 2 p.m., almost three hours later, having finally received some reasonable reassurance that the Lewis residence was in minimal danger of imminent collapse. And at least *Mrs* Lewis was now somewhat happier in her mind.

It soon became apparent to Lewis that during his absence someone – the doughnut-addicted Dixon? the pea-brained

Palmer? – had been back out to Jowett Place; and Morse himself (what *else* had he been up to?) now sat purring like some cream-crammed orange-eyed long-hair as he surveyed the evidence before him on his desk – ready, it appeared, to lead the way along the path of true enlightenment.

'Clue Number One.' Morse opened the magnum opus of Diogenes Small and lovingly contemplated the bookmark: 'Greetings from Erzincan'. 'All right, Lewis?

'Clue Number Two.' He held up the postcard from Tashkent, turned it over, and read out its brief message once more: '"Travelling C 250 K E". Not too bright, were we? It means exactly what it says: Travelling about two hundred and fifty kilometres east, east of Tashkent, where we find, Lewis – the Susamyr Valley in Kirgyzstan.

'Clue Number Three. Dear old Toot-and-come-in – another postcard, another message, pretty certainly in the same handwriting: "Cairo's bloody hot but wish you were here." Remember? Signed "B".

'Clue Number Four.' Morse picked up the couplet from 'Last Poems'. 'Lines from a love poem, Lewis – with the seas between the pair of them – written from Los Angeles – the place to which the letter was re-addressed by Mrs S-G in the story. Remember? And we know *why* he went to all these places, don't we?'

Lewis didn't. But he nodded.

Why not?

'Then there was Clue Number Five – that walloping great clue *you* found straightaway: the fact that Sheila Poster had worked in the *Geology* Department here. Huh! I was blind.

'Then there was Clue Number Six . . . from *The Times*

crossword yesterday . . . Well, no, perhaps that was just a coincidence.

'And to cap it all you tell me about those almighty cracks in your bedroom wall . . .'

'*Crack* – only *one* crack, sir – in the *kitchen*, actually.'

Morse waved his right hand as if dismissing such trivial inaccuracies as of minor moment.

'*And*, Lewis, the dates all match – *all* of 'em. In each case they fall about ten days or a fortnight after the events – I've checked 'em with a lovely girl called Eunice Gill in the OUP cartographical section.'

(What *hadn't* Morse done, Lewis was beginning to wonder.)

'And she faxed me this,' continued Morse.

Lewis took the sheet and read a newspaper paragraph, dated 28.xi.92:

EARTHQUAKE SUMMIT

Following the major earth tremors which recently shook central Los Angeles, seismologists from all over the world, including the UK, will be assembling in Sacramento early in the new year to discuss improvements in the forecasting of potential disasters. No conference of similar scale has previously been held, and its anticipated 6-week duration reflects the urgency which is attached to this cosmic problem.

It had all taken Lewis far too long, of course; but now he let the information sink in. And finally he spoke:

'So what we need is a list of the delegates at the conference. Shouldn't take—'

But he got no further, for Morse handed him a sheet on which the members of the UK delegation were listed.

'Good man – Sergeant Dixon – you know,' said Morse.

Lewis ignored the tribute. 'None of 'em with the initial "B", though.'

'Why not try "R"?' asked Morse quietly.

So an embarrassed Lewis tried 'R', and looked again at the middle name of the five: Robert Grainger, D.Phil., MA.

'So all we need is to find out his address—'

'Cumnor Hill, Lewis. Not far off, is it? Palmer traced him. Good man – Palmer – you know.'

PART FOUR

White on a throne or guarded in a cave
  There lives a prophet who can understand
Why men were born . . .

(James Elroy Flecker, *The Golden Journey to*
Samarkand)

'Why do you think he did it?' asked Lewis as they drove
along the Botley Road.

'Grainger's possible motives, you mean? Well, he was hot
favourite for the chair in Geology – you've just discovered
that for yourself. Great honour, you know, having a prof-
essorial chair at Oxford. Biggest prize of the lot. For some
people.'

Lewis nodded, for he half understood now, and himself
took up the thread: 'And Sheila Poster was going to ruin it
all. Just as he's going to claim his birthright, he's suddenly
faced with the prospect of scandal and failure and divorce
. . . and the nightmare of some squawking infant into the
bargain.'

Morse was unusually slow in his reply as they started to
climb Cumnor Hill. 'I wouldn't know about those last two
things, Lewis.'

*

206

They walked along the flagged path that bisected the well-tended lawn, weedless even in winter, and knocked on a front door which was immediately opened by a prematurely grey-haired man, slimly built, in his late forties or so, his eyes looking at them over half-lensed spectacles.

'You're the police, I suppose?'

Morse showed his warrant. 'Dr Grainger?'

For a few seconds the man hesitated. Then stood back and ushered his visitors into a well-appointed lounge, three of its walls completely lined with books.

'Yes. I suppose we'd better get it over with.'

He spoke quite slowly, and without emotion – at least to begin with. Yes, he knew that Sheila Poster had been murdered. He'd read it in the *Oxford Mail*. Yes, he'd had an affair with her; she'd been putting pressure on him to leave his wife and go to live with her; she'd told him she was pregnant – though he'd doubted the claim. His wife now knew most of the truth, but had only become directly involved because Sheila had contrived somehow to get a job as a cleaning-woman in the house there, and then had sought to poison the marital relationship – what little there was left of it . . .

It was at this point that the belittled Lewis (seemingly to Morse's mild amusement?) decided to assert himself.

'It'll be up to *Mrs* Grainger to give us details about her side of things, sir. You yourself weren't here, were you, when Miss Poster was working for your wife?'

Grainger, who hitherto had been speaking directly to Morse, now turned his eyes upon Lewis.

'You mean you're not prepared to take *my* word about what my wife has told me?'

207

COLIN DEXTER

'We're not here to answer questions, Dr Grainger – we're here to ask them,' snapped Lewis.

Irritatedly, Grainger turned back to Morse. 'Is it necessary for us to have this man with us, Inspector? I am *not* used to being spoken to in this way and I find it wholly and unnecessarily offensive!'

'This is a *murder* enquiry, sir,' began Morse rather lamely. 'You must understand—'

'But I *do* understand. And I'm telling you you're wasting your time if you think you'll find any murderer in *this* house.'

'Where were you on Sunday night?' asked Morse quietly.

'Huh! I'll tell you. I was in America – that's where I was.'

'And you can prove that?'

Grainger stood up, and followed by Lewis walked over to a bureau on which, beside a framed wedding-photograph, lay an envelope (as it proved) of travel documents. He handed it to Morse.

'As you'll see, I arrived back only yesterday afternoon – Monday. The plane, believe it or not, landed punctually at 4.15 p.m. I caught the Heathrow bus just after five o'clock, and I got to Oxford about quarter-to seven.'

'It'll certainly be pretty easy to check up, then,' said Lewis, smiling serenely; and it was Morse who now looked round at his sergeant, more in admiration than in anger. Yet he himself sat silent and listened only, as Grainger snarled at Lewis once more, the antagonism between the two men now almost physically tangible.

'Oh yes. It'll hardly require a man of your calibre to check up on *that*. And it'll be pretty easy to check up on my wife as well. But let me tell you something, Sergeant! It won't be *you* who sees her. Is that clear? She's extremely upset – and you

208

can understand why, can't you? Sheila was here *working* for her until a fortnight or so ago. All right? Now *you* might get a bit blasé about murders, Sergeant – but other people *don't*. My wife is under sedation and she's not going to see *anyone* – not today she isn't. And she won't see *you*, in any case! Your inspector here sounds a reasonably humane and civilized sort of fellow – and perhaps there are still a few others like him in the Force. So any of *them* can see my wife. All right? But it won't be *you*, Sergeant. Why? *Because I say so!*'

Phew!

Morse now intervened between the warring parties: 'That'll be fine, sir. Have no fears! I'll be interviewing your wife myself. But . . . but it would help us, sir, if you *do* happen to know where Mrs Grainger was on Sunday night?'

'She went to some gala do in London with one of her friends – lady-friends. As I understand it, the pair of them missed the 11.20 from Paddington and had to catch the 12.20 – the "milk-float", I think they call it – landing up here at about 2 a.m. They got a taxi home from the station. That's all I know.'

'Have you got this friend's telephone number?'

'You won't need it. She lives next door.'

Grainger pointed vaguely to the right; and Morse nodded his unspoken instruction to Lewis.

And Lewis left.

Morse was already seated in the Jaguar when Lewis rejoined him ten minutes later.

'He's right, sir. They got back here to Cumnor about half-past two in the early hours of Monday morning.'

Morse showed no emotion, for he'd fully expected confirmation of Mrs Grainger's alibi.

And he began to explain.

'You see, Lewis, it's not the *who*-dunnit aspect of this particular case that's really important – but the *why*-dunnit. *Why* was Sheila Poster murdered? She must surely have posed a threat to someone, either a man or a woman. And more likely a man, I'm thinking. She must have stood in the way of some man's hopes and calculated advancement. So *much* of a threat that when she refused to compromise, at some showdown between them, she was murdered precisely for that refusal of hers. So we'd no option but to work backwards – agreed? And we knew *her* side of things, to some extent, from the story she wrote. Now *some* things in that story reflected actuality fairly closely, didn't they? The Graingers' house – "The Grange", huh! – her job there – her affair with the husband – her overwhelming wish to force the issue with the wife—'

'Don't forget the baby, sir!'

'No, I won't forget the baby. But Grainger didn't seem to think she was telling the truth about that, did he?'

'She *was* pregnant, though.'

'Yes, she was telling the truth about being pregnant. In fact, she was telling a whole lot more of the truth perhaps than she was prepared to admit – even to herself. Let's make a hypothetical case. What, say, if she really wanted to murder *not* the married couple she was telling herself she hated? What if – in her story – she wanted to murder the very people she *did* in fact murder: the lady-of-the-house and *that lady's lover*? What if the pair of *them* had fallen deeply in love? What if – again as in the story – the lady-of-the-house had been only too glad to learn of her husband's infidelity? Because then she could divorce him, and marry her new lover . . . the man who stood by the flower-beds and tended the lawns there . . .'

'The man who came in for a cup of coffee, sir.'

'Perhaps so. But don't forget she wasn't just telling us a string of *facts* in the story – she was making a whole lot of it up as she went along.'

'Really, sir?'

Lewis, as Morse could just about make out in the gloaming, was smiling quietly to himself.

'What the hell's got *into* you, Lewis? You antagonize one of our leading witnesses; you go off and find an unshakeable alibi for his missus; and now you sit there grinning like a Cheshire—'

'By the way, sir, they do have a cat – I asked next door. "Johnson", its name is.'

'You've nothing *else* to tell me, have you?' asked Morse, looking curiously at his sergeant.

'Actually, there is, sir – yes.'

'Out with it, man!'

'Yesterday, sir, when we interviewed Paul Bayley, he said he'd been with his girlfriend all night.'

'You told me that. You told me you'd checked.'

'I did check. Bayley told me she was in the middle of moving flats that very day – seemed she'd been a little bit too generous with her favours for the landlord's liking; and – just temporarily, mind – she was registered as of no fixed address. But Bayley said she'd almost certainly be in the City Centre Westgate Library – where she went most mornings – in the Local History Section—'

'Where she was!'

Lewis nodded. 'Doing some research on Nuneham Courtenay and the Deserted Village. So she told me.'

'Well?'

'Well . . . that's about it.'

'Is it?'

'She's a very beautiful woman, sir.'

'More beautiful than Sheila Poster?'

'I'd say so. More to my taste, anyway.'

'And most men would fancy her?'

'If they had the chance.'

'And Bayley *did* have the chance.'

'I'm pretty sure he did. He's been in Jowett Place for about four months or so now. Unemployed for a start; but then *in* work – so his landlord says.'

'His landlord? When did you see *him*?'

'He called in yesterday lunchtime, when you were in the pub. And from what he said—'

'You didn't mention this before.'

'Thought I'd just do a bit of investigation off my own bat, sir. You didn't mind?'

'See if *you* could solve the case, you mean?'

'Try to, yes. And the landlord said it was Sheila Poster who'd told Bayley about the vacancy in the flat upstairs and who'd put in a good word for him, you know – gave him a good-behaviour reference. Not only that, though. I reckon she was the one who told Bayley about the odd-job vacancy going up at the Graingers' place.'

'Phew!' Morse whistled quietly. 'You're saying *Bayley* was the odd-job man?'

'I'm saying exactly that, sir!'

'You're *sure* of this?'

'Not yet,' replied Lewis, beaming happily.

'Let me get this clear. You're suggesting that Bayley goes to work for Mrs Sylvia Grainger – she falls for *him* – he falls for *her* – she knows her husband's having an affair with the *charwoman* – she's proof of it. Then' (Morse paused slightly for dramatic effect) 'just when things are looking hunkydory, this charwoman claims she's pregnant. Not by Grainger, though . . .'

'. . . but by *Bayley*. Yes, sir.'

'And Bayley goes down on Sunday night – has it out with her – she refuses to play ball – and she gets herself murdered. Is that the idea?'

'Exactly!'

'But Bayley's got an alibi! This local history woman of yours – she says she was with him all night.'

'From about 9 p.m. to 7 a.m. the following morning. Correct. Slept on the floor together in a friend's house in Cowley somewhere – she refuses to say exactly where.'

'She's probably trying to protect her friends or something.'

'Or something,' repeated Lewis.

'Just you bear in mind all the adverse publicity we're getting about "confessions under duress", OK? We've got to tread carefully, you know that.'

It was still only four o'clock, yet already the afternoon had darkened into early dusk.

'Can you guess, sir, why Dr Grainger was so worried about *me* interviewing his wife?'

'He probably thought you were a bit crude, Lewis –

preferred a sensitive soul like me. And by the way, don't forget that there are few in the Force more competent at that sort of thing than me.'

'You can't think of any other reason?'

'*You* obviously can.'

Lewis savoured his moment of triumph. 'Did you see the wedding-photo just now – the one Dr Grainger had on the bureau?'

'Well, yes – at a distance.'

'Beautiful woman, Mrs Grainger – *very* beautiful.'

'Taken quite a few years ago, that photo – she's probably changed since then.'

'No! You're wrong about that, sir.'

'How do *you* know?'

'Because I met her very recently. Met her yesterday morning, in fact. In the Westgate Library. She told me her name was Wendy Allsworth. But it isn't, sir. It's *Sylvia Grainger.*'

'Extraordinary!' said Morse, his voice strangely flat.

'You don't sound all that surprised.'

'Just tell me one thing. When you took the statement from – from Mrs Grainger, do you think she knew about the murder?'

'No, I don't.'

'*You* didn't tell her?'

'No. So unless they planned things—'

'Very doubtful!' interposed Morse.

'—Bayley must have rung her up early that morning.'

'Do you think *he* told her?'

'I don't think so. If she'd known it was a murder enquiry . . . No, I don't think he told her.'

'I agree. She was prepared to go a long way – *did* go a long way. Not that far, though.'

Lewis hesitated. 'You'll excuse me for saying so, but as I said you don't sound very *surprised* about all this.'

'What? Of course I am. From where I sat I couldn't have recognized the *Queen* if she'd been in that photo. The old eyes are not as sharp as they were.'

'You *knew*, though, didn't you?' asked Lewis quietly.

'Not *all* of it, no,' lied Morse.

Yet Lewis's silence was saddeningly eloquent, and Morse finally nodded. Then sighed deeply.

'I've always *told* you, Lewis, haven't I? The person who finds the body is going to be your prime suspect. That's always been my philosophy. It's *compulsive* with these murderers – they want their victim *found*. It'd send 'em crackers if the body lay undiscovered somewhere for any length of time.'

'So?' asked Lewis dejectedly.

'So! So I had Bayley brought in this morning – this lunchtime.'

'While I was with the builder.'

'Yes. And Bayley continues to be detained at Her Majesty's Pleasure.'

'You interviewed him yourself?'

'Yes. As I just told you, there's no one in the Force so firmly and fairly competent as me – not in that line of business.'

Lewis was smiling wryly now – first nodding, then shaking his head. He might well have known . . .

He nodded towards the Graingers' home: 'Shall we go and take *her* in as well?'

'Actually she's, er, she's already helping with our enquiries.'

Lewis almost exploded. 'But you *can't* – you *can't* mean . . .'

'I do, yes. I had Bayley tailed and he went out to meet Sylvia Grainger – in the bar at The Randolph – about a quarter to twelve, that was. She'd told her husband she was going to her sister's for a few hours. That's what she said. So! So there's really not much point in us sitting here freezing any longer, is there?'

Lewis turned the key in the ignition, the Jaguar spurted into life, and the two detectives now sat silently side by side for several minutes as they drove back down into Oxford.

It was Lewis who spoke first: 'You know, it really is nonsense what you say, sir – about the first person finding the body. I just don't know where the *evidence* is for that. And then you say it's "compulsive" – didn't you say that? – for murderers to want the body found. But some of 'em take enormous time and trouble for the body *never* to be found.'

'You're right, I agree. I was exaggerating a bit.'

'So what *did* make you think it was Bayley? There must have been *something*.'

'It's all these wretched crosswords I do. You meet some odd words, you know. The first time I saw Bayley in his room I thought what a great big fat-arsed sod he was. And then, this morning, I read Sheila Poster's story again – and well, things went sort of "click". You remember that long word Sheila Poster used – about the odd-job man? Mind you, she *was* an English graduate.'

Lewis did remember, but only vaguely; he'd look it up once they got back to HQ.

'It was always going to be a straightforward case,' continued Morse. 'We'd have been sure to find out where Bayley had been working, sooner or later.'

'"Sooner or later",' repeated Lewis. 'And for once I thought it was me who was sooner. It's just like I said: I've got a second-class mind – I'm just like a second-class—'

'Ah! That reminds me. Just pull in here a minute, will you?'

Lewis turned into a slip-road alongside a row of brightly lit shops just before the Thames Valley Police HQ buildings.

'Where exactly—?'

'Here! Here's fine.'

Morse jabbed a finger to the left, and Lewis braked outside a sub post-office.

'Just nip in and get me a book of stamps, please.'

'First- or second-class?' For some reason Lewis was feeling reasonably happy again.

'No need to go wild, is there? I'll have one book of second-class, all right? These days they get there almost as quickly as first, you know that.'

Morse had been pushing his hands one after the other into the pockets of overcoat, jacket, trousers – seemingly without success.

'You'll never believe it, Lewis, but . . .'

'I think I will, sir. Remember what that fellow Diogenes Small wrote about people's flights of imagination?'

'You've been soaring up there yourself, you mean?'

'Not quite, no. All I'm saying is it wouldn't take a detective to see what you're trying to tell me.'

'Which is?'

'You haven't got any money.'

'Ah!'

217

Morse looked down silently at the car-mat; and Lewis, now smiling happily, opened the driving-seat door of the Jaguar, and was soon to be seen walking towards the premises of the sub post-office in Kidlington, Oxon.

MONTY'S
REVOLVER

> Women sometimes forgive those who force an opportunity, never those who miss it.

> (Talleyrand)

It wasn't often that Professor Rawlins bothered her with his personal letters. Occasionally, though – like this afternoon; and like yesterday afternoon, come to think of it. But he always insisted on putting his own stamps on such letters, never allowing them through the Department's franking-machine. Bit too obviously self-righteous, she thought. She glanced at the tiny gold watch (a wedding present) on her left wrist: almost a quarter to five. TGFF. Thank God For Friday!

Rawlins took off his half-glasses, pinched the top of his nose, turned over a page of his desk diary, lit another cigarette, and looked across at Carol Summerson.

'Professor Smithson's coming on Monday morning. Will you nip out first thing and get me a bottle of Glenfiddich?'

Carol made a note, closed her shorthand book, uncrossed her elegant legs, and smiled as she looked at him. And he, half smiling himself, looked back across at her; and she felt pleasingly surprised. (Or was it surprisingly pleased?) There had been so few moments of real communication between them during the three months she'd been working for him – the man she'd more than once heard described as 'the cleverest fellow in Oxford'.

She was glad to get out of his office, though. He would never open the window and the smell in the room was invariably horrid. How she wished he'd stop smoking! (John never smoked, thank goodness.) How old was he? Sixty? Overweight, and with a chest that sounded like a loose-strung harp, he was just the sort to die before his time from heart trouble or lung cancer or chronic bronchitis or emphysema – or like as not the whole lot of them listed on his death certificate. Why didn't his *wife* do something about him, for Christ's sake?

'Good night, sir,' she heard herself say; and for a moment she fancied that she'd almost like to look after him herself.

John was waiting for her, sitting on his wife's swivel-chair and turning over the papers that lay on her desk. (He always picked Carol up on Fridays.) While she was out in the cloak-room, he looked through a few more recent carbons, each neatly stapled to its originating letter. One carbon in particular caught his eye:

Dear Jack,

Glad you still remember me and – yes! – I still keep the old collection going. But anything that belonged to Monty is sure to spark off some keen bidding – all a bit too high for me. As you say, though, the reserve price seems fair enough.

How long is it since we met? Seven – eight years? Marion died six years ago – malignant tumour. Not unexpected, but all desperately sad and very upsetting for the boys. I remarried two years later, and since then I've had another son! – and another!! – and another!!! Do you know the odds against a penny coming down *six* times on the trot?

If you're ever near Oxford, let me know. I promise not to show you round the Department.

Sincerely yours,

Carol looked at her husband as she re-entered her office. At twenty-two, he was a year younger than herself; yet in many ways since their marriage two years previously, he'd shown himself the more mature, the more dependable, of the two. There had been a few patches of squabbling – mostly her fault; and the one continuing sadness . . . But she was glad she'd married him.

That, at least, is what Carol Summerson was telling herself that December afternoon.

'You reading my boss's correspondence again?'

He nodded.

'Interesting?'

'Not really.'

As she unhooked her coat from the wall-cupboard, John glanced quickly at the originating letter, stapled behind the carbon he had just been reading. A letterhead announced a 'J. Wingate, Gunsmith', with an address in Guildford, the letter itself reporting the forthcoming auction of a revolver that had belonged to Field Marshal Bernard Montgomery – reserve price £3,000.

'I didn't know he was interested in revolvers,' said John, unlocking the nearside door to the Metro.

'I've told you *before*. You shouldn't read—'

'Didn't mind, did you?'

'Course not!' She brushed her full lips against his cheek as she fastened her safety-belt.

'His big hobby. One of the girls went to his house once when he'd got bronchitis or something and she said he'd got all these revolvers like in cases sort of thing hanging round the walls. Not very nice really, is it? You'd think that with all those young children—'

She stopped suddenly and a silence fell between them.

*

223

At 5.20 p.m. Rawlins locked the door of his office and left the Department. Florence (at thirty-two, exactly half his age) would have the fish all ready. TGFF. Thank God For Florence!

That night, for no immediately apparent reason, Frank Rawlins dreamed of Carol Summerson.

It was just before 11 a.m. the following Monday that Smithson arrived. Carol was not introduced to him, but from her adjacent room she could hear his voice; could hear, too, the occasional gurgle of Glenfiddich and the clink of the office glasses. Just over an hour later, after the pair of them had walked past her window, she entered Rawlins' office, took the two glasses, washed them out in the ladies' loo, and bent down to put them back in the cupboard beside the bottle – now empty.

'Hello!'

She hadn't heard him come back in, and she felt slightly confused as he steered her by the elbow into her own office.

'Don't you think it's about time I treated my confidential secretary to lunch?'

He looked – and sounded – surprisingly sober; and she felt flattered. Soon he was holding her coat ready, and she was slipping her arms into the sleeves.

Easily.

He was interesting – no doubt about that. He told her of the time he and Smithson had worked together in a VD clinic in

224

Vienna; and as he reminisced of this and other experiences Carol felt herself enriched, and newly important.

'Another?'

'I've had enough, thank you.'

'Nonsense!' He picked up her glass and made his slightly unsteady way to the bar once more.

Her third gin-and-tonic tasted strong. Nice, though! Was it a double? His own drink looked very much like the orange juice he'd promised himself; and after he'd left her to visit the gents' she took a sip of it: it tasted even more strongly of gin than hers.

'We'd better be getting back, sir.'

'Yes.'

'Thanks for a lovely lunch.'

'Carol! I've had a lot to drink – you know that. But I just want you to know how ver' much I'd like to go to bed with you this afternoon.'

Carol's heart sank.

'Don't be silly! Come on, let's get back!'

He was hurt, she knew that; a bit ashamed, too. And as they walked back he tried so very hard to sound his usual sober self.

That night Carol Summerson dreamed of Frank Rawlins. Erotically.

Carol's rise came through in mid-January, and she was thrilled.

'I'm ever so grateful, sir.'

'You deserve it.'

'Will you come out one day and have lunch with *me*?'

'When?'

'Whenever you're free.'

'Today?'

'Today!'

She saw to it that he drank almost all the wine, and she insisted on buying him a glass of brandy after their meal. They were sitting close together now, and gently she moved her right leg against the rough tweed of his trousers. And, just as gently, he responded, saying nothing, yet saying everything.

'Another brandy?' she ventured.

Rawlins looked down at his empty glass, and smiled a little sadly.

'Have you ever thought how wonderful it would be to have a quiet, civilized little place all to yourself where—'

He stopped, and there was a long silence between them before Carol spoke softly in his ear.

'But I've *got* a nice little place out at Wheatley. You see, John's away for a few days . . .'

Seven weeks later, Carol's GP told her that she was quite definitely pregnant.

On the Friday evening of that same week, John Summerson called as usual to collect his wife. It was quarter to five – exactly so – when he walked through into Rawlins's office and sat down in the chair that his wife had just vacated.

Over his glasses, Rawlins' eyes registered puzzlement: it was as though a new boy had just strolled into the Masters' Common Room.

'Can I help you? John – isn't it?'

'You had sex with my wife.' Summerson spoke quietly, firmly – defying all denial.

'Where on earth did you get such—?'

'You're lying!'

'Look here! You can't be serious—'

'She's pregnant!'

'But you can't—'

'I *watched* you!' hissed Summerson.

'But you—'

'Shut up! I'm not the father. I can *never* be a father. You do understand what I'm saying, don't you?'

'Yes,' answered Rawlins softly.

'Did you *enjoy* it?' The young man's eyes were blazing with a terrible anguish.

'I just—'

'*Shut up!*'

Rawlins sank back in his chair, his shoulders sagging.

'I'm redundant now,' continued Summerson. 'They gave me £3,000 for the five years I worked there. There's not *much* you can do with £3,000, is there, Professor?'

Rawlins closed his eyes and thought of his sons and thought of Florence and thought of himself, too: he knew exactly what £3,000 might possibly have bought.

When he opened his eyes he saw the revolver in Summerson's right hand – a British Enfield .380, Number 2, Mark 1, the wooden stock a dirty nicotine-brown, the gunmetal of the fluted barrel as clean and gleaming as a polished stone. Summerson swivelled the revolver round until it pointed straight at Rawlins' heart, and his finger squeezed the trigger until the hammer lifted to the limit of the catch.

'Pretty accurate, they tell me, at such close range as this, Professor!'

Rawlins said nothing, his eyes seemingly mesmerized as he stared at the cylinder-chamber. But now the revolver was no longer pointing at him; for with slow deliberation Summerson turned it round upon himself and brought the tip of the shining barrel up against his own right temple, where the index finger of his right hand finally exacted that minimal extra pressure on the double-action trigger, and the hammer drove against the cylinder-chamber.

The children had eaten half an hour previously, and Florence Rawlins looked down sadly at the juiceless fillet that lay beneath the low-burning grill. Why couldn't Frank be more thoughtful?

Six o'clock.

Ten past.

Twenty past.

At half-past six she rang his private office number, but there was no reply.

'Fine! Fine!' The young gynaecologist had repeated. 'No problems. Now you'll promise not to smoke, won't you?' 'I promise.' Of course she wouldn't smoke! Her thoughts drifted back happily to Rawlins . . . With a father like Rawlins, it would surely be a *boy* – and pretty certainly a *clever* little boy, at that! She'd longed to be a mother ever since she'd been a young girl, when she'd played incessantly, obsessively almost, with her dollies – dressing them, combing their lank locks, bending their stiff joints before propping them up against the backs of chairs . . .

Six weeks after that first ante-natal clinic, an oblong parcel was delivered to the Rawlins' residence, where later in the day the Professor of Forensic Medicine inspected its contents with enthusiasm. The new case would naturally take pride of place, perhaps just inside the front entrance, he thought. He fitted the revolver carefully inside the specially constructed case, closed the glass cover, and held the exhibit up against some imaginary hook on the facing wall. Not a bad reward, really, for being trapped into exercising his dubiously enviable knack of procreating male offspring with even the most perfunctory ejaculation. And even that extraordinary afternoon when young Summerson had pointed the revolver at his heart hadn't been all that traumatic an experience really, because long before the final, cosmically anticlimactic 'click' he had known (as any expert in the field would have known) that there were no bullets in the open chambers of the revolver – not a single one. For all that though, it had been a great relief when the revolver had at last been lowered, and a genuine surprise when Summerson had presented it to him across the desk – reward for services rendered, so to speak. And he really *had* needed those two large whiskies, although he'd afterwards agreed with a worried, tearful Florence that he should have told her he'd be late.

On September 29 of that same year, a baby was delivered on the third floor of the Maternity Hospital up at Headington, and the young father had the name all ready. The gunsmith from Guildford may not have bothered to work out any mathematical odds, but John Summerson had calculated the chances of a penny coming down heads for a *seventh* time; and at 128:1, they'd seemed to him wildly improbable.

They called the lovely little girl 'Francesca'.

THE
CARPET-BAGGER

He who is conceived in a cage
Yearns for the cage.

(Yevtushenko, *Monologue of a Blue Fox on an Alaskan Animal Farm*)

1

There were longish periods now when the A34 was quiet, almost completely free of the swishing traffic. Only up there along the lay-by, two 'Long Vehicle' lorries ahead, was there still any continuum of activity – where at the side of a converted white caravan a single electric light bulb illuminated MACS SNAX – Open 24 Hour's.

Though with little formal education behind him, Danny had still felt the itch to transpose that single apostrophe from the last word to the first when, three-quarters of an hour earlier, he'd walked along to the serving-hatch and ordered a cup of tea and a Melton Mowbray pork-pie. Two other drivers had stood there then, chatting in desultory fashion and intermittently stamping their feet, their white plastic cups of piping-hot tea steaming brightly in the cold air of that late-January night. But apart from swopping first names, the three of them had said little to each other.

Now, back in the cab of the furniture van, Danny began to realize how very cold he was. Yet he told himself that 'cold' was only a relative concept and was trying to convince himself that he was only *relatively* cold. As with many things in life, it was all a question of mind over matter. His feet *felt* bloody frozen – Christ, they did. But they weren't *really* frozen, were they, Danny boy? What if he were standing barefoot on the far North Pole? He'd always believed there was just that one square yard of ice and snow comprising yer actual North Pole, and no one yet had managed to persuade him otherwise.

There were two newspapers in the cab: the *Daily Telegraph* (oddly?) and a late edition of the *Oxford Mail*. And newspapers were super for insulation, everyone knew that. Just stick a few sheets all the way round between your shirt and your jumper : . .

He looked at his wrist-watch: half-past midnight, just gone.

It had been most unlike him to make one mistake – let alone two – on such an important day. How stupid, in the first place, to have left his faithful old army greatcoat behind! And absolutely bloody stupid to have drunk more than a little too much that lunchtime, because more than a little had amounted to more than a lot and he had spent far more than he could really afford of his meagre savings.

At a service station just north of Oxford he had stopped to buy two litre bottles of Spring Water – as well as the *Oxford Mail* – prior to pulling into the next lay-by, just before the M40 interchange. It was a bit naïve, he knew, but he'd always believed that considerable quantities of water must significantly, and soon, serve to dilute and thereby to diminish the alcoholic level in the human bloodstream. And so it was that, an hour earlier, he'd forced himself to swallow all that flat and tasteless fluid to the final drop.

How come he'd been so careless?

Nervousness partly; and partly the exhilaration of the chase – of the fox keeping a few furlongs ahead of the yapping hounds. Perhaps the fox wasn't really exhilarated at all though – just frightened. Like he was, if he were honest with himself.

Just a bit.

Yet as he now sat behind the steering-wheel in the darkened cab, he couldn't really believe he'd find himself in much trouble with the police that night. He wasn't sure whether they *could* nick him for being over the limit in charge of a stationary vehicle. But they'd still need *some* reason for breathalysing him, wouldn't they? They'd have one if they spotted the number-plate, of course. But that was a pretty unlikely possibility, he reckoned. He hadn't read much of the *Oxford Mail*, but he'd seen one of its front-page headlines – OXON POLICE 'UNABLE TO COPE' WITH CRIME – and at least that was a nugget of encouragement in a naughty old world. A vehicle, so it seemed, was stolen every something seconds in the Thames Valley region and that was very good news indeed – considerably lengthening the odds against him being caught.

No. There was something else that was worrying him much more: the wretched 'tachometer' just to the left of the steering-wheel – a device (as he was now learning) that showed details of speeds and times, of stoppings and startings. He just couldn't *understand* the thing, that was the trouble. Nor the pile of paper discs, looking like so many CDs, that stood beside it – discs marked 'Freightchart', with lines and spaces and boxes for Name and Base and Destination and Cargo and Date and Mileage and God knows what else. Confusing. Unfamiliar. He could gauge all the other risks all right; but not this one. Perhaps the police couldn't give him a random breath-test. But could they give him a random tacho-test?

He switched on the dimmish light in the roof of the cab and picked up one of the white discs, noting that two lines had already been completed, presumably in the cheap blue Biro that lay beside the pile: SMITH, JOHN; Southampton.

Danny shook his head; and turned to the *Oxford Mail* again.

The main editorial picked up the page-one article on car-related crime, and Danny smiled to himself as he read the last few sentences:

The truth is that some of us, especially in the present cold snap, find it difficult enough to start our cars anyway – in spite of the considerable advantage of possessing our own car-keys. So how is it that even some comparatively incompetent car thief can enter our vehicles in a matter of seconds, twist a couple of wires together (so we're told), and be seen two minutes later outpacing a pursuing police car along the nearest motorway? Come on, you manufacturers! Let's have a bit more resource and ingenuity in a fully committed nationwide crusade against this growing social evil.

Danny inclined his head slightly to the right and wondered what exactly the manufacturers *could* do – given the nature of electric current. And already it was considerably more difficult than the editor was suggesting. Four minutes it had taken him with this particular van at Southampton – a ramshackle heap that'd have about as much chance with a police car as a moped would with Nigel Mansell.

Brrr . . . was it cold, though! And getting colder.

He could have turned on the engine for a quarter of an

hour or so, but he was reluctant to waste any diesel. There was a long journey north ahead of him; and while he reckoned he'd be safe enough on the busy daytime motorways, he didn't really want to stop again. At the same time he daren't drive any further, either – not until he'd had a few hours' rest; or kip, if he were lucky. Twice, only an hour or so since, he'd almost fallen asleep at the wheel, his eyes slowly drooping downwards . . . and further downwards, until his head followed them, only – suddenly! – to jerk upright in panic as consciousness reasserted itself.

Death had never figured prominently among his deepest fears, but he'd hardly had much of an innings as yet. And with all that cargo sitting there just behind him, well, it would have been criminal – *extra* criminal – to take any needless risks.

Thinking of all that cargo, though . . .

Why'd it taken him so long to think of it?

Earlier he'd leafed through the bundle of inventories and invoices, and counted at least – what, eighty? – eighty or more oriental rugs and carpets from Turkey, from Persia, from the Caucasus, from places sounding like Something-stan, with prices ranging from £4,500 (several such from Isfahan) to the cheapest (huh!) at only a thousand or so apiece. Danny's skill at scoring for his local darts team had once been legendary and his mind dwelt lovingly now on those accumulated spondulicks.

But the carpets weren't just precious, were they? They'd be *warm* too. Climb into the back, lie down under a couple of those beautifully embroidered beauties and – like his mum used to say – he'd soon be as snug as a bug in a rug.

A Persian rug.

There was no key to be found for the rear doors, but opening locks was Danny's hobby; his specialism. Some few people, he knew, could finish a fiendish crossword puzzle in a matter of minutes; a few others could spot a master-move to some complex chess problem in hardly any time at all. And he was like that with opening locks.

Only quicker.

And immediately disappointed.

Inside, no neatly laid-out pile of carpets presented itself for him to lie on, like the princess on the mattresses. Instead, facing him, from floor to ceiling, lying lengthways along the sides of the van, stood a honeycomb of tightly packaged carpets rolled up in their thick cardboard cylindrical wrappings. Jes-*us*! Even with an outsize Stanley knife it'd probably take him half an hour to liberate only *one* of them. And he couldn't just slide one out and carve it up in the middle of the lay-by, now could he?

Aagh! Forget it.

He walked back, clambered up the two metal foot-holds, and sat once more in the front cab, now grown even chillier. One bit of luck, though. The *Daily Telegraph* proved to be a pretty substantial broadsheet, and he was dividing the multi-paged wodge in half when he spotted the headline, in the Home News section, and was soon reading the article beneath it:

TRUSTY ABSCONDS

Wiltshire Police report the escape of Daniel Smithson from Winchester Gaol, where most recently he was serving a four-year sentence for robbery.

For the last three months it appears that Smithson had

been privileged to enjoy the maximum range of freedom within the prison régime, and indeed during the past week had been working in a garden adjacent to the prison with a brick wall only some four feet high separating him from the outside world.

Although prison authorities are unwilling to give specific details, it is understood that the ex-soldier Smithson, who for the last twelve years has seen little except the inside of a cell in one of HM prisons, was due for release shortly.

Aged forty-three, he is five feet seven inches in height, of slim-to-medium build, and has shortish brown hair. Lightly tattooed on the back of the lower knuckles of the left hand are the letters I – L – Y – K, supposed by fellow prisoners to commemorate a former girlfriend: 'I Love You Kate'.

The escapee has no record of any criminal violence, and it is the view of the prison officers at Winchester that he poses no threat whatsoever to the public at large. An early re-arrest is expected.

Characteristically, Danny tilted his head to the right, and glanced through the article again. Then nodded to himself. There *were* people who couldn't cope with life outside the Rules and Regulations of an institution – just as there were people (hadn't he just read it?) who couldn't quite cope with all this crime. And it was easy to read between the lines of that last couple of sentences, wasn't it? 'No need to clap the darbies round the poor sod's wrists. Nah! He'll probably soon be knocking on the gates o' the nearest nick hisself.'

Funny old business, life. Full o' pitfalls – full of opportunities, too. Just watch out for the first – and make sure you grab hold o' the second. Common sense, innit? That's what his dad had told him.

Danny clasped his hands, left over right, and rubbed them vigorously together against the numbing cold. And even as he did so, he found himself looking down at the lower knuckles of his upper hand.

2

'I coulda scored the bloody thing in me carpet slippers, honest I could.'

'You reckon?'

'And if Oxford hadn't buggered up that last-minute penalty—'

'You'da won a fortune.'

'Third divi on the treble-chance.'

'About sixpence.'

'We've gone decimal, Sarge – remember?'

PC Watson accelerated up the slip-road into the A34 (N) from the Pear Tree roundabout, noting as he did so the miraculously civilized deceleration of a couple of cars behind him.

'Better take a gander somewhere, I s'pose,' suggested Sergeant Hodges a couple of miles further on, pointing to one of the several lay-bys on the twin-track road that led up to the M40 interchange.

No snack bar here. Just the black hulks of two juggernauts; and tucked in behind them an old man in an old car studying an old map.

'Need any help, sir?'

'No!'

Sod you then, thought Watson, as he moved forward past the two container-lorries.

At the far end of the lay-by – not spotted earlier – was a Jaguar of indeterminate colour: 'indeterminate' partly because during the hours of darkness light reflected oddly from the metallic sheen of some cars; and partly because Watson was in any case wholly colour-blind between the reds and the blues.

But he made no further advance as he saw the grey head of the driver jerk round and the dusky-headed young maiden beside him hasten to fasten up the buttons on her blouse.

'Any joy?' asked Hodges.

Watson shook his head as he got back into the car. 'Well, 'cept for the fellow up front there in the Jag, perhaps.'

Half a mile or so further along, Hodges nodded again to his left, and this time the Vauxhall Senator pulled in behind a furniture van.

'Coffee for me, Barry. Not too much milk, and two sugars, please.'

But Watson was no more than a few seconds into his mission before he stopped and stared. When (only an hour since) he'd glanced through the briefing-files and the traffic telexes back in Kidlington Police HQ, the last three letters of one particular stolen vehicle had caught his notice. How otherwise? For those last three letters were the initials of his own name, Barry Robert Watson; and here, on the van in front of him, was the registration number C 674 BRW.

There was always an awful lot of luck needed in apprehending villains, Watson had already learnt that – unless you were looking for a ginger-bearded giant, with a wooden leg, and a dinosaur tattooed on his balding head. And this *was* a bit of luck. Surely so.

Back in the police car, Hodges rang through to the Control Room at HQ, where within only a few seconds an operator read from his Police National Computer screen that the said vehicle, reg. C 674 BRW, had been stolen earlier that evening in Southampton. The number had appeared in the Thames Valley briefing-files only because there seemed to be some suggestion that the vehicle might be heading north. Along the A34. Up into Oxfordshire.

His head cushioned on his arms, the driver appeared to be deeply asleep, since only after a series of staccato raps on the cab window did he raise his head above the steering-wheel.

'This your vehicle?' bawled Watson.

'Wha'?'

'Police!'

The driver slowly wound down his window. 'Wha's the trouble, mate?'

'This your vehicle?'

'Wha', this? I wouldn't have it if you gev it me!'

'Let's see your licence, please.'

'What licence?'

'Not your bloody *dog* licence, is it!'

'You got so many days on producin' yer licence, you know that.'

'Haven't got one – is that what you're saying?'

'Not on me, no.'

'What's your name?' (It was Hodges who took over now.)

'John Smith.'

'Sorry, yeah. Shoulda known.'

'Anything else I can help you with?'

'You'd better get down and come along with us.'

'Have I got any option, mate?'

'Not much.'

'Hold on a tick, then. I'd better just fill in the old tacho thing here. Got to keep yer records up to date, you know – 'specially if you get delayed a bit.'

'Yeah, well, let's say you look like getting delayed a bit.'

Beckoning Watson to the other side of the van, and with one foot now on the lower foot-hold, Hodges raised himself to look into the cab, where he saw the driver filling in a white tachometer disc – writing slowly and innocently enough with a cheap blue Biro.

The driver of the lorry in front walked back to the van.

'Everything OK, Officer?'

Hodges nodded and stepped down. 'No problems.'

'Everything OK, Danny?' continued the other, as the cab-door now opened.

'Fine, yeah! Just forgot me licence, din I?'

'"Danny", eh?' remarked Sergeant Hodges as he steered the man into the near-side rear seat of the Vauxhall, con-scious that the slimly built, quietly spoken man beside him hardly fitted the stock profile of any tearaway joyrider.

'Yeah! What do we call you?' added PC Watson over his shoulder.

'"Mr Smith"?' suggested Danny quietly.

243

3

If the Custody Suite at Bicester Police Station is not a match for the British Airways Club Class lounge at Heathrow, it is at least a well-lit, well-ventilated room – separated from the cell-area, and affording its present occupant a comfortable enough introit into his temporary detention.

In the presence of the arrested person himself (in the presence too of PC Watson) Sergeant Russell, the Custody Officer, standing in shirt-sleeves at a tall desk, has recited the statutory 'Notice to Accused Persons', and is now completing the Custody Record, as the law requires of him. Russell is an older man, a stickler for procedure, and he fills in the lengthy sections with scrupulous care. He has already made the decision to authorize the continued custody of the prisoner.

'Let me just put it to you once more, lad. What's your real name?'

'Told you, din I? How many more times I got to tell you?'

Russell sighs wearily. There is little he can do if the man persists in such manifest falsehoods.

Yet Danny does so persist; has been so persisting for the past half-hour – ever since he'd slid a letter addressed to him beneath the driver's seat in the front of the cab; ever since he'd jumped down into the strong arms of the law. Literally so.

'Still no news of your address?'

'No fixed abode, innit? Told you, din I? I'm a new-age traveller.'

'Occupation, then – "Traveller". OK?'

'Yeah.'

'And you travelled down here in a vehicle stolen from a depot in Southampton at approximately 9.35 p.m. yesterday evening, right?'

'Who told you that?'

'Relax! I've got to put *summat* down here, that's all – in the "Grounds for Detention" bit. Don't you understand that?'

Russell collects together his sheets of white A4, and prepares to call it a day. Or a night. 'I just hope the Southampton boys've got as much patience as I have, that's all.'

'Do we fingerprint him?' asks Watson.

'We do not! We follow the rule-book; and the rule-book says he's got the right to a nice hot cuppa, if he wants one.'

Danny very much wants one, for his mouth is dry. But he is suddenly frightened and in danger of losing his self-control.

'You can't bloody keep me 'ere!' The voice has grown harsh, the muscles are tightened in the neck. There is, for the first time since the arrest, a strong hint of a tightly coiled spring within the prisoner's sinewy frame. His head moves forward over the desk which separates him from his interlocutor.

'Constable!' Russell is fully prepared; he experiences no fear, as he steps towards the door at the back of the room which leads to his office. 'Put the cuffs on him, will you? I shan't be more'n a minute or two—'

'No!'

As suddenly as it has appeared, the tension has now gone. The voice is quiet once more; the muscles once more relaxed. The man breathes out a long, deep sigh, then holds up his hands in a gesture of mock surrender.

And Russell steps back to the desk, lays down the Custody Record, and takes out his pen again.

'OK. Let's be having things, lad.'

Ten minutes later, from his own office, Sergeant Russell has introduced himself, and is speaking on the telephone to a Senior Prison Officer at Winchester.

'You've got somebody there who's just scarpered, I think? Rather you *haven't* got somebody there, if you see what I mean. Name o' Smithson.'

'Oh God, no!'

'Pardon?'

'Just keep him, will you?'

'We *are* keeping him. He's here – at Bicester – locked in his cell.'

'Excellent! As I say, just keep him there.'

'What's *that* supposed to mean?'

'It means we don't want him back here, that's what.'

'I'm not with you.'

'Either keep him, or lose him, that's what I'm saying. Yes . . . Not a bad idea that, Sergeant. Why don't you just *lose* him, and do us all a bloody favour?'

There is a chuckle at the Winchester end of the line before the voice continues, in a more serious vein, to explain these strange rejoinders.

Daniel Smithson had joined the army at the age of sixteen, as a boy-soldier; become a mercenary in Africa at the age of twenty-two; served in the SAS for six years after that; and then . . . and then served somewhere else – in prison, for virtually the whole of the past twelve years, his offences ranging from petty theft to hefty larceny. *And* (and this was the real point) the magistrates and the judges and the prison authorities were all becoming increasingly undecided about how to deal with the fellow. What he'd do was this. He'd keep his nose immaculately clean, cause no trouble to any-body, and end up by getting a 'trusty' job. Then, well, he'd bugger off a day or two before he was due for release. Huh! Once outside, he'd pinch as much as his pockets could accommodate, nick a car, live it up for a few days; then (inevitably) get re-arrested, and return to his old haunts and his old mates, with the Prison Governor treating him like the Prodigal Son. The simple truth was that Smithson just couldn't settle down outside the prison walls: he needed – enjoyed! – the stable routine of a familiar nick. Though not a big fellow, he was a strong and wiry one, and his SAS history had reached the prison well ahead of him. No one buggered about (if that was the right word) with Mr Danny Smithson.

'Oh no, Sergeant. No one.'

One thing has been troubling Russell during the recital of the Winchester prisoner's CV: the fact that his man hardly looks the part of some ex-SAS paratrooper, or whatever; and Russell puts his thoughts into words.

'You sure we've got the right fellow – the fellow you're talking about?'

'Put him on the line, if you like. I'll soon tell you.'

'No, I don't think I can allow that.'

'Easy enough to tell, anyway. He's got some letters tattooed

247

on the back of one of his hands – left hand, I think it is. They mentioned it in the papers. Hold on! Shan't be a tick.'

In fact four minutes drag by before the Prison Officer reads from a folder; and Russell listens carefully.

'I'll go and check straightaway. Shan't be a tick.'

Danny is not asleep. He sits on the side of the bed, staring at the floor – and looking up with no apparent interest as Russell unlocks the door.

'Just lift up your hands, will you, Danny Boy.'

The prisoner lifts up his hands as if, once again, he is surrendering to the foe.

'Good. Now turn your hands round, please.'

So Danny turns his hands round; and on the lower joints of the fingers on his left hand Russell reads the letters I – L – Y – K.

This time it is the Winchester end which has waited through four long minutes.

'Well?'

'Yep – it's him, all right. When'll you be coming to fetch him?'

'Not before breakfast, I'll tell you that! We'll let you know.'

'OK.'

'By the way, what exactly are you holding him on?'

'Theft of vehicle; theft of goods in transit; driving without a licence; driving without—'

'Same old stuff.'

'Same old sentence, like as not.'

'Unless some judge suddenly decides to show a bit o' sense and refuses to lock the silly sod away again.'

Russell is not prepared to enter any penological discussion, and prepares to sign off.

'Thanks anyway. Will you be coming yourself?'

'Me? God, no. I'll be seeing him soon enough.'

'And no handcuffs, you say.'

'That's it. No need. Let him have a stroll round Bicester after breakfast by all means – no problem. No cuffs, though. He's one of those who can't stand any physical contact with people. Know what I mean?'

'Doesn't sound as if he'll give us any trouble, anyway.'

'I wouldn't go quite so far as that.'

'What do you mean?'

'Nothing really. Just don't be surprised if he – well, if he strings you along a bit. Know what I mean? He's a bit of a joker is our Danny. Always was. Probably ask you for a bottle of champers for breakfast – say it's doctor's orders.'

'We do a nice little line in tea-bags down here in Bicester.'

'Cheers then.'

'Cheers.'

PC Watson has finished his report, and now looks in for the last time at his prisoner.

'Anything you want?'

Danny shakes his head. 'Unless you'd like to gimme me Biro back.'

Returning to the Custody Suite, Watson passes on the request; and Sergeant Russell looks down, first at the cash envelope, then at the property bag – from the latter finally taking out the cheap blue pen with which Danny had written on the tacho-disc.

'No harm, I suppose. He probably wants to write a poem on the loo-paper.'

4

At 8.20 a.m. the minibus from Winchester arrived in the front yard of Bicester Police Station, where one of the two prison personnel immediately alighted and reported to the Information Desk.

Everything was ready.

Driven now into the yard behind the main building ('Police Vehicles Only'), the minibus was backed up alongside the wall, its rear window coming to a halt only a few feet from the single external door of the Custody Suite.

The prisoner had not after all ordered champers for breakfast; instead he had done splendid justice to the sausages and beans brought to him an hour earlier. Yet he did make one request when the cell door was again unlocked for his departure, just after 8.30 a.m. Two spare blankets were folded beside the bed, and he'd asked if he could have one to put round him on the journey. He had no overcoat; it was a cold morning.

Not very much to ask at all really, was it?

It had all happened so very suddenly that no one afterwards had any particularly clear picture of the events. But it went something like this . . .

As he was walking through the exit door from the Custody

Suite, the blanket which the prisoner was holding about his head and shoulders was dramatically whisked away and equally dramatically whipped over the head and shoulders of the tall, bearded officer who was about to unlock the near-side door of the minibus. Then, dodging lightly past him, the prisoner sprinted the thirty or so yards to the tall beech-hedge which enclosed the rear yard. The hedge was strengthened by a six-foot meshed-wire fence – the fence, in turn, supported every six or seven yards by concrete posts. These posts were some five feet in height, finishing a foot or so below the top of the hedge. One of the posts – and only one – was itself strengthened by a concrete strut which formed an angle of 45 degrees to the ground and which joined the post roughly halfway up, looking rather like a lambda in the Greek alphabet.

At full speed the prisoner leapt at this structure, his left foot landing firm on the top of the strut, his right foot equally firm on the top of the post; and then, propelled by such twin leverage, he had cleared the beech-hedge by several inches, landing neatly on the grass of a school playing-field beyond. Someone later said it was a bit like watching a Russian gymnast clearing a vaulting-horse at the Olympics.

The prisoner was gone.

Neither of the heavy Winchester men could hope to match such a nimble-footed feat of levitation; and it was ten minutes before a wailing police car, forced to take the long way round the front of the station, was criss-crossing the maze of streets in the King's End estate behind, where (it was believed) the prisoner was last sighted.

But not sighted again.

5

The loo-paper in the cells at Bicester may by no means be described as 'Savoy Soft', stiffly reluctant as it is to accommodate itself to the contours of the average human backside. Yet (as Sergeant Russell had earlier intimated) it makes unexpectedly fine writing-paper; and it was two sheets of this paper which one of the cleaners found just before lunchtime that same day – between the folds of the remaining blanket in the cell which had housed the escaped prisoner.

The escape had caused no little embarrassment to the officers concerned, and (worse still) would almost certainly hit the national headlines the following day. Thus it was that Chief Inspector Page of Thames Valley CID (no less) had little compunction in summoning the now off-duty officers Russell, Hodges, and Watson, to his office in Kidlington at 11 a.m. to review the matter – and the cleaner's discovery.

The spelling and punctuation were both a bit shaky, but the import of the letter could hardly have given a clearer answer to what had hitherto seemed the increasingly bewildering question of the escaped man's identity:

The Torygraph did it, very useful paper and a lot of criminals vote tory. It was Smithson give me the idea because we got the same name see. If he got nicked he gets good treatment but if I got nicked no, so what about him and me changing places for a little wile and no harm done is it? Besides, probably gives me a best chance of scarpering – lots of that now days, perhaps its the resession to blame like for every thing else. There was just that one problem, that tatoo I read about and when you coppers thought I was filling in the old tacko with the blue byro I was just writing out them four letters on the old nuckles see, easy! Then I done a pretty good job really with all that stuff about me name, dont you think so? Well well Danny Smithson boy, I wonder where you are, have <u>you</u> desided to keep out this time, why not?

I'll leave this letter in the bottom blanket because I've got ideas with the top one. If I get away what a big laugh for me when you find it, and if I dont its your turn for the big laugh
Samuel (Danny) Lambert
PS you can give me old comb and spare hanky to Oxfam or the Sally army, its up to you

Newly recruited to the Force, PC Watson was glad to have someone to chat with – even a subdued-looking Sergeant Russell – as they stood in the lunch queue in the HQ canteen.

'Rotten bit o' luck, Sarge . . .' he began.

'You make your own luck, lad. I shoulda been far more careful checking out that tattoo.'

'I was thinking more about both of 'em being named "Danny".'

'*Nick*named, you mean – one of 'em.'

'Yeah. I mean, there's your "Pongo" Warings . . .'

'And your "Nobby" Clarks . . .'

'How come your "Danny" Lamberts, though?'

'Dunno.'

The queue moved a couple of feet, and the plain-clothes man in front of them turned round to proffer a suggestion:

'Might be someone from Stamford? Stamford in Lincolnshire? Lamberts there often get called "Danny", after Daniel Lambert – fellow who weighed fifty-two stone odd – still in the Guinness Book of Records.'

'Who's *he* when he's at home?' asked Watson, after they'd been served.

'You don't know?'

Watson shook his head.

'That, my lad, was Chief Inspector Morse.'

Watson frowned slightly. He'd never heard of the man; yet for a fleeting second he'd thought he'd almost recognized the profile as that grey head had turned towards them in the queue . . .

Next morning, the Governor of HM Prison Winchester received a full report on the case, now becoming widely known as the 'Cock-up at Bicester Corral', including a photocopy of the letter found in the escapee's cell. He immediately summoned the Senior Prison Officer from D Wing, where Smithson had spent so many comparatively contented months and years.

'You'll be interested in this.' The Governor handed over the file.

Price, a thick-set Irishman, sat down and began reading.

'No news of our Danny?' interrupted the Governor.

Price shook his head. Then, halfway through the letter, his eyes suddenly widened with a new and startling notion.

'You don't think, sorr . . . ?' he began slowly, pointing to the letter.

The Governor groaned, permitting himself also, albeit briefly, to contemplate the unimaginable.

'Don't tell me *that*! Please! Don't tell me it's *Smithson's* writing?'

Price studied the writing of the letter again. 'Yes, sorr. I'm sorry. But I'm pretty sure it is.'

And for a few moments the two men sat there in silence, each of them visualizing their erstwhile prisoner perched aloft in the cabin of a stolen van, and carefully over-tracing his own tattoos with a cheap blue Biro pen . . .

LAST CALL

> Wives invariably flourish when deserted; it is the deserting
> male who often ends in disaster.
>
> (William McFee)

Not too carefully – not carefully at all really – Morse looked down at the man lying supine on the double bed, dressed only in an unbuttoned white shirt, Oxford-blue pants, and black socks. The paleness of the man's skin precluded the probability of any recent holiday on the Greek islands – with only the dullish-red V below the throat suggesting the possibility of any life outside the executive-suited higher echelons of British management.

Late forties, by the look of him; a firmly built man, with a pleasantly featured, clean-shaven face, and frizzy, grey-flecked hair. The jacket of a subfusc herring-bone suit was hanging inside the open-doored wardrobe, a maroon tie over it; and neatly aligned at the near side of the bed was a pair of soft black leather shoes.

A methodical, successful businessman, thought Morse.

A quiet knock on the door of Room 231 of The Randolph Hotel heralded the arrivals of Sergeant Lewis and Dr Laura Hobson – the latter immediately stepping forward to peer down at the dead man's face. Blood was still seeping slowly from a deep gash that slanted over the closed right eye like some monstrous acute accent. But there was no other sign of red in the face, for the lips were a palish shade of purple.

'Probably had a heart attack,' volunteered the pathologist.

Lewis looked down at the Corby trouser-press, standing to

the left of the bathroom door, on which a pair of subfusc herring-bone trousers were draped over the opened leaf.

'Probably bashed his head on that?' suggested Lewis.

And Morse nodded.

The cream paint of the left-hand door-jamb was splashed with elongated flecks of scarlet, and two feet inside the bathroom itself, on the blue-and-white tiled floor, was a patch of darkly dried blood.

'If he'd tripped it could have brought on a heart attack, don't you think, sir?'

Again Morse nodded. 'And if he'd had a heart attack he could have tripped and cracked his head, yes.'

Turning her head momentarily towards them, Dr Hobson put the situation rather more simply: 'Which came first – the chicken or the egg?'

'The chicken?' said Morse.

But the blonde pathologist was clearly in favour of an each-way bet. 'Like as not it happened contemporaneously.'

Lewis's eyebrows shot up. 'Big word, that.'

Dr Hobson smiled at him, attractively. 'I've finished with it for now, Sergeant. It's all yours if you'd like to have it.'

On the dressing table to the right of the bathroom door, beside the phone, lay two items which had been recovered from the bathroom floor: a calibrated syringe, its orange hood still in place over the needle; and the glass fragments of what had been a small phial, some three inches long, which had contained (as indicated by its label) 'Human Actrapid Insulin' – the colourless liquid having almost completely seeped away into a layer of white tissue-paper.

For a minute or so longer, Chief Inspector Morse stood exactly where he was, visualizing much – visualizing almost everything, perhaps – of what had happened there on the threshold of the bathroom, his eyes finally concentrating on the telephone, its receiver cradled firmly on its base.

Then he announced his strategy: 'I think we'll just nip down to the bar, Lewis – while Doctor Hobson finishes off here.' He looked at his wrist-watch. 'That's two nights running I've missed *The Archers*. For nothing, too – there's been no murder here.'

But before leaving Room 231, he dipped a hand gently into the inside breast-pocket of the dead man's jacket, withdrawing a wallet of pigskin leather.

'Do we know who found him – and how?' asked Lewis, as the two detectives walked down the grandly wide staircase to the reception area of The Randolph.

'That's exactly what I hope you're going to find out for me.'

Three-quarters of an hour later Sergeant Lewis had discovered all there was to be known. Not much, but enough. And he reported to Morse.

Sherwood had reserved the double-bedded, en suite, five-star room by phone only the previous evening – with no opportunity thus afforded for any written confirmation. He had booked in, on his own, at about 5.40 p.m. But the form, duly completed at reception, was comparatively uninformative: **Name(s)** – 'Sherwood'; **Home Address** – '53 Leominster Drive, Shrewsbury'; **Signature** – 'Peter Sherwood'. The two boxes beside the questions **Are you here on**

business? On Leisure? remained unticked, and the space for **Car Registration** was completed with a dismissive dash. That was all, except for a tick in the **Cash** box alongside **How do you intend to settle your account?**

The Guest Registration Card thus negotiated, £140 (in twenties) had been paid; and no further details were disclosed by Sherwood or demanded by the chicly uniformed receptionist. Any wake-up call in the morning? 'No.' Any newspaper? 'Yes – the *Telegraph*.' Sherwood had taken the key, politely declined the offer of help with his two suitcases, and that was that.

No woman on the scene – no one remembered a woman at all.

Sherwood was scheduled to attend a two-day conference on Computer Technology being held at Rewley House – very close by, just up at the top of St John Street, almost immediately opposite The Randolph.

Now clearly of importance had been two telephone calls. The first, probably an outside call, asking to be put through to Mr Sherwood; the second, presumably made from inside the hotel, reporting to the operator that medical assistance was urgently required in Room 231. The Senior Concierge, Roy Harden, had immediately gone up to the room, where he'd found the door slightly ajar – and Sherwood lying across the threshold of the bathroom. Already dead by the look of him. From the room itself Harden had promptly telephoned the house-doctor; and then the manager, with whose assistance two minutes later he'd carried Sherwood's body over to the bed. A room-maid had cleared up the broken glass from the bathroom – for there seemed to be no suspicious circumstances at the time. It was only because of the house-doctor's marginal unease over the head wound that the manager had deemed it prudent to call in the police. Just to be on the safe side.

'What do you think so far?' asked Morse.

'Same as you, sir. *Cherchez la belle femme.* He's off to another conference – he invites his mistress – they know how to work things – he has a heart attack – she's scared out of her wits – rings for the doc – and then gets pretty smartish out of it.'

'Ye-es . . .' Morse picked up the dead man's wallet. 'No railway tickets in here, Lewis.'

'So?'

'They don't very often *collect* railway tickets from passengers these days, do they?'

Lewis followed the drift of Morse's thinking. 'They probably came by car, you mean?'

'*Her* car, like as not. He tells his wife he's going to the railway station, and his lady-love picks him up there. Then when she gets him here, she just nips off and parks her car somewhere nearby – and there's no need for anyone to know her registration number or anything. Very neat. Very easy.'

Lewis nodded agreement. 'It's getting easier all the time to commit adultery.'

Morse looked up sharply. 'Let's be slightly more accurate about things, Lewis. What you mean is that the preconditions for adultery are easier to handle: fewer eyebrows raised; fewer questions asked; fewer details to be filled in; just fork out your fee for the room . . . But whether it's really become emotionally easier, psychologically easier . . . *physically* easier – well, I just wouldn't know, would I?'

Saving Lewis the possible embarrassment of any reply, the young pathologist now appeared beside them in the Chapters Bar.

Morse beamed happily, and pushed forward his emptied glass. 'Ah, Doctor Hobson! What'll you have to drink? Lewis here is in the chair.'

But Dr Hobson shook her pretty head. 'I can't stay, I'm afraid.'

'Pity!'

'You're feeling all right, Chief Inspector?'

'Pardon?'

'They told me the only thing you ever wanted from any pathologist was an estimated time of death.'

'Oh, I know that already,' replied Morse. 'Six o'clock – to the minute, I'd say.'

Laura Hobson smiled, refusing to rise to the bait. 'About six o'clock, yes. I hope you don't expect me to be *quite* so precise as you, though? I'm just a humble medical scientist myself. No foul-play, though. I'm fairly sure of that.'

'*Fairly* sure?'

'As I say, I'm just a scientist. Good night.'

'He was a neat and tidy enough man,' resumed Lewis. 'The bag he'd packed for himself – well, it was all laid out with sort of military precision. You know, socks, hankies, spare pants, washing kit – all in their proper compartments.'

'Condoms?'

'Yes, sir, in a little compartment at the front.'

'It's all very sad, isn't it?'

'More sad for the wife, if you ask me.'

'It was the wife I was thinking of,' replied Morse quietly.

Lewis thought it wise to change tack. 'You seem very sure about the time?'

'There's a Diabetic Card here in the wallet, giving details and times of daily injections: 7 a.m.; 6 p.m.; 10.30 p.m. "Military precision", did you say? I think you're right.'

'We'd know it was just before or just after six anyway, wouldn't we? From the telephone calls, I mean.'

'Ye-es.'

'Who do you think made the first call, sir?'

'Same woman who made the second. She rang from a phone-box outside – said she'd parked OK – asked him for the room number – told him to leave the door slightly ajar – promised she'd be with him in just a few minutes . . .'

'. . . saw him lying there – realized he was dead – and rang for help.'

'Where did she ring from, though?' asked Morse slowly.

'Bedroom, I should think?'

'I wonder . . . She'd have to stand just over him when she rang, wouldn't she?'

'Not everybody's quite so put off by dead bodies as you, sir.'

The Senior Concierge, now re-summoned, briskly confirmed his earlier evidence, and Morse had only one additional question.

'Was the telephone off the hook when you went into the room?'

'Yes, sir. Dangling on the cord.'

'And you replaced it?'

'I replaced it.'

'I see.'

'Should I have left it?'

'No, no!' For some reason Morse seemed almost relieved, and the concierge left.

'I wish all our witnesses were as bright and unequivocal as Mr Harden, Lewis!'

'Important, is it, this phone business?'

'No. I don't think so. Not now.'

Lewis looked at his watch. 'We shall have to do something about his wife, sir.'

'You know the routine better than I do.'

Yes, Lewis did.

'Tell 'em to be gentle with her. Just to say her husband's had a fatal heart attack. We can arrange transport – well, *they* can – if she wants to come to Oxford tomorrow. Not tonight, though. Get her local GP in. Well – you know the ropes.'

Morse drained his beer and his eyes reflected the curious sadness he clearly felt for the woman left alone that night in Shrewsbury.

'Another pint?' suggested Lewis.

But Morse shook his head and stood up to go, the pigskin wallet held tightly in his right hand.

Three-quarters of an hour later, a police car drew up outside the double-garaged property that stood at 53 Leominster Drive, Shrewsbury. Accompanying the police sergeant was a young smartly-attractive WPC, who did the talking:

'Mrs Sherwood?'

'Yes?'

'I'm afraid we've got some bad news for you.'

Sometimes the police had the lousiest job in the whole world.

Mid-morning the following day Morse had received Dr Hobson's preliminary report:

> Heart attack – death following almost immediately. Little or no chance of survival, even if any more sophisticated treatment had been available earlier. _Massive_ h.a. Subject a heavily-dependent insulin diabetic, with (probably) high blood-pressure. Often a risky – sometimes fatal – combination. Every indication that onset of h.a. precipitated subject's imbalance and collapse, with head injury incurred only subsequently. Blood sugar at time of death: 26.8. _Very_ high.
>
> Doing one or two other little tests. Will keep you informed.
>
> L.H.

And now Lewis read through the findings.

'Things seem to have happened, er, contemporaneously, sir.'

'Clears it up, certainly, as far as I'm concerned.'

'Mrs Sherwood's coming down this morning. Identify the body and . . .'

Morse nodded. 'Keep her out of The Randolph, if you can. No need for her to know anything about the room or . . . or anything.'

COLIN DEXTER

'I suppose not.'

'Look! Nobody's going to profit from parading any dirty linen, agreed?'

'Least of all Mrs Sherwood.'

'*And* her family.'

'OK.'

'Have we discovered much about her?'

Lewis consulted his note-book.

'Aged forty-five; son and daughter – both early twenties; she works part-time; bags o' money; everybody seemed to think the marriage was fine.'

Morse nodded sombrely. 'Death's bad enough, but ... Remember that Greek Archbishop, Lewis? Had a heart attack in his local knocking-shop at Athens? Poor sod!'

'At least he hadn't got a wife.'

'How do *you* know?'

'Perhaps *Mrs* Sherwood was having a bit on the side, too.'

But Morse appeared not to be listening. He took from the dead man's wallet a passport-sized colour photograph of a duskily tressed and deeply-tanned young beauty, wearing thinly rimmed schoolma'amish spectacles, and looking half-seriously into the camera – yet with lips beginning to curl in a sensuous smile.

'Lovely!' said Morse. 'Lovely!'

'And that's ... ?'

'That's *Mr* Sherwood's "bit on the side", as you so elegantly phrase things.'

Then Morse, after glancing briefly at the back of the photo, slowly tore it into smaller and smaller pieces.

'Destroying evidence, that is. Could be valuable in the case—'

268

'*What* case?'

Lewis shrugged. 'You're in charge, sir.'

Morse was now on his feet. 'Just nip me down to Oxford, will you? Railway station for a couple of minutes – then on to St Aldates. What time's Mrs Sherwood due here?'

'Eleven-thirty. Driving down – dunno if it's the Rolls or the BMW, though!'

Morse shot off at an odd angle: 'Do you believe in any after-life, Lewis?'

'Not sure, really. What about you?'

'No, not me. I think death's just a process of chemical disintegration.'

'Perhaps *she* could tell us – Mrs Sherwood. She took a Chemistry degree at Cambridge.'

'How on earth did you find that out?'

Lewis too now rose. 'I'm a detective, sir, remember?'

'She must have been a clever lass at school.'

'But you still don't want to see her?'

'No.'

As he'd promised, Morse spent only a brief while inside Oxford railway station; and five minutes later Lewis was driving down St Aldates, when Morse peremptorily announced a slight change of plan. It was just after 11 a.m.

'Drop me anywhere here! I'll just nip in to see how the landlord is.'

He gestured vaguely to the Bulldog, and Lewis brought the police car to a stop opposite Christ Church.

'Just give this to Mrs Sherwood, will you?'

Lewis took the proffered wallet. 'No more photos in it?'

'Only one of the four of 'em: mum and dad and the two kids. Everything's all right now.'

Lewis had arrived back at Kidlington HQ at 2 p.m. to find that the chief had not yet returned – from wherever.

Mrs Sherwood had been a quarter of an hour late (in the BMW), and Lewis had looked quickly through the contents of her late husband's wallet as he'd waited in a small ante-room in the Pathology Institute. The usual plastic cards were there, relating to monies and memberships; £110 in bank-notes; the family photograph that Morse had mentioned (but no others); and something else, yes – two green-and-orange British Rail tickets, one 'Out' and one 'Return', between Shrewsbury and Oxford. Neither had received the attention of any ticket-collector's clip. Yet they looked genuine enough. *Were* genuine enough, except for the fact that the date printed on each of them was not yesterday's – but today's.

Lewis smiled wryly to himself.

Mrs Pamela Sherwood had turned out to be a slim, well-groomed, delicately featured woman – distressed, yes, but well in control. Lewis himself never really knew what to do or what to say in times of bereavement; but that was exactly why (as Morse well knew) he performed the job so success-fully, since it was not unusual on such sad occasions for roles to be reversed and for the bereaved themselves to feel an instinctively reciprocal sympathy with the good sergeant.

As now.

Over coffee, and after identifying her husband's body, Mrs Sherwood herself had looked quickly through the contents of the wallet, her eyes intent as she took out one item after another, including the tickets.

One item after another . . . except of course for the photograph of the dusky siren whose features for a little while had recently held the Chief Inspector mesmerized.

But it was the message on Morse's Ansaphone which displaced any thoughts of Mrs Sherwood; a message left by the manager of The Randolph; a message which Lewis, now for the third time, replayed as he waited for Morse to return.

Bamber Goodall here, Chief Inspector. I had a personal call this morning just before twelve. A woman, youngish woman by the sound of her, said she'd got to speak to me and I accepted the call. She said she was feeling guilty because she was the woman who was going to stay with Mr Sherwood. She said she'd driven him down in her own car. She'd kept out of the way when he'd booked in, and when he'd gone up to the room with their luggage. Then he'd come down again, given her the room-key, and said he'd expect her in about ten or fifteen minutes, after she'd parked the car – which she had done, up in Norham Gardens. It seems they'd both been worried about leaving the car in the hotel garage. Then when she got back and walked up to their room she'd opened the door to find him lying there, and she'd just 'panicked' – her word – and grabbed her case – still unopened – and got the hell out of things. She drove out to the Cotswolds, and then back home this morning. She was still feeling awful about it, she said. Somehow she'd known he was dead – though she didn't say *how* she knew. Well, that's it really. When I said she ought to talk to the police she said she couldn't. I tried

271

to keep her talking but it was no good. She just kept saying that if only Mrs Sherwood could be kept out of it all – you know – kept in the dark about things, about *her*, well, she'd be extremely grateful. So that's it, really. I'll be in the hotel here till about eight-thirty this evening . . . if you want me.

During the replay of this message, Lewis had been conscious that Morse was standing beside him, listening (it seemed) intently; and as Goodall signed off, Lewis noted that Morse's eyes were shining with excitement; and impatience too – like a camel sniffing the coolness of the air and eager to ride forth at evening from the wells . . .

Although Lewis himself would not have made that particular simile.

Morse's verdict, whispered and intense, was barely audible in the now silent office:

'She did it! She murdered him!'

For a few moments Lewis looked across the desk with mouth agape, like a young lad bidden to display his tonsils to the doctor. He would have asked about that unspecified 'She', but already Morse had picked up the phone, asking to be put through to the Path lab – urgently. And as he covered the speaker with the palm of his left hand, he gave his instructions:

'Go and take a full statement from the manager, Lewis. I want to know *exactly* what she told him. *Verbatim*, as far as—

'Ah, Doctor Hobson?'

*

272

'*You* can drive back,' Morse had said the following morning when just after 10 a.m. he himself took the wheel of the maroon-coloured Jaguar and began the drive up to Shrewsbury, via Motorways 40, 42, 6, and 54. One hundred and ten miles. No Services. An hour and a half. Lewis, whose only indulgence in life (apart from eggs and chips) was speedy driving, would have cut fifteen minutes off the time.

Did cut fifteen minutes off, on the return journey.

'Difficult to know why anyone'd ever want to go from Shrewsbury to Oxford by British Rail,' declared Lewis, as Morse pulled up outside the elegantly appointed, detached house that stood at 53 Leominster Drive.

'Mrs Sherwood,' began Morse, 'we have some difficult things to tell you. When your husband went off to Oxford, we have every reason to believe, I'm afraid, that he'd arranged to spend two nights with a woman-friend – with a mistress – in The Randolph Hotel. She'd driven him down to Oxford in her own car—'

Mrs Sherwood shook her head and closed her eyes, like a young girl refusing to believe that Santa Claus was just a dream.

'You've got it all wrong! He went to Oxford by *train* – I took him to the station myself. He knew he'd be having quite a lot to drink at the conference—'

'He went to Oxford by *car*,' countered Morse. 'His mistress drove him there.'

'But that's *nonsense*! I've got the rail tickets—'

'Show me!'

273

From her handbag, Mrs Sherwood took out her husband's wallet; and from the wallet, the two tickets – which she handed to him.

'*We* decided to buy these for you, Mrs Sherwood, because we wanted to spare you some of the anguish and the pain of all this trouble. And if you'd been more observant, you'd have spotted the wrong date on them. Until yesterday, you see, we'd no suspicion at all that your husband's death was due to anything but natural causes.'

Her eyes flicked up sharply. 'And now you're saying . . . ?'

Morse made no direct answer, but looked away from those compelling eyes, and slowly tore the rail tickets into smaller and smaller pieces, just as earlier he'd torn the photograph.

'Did you know your husband's mistress?'

For a while it seemed that Mrs Sherwood would challenge the premiss of Morse's brutal question. But she didn't.

'I know her.'

'We did find a photograph,' continued Morse, 'but foolishly I tore it up, because, as I say, we wanted to—'

'She was hardly the first, Chief Inspector.'

'Please tell me who she is and where we can find her.'

But Mrs Sherwood shook her head as she stared into some middle distance. 'I felt jealous about his other women – of course I did. But I *envied* this one. I'd found out a few things about her and I think she was everything to Peter that I'd never been. You see, I'm so very careful and tight about life – about emotions, money, everything. And she's open and vivacious, and wonderful in bed, for all I know . . .'

'And very young,' added Morse cruelly.

'About half Peter's age, yes. Perhaps that's what hurt more than anything.'

'But who *is* she, Mrs Sherwood?'

Morse had lifted his fiercely blue eyes to challenge hers. Yet to no avail; and it was Lewis who pursued the questioning.

'We're interested in two telephone calls, Mrs Sherwood, made about the time your husband died: one just before six o'clock; and one five or ten minutes later. At first we believed both calls were made by the same person. Yesterday, though, a woman rang and admitted making the second call – the one asking for a doctor – but she claimed quite certainly that she hadn't made any earlier call – a call, we thought, possibly asking for your husband's room-number, or whatever it was she needed to know. She said she already *knew* the room-number: he'd gone upstairs with the luggage after checking in, and then come down and actually *given* her the key – before she drove off to park the car somewhere. So what reason could she have had for ringing him?'

Mrs Sherwood shrugged her thin shoulders. 'Doesn't seem much point, does there?'

'Do you think it was one of his other lady-loves?'

'Could have been—'

'*You*, perhaps?' broke in Morse, very quietly.

Rising from her armchair, Mrs Sherwood walked over to the french window and stood gazing out across the wide lawn.

'Is a wife not allowed to ring her husband? At least he almost always told me *where* he was staying, if not who he was staying with.'

'What time did you make the call?' continued Morse.

'Six – sixish? As you say.'

'Before or after?'

'Does it matter?'

'You said you're – what was it? – a bit tight and careful about things like money.'

She nodded. 'Silly really. We'd plenty of money – two salaries coming in.'

'You work in a pharmaceutical lab, I think?'

'Part-time, yes.'

'And you're a Chemistry graduate.'

'Huh! You know all about me. But all you really want to know is about *her*. Am I right?'

'I'd like to know *more* about you, though. For example, the phone-rate gets cheaper after six o'clock, doesn't it? So why didn't you wait till *after* six o'clock – it was only a matter of a few minutes.'

'I didn't think.'

'Come on, Mrs Sherwood! You can do better than that.'

'No, I can't.'

'You'll have to, if you want us to find out who murdered your husband.'

She turned from the window, and in the pale face the eyes were now ablaze.

'Murdered?'

'Yes, murdered.'

'But you're wrong! He died of a heart attack. That's what they told me – the medical people – in Oxford.'

'We've had a further report from the police pathologist, Mrs Sherwood. Sergeant!'

Lewis now read out the relevant extract from Dr Hobson's second report:

The glass capsule had shattered into small pieces, and the
liquid contents had been almost entirely spilled. Our analysis

however shows that the original insulin within the capsule
had been injected with Sodium Fluoroacetate, a substance
readily soluble in water; and extremely poisonous even in the
smallest quantity, interfering fatally and almost immediately
as it does with the Krebs cycle of metabolism. For obvious
reasons this substance is never openly available to the
general public.

'But would be available,' added Morse slowly, 'to someone
working in a pharmaceutical lab.'

'My husband died of a heart attack! I was told so. Are you
now saying he didn't?'

'No.'

'So please tell me what you *are* saying! What's all this
about murder?'

'*You* wished to murder your husband, Mrs Sherwood. *You*
poisoned the insulin capsule. That's what I'm saying.'

She turned to stare out of the window again.

'And if I did?' she asked finally.

'I don't know,' replied Morse simply. 'But I believe you
intended to poison your husband. You'd lived with him for
twenty-odd years and you knew him to be an extremely
meticulous and methodical man. You knew perfectly well
that in Oxford, just as here at home, he'd almost certainly
be taking his insulin at six o'clock that evening. And the
reason you rang him up just *before* six o'clock was to make
sure he *didn't* inject himself from the capsule you'd poisoned.
Please tell me if I'm wrong, Mrs Sherwood! But I think
that in spite of all that had happened, in spite of all his
infidelities, you didn't hate him *quite* enough to go through
with your plan. In the last analysis, you wanted him to stay

277

alive. Perhaps you even hoped he'd come to love you once again.'

She nodded weakly, and spoke in a sing-song voice as if the events she now described were distanced and unreal.

'Five to six, it was when I rang. The line was engaged at first and I began to panic. But then I *did* get through. It was just like when I was a girl; when I used to play little games with myself. I just asked him if he was going to sleep with her that night . . . I wanted to shock him, you see . . . And if he said "no", I was going to tell him about the insulin.'

She stopped.

'And if he said "yes"?'

'It never got that far. I just – I just heard a great crash.'

'Don't you think you may have murdered him just as surely as if you'd poisoned him yourself?'

She shook her head, more in bewilderment, it seemed, than in denial. 'What will happen to me?'

'I just don't know,' said Morse.

At the front door, she laid a hand lightly on his arm, and lowered her eyes.

'It was very kind of you – what you did.'

'But you won't tell me who this other woman is?'

'No.'

Once the Jaguar had disappeared from view, Mrs Sherwood moved back inside the house, a semi-smile upon her lips.

Too clever for his own good, that man! She'd played it mostly by ear, of course. But how easy he'd made it for her! With *him* pointing out the escape route she'd so desperately been seeking after his mention of the Sodium Fluoroacetate; *him* suggesting the blessedly mitigating circumstance that it was she, Pamela Sherwood, who had rung her husband; *she* who had tried not to *cause*, but to *prevent* her husband's death. Why he'd even told her the time of that telephone call – a call she'd never made, of course.

Oh, she'd willingly enough have faced the consequences of poisoning her husband, because above all things in life she'd wanted him dead. But now? If by some happy chance she were to be seen as guilty only of causing him a heart attack – well, she'd settle for that all right. Why not? He was dead, that was the main thing. And that Jane bloody Ballantyre – pox-ridden strumpet! – would have to seek some other demerara daddy now.

'You *were* kind, you know,' said Lewis as he drove the Jaguar out of Leominster Drive.

'How come?'

'Well, the photo—'

'"Stupid", do you mean?'

'—and the rail tickets.'

'You think so?'

'Yes, I do. You probably know you haven't got a reputation for being too generous with money—'

'No?'

'—but I reckon underneath you're a bit of an old softie, really. I mean, forking out of your own pocket for those tickets . . .'

Morse opened his mouth as if to reply; but decided against

it. He *would* (he promised himself) inform Lewis about the expenses claim he had already submitted for £26 – but not for the time being.

'Where to now, sir?'

'We're going to try to trace Peter Sherwood's mistress.'

'But – but haven't we cleared things up?'

'What? You didn't believe all that stuff we got from Mrs Sherwood, did you?'

'You mean – you mean *you* didn't?'

'Lewis! Lewis! Why do you think she refused to tell us anything about her husband's latest conquest?'

Lewis had no idea, and mercifully Morse continued.

'Because our dusky maiden is the only one who knows the truth in this case. And Mrs Sherwood doesn't *want* us to know the truth, does she?'

'Perhaps not,' mumbled Lewis, uncomprehendingly.

'So you ask me where we're going? Well, it's a longish shot, but not a hopeless one. The initials on the back of the photo were "JB"; she looked deeply tanned—'

'Perhaps she's just back from a topless two weeks in Torremolinos.'

'You know, Lewis, you don't often come out with such a splendid sentence as that.'

Lewis felt better. 'You mean she might belong to a local health centre?'

'Lying on a sun-bed, yes. And if Mrs Sherwood was able to find out a few things about her—'

'—she might not live a million miles from Leominster Drive.'

'Exactly so.'

'Sounds like my sort of job, sir.'

'Just what I was thinking, Lewis. So, if you'll just drop me off at the nearest pub?'

Late that same afternoon, in a luxury flat rather less than a mile from the Sherwood residence, a dark-haired, totally and fatally attractive young woman, wearing thinly rimmed, schoolma'amish spectacles, was still in an agitated frame of mind.

For she knew that she had killed her lover.

Had it been foolish to ring the manager of The Randolph? Certainly the questions he'd asked were disturbingly shrewd; yet her conscience had compelled her to do something. Yes, even she had a conscience . . .

It had been five minutes to six when she'd finally managed to park the car – up in Norham Gardens, rather further out than she'd anticipated. But at least a telephone booth had stood near by, and (as arranged) she'd dialled the hotel and been put through without delay. And virtually verbatim could she recall that brief – that *fatal* – conversation:

'Peter?'

'Jane!'

'Everything OK?'

'Will be once you get here. Room 231.'

'Is it nice?'

'Lovely double bed!'

'I can hardly wait.'

'I'll leave the door ajar.'

'Peter?'

'Yes?'

'I'm wanting you like crazy.'

281

'Jane! Please don't say things like that!'

'Why on earth not?'

'You make me – you make me so *excited*—'

That was when she'd heard a great crash, although the terrible truth had not immediately dawned upon her consciousness . . .

Who the two men were she now saw walking up to the block of flats, she hadn't the faintest notion. But they looked a well enough heeled pair, and the posh car parked at the kerbside hardly suggested a couple of double-glazing double-dealers. And when she answered the door-bell (yes, they had called to see *her*) she acknowledged to herself that she could really rather fancy one of the two men, the one whose hair looked somewhat prematurely grey. For in spite of her anxieties, she was already casting round (as Mrs Sherwood had suspected) for some replacement demerara daddy.

'Jane Ballantyre?'

She smiled invitingly. 'Can I help you, gentlemen?'

'You know, I rather think you can,' said the man whose hair looked somewhat prematurely grey.

SERVICE OF
ALL THE DEAD

I had rather be a doorkeeper in the house of
my God: than to dwell in the tents of ungodliness

(Psalm 84, v. 10)

The First Book
of Chronicles

CHAPTER ONE

LIMPLY THE REVEREND Lionel Lawson shook the last smoothly gloved hand, the slim hand of Mrs Emily Walsh-Atkins, and he knew that the pews in the old church behind him were now empty. It was always the same: whilst the other well-laundered ladies were turning their heads to chat of fêtes and summer hats, whilst the organist played his exit voluntary, and whilst the now discassocked choirboys tucked their T-shirts into flare-line jeans, Mrs Walsh-Atkins invariably spent a few further minutes on her knees in what had sometimes seemed to Lawson a slightly exaggerated obeisance to the Almighty. Yet, as Lawson knew full well, she had plenty to be thankful for. She was eighty-one years old, but managed still to retain an enviable agility in both mind and body; only her eyesight was at last beginning to fail. She lived in north Oxford, in a home for elderly gentlewomen, screened off from the public gaze by a high fence and a belt of fir-trees. Here, from the front window of her living-room, redolent of faded lavender and silver-polish, she could look out on to the well-tended paths and lawns where each morning the resident caretaker unobtrusively collected up the Coca Cola tins, the odd milk bottle and the crisp packets thrown over by those strange, unfathomably depraved young people who, in Mrs Walsh-Atkins' view, had little right to walk the streets at all – let alone the streets of her own beloved north Oxford. The home was wildly expensive; but Mrs W.-A. was a wealthy woman, and each Sunday morning her neatly sealed brown envelope, lightly laid on the collection-plate, contained a folded five-pound note.

'Thank you for the message, Vicar.'

'God bless you!'

This brief dialogue, which had never varied by a single word in the ten years since Lawson had been appointed to the parish of St Frideswide's, was the ultimate stage in non-communication between a priest and his parishioner. In the early days of his ministry, Lawson had felt vaguely uneasy about 'the message' since he was conscious that no passage from his sermons had ever been declaimed with particularly evangelistic fervour; and in any case the rôle of some divinely appointed telegram boy was quite inappropriate – indeed, quite distasteful – to a man of Lawson's moderately high-church leanings. Yet Mrs Walsh-Atkins appeared to hear the humming of the heavenly wires whatever his text might be; and each Sunday morning she reiterated her gratitude to the unsuspecting harbinger of goodly tidings. It was purely by chance that after his very first service Lawson had hit upon those three simple monosyllables – magical words which, again this Sunday morning, Mrs Walsh-Atkins happily clutched to her bosom, along with her Book of Common Prayer, as she walked off with her usual sprightly gait towards St Giles, where her regular taxi-driver would be waiting in the shallow lay-by beside the Martyrs' Memorial.

The vicar of St Frideswide's looked up and down the hot street. There was nothing to detain him longer, but he appeared curiously reluctant to re-enter the shady church. A dozen or so Japanese tourists made their way along the pavement opposite, their small, bespectacled cicerone reciting in a whining, staccato voice the city's ancient charms, his sing-song syllables still audible as the little group sauntered up the street past the cinema, where the management proudly presented to its patrons the opportunity of witnessing the intimacies of Continental-style wife-swapping. But for Lawson there were no stirrings of sensuality: his mind was on other things. Carefully he lifted from his shoulders the white silk-lined hood (M.A. Cantab.) and turned his gaze towards Carfax, where already the lounge-bar door of the Ox stood open. But public houses had never held much appeal for him. He sipped, it is true, the occasional glass of sweet sherry at some of the diocesan functions; but if Lawson's soul should have anything to answer for when the archangel bugled the final trumpet it would certainly not be the charge of drunkenness. Without disturbing his carefully parted hair, he drew the long white surplice over his head and turned slowly into the church.

Apart from the organist, Mr Paul Morris, who had now reached the last few bars of what Lawson recognized as some Mozart, Mrs Brenda Josephs was the only person left in the main body of the building. Dressed

5

in a sleeveless, green summer frock, she sat at the back of the church, a soberly attractive woman in her mid- or late thirties, one bare browned arm resting along the back of the pew, her finger-tips caressing its smooth surface. She smiled dutifully as Lawson walked past; and Lawson, in his turn, inclined his sleek head in a casual benediction. Formal greetings had been exchanged before the service, and neither party now seemed anxious to resume that earlier perfunctory conversation. On his way to the vestry Lawson stopped briefly in order to hook a loose hassock into place at the foot of a pew, and as he did so he heard the door at the side of the organ bang shut. A little too noisily, perhaps? A little too hurriedly?

The curtains parted as he reached the vestry and a gingery-headed, freckle-faced youth almost launched himself into Lawson's arms.

'Steady, boy. Steady! What's all the rush?'

'Sorry, sir. I just forgot ...' His breathless voice trailed off, his right hand, clutching a half-consumed tube of fruit gums, drawn furtively behind his back.

'I hope you weren't eating those during the sermon?'

'No, sir.'

'Not that I ought to blame you if you were. I can get a bit boring sometimes, don't you think?' The peda-gogic tone of Lawson's earlier words had softened now, and he laid his hand on the boy's head and ruffled his hair lightly.

Peter Morris, the organist's only son, looked up at Lawson with a quietly cautious grin. Any subtlety of tone was completely lost upon him; yet he realized that everything was all right, and he darted away along the back of the pews.

'Peter!' The boy stopped in his tracks and looked round. 'How many times must I tell you? You're not to run in church!'

'Yes, sir. Er – I mean, no, sir.'

'And don't forget the choir outing next Saturday.'

''Course not, sir.'

Lawson had not failed to notice Peter's father and Brenda Josephs talking together in animated whispers in the north porch; but Paul Morris had now slipped quietly out of the door after his son, and Brenda, it seemed, had turned her solemn attention to the font: dating from 1345, it was, according to the laconic guide-book, number one of the 'Things to Note'. Lawson turned on his heel and entered the vestry.

Harry Josephs, the vicar's warden, had almost fin-ished now. After each service he entered, against the appropriate date, two sets of figures in the church register: first, the number of persons in the congrega-tion, rounded up or down to the nearest five; second, the sum taken in the offertory, meticulously calculated to the last half-penny. By most reckonings, the church of St Frideswide's was a fairly thriving establishment. Its clientèle was chiefly drawn from the more affluent sectors of the community, and even during the Univer-sity vacations the church was often half-full. It was to be expected, therefore, that the monies to be totalled by the vicar's warden, then checked by the vicar himself, and thereafter transferred to the church's number-one account with Barclays Bank in the High, were not inconsiderable. This morning's takings, sorted by denominations, lay on Lawson's desk in the vestry: one five-pound note; about fifteen one-pound notes; a score or so of fifty-pence pieces and further sundry piles of smaller coinage, neatly stacked in readily identifiable amounts.

'Another goodly congregation, Harry.' 'Goodly' was a favourite word in Lawson's vocabulary. Although it had always been a matter of some contention in theological circles whether the Almighty took any great interest in the counting of mere heads, it was encouraging, on a secular assessment, to minister to a flock that was at least numerically fairly strong; and the word 'goodly' seemed a happily neutral word to blur the distinction between the 'good', by purely arithmetical reckoning, and the 'godly', as assessed on a more spiritual computation.

Harry nodded and made his entries. 'Just check the money quickly if you will, sir. I made it a hundred and thirty-five in the congregation, and I make it fifty-seven pounds twelve pence in the collection.'

'No ha'pennies today, Harry? I think some of the choirboys must have taken my little talk to heart.' With the dexterity of a practised bank clerk he riffled through the pound notes, and then passed his fingers over the piles of coins, like a bishop blessing heads at a confirmation service. The addition of monies was correct.

'One of these days, Harry, you're going to surprise me and make a mistake.'

Josephs' eyes darted sharply to Lawson's face, but

the expression there, as the minister put his signature to the right-hand column of the church register, was one of bland benignity.

Together vicar and warden placed the money in an ancient Huntley & Palmer biscuit tin. It looked an unlikely repository for any great store of wealth; but when at one of its recent meetings the church council had discussed the problem of security no one had come up with any brighter suggestion, except for the possibility that a slightly later vintage of a similar tin might perhaps more firmly corroborate the notion that the receptacle open to view on the back seat of Josephs' Allegro contained nothing more precious than a few ginger-snaps and arrowroots left over from a recent social.

'I'll be off, then, Vicar. The wife'll be waiting.'

Lawson nodded and watched his warden go. Yes, Brenda Josephs would be waiting; she had to be. Six months previously Harry had been found guilty on a charge of drunken driving, and it was largely through Lawson's plea for mitigation that the magistrate's sentence of a fifty-pound fine and one year's suspension had seemed so comparatively lenient. The Josephs' home was in the village of Wolvercote, some three miles north of the city centre, and buses on Sundays were a rarer sight than five-pound notes on a collection-plate.

The small vestry window looked out on the south side of the church, and Lawson sat down at the desk and stared blankly into the graveyard where the grey, weathered tombstones tilted at their varied angles from the vertical, their crumbling legends long since overgrown

9

with moss or smoothed away by centuries of wind and rain. He both looked and felt a worried man, for the simple truth was that there should have been *two* five-pound notes in the collection that morning. Was there just a possibility, though, that Mrs Walsh-Atkins had at last exhausted her store of five-pound notes and put five separate one-pound notes into the collection? If she had, though, it would have been the first time for – oh, years and years. No. There was a much more probable explanation, an explanation that disturbed Lawson greatly. Yet there was still the slimmest chance that he was mistaken. 'Judge not that ye be not judged.' Judge not – at least until the evidence is unequivocal. He took out his wallet and from it drew a piece of paper on which earlier that same morning he had written down the serial number of the five-pound note which he himself had sealed in a small brown envelope and placed in the morning collection. And only two or three minutes ago he had checked the last three numbers of the five-pound note which Harry Josephs had placed in the biscuit tin: they were not the numbers he had written down.

Something of this sort Lawson had suspected for several weeks, and now he had proof of it. He should, he knew, have asked Josephs to turn out his pockets on the spot: that was his duty, both as a priest and as a friend (friend?), for somewhere on Josephs' person would have been found the five-pound note he had just stolen from the offertory. At last Lawson looked down at the piece of paper he had been holding and read the serial number printed on it: AN 50 405546. Slowly he lifted his eyes and stared across the churchyard once more. The sky had grown suddenly overcast, and when half an hour later he walked down to the vicarage in St Ebbe's the air was heavy with the threat of rain. It was as if someone had switched off the sun.

CHAPTER TWO

ALTHOUGH HE PRETENDED still to be asleep, Harry Josephs had heard his wife get up just before seven, and he was able to guess her movements exactly. She had put on her dressing-gown over her nightdress, walked down to the kitchen, filled the nettle, and then sat at the table smoking her first cigarette. It was only during the past two or three months that Brenda had started smoking again, and he was far from happy about it. Her breath smelt stale, and the sight of an ash-tray full of stubs he found quite nauseating. People smoked a lot when they were worried and tense, didn't they? It was just a drug really, like a slug of aspirin, or a bottle of booze, or a flutter on the horses . . . He turned his head into the pillow, and his own anxieties once more flooded through his mind.

'Tea.' She nudged his shoulder gently and put the mug down on the small table that separated their twin beds.

Josephs nodded, grunted, and turned on to his back, watching his wife as she stood in front of the dressing-table and slipped the nightdress over her head. She was thickening a little round the hips now, but she was still leggily elegant and her breasts were full and firm. Yet

12

Josephs did not look at her directly as she stood momentarily naked before the mirror. Over the past few months he had felt increasingly embarrassed about gazing at her body, as if somehow he were intruding into a privacy he was no longer openly invited to share.

He sat up and sipped his tea as she drew up the zip at the side of her nigger-brown skirt. 'Paper come?'

'I'd have brought it up.' She bent forward from the waist and applied a series of cosmetic preparations to her face. Josephs himself had never followed the sequence with any real interest.

'Lot of rain in the night.'

'Still raining,' she said.

'Do the garden good.'

'Mm.'

'Had any breakfast?'

She shook her head. 'There's plenty of bacon, though, if you – ' (she applied a thin film of light pink to her pouting lips) ' – and there's a few mushrooms left.'

Josephs finished his tea and lay back on the bed. It was twenty-five past seven and Brenda would be off in five minutes. She worked mornings only at the Radcliffe Infirmary, at the bottom of the Woodstock Road, where two years ago she had taken up her nursing career once again. Two years ago! That was just after . . .

She came across to his bedside, lightly touched her lips to his forehead, picked up his mug, and walked out of the room. But almost immediately she was back again. 'Oh, Harry. I nearly forgot. I shan't be back for lunch today. Can you get yourself something all right?

I really must go and do some shopping in town. Not that I'll be late – three-ish at the latest, I should think. I'll try to get something nice for tea.'

Josephs nodded and said nothing, but she was lingering by the door. 'Anything you want – from town, I mean?'

'No.' For a few minutes he lay quite still listening to her movements below.

'By-ee!'

'Goodbye.' The front door clicked to behind her. 'Goodbye, Brenda.'

He turned the bedclothes diagonally back, got up, and peered round the side of the curtained window. The Allegro was being backed out carefully into the quiet, wet street and then, with a sudden puff of blue exhaust smoke, was gone. To the Radcliffe was exactly 2.8 miles: Josephs knew that. For three years he had made the identical journey himself, to the block of offices just below the Radcliffe where he had worked as a civil servant after his twenty years' service in the forces. But two years ago the staff had been axed following the latest public-expenditure cuts, and three of the seven of them had been declared redundant, including himself. And how it still rankled! He wasn't the oldest and he wasn't the least experienced. But he was the least experienced of the older men and the oldest of the less experienced. A little silver handshake, a little farewell party, and just a little hope of finding another job. No, that was wrong: almost no hope of finding another job. He had been forty-eight then. Young enough, perhaps, by some standards. But the sad truth had slowly seeped into his soul: no one really wanted him any longer. After more than a year of dispiriting idleness, he had, in fact, worked in a chemist's shop in Summertown, but the branch had recently closed down and he had almost welcomed the inevitable termination of his contract. He – a man who had risen to the rank of captain in the Royal Marine Commandos, a man who had seen active service against the terrorists in the Malayan jungles – standing politely behind the counter handing over prescriptions to some skinny, pale-faced youth or other who wouldn't have lasted five seconds on one of the commando assault-courses! And, as the manager had insisted, saying 'Thank you, sir,' into the bargain!

He shut the thought away, and drew the curtains open.

Just up the road a line of people queued at the bus-stop, their umbrellas raised against the steady rain which filtered down on the straw-coloured fields and lawns. Lines he had learned at school drifted back into his mind, serving his mood and seeming to fit the dismal prospect before him:

> And ghastly thro' the drizzling rain
> On the bald street breaks the blank day.

He caught the 10.30 a.m. bus into Summertown, where he walked into the licensed betting-office and studied the card at Lingfield Park. He noticed that by some strange coincidence The Organist was running in the two-thirty, and Poor Old Harry in the four o'clock. He wasn't usually over-influenced by names, but when he recalled his lack of success through undue reliance on the form-book he suspected that it might have been more profitable if he had been. In the ante-post betting odds, The Organist was one of the co-favourites, and Poor Old Harry wasn't even quoted. Josephs walked along the series of daily newspapers affixed to the walls of the office: The Organist was napped in a couple of them; Poor Old Harry seemed to have no support whatsoever. Josephs allowed himself a rueful grin: probably neither of them was destined to be first past the post, but ... why not? Take a chance, Harry boy! He filled in a square white betting-slip and pushed it over the counter with his money:

Lingfield Park: 4 p.m.
£2 win: Poor Old Harry.

A year or so previously, after purchasing two tins of baked beans from a supermarket, he had been given change for one pound instead of for the five-pound note he knew he had handed over. His protestations on that occasion had necessitated a full till-check and a nervy half-hour wait before the final justification of his claim; and since that time he had been more careful, always memorizing the last three numbers of any five-pound note he tendered. He did so now, and repeated them to himself as he waited for his change: 546 ... 546 ... 546 ...

The drizzle had virtually stopped when at 11.20 a.m. he walked unhurriedly down the Woodstock Road.

Twenty-five minutes later he was standing in one of the private car parks at the Radcliffe where he spotted the car almost immediately. Threading his way through the closely parked vehicles, he soon stood beside it and looked through the offside window. The milometer read 25,622. That tallied: it had read 619˙before she left. And if she now followed the normal routine of any sensible person she would walk down into Oxford from here, and when she got home the milometer would read 625 – 626 at the most. Finding a suitable vantage-point behind a moribund elm tree he looked at his watch. And waited.

At two minutes past twelve the celluloid doors leading to E.N.T. Outpatients flapped open and Brenda Josephs appeared and walked briskly to the car. He could see her very clearly. She unlocked the door and sat for a few seconds leaning forward and viewing herself in the driving-mirror, before taking a small scent-bottle from her handbag and applying it to her neck, first to one side, then to the other. Her safety-belt remained unfastened as she backed none too expertly out of the narrow space; then the right blinker on as she drove out of the car park and up to the Woodstock Road; then the orange blinker flashing left (left!) as she edged into the traffic departing north and away from the city centre.

He knew her next moves. Up to the Northern Ring Road roundabout, there cutting through Five Mile Drive, and then out on to the Kidlington Road. He knew his own move, too.

The telephone kiosk was free and, although the local

directory had long since been stolen, he knew the number and dialled it.

'Hello?' (A woman's voice.) 'Roger Bacon School, Kidlington. Can I help you?'

'I was wondering if I could speak to Mr Morris, Mr Paul Morris, please. I believe he's one of your music teachers.'

'Yes, he is. Just a minute. I'll just have a look at the timetable to see if . . . just a minute . . . No. He's got a free period. I'll just see if he's in the staff-room. Who shall I say?'

'Er, Mr Jones.'

She was back on the line within half a minute. 'No, I'm afraid he doesn't seem to be on the school premises, Mr Jones. Can I take a message?'

'No, it doesn't really matter. Can you tell me whether he's likely to be at school during the lunch-hour?'

'Just a minute.' (Josephs heard the rustling of some papers. She needn't have bothered, though, he knew that.) 'No. He's not on the list for lunches today. He usually stays but—'

'Don't worry. Sorry to have been a nuisance.'

He felt his heart pounding as he rang another number – another Kidlington number. He'd give the bloody pair a fright! If only he could drive a car! The phone rang and rang and he was just beginning to wonder . . . when it was answered.

'Hello?' (Just that. No more. Was the voice a little strained?)

'Mr Morris?' (It was no difficulty for him to lapse into the broad Yorkshire dialect of his youth.)

'Ye-es?'

'Electricity Board 'ere, sir. Is it cónvénient for us to come along, sir? We've—'

'Today, you mean?'

'Aye. This lunch-taime, sir.'

'Er – er – no, I'm afraid not. I've just called in home for a second to get a – er – book. It's lucky you caught me, really. But I'm due back at school – er – straight away. What's the trouble, anyway?'

Josephs slowly cradled the phone. That would give the sod something to think about!

When Brenda arrived home at ten minutes to three, he was clipping the privet hedge with dedicated precision. 'Hello, love. Have a good day?'

'Oh. Usual, you know. I've bought something nice for tea, though.'

'That's good news.'

'Have any lunch?'

'Mouthful of bread and cheese.'

She knew he was telling a lie, for there was no cheese in the house. Unless, of course, he'd been out again . . .? She felt a sudden surge of panic as she hurried inside with her shopping bags.

Josephs continued his meticulous clippings along the tall hedge that separated them from next door. He was in no hurry, and only when he was immediately alongside the offside front door of the car did he casually glance at the fascia dials. The milometer read 25,633.

COLIN DEXTER

As he always did, he washed up after their evening meal by himself, but he postponed one small piece of investigation until later, for he knew that as surely as night follows day his wife would make some excuse for retiring early to bed. Yet, strange as it seemed, he felt almost glad: it was he who was now in control of things. (Or, at least, that is what he thought.)

She was on cue, all right – just after the news headlines on BBC 1: 'I think I'll have a bath and an early night, Harry. I – I feel a bit tired.'

He nodded understandingly. 'Like me to bring you a cup of Ovaltine?'

'No, thanks. I shall be asleep as soon as I hit the pillow. But thanks anyway.' She put her hand on his shoulder and gave it the slightest squeeze, and for a few seconds her face was haunted by the twin spectres of self-recrimination and regret.

When the water had finished running in the bathroom, Josephs went back into the kitchen and looked in the waste bin. There, screwed up into small balls and pushed right to the bottom of the débris, he found four white paper bags. Careless, Brenda! Careless! He had checked the bin himself that same morning, and now there were four newcomers, four white paper bags, all of them carrying the name of the Quality supermarket at Kidlington.

After Brenda had left the next morning, he made himself some coffee and toast, and sat down with the *Daily Express*. Heavy overnight rain at Lingfield Park had upset a good many of the favourites, and there were no congratulatory columns to the wildly inaccurate prognostications of the racing tipsters. With malicious glee he noticed that The Organist had come seventh out of eight runners; and Poor Old Harry – had won! At sixteen to one! Whew! It hadn't been such a blank day after all.

CHAPTER THREE

THE LAST LESSON of the week could hardly have provided a more satisfactory envoi. There were only five of them in the O Level music group, all reasonably anxious to work hard and to succeed, all girls; and as they sat forward awkwardly and earnestly, their musical scores of Piano Sonata Opus 90 on their knees, Paul Morris vaguely reminded himself how exquisitely Gilels could play Beethoven. But his aesthetic sense was only minimally engaged, and not for the first time during the past few weeks he found himself wondering whether he was really cut out for teaching. Doubtless, these particular pupils would all get decent O Level grades, for he had sedulously drilled the set works into them – their themes, their developments and recapitulations. But there was, he knew, little real radiance either in his own exposition of the works or in his pupil's appreciation of them; and the sad truth was that what until so recently had been an all-consuming passion was now becoming little more than pleasurable background listening. From Music to Muzak – in three short months.

Morris had moved from his previous post (it was almost three years ago now) primarily to try to forget that terrible day when the young police constable had come to tell him that his wife had been killed in a car accident; when he had gone along to the primary school to collect Peter and watched the silent, tragic tears that sprang from the boy's eyes; and when he had wrestled with that helpless, baffled anger against the perversity and cruelty of the Fates which had taken his young wife from him – an anger which over those next few dazed and despairing weeks had finally settled into a firm resolve at all costs to protect his only child whenever and wherever he could. The boy was something – the only thing – that he could cling to. Gradually, too, Morris had become convinced that he had to get away, and his determination to move – to move anywhere – had grown into an obsession as weekly the Posts Vacant columns in *The Times Educational Supplement* reminded him of new streets, new colleagues, a new school – perhaps even a new life. And so finally he had moved to the Roger Bacon Comprehensive School on the outskirts of Oxford, where his breezy interview had lasted but fifteen minutes, where he'd immediately found a quiet little semi-detached to rent, where everyone was very kind to him – but where his life proved very much the same as before. At least, until he met Brenda Josephs.

It was through Peter that he had established contact with St Frideswide's. One of Peter's friends was a keen member of the choir, and before long Peter had joined, too. And when the aged choirmaster had finally retired it was common knowledge that Peter's father was an organist, and the invitation asking him to take over was accepted without hesitation.

Gilels was lingering *pianissimo* over the last few bars when the bell sounded the end of the week's schooling. One of the class, a leggy, large-boned, dark-haired girl, remained behind to ask if she could borrow the record for the weekend. She was slightly taller than Morris, and as he looked into her black-pencilled, languidly amorous eyes he once more sensed a power within himself which until a few months previously he could never have suspected. Carefully he lifted the record from the turntable and slipped it smoothly into its sleeve.

'Thank you,' she said softly.

'Have a nice weekend, Carole.'

'You, too, sir.'

He watched her as she walked down the steps from the stage and clattered her way across the main hall in her high wedge-heeled shoes. How would the melancholy Carol be spending her weekend? he wondered. He wondered, too, about his own.

Brenda had happened just three months ago. He had seen her on many occasions before, of course, for she always stayed behind after the Sunday morning service to take her husband home. But that particular morning had not been just another occasion. She had seated herself, not as usual in one of the pews at the back of the church, but directly behind him in the choir-stalls; and as he played he'd watched her with interest in the organ-mirror, her head slightly to one side, her face set in a wistful, half-contented smile. As the deep notes died away around the empty church, he had turned towards her.

'Did you like it?'

She had nodded quietly and lifted her eyes towards him.

'Would you like me to play it again?'

'Have you got time?'

'For you I have.' Their eyes had held then, and for that moment they were the only two beings alive in the world.

'Thank you,' she whispered.

Remembrance of that first brief time together was even now a source of radiant light that shone in Morris's heart. Standing by his side she had turned over the sheet-music for him, and more than once her arm had lightly brushed his own . . .

That was how it had begun, and how, he told himself, it had to end. But that couldn't be. Her face haunted his dreams that Sunday night, and again through the following nights she would give his sleeping thoughts no rest. On the Friday of the same week he had rung her at the hospital. A bold, irrevocable move. Quite simply he had asked her if he could see her some time – that was all; and just as simply she had answered 'Yes, of course you can' – words that re-echoed round his brain like the joyous refrain of the Seraphim.

In the weeks that followed, the frightening truth had gradually dawned on him: he would do almost anything to have this woman for his own. It was not that he bore any malice against Harry Josephs. How could he? Just a burning, irrational jealousy, which no words from Brenda, none of her pathetic pleas of reassurance could assuage. He wished Josephs out of the way – of course he did! But only recently had his conscious mind accepted the stark reality of his position. Not only did he wish Josephs out of the way: he would be positively happy to see him dead.

'You stayin' much longer, sir?'

It was the caretaker, and Morris knew better than to argue. It was a quarter past four, and Peter would be home.

The regular Friday evening fish and chips, liberally vinegared and blotched with tomato sauce, were finished, and they stood together at the kitchen sink, father washing, son drying. Although Morris had thought long and hard about what he would say, it was not going to be easy. He had never before had occasion to speak to his son about matters connected with sex; but one thing was quite certain: he had to do so now. He remembered with devastating clarity (he had only been eight at the time) when the two boys next door had been visited by the police, and when one of the local ministers had been taken to court, and there convicted and sentenced to prison. And he remembered the new words he had then learned, words that his school-fellows had learned, too, and laughed about in lavatory corners: slimy words that surfaced ever after in his young mind as if from some loathsome, reptilian pool.

'I think we may be able to get you that racing bike in a couple of months.'

'*Really*, Dad?'

'You have to promise me to be jolly careful . . .'

But Peter was hardly listening. His mind was racing as fast as the bike was going to race, his face shining with joy . . .

'Pardon, Dad?'

'I said, are you looking forward to the outing to-morrow?'

Peter nodded, honestly if comparatively unenthusiastically. ''Spect I'll get a bit fed up on the way back. Like last year.'

'I want you to promise me something.'

Another promise? The boy frowned uncertainly at the serious tone in his father's voice, and rubbed the tea-towel quite unnecessarily round and round the next plate, anticipating some adult information, confidential, and perhaps unwelcome.

'You're still a young lad, you know. You may think you're getting a bit grown-up, but you've still got a lot to learn. You see, some people you'll meet in life are very nice, and some aren't. They may seem nice, but – but they're not nice at all. It sounded pathetically inadequate.

'Crooks, you mean?'

'In a way they're crooks, yes, but I'm talking about people who are bad inside. They want – strange sorts of things to satisfy them. They're not normal – not like most people.' He took a deep breath. 'When I was about your age, younger in fact . . .'

Peter listened to the little story with apparent unconcern. 'You mean, he was a queer, Dad?'

'He was a homosexual. Do you know what that means?'

''Course I do.'

'Listen, Peter, if any man ever tries anything like that – anything! – you have nothing at all to do with it. Is that clear? And, what's more, you'll tell me. All right?'

Peter tried so very hard to understand, but the warning seemed remote, dissociated as yet from his own small experience of life.

'You see, Peter, it's not just a question of a man – touching' (the very word was shudderingly repulsive) 'or that sort of thing. It's what people start talking about or – or photographs that kind of—'

Peter's mouth dropped open and the blood froze in his freckled cheeks. So *that* was what his father was talking about! The last time had been two weeks ago when three of them from the youth club had gone along to the vicarage and sat together on that long, black, shiny settee. It was all a bit strange and exciting, and there had been those photographs – big, black and white, glossy prints that seemed almost clearer than real life. But they weren't just pictures of *men*, and Mr Lawson had talked about them so – so naturally, somehow. Anyway, he'd often seen pictures like that on the racks in the newsagent's. He felt a growing sense of bewilderment as he stood there by the sink, his hands still clutching the drying-cloth. Then he heard his father's voice, raucous and ugly, in his ears, and felt his father's hand upon his shoulder, shaking him angrily.

'Do you hear me? Tell me about it!'

But the boy didn't tell his father. He just couldn't. What was there to tell anyway?

CHAPTER FOUR

THE COACH, A wide luxury hulk of a thing, was due to leave Cornmarket at 7.30 a.m., and Morris joined the group of fussy parents counterchecking on lunch bags, swimming gear and pocket money. Peter was already ensconced between a pair of healthily excited pals on the back seat, and Lawson once more counted heads to satisfy himself that the expedition was fully manned and could at last proceed. As the driver heaved round and round at the huge horizontal steering-wheel, slowly manœuvring the giant vehicle into Beaumont Street, Morris had his last view of Harry and Brenda Josephs sitting silently together on one of the front seats, of Lawson folding his plastic raincoat and packing it into the overhead rack, and of Peter chatting happily away and like most of the other boys disdaining, or forgetting, to wave farewell. All *en route* for Bournemouth.

It was 7.45 a.m. by the clock on the south face of St Frideswide's as Morris walked up to Carfax and then through Queen Street and down to the bottom of St Ebbe's, where he stopped in front of a rangy three-storeyed stuccoed building set back from the street behind bright yellow railings. Nailed on to the high wooden gate which guarded the narrow path to the front door was a flaking notice-board announcing in faded capitals ST FRIDESWIDE'S CHURCH AND OXFORD PASTORATE. The gate itself was half-open; and as Morris stood self-consciously and indecisively in the deserted street a whistling paper boy rode up on his bicycle and inserted a copy of *The Times* through the front door. No inside hand withdrew the newspaper, and Morris walked slowly away from the house and just as slowly back. On the top floor a pale yellow strip of neon lighting suggested the presence of someone on the premises, and he walked cautiously up to the front door where he rapped gently on the ugly black knocker. With no sound of movement from within, he tried again, a little louder. There must be someone, surely, in the rambling old vicarage. Students up on the top floor, probably? A housekeeper, perhaps? But again as he held his ear close to the door he could hear no movement; and conscious that his heart was beating fast against his ribs he tried the door. It was locked.

The back of the house was enclosed by a wall some eight or nine feet high; but a pair of gates, with NO PARKING amateurishly painted in white across them, promised access to somewhere, and turning the metal ring Morris found the gate unlocked. He stepped inside. A path led alongside the high stone wall beside an ill-tended stretch of patchy lawn, and quietly closing the gates behind him Morris walked up to the back door, and knocked with a quiet cowardice. No answer. No sound. He turned the door-knob. The door was unlocked. He opened it and went inside. For several seconds he stood stock-still in the wide hallway, his eyes unmoving as an alligator's. Across the hall *The Times* protruded downwards through the front-door letter-box like the tongue of some leering gargoyle, the whole house as still as death. He forced himself to breathe more naturally and looked around him. A door on his left was standing ajar, and he tiptoed across to look inside. 'Anyone there?' The words were spoken very softly, but they gave him an odd surge of confidence as though, should anyone be there, he was obviously trying to be noticed. And someone was there; or had been, until very recently. On a formica-topped table lay a knife, stickily smeared with butter and marmalade, a solitary plate strewn with toast crumbs, and a large mug containing the dregs of cold tea. The remains, no doubt, of Lawson's breakfast. But a sudden shudder of fear climbed up Morris's spine as he noticed that the grill on the electric cooker was turned on full, its bars burning a fierce orange-red. Yet there was the same eerie stillness as before, with only the mechanical tick-tock of the kitchen clock to underline the pervasive silence.

Back in the hallway, he walked quietly across to the broad staircase, and as lightly as he could climbed up to the landing. Only one of the doors was open; but one was enough. A black-leather settee was ranged along one side of the room, and the floor was fully carpeted. He walked noiselessly across to the roll-top desk beside the window. It was locked, but the key lay on the top. Inside, two neatly written sheets of paper – on which he read the text and notes for some forth-coming sermon – lay beneath a paper-knife, curiously fashioned in the shape of a crucifix, the slitting-edge, as it seemed to Morris, wickedly (and quite needlessly?) sharp. He tried first the drawers on the left – all of them gliding smoothly open and all of them apparently fulfilling some innocent function; and the same with the top three drawers on the right. But the bottom one was locked, and the key to it was nowhere to be seen.

As a prospective burglar Morris had anticipated the stubbornness of locks and bolts only to the extent of a small chisel which he now took from his pocket. It took him more than ten minutes, and when finally the bottom drawer lay open the surrounding oblong frame was irreparably chipped and bruised. Inside lay an old chocolate-box, and Morris was slipping off the criss-cross of elastic bands when a slight sound caused him to whip round, his eyes wide with terror.

Standing in the doorway was a man with a lathered face, his right hand holding a shaving-brush, his left clutching a dirty pink towel about his neck. For a second Morris felt a shock that partly paralysed his terror, for his immediate impression was that the man was Lawson himself. Yet he knew he must be mistaken, and the logic that for a moment had threatened to disintegrate was swiftly reasserting itself. The man was about the same height and build as Lawson, yes. But the face was thinner and the hair was greyer; nor was the man's voice, when finally he spoke, in any way like Lawson's own, but a voice and a mode of expression that seemed to mask a curious combination of the cultured and the coarse:

'May I ask what the 'ell you're doing 'ere, mate?'

Morris recognized him then. He was one of the drop-outs who sometimes congregated in Bonn Square or Brasenose Lane. Indeed, Lawson had brought him to church a few times, and there was a whisper of rumour that the two men were related. Some had even suspected that the man was Lawson's brother.

At Bournemouth the sun shone brightly out of a clear sky, but the wind was chill and blustery, and Brenda Josephs, seated in an open deck-chair, envied the other holiday-makers who sat so snugly, it seemed, behind their striped wind-breaks. She felt cold and bored – and more than a little disturbed by that little remark of Harry's on the coach: 'Pity Morris couldn't make it.' That was all. That was all . . .

The boys had thrown themselves around with phenomenal energy: playing beach football (Harry had organized that), running into the sea, clambering up and down the rocks, guzzling Coke, guttling sandwiches, crunching crisps, then back into the sea. But for her – what an empty, fruitless day! She was officially the 'nurse' of the party, for invariably someone would feel sick or cut his knee. But she could have been with Paul all day. All day! No risk, either. Oh God! She couldn't bear to think of it . . .

The farther stretches of the sea twinkled invitingly in the sun, but along the shore-line the crashing breakers somersaulted into heavy spray. It was no day for tentative paddlers, but huge fun for the boys who were still leaping tirelessly against the waves, Lawson

with them, white-skinned as a fish's underbelly, laughing, splashing, happy. It all seemed innocent enough to
Brenda, and she couldn't really believe all that petty
church gossip. Not that she liked Lawson much; but
she didn't dislike him, either. In fact she'd thought
more than once that Lawson must suspect something
about herself and Paul; but he'd said nothing . . . so far.

Harry had gone for a walk along the esplanade, and
she was glad to be left to herself. She tried to read the
newspaper, but the sheets flapped and billowed in the
breeze, and she put it back into the carrier bag,
alongside the flask of coffee, the salmon sandwiches,
and her white bikini. Yes. Pity about the bikini . . . She
had become increasingly conscious of her body these
past few months, and she would have enjoyed seeing
the young lads gawping up at her bulging breasts. What
was happening to her . . .?

When Harry returned an hour or so later it was quite
clear that he had been drinking, but she made no
comment. As a concession to the English summer he
had changed into a pair of old shorts – long, baggy
service-issue in which (according to Harry) he and his
men had flushed the Malaysian jungles of all the
terrorists. His legs had grown thinner, especially round
the thighs, but they were still muscular and strong.
Stronger than Paul's, but . . . She stemmed the gather-
ing flood of thoughts, and unfolded the tin-foil round
the sandwiches.

She averted her eyes from her husband as he slowly
masticated the tinned salmon. What *was* happening to
her? The poor fellow couldn't even eat now without

34

her experiencing a mild disgust. She would have to do something, she knew that. And soon. But what *could* she do?

It was not on that joyless day at Bournemouth (although it was very soon after) that Brenda Josephs recognized the ugly fact that had been standing at the threshold of her mind: she now hated the man she had married.

'Have you heard that somebody might be helping himself from the collection? It's only a rumour but . . .' It was the following morning when Morris heard the first whisperings; but in his mind – as in many others' – the alleged hebdomadal thefts were already firmly substantiated in the higher courts of heaven and now stood only in need of a little terrestrial corroboration. There were – surely – only two obvious opportunities, and two possible suspects: Lawson at the altar and Josephs in the vestry. And during the penultimate verse of the offertory hymn Morris turned the organ-mirror slightly to the right and adjusted the elevation so that he had a good view of the large, gilt crucifix standing on the heavily brocaded altar cloth; and of Lawson holding high the collection-plate, then lowering it and leaning forward in a tilted benediction before handing it back to the vicar's warden. It had been impossible to see Lawson's hands clearly, but nothing had been taken – Morris could have sworn to it. So it must be that contemptible worm Josephs! Much more likely – counting the cash all alone in the vestry. Yes. And yet . . . And yet, if the church funds *were* being pilfered, wasn't there a much likelier culprit than either? The scruffy-looking man from the Church Army hostel, the man who had been there again this morning, sitting next to Josephs at the back of the church, the man Lawson had befriended – and the man whom Morris himself had encountered the previous morning in the vicarage.

A few minutes later he closed the organ-door quietly behind him and managed a cheerful 'Good morning' to Mrs Walsh-Atkins as she finally rose from her knees. But in truth he was far from cheerful; and as he walked slowly up the central aisle his mind for once was not wholly preoccupied with thoughts of Brenda Josephs, whom he could now see waiting for him by the font. Like Lawson at this time a week ago, he felt a very worried man.

CHAPTER FIVE

ON WEDNESDAY OF the same week, no one seemed to mind the woman as she stood by the shop window examining with slow deliberation one bulky sample-book after another. 'Just looking,' she told the assistant. She'd known what would happen, of course: from the bus-stop in Woodstock Road he would walk down South Parade (where Cromwell had once arranged his Roundheads), turn right into Banbury Road, and then go into the licensed betting-office just opposite the carpet-shop. And he had already done so. She knew, too, that he would have to come out sooner rather than later, since he was due home for lunch – lunch with *her* – at about one o'clock; and he had another call to pay before then, had he not?

It was 11.20 a.m. when Harry Josephs at last emerged, and his wife drifted quietly behind a line of vertically stacked linoleum rolls, watching him. Back up to South Parade, where he pushed the button at the pelican crossing and waited to cross the Banbury Road. Just as she'd thought. She left the shop with a guilty 'Thank you', and kept well behind him as he walked with his slightly splay-footed gait up towards north Oxford, his brown suit clearly visible beyond the other pedestrians.

He would turn right very soon now (how much she knew!) into Manning Terrace; and she skipped and waltzed her way in and out of the prams as soon as he disappeared. He was on the right-hand side of the terrace, about seven or eight houses along, and he would be stopping just about there (yes!) and walking up the short path to one of the front doors. She knew not only the number of the house but also the woman who lived there; knew the style and colour of her hair even – long and prematurely grey, like the strand she'd found on Harry's suit one day the previous week. Ruth Rawlinson! That was the name of the woman who lived at number 14, the woman whom her husband had been seeing; and it was all just as Lionel Lawson had told her it was. She hurried back to the Summertown car park. She would just have time to put in a brief appearance at the Radcliffe Infirmary, and to tell the nursing officer that her dental appointment had taken much longer than expected and that she'd make up the time tomorrow.

As she drove down into Oxford her lips were curled in a cruelly contented smile.

At 8 p.m. on the Wednesday of the following week, Ruth Rawlinson took little notice when she heard the click and the creak of the north door opening. People often came in to look around, to admire the font, to light a candle, to pray even; and she silently wiped her wet cloth over the wooden floor of the pew behind one of the pillars in the south aisle. The stranger, whoever he might be, was now standing still, for the echo of his footsteps had died away in the empty, darkening church. This was just about the time when the place could get almost eerie – and time for Ruth to go home. Of indeterminate age, anywhere between mid-thirties and late forties, she wiped her pale forehead with the back of her wrist and brushed back a wisp of straggling hair. She'd done enough. Twice a week, on Mondays and Wednesdays, she spent about two hours in St Frideswide's (usually in the mornings), cleaning the floors, dusting the pews, polishing the candlesticks, turning out the dying flowers; and once every three months washing and ironing all the surplices. For these good works her motives were obscure, not least to Ruth herself: sometimes she suspected they sprang from an almost pathological need to escape for a brief while her demanding, discontented, self-centred invalid of a mother, with whom she shared her house; at other times, especially on Sundays, she felt her motives sprang from a deeper source, for she found herself profoundly moved in spirit by the choral mass, especially by Palestrina, and then she would approach the altar of the Lord to partake the host with an almost mystical sense of wonder and adoration.

The footsteps had started again, and as they moved slowly up the central aisle she peered over the top of the pew. He looked somehow familiar, but he was half turned away from her and for a while she failed to recognize him: his subfusc suit seemed of good quality cloth, though loose-fitting and shabby; and his face (so far as she could see it) was matted with greyish stubble.

He peered vaguely across the pews, first to the left, then to the right, before stopping at the chancel steps. Was he looking for something – or someone? Instinctively Ruth felt it better if he remained unaware of her presence, and very very quietly she wiped the cloth over the winking suds.

The north door clicked and groaned again, and she dipped the soapy cloth more boldly into the dirty water; but almost immediately her body froze over the bucket.

'You came, then?'

'Keep your voice down!'

'There's nobody here.'

The newcomer walked down the central aisle and the two men met half-way. They spoke in hushed voices, but the few snatches of their conversation that carried to Ruth's ears were readily and frighteningly comprehensible.

'. . . given you more than enough already and you're not getting a penny more . . .'

'. . . *told* you, Mister Morris. It's just to tide me over, that's all. And I'm sure you wouldn't want me to tell my brother . . .' The voice seemed a curious combination of the cultured and the coarse.

The ugly word 'blackmail' rose to the surface of Ruth's mind; but before she could learn more the door had opened again to admit a small group of tourists, one of whom in a nasal twang was soon admiring 'that cute lil farnt'.

*

Half of the long school holiday had now passed and the August sun shone gloriously. Brenda and Harry Josephs were in Tenby for a week; Lawson had just come back from a brief holiday in Scotland; Peter Morris was away at scout camp; and his father was decorating the staircase – amongst other things.

It was at 1.30 p.m. that he was sitting in the Old Bull at Deddington and deciding that he oughtn't to drink any more. After all, he had to drive home. And he had the additional responsibility of a passenger.

'I think we ought to go now,' he said.

Carole nodded, and drained her third Babycham. From the start she had felt embarrassment at being with him, and things hadn't been helped much by the way he'd been speaking to her – so naturally! So unendearingly! It wasn't at all what she'd expected. Or hoped. She'd been in a pub before, of course – quite a few times; but only for a giggle round the juke-box with some of the others from school. But this? The whole thing had been a ghastly mistake, somehow; and yet it could have been so very different . . .

The car was parked at the far end of the tarmac behind the pub, and Morris politely unlocked and opened the door for his passenger before getting into the driver's seat and fitting the key into the ignition.

'You won't say anything at all about this, will you?'

''Course I won't.'

'You mustn't tell anyone.'

'I shan't tell a soul,' she said. Her eyes, the lids shaded in a lurid blue, were dull with disappointment.

41

Morris took a deep breath. 'Put your safety belt on, my girl. Better safe—'

He leaned over to help fix the awkward thing, and was aware of the softness of her breast against his arm. With what seemed almost paternal affection he took her hand in his; and as she turned her head towards him he put his mouth lightly to hers and felt her full lips softly cushioning his own. He had meant no more than that; but he lingered there as the girl's lips gently – yet so perceptibly! – pushed forward against his own. And still he lingered, savouring long the sensual delight. He put his arm along the seat, easing her more closely towards him; and then the tip of her tongue tentatively tried the entrance to his mouth, and the smouldering smoke burst forth in a blazing flame . . . Eagerly she pulled down his hand to her naked thigh, and her legs opened slowly and invitingly, like the arms of a saint in a holy benediction.

They broke away from each other guiltily as a car backed into the space beside them, and Morris drove off to Kidlington, dropping her (where he had picked her up) on the north side of the village.

'Would you like to come to see me sometime?' They were the first words that either of them had spoken on the way back.

'When do you mean?'

'I dunno.' His throat was very dry. 'Now?'

'All right.'

'How long will it take you from here?'

'Ten minutes.'

'You'd better come in the back way.'

42

'All right.'

'I want you, Carole!'

'I want you, sir.' ('Sir'! My God! What was he doing?)

'Be as quick as you can.'

'I will, don't worry.'

In the kitchen he opened a bottle of Beaujolais, fetched two glasses from the living-room, and looked yet again at his watch. Just another five minutes. Come on, Carole! ... Already in his mind he was unfastening the buttons down the front of her white blouse, and his hands were slipping inside to fondle her breasts ... He breathed deeply and waited with an almost desperate impatience.

When finally he heard the timid knock, he walked to the back door like a man newly ushered through the gates of Paradise.

'Good afternoon,' said Lawson. 'I hope I've not called at an inconvenient time? I wonder if I can come in and talk to you. It's – er – it's rather important.'

The Second Book
of Chronicles

CHAPTER SIX

BUT FOR HIS dilatoriness and indecisiveness Detective Chief Inspector Morse would have been cruising among the Greek islands. Three months earlier, in January, he had discussed Easter bookings with the Town and Gown travel agency, taken home a Technicolor brochure, rung up his bank manager to discover the going rate for the drachma, bought a slim Modern Greek phrase-book, and even managed to find his passport again. He had never been to Greece; and now, a bachelor still, forty-seven years old, he retained enough romance in his soul to imagine a lazy liaison with some fading film star beside the wine-dark waves of the Aegean. But it was not to be. Instead, on this chilly Monday mid-morning in early April, he stood at a bus-stop in north Oxford, with a fortnight's furlough before him, wondering exactly how other people could organize their lives, make decisions, write a letter even.

Still no bus in sight.

A heavily pregnant mother pushed a rickety, collapsible pram into the shelter, unstrapped the infant within it, and then stuck her head out to admonish her slightly older offspring, already exhibiting, as it seemed to Morse, the lively potential of a fully fledged criminal. 'Stop frowin' dem bricks, Jason!'

Jason! Jason and the Argonauts sailing up to the Hellespont . . . Morse felt he could have done without the reminder – the second reminder, in fact, that morning; for Radio Oxford had just broadcast an interview with the new vicar of St Frideswide's, recently returned from a fortnight in a monastery on the island of Patmos.

Morse stood aside to allow Jason's formidable mother to enter the bus first. She asked for 'St Frideswide's', and as she fiddled one-handedly in her purse the other passengers watched in helpless silence as the hero of the *Argosy* wiped his filthy shoes over the nearest seat-cover.

Morse knew where St Frideswide's was, of course: one of the string of ecclesiastical edifices along Cornmarket . . . where there had been some rather curious occurrences the previous Autumn . . . when he himself had been away on an eight-week secondment in west Africa . . .

'Where to, mate?'

'Er' (it was more than a year since Morse had been on a bus) 'St Frideswide's, please.' It was as good a stop as any for the Ashmolean, and Morse had promised himself an hour or so in the galleries: it would be good to see the Tiepolo again; and the Giorgione.

But he saw neither that morning.

Whilst Mrs Jason was extricating his pram from the luggage-rack, the triumphant young vandal himself was already at large in the street, and very soon the bottom half of a notice affixed to the church railings was torn from its moorings.

''Ow many times 'ave I *told* you, Jason?' This rhetorical question was accompanied by a clumping clout across the youngster's ears, and the bawling brat was finally dragged away.

The notice now read: ST FRIDESWIDE'S EASTER JUMBLE SALE. That was all. Any details of date, time and place had vanished with the passing of Jason.

Morse was a believer neither in the existence of God nor in the fixity of the Fates. About such things he never quite knew what he should think; and, like Hardy's, his philosophy of life amounted to little more than a heap of confused impressions, akin to those of a bewildered young boy at a conjuring show. Yet, as he looked back, it seemed somehow pre-ordained that his steps should take him on only one course that morning; and he took that course now as, in obedience to some strangely compelling impulse, he walked the few steps across the pavement and unlatched the door at the north porch of St Frideswide's.

CHAPTER SEVEN

As a schoolboy, Morse had once paid a few shillings for a book on architecture and had traipsed around a good many churches, earnestly tracing the development of Early English into Gothic. But the enthusiasm, like so many, had been short-lived. And as he stood in the vaulted silence, looking down the central aisle towards the altar, with the heavily curtained vestry to the right behind him, few of the architectural features were familiar any longer; and his mind, whilst not uninformed, remained maddeningly blank – like that of an amnesic ornithologist at a duck-pond. A ring of candles burned around the effigy of some saint or other, and an occasional elongated asterisk of light was reflected in a gleaming flash from an adjacent crucifix. The air was heavy with incense.

As he walked slowly towards the chancel, Morse realized that he'd been wrong about the silence, though. Somewhere he could hear a quiet, rhythmic scratching noise, like that of a church mouse scampering about in the wainscoting. But the noise was too regular for that; and suddenly Morse knew that he was not alone. A grey head rose above the level of the front pew and nodded neutrally as the visitor stopped alongside. She wiped her pale forehead with the back of her wrist and blew a stray hair from her vision before bending over her work once more, the concentric rings of soap on the wooden floor dissolving beneath her wiping-cloth, the bucket rattling as she moved to the next rectangle.

'Good morning.' Morse smiled amiably as he looked down at her. 'You don't seem to have got any of those brochure things – you know, telling people what to look at.'

'No. We ran out last week, but the Vicar's having some more printed.'

'The Vicar? That's Mr Lawson, isn't it?'

'No, it isn't.' Her large brown eyes looked up at him cautiously, and she suddenly seemed a good deal younger than he'd thought. 'It's Mr Meiklejohn. He's been here since last November.'

'I must have been thinking of one of the other churches.'

'No. Mr Lawson *was* here.' She hesitated. 'He – he died last October.'

'Oh dear. I'm sorry about that.'

For a few seconds there was silence between them.

'I think you knew he was dead,' said the woman quietly.

Morse blinked at her happily. 'Did I?'

'You're another one of those reporters, aren't you?'

Morse shook his head and told her. He was a police officer attached to the Thames Valley Police H.Q. in Kidlington – not to the City Police in St Aldates; he'd heard vaguely about the case but had never been on it himself; in fact, he'd been out of the country at the time.

'Were you involved in any way?' he asked.

'As a matter of fact I was, yes.'

'Pardon?' She spoke so very quietly now that Morse took a step nearer to her.

'I was here in the church on the night of the murder.'

'I see. Do you mind telling me something about it?'

She dried her hands along her faded blue jeans, worn almost threadbare at the knees, and stood up. 'Wait a minute.'

There was a natural elegance about her walk, and Morse's eyes followed her with a slightly quickened interest as she disappeared somewhere at the back of the church, and re-emerged a minute later carrying a brown handbag. She had taken the opportunity to arrange her straggling hair, and Morse began to realize that she must once have been an attractive woman.

'Here you are.' She handed him a cheap brown envelope containing several cuttings from the *Oxford Mail*, and Morse sat down in the pew opposite her and carefully unfolded the thin sheets. The first cutting was dated Tuesday, 27 September of the previous year:

CHURCHWARDEN MURDERED DURING SERVICE

WHILST the congregation was singing the last hymn, Mr H. A. Josephs was last night stabbed to death in the vestry of St Frideswide's Church, Cornmarket.

Chief Inspector Bell of the Oxford City Police, who is in charge of the murder enquiries, told our reporter that Mr Josephs, one of the two churchwardens at St Frideswide's, had just taken the collection and was almost certainly counting it as he was attacked.

When the police arrived there was no sign of the collection-plate itself or of the money. Inspector Bell said that if robbery had been the sole motive the murder was doubly tragic, since only a dozen or so people had attended the evening service, and the offertory could have amounted at most only to about two or three pounds.

Several members of the congregation had heard sounds of some disturbance at the back of the church, but no one suspected that anything was seriously wrong until Mr Josephs had shouted for help. The vicar,

the Reverend L. Lawson, immediately suspended the service and summoned the police and the ambulance, but Mr Josephs died before either could arrive.

The knife used by the murderer was of a dull, golden colour, cast in the shape of a crucifix, with the blade honed to a razor sharpness. Police are anxious to hear from anyone who has knowledge of such a knife.

Mr Josephs, aged 50, was married and lived in Port-Meadow Drive, Wolvercote. He came to Oxford after the bar brilliantly pushed over left-foot shot was serving as a regular officer in the Royal Marine Commandos and saw active service in Malaya. Until two years ago he worked for the Inland Revenue Department. There are no children. The inquest is to be held next Monday.

Morse quickly read through the article again, for there were a couple of things, quite apart from the extraordinary typography of the last paragraph, that puzzled him slightly.

'Did you know him very well?'

'Pardon?' The woman stopped her scrubbing and looked across at him.

'I said did you know Josephs well.'

A flicker of unease in those brown eyes? Had she heard him the first time?

'Yes, I knew him quite well. He was a churchwarden here. It says so, doesn't it?'

Morse let it go and turned his attention to the second cutting, dated Tuesday, 4 October:

INQUEST RIDDLE

THE inquest on Mr H. A. Josephs, who was stabbed to death last week at St Frideswide's Church, was adjourned yesterday after a twenty-minute hearing, but not before the court had heard some startling new evidence. The post-mortem report on Mr Josephs showed that a lethal quantity of morphine was present in the stomach, but it seemed clear that it was the stab-wound which had been the immediate cause of death.

Earlier, Mr Paul Morris, of 3 Home Close, Kidlington, had given evidence of formal identification. He had been the organist during the service and was in fact playing the last hymn when Mr Josephs was murdered.

Another witness, Miss Ruth Rawlinson, of 14 Manning Terrace, Summertown, said that she heard noises coming from the vestry during the singing of the last hymn, and had turned to see Mr Josephs call out and slump beside the vestry curtains.

Chief Inspector Bell, of the Oxford City Police, informed the Coroner that he was as yet unable to re-

port on any firm develop-
ments in the case but that
enquiries were proceeding.
The Coroner extended his
deepest sympathy to Mrs
Brenda Josephs, the de-
ceased's wife.

The funeral service will be
held at St Frideswide's on
Thursday at 2.30 p.m.

The narrative was bald, but interesting enough,
wasn't it? What was morphine doing in the poor
beggar's innards? Somebody must have wanted him out
of the way pretty badly, and that somebody had so far
got away with it and was still walking around – probably
walking around the streets of Oxford – a free man. Or
a free woman perhaps, he reminded himself, as he
glanced across the aisle.

Morse looked about him with renewed interest. He
was actually sitting a few yards from the scene of the
crime, and he tried to imagine it all: the organ playing,
the few members of the congregation standing, heads
bowed over their hymn books – one minute, though!
Where was the organ? He got to his feet and walked up
the broad, shallow steps of the chancel. Yes. There it
was, on the left-hand side behind two rows of choir-
stalls, with a blue curtain stretched across in front of it
to hide the body of the organist; and a mirror, too, fixed
just above the high top manual, so that, however much
he was concealed from the view of all others, the organist himself could keep an observant eye on the minister
and the choir – and on the congregation as well, if he
wanted to. If you swung the mirror round a bit ...
Morse sat himself behind the curtain on the organ-seat
and looked into it. He could see the choir-stalls behind

him and the main body of the chancel. Mm. Then, like a nervous learner before starting off on a driving test, he began adjusting the mirror, finding that it moved easily and noiselessly: up and down, right and left – wherever he wanted it. First, to the right and slightly down, and he found himself looking straight at the intricately woven gold design on the front of the green altar-cloth; then to the left and down, and he could see the head and shoulders of the cleaning woman, her elbows circling sedulously over the soapy suds; then further still to the left and up slightly, almost as far as the mirror would go – and Morse suddenly stopped, a needle-sharp sensation momentarily flashing across his temples. So very clearly he could now see the front curtains of the vestry, could even see the fold where they would swing back to let the choir on its way; the fold where they had once opened – perhaps only slightly? – to reveal the figure of a man shouting desperately above the swell of the organ notes, a man with a knife stuck firm and deep through his back, a man with only a moment or two to live . . . What if the organist – Morris, wasn't it? – had actually been looking at the vestry curtains during those fateful, fatal seconds? What if he'd seen something? Something like . . .

The rattle of the pail brought his airborne fancies down to earth. What possible reason could Morris have had for turning the mirror to such an improbable angle as he played the last hymn? Forget it! He turned on the smooth bench and looked over the curtain. The cleaner was packing up by the look of things, and he hadn't read the other cuttings yet. But before he got off the bench his mind again took wing and was floating as effortlessly as a kittiwake keeling over the cliffs. It was the organ-curtain . . . He was himself a man of just over medium height, but even someone three or four inches taller would be fairly well concealed behind that curtain. The back of the head would be showing, but little else; and if Morris was a small man he would have been almost completely concealed. Indeed, as far as the choir and congregation were concerned, the organist might . . . might not have been Morris at all!

He walked down the chancel steps. 'Mind if I keep these cuttings? I'll post them back to you, of course.'

The woman shrugged. 'All right.' It seemed a matter of little concern to her.

'I don't know your name, I'm afraid,' began Morse, but a small middle-aged man had entered the church and was walking briskly towards them.

'Morning, Miss Rawlinson.'

Miss Rawlinson! One of the witnesses at the inquest. Well, well! And the man who had just come in was doubtless Morris, the other witness, for he had already seated himself at the organ, where a few switches were clicked on and where a whirr of some hidden power was followed by a series of gruff bass blasts, as if the instrument were breaking wind.

'As I say, I can post 'em,' said Morse, 'or pop 'em through your letter-box. 14 Manning Road, isn't it?'

'Manning *Terrace*.'

'Oh yes.' Morse smiled at her good-naturedly. 'Memory's not what it was, I'm afraid. They tell me we lose about 30,000 brain cells a day once we're past thirty.'

'Just as well we all have plenty to start with, Inspector.' There was perhaps just a hint of mockery in her steady eyes, but Morse's lightheartedness had evoked no reciprocal response.

'I'll just have a quick word with Mr Morris before—'

'That's not Mr Morris.'

'Pardon?'

'That's Mr Sharpe. He was deputy organist when Mr Morris was here.'

'And Mr Morris isn't here any longer?' said Morse slowly.

She shook her head.

'Do you know where he's gone?'

Did she? Again there seemed some hesitation in the eyes. 'N-no, I don't. He's left the district. He left last October.'

'Surely he must have—'

'He left his post at the school and, well, he just went.'

'But he must have—'

She picked up the bucket and prepared to leave. 'Nobody knows where he went.'

But Morse sensed she was lying. 'It's your duty to tell me, you know, if you've any idea at all where he went.' He spoke now with a quiet authority, and a flush arose in the woman's cheeks.

'It's nothing really. Just that he – he left at the same time as someone else. That's all.'

'And it was fairly easy to put two and two together?'

She nodded. 'Yes. You see, he left Oxford the same week as Mrs Josephs.'

58

CHAPTER EIGHT

MORSE LEFT THE church and strolled over to the snack bar.

'One coffee, please,' he said to the girl lounging by the pay-desk.

'If you go an' si' down, one of the girls'll come.'

'Oh.' It all seemed a roundabout business.

He sat and stared abstractedly through the large window, flecked now with drizzle, and watched the people walking to and fro along Cornmarket. Immediately opposite him, fencing in the church and the churchyard, were the sharply pointed, black-painted railings of St Frideswide's, against which a bearded, damp-looking tramp was leaning uncertainly, a bottle of something hanging loosely in his lefthand.

'Order, please?' It was the same waitress.

'You just had it,' snapped Morse.

'I'm sorry, sir, bu'—'

'Forget it, luv.'

He left and walked back across the street.

'How goes it, brother?'

The tramp looked at Morse warily through an incongruous pair of dark sunglasses: unsolicited interest in his well-being was quite clearly no everyday occurrence. 'Could do wiv a cup o' tea, guv.'

Morse pushed a couple of ten-pence pieces into a surprisingly clean hand. 'Do you usually stand here?'

'Nah. Usually be'ind Brasenose College. Makes a change, though, don't it?'

'Some nice kind people come out of the church, do they?'

'Sometimes.'

'You know the minister here?'

'Nah. Tell yer to push off, like as not, this one. Knew the other one, though. Real gent he was, guv. Sometimes 'e'd take yer down to the vicarage an' give yer a real square meal, 'e would.'

'Is he the one who died?'

The tramp looked at Morse with what could have been a glint of suspicion behind the dark lenses, and took a swig on the bottle. 'Christ, you can say that again, mister.' He shuffled along the railings towards Carfax, and was gone.

Morse crossed the road yet again, and walked past the snack bar, past a well-stocked bicycle-shop, past the cinema, and then turned left into the curving sweep of Beaumont Street. Momentarily he debated between the Ashmolean, just opposite on his right, and the Randolph, immediately on his left. It wasn't a fair contest.

The cocktail-bar was already quite full as Morse waited rather impatiently for a group of Americans to sort out their gins and tarnics. The barmaid wore a low-cut dress and Morse watched with what he told himself was a fascinated indifference as she finally leaned forward over the beer pump to pull his order. She was too young, though – no more than twenty-odd – and Morse was beginning to formulate the philosophy that men were attracted to women of roughly their own age – well, give or take ten years or so either way.

He sat down, savoured his beer, and took out cutting number three from his pocket. It was dated Wednesday, 19 October.

TRAGIC FALL FROM CHURCH TOWER

YESTERDAY morning the Reverend Lionel Lawson fell to his death from the tower of St Frideswide's Church in Cornmarket. Only ten minutes earlier he had conducted the regular 7.30 a.m. Communion Service, and two members of the congregation were among the first to discover the tragedy.

The church tower, formerly a favourite viewing-point for tourists, has been closed to the public for the last two years as signs of crumbling have become evident in the stone fabric on the north side. But the tower was not considered unsafe, and only a year ago workmen had been up to check the leads.

Mr Lawson, a bachelor, aged 41, had been vicar of St Frideswide's for almost eleven years. He will be remembered above all, perhaps, for his social work, since in addition to his deep involvement with the church's flourishing youth activities he invariably took a compassionate interest in the plight of the homeless, and there can be few regular down-and-outs in Oxford who have not at some time or another enjoyed his hospitality.

As a churchman he made no apologies for his High Anglican views, and although his strongly voiced hostility towards the ordination of women was not universally popular his large and loyal congregation will mourn the death of a dear friend and pastor. He studied theology at Christ's College, Cambridge, and later at St Stephen's House, Oxford.

Only last month Mr H. A. Josephs, churchwarden of St Frideswide's, was found stabbed to death in the church vestry.

Mm. Morse looked at the last sentence again and wondered why the reporter had deemed it his duty to stick it in. Wasn't there a bit too much of that *post hoc, propter hoc* suspicion about it? Yet a murder followed very shortly afterwards by a suicide was by no means uncommon, and the reporter would hardly have been the only one to suspect some causal connection. For if Lawson had somehow managed to murder Josephs, then it was surely only honourable and proper for a servant of the Lord to be stricken so sorely in conscience as to chuck himself off the nearest or most convenient pinnacle, was it not?

Morse drained his beer, fiddled in his pockets for some more change, and looked vaguely around him. A woman had just walked up to the bar and he studied her back view with growing interest. A good deal nearer his own age than the barmaid, certainly: black-leather, knee-length boots; slim figure; tight-belted, light-fawn raincoat; spotted red headscarf. Nice. On her own, too.

Morse sauntered up beside her and heard her order a dry Martini; and the thought crossed his mind that all he had to do was to pay for her drink, ask her over to his lonely corner, and talk of this and that in a quiet, unassuming, intelligent, fascinating, masterly way. And then – who knows? But a middle-aged customer had risen from his seat and clapped a hand on her shoulder.

'I'll get that Ruth, love. You sit down.'

Miss Rawlinson unfastened her headscarf and smiled. Then, as she appeared to notice Morse for the first time, the smile was gone. She nodded – almost curtly, it seemed – and turned away.

After his third pint, Morse left the cocktail-bar and from the foyer rang through to the City Police Station. But Chief Inspector Bell was on holiday, he was told – in Spain.

It was a long time since Morse had undertaken any extended exercise, and he decided on impulse to walk up to north Oxford. Only half an hour, if he stepped it out. As if to deride his decision, bus after bus passed him: Cutteslowe buses, Kidlington buses, and the eternally empty Park and Ride buses, subsidized at huge cost by the City Fathers in the vain hope of persuading shoppers to leave their cars on the outskirts. But Morse kept walking.

As he came up to the Marston Ferry crossroads he watched, almost mesmerized, as a north-bound car pulled out of the inside lane into the path of an overtaking motor-cycle. The rider was thrown slithering to the other side of the road where his white helmet hit the kerb with a sickening thwack, and where the nearside wheel of a south-bound lorry, for all its squealing brake-power, ran over the man's pelvis with an audible crunch.

Others on that scene showed, perhaps for the first time in their lives, a desperate courage born of the hour: figures knelt by the dying man, and coats were laid over his crushed body; a young man with greasy shoulder-length hair took upon himself the duties of a traffic policeman; a doctor was on his way from the Summertown Health Centre on the corner; the ambulance and police were already being summoned.

But Morse felt his stomach tighten and twist in a spasm of pain. A light sweat had broken out on his forehead, and he thought he was going to vomit as he averted his eyes and hurried away. The sense of his inadequacy and cowardice disgusted him, but the physical sickness prowling in his bowels drove him on, farther and farther up the road, past the Summertown shops, and at last to his home. Even the Levite had taken a quick look before passing by on the other side.

What it was about road accidents that threw him so completely off balance, Morse had never quite been able to understand. Many a time he had been on the scene of a murder, and examined a brutally mutilated corpse. With an ugly distaste, certainly; but with nothing worse. Why was it, then? Perhaps it was something to do with the difference between death and the *process* of dying, certainly of dying in a writhing agony after a road accident. Yes, it was the *accidental* angle of things; the flukey, fortuitous nature of it all; the 'if only' of being just a few yards, just a few inches even, from safety; of being just a second, just a fraction of a second, earlier – or later. It was all that Lucretian business about the random concourse of the atoms, hurtling headlong through the boundless void, colliding occasionally like billiard balls, colliding like a car against a motor-bike. All so pointless, somehow; all so cruelly haphazard. Occasionally Morse considered the ever-decreasing possibility of having a family himself, and he knew that he might be able to face some terrible illness in those he loved; but never an accident.

In the distance sounded the urgent two-toned siren of an ambulance, like some demented mother wailing for her children.

Morse picked up his one pint of milk and shut the door of his bachelor flat behind him. Not the best of starts to a holiday! He selected Richard Strauss's *Vier Letzte Lieder*, but a sudden thought flashed through his mind, and he put the record down again. In the Randolph he had quickly read through cutting number four, the newspaper account of the inquest on Lawson; little of interest there, he'd thought. But had he been right? He read it through again now. The poor fellow had obviously been a terrible sight, his body violently crushed by his fall, his skull – Yes! That is what had clicked in Morse's mind as he had lifted the lid of the record-player. If he himself had been unwilling to look at the face of a dying motor-cyclist, had those two witnesses looked as closely as they should have done at that sadly shattered skull? All he needed now was a little information from the official report of the coroner's hearing; and, knowing the coroner very well, he could get that little information straight away – that very afternoon.

Ten minutes later he was asleep.

CHAPTER NINE

AVOIDING THE MAN'S look, Ruth Rawlinson finished her second Martini and stared at the slice of lemon at the bottom of her glass.

'Another?'

'No, I mustn't. Really. I've had two already.'

'Go on! Enjoy yourself! We only live once, you know.'

Ruth smiled sadly. It was just the sort of thing her mother kept saying: 'You're missing out on life, Ruthie dear. Why don't you try to meet more people? Have a good time?' Her mother! Her grumbling, demanding, crippled mother. But still her mother; and she, Ruth, her only child: forty-one years old (almost forty-two), a virgin until so recently, and then not memorably deflowered.

'Same again, then?' He was on his feet, her glass held high in his hand.

Why *not?* She felt pleasantly warm somewhere deep down inside her, and she could always go to bed for a few hours when she got home. Monday afternoon was her mother's weekly bridge session, and nothing short of a nuclear attack on north Oxford could ever disturb those four mean old women as they grubbed for penalty points and overtricks at the small green-baize table in the back room.

'You'll have me drunk if you're not careful,' she said.

'What do you think I'm trying to do?'

She knew him fairly well now, and she watched him as he stood at the bar in his expensively cut suit: a few years older than herself, with three teenage children and a charming, intelligent, trusting wife. And he wanted *her*.

Yet for some reason she didn't want him. She couldn't quite bear the thought of being intimate with him – not (she reminded herself) that she really knew what intimacy was all about . . .

Her eyes wandered round the room once more, in particular to a point in the farthest corner of the room. But Morse had gone now, and for some unfathomable reason she knew she had wanted him to stay – just to *be* there. She'd recognized him, of course, as soon as she'd walked in, and she had been conscious of his presence all the time. Could she get into bed with *him?* It was his eyes that fascinated her; bluey-grey, cold – and yet somehow vulnerable and lost. She told herself not to be so silly; told herself she was getting drunk.

As she slowly sipped the third Martini, her companion was busily writing something on the back of a beer-mat.

'Here we are, Ruth. Be honest with me – please!'

She looked down at what he had written:

Tick the box which
in your opinion is nearest

> to your inclinations. Will
> you let me take you to bed
>
> | this week? | ❑ |
> | next week? | ❑ |
> | this year? | ❑ |
> | next year? | ❑ |
> | sometime? | ❑ |
> | never? | ❑ |

It made her smile, but she shook her head slowly and helplessly. 'I can't answer that. You know I can't.'

'You mean it's "never"?'

'I didn't say that. But – you *know* what I mean. You're married, and I know your wife. I respect her. Surely—'

'Just tick one of the boxes. That's all.'

'But—'

'But you'll disappoint me if you tick the last one, is that it? Go on, then. Disappoint me. But be honest about it, Ruth. At least I shall know where I stand.'

'I like you – you know that. But—'

'You've got plenty of choice.'

'What if none of the answers is the right one?'

'One of 'em must be right.'

'No.' She took out her own pen and wrote in a single word before 'sometime': the word 'perhaps'.

Unlike Morse, she didn't sleep that afternoon. She felt fresh and alive, and would have done a few odd jobs in the garden but for the persistent drizzle. Instead she revised the lines for her part in the play. Friday was looming frighteningly near, and the cast was rehearsing at 7.30 p.m. that evening. Not that a tuppenny-ha'penny play at a church social was all that grand; but she was never happy about doing even the smallest things half-heartedly – and they always had a good audience.

Morse himself woke up with a shudder and a grunt at 3 p.m., and slowly focused upon life once more. The newspaper cuttings still lay on the arm of his chair, and he collected them together and put them back in their envelope. Earlier in the day he had allowed things to get out of perspective. But no longer. He was on holiday, and he was going to *have* a holiday. From his bookshelf he hooked out a thick volume; and just as the Romans used to do it with the Sibylline Books, just as the fundamentalists still do it with the Holy Scriptures – so did Morse do it with the *A.A. Hotels of Britain*. He closed his eyes, opened the book at random, and stuck his index finger half-way down the left-hand page. There she was. Derwentwater: *Swiss Lodore Hotel*. Keswick, three miles S. along the . . . He rang the number immediately. Yes, they had a single room with private bath. How long for? Four or five nights, perhaps. All right. He'd be leaving straight away, and be there about – oh, about nine or ten. Good.

Evesham – about an hour, if he was lucky. Along the old Worcester Road. M5 and M6 – 80 m.p.h. in the fast lane. Easy! He'd be there in time for a slap-up meal and a bottle of red wine. Lovely. *That's* what holidays were all about.

CHAPTER TEN

THE REVEREND KEITH MEIKLEJOHN exuded a sort of holy enthusiasm as he stood at the door of the church hall. Obviously there was going to be a big audience, and in between the unctuous Good evenings, how nice of you to comes, he debated the wisdom of fetching some of the old chairs from the store-room. It was only 7.20 p.m., but already the hall was two-thirds full. He knew why, of course: it was the Sunday School infant classes' tap-dance troupe, with its gilt-edged guarantee of attracting all the mums and aunts and grandmas. 'Hello, Mrs Walsh-Atkins. How very nice of you to come. Just a few seats left near the front...' He despatched two reluctant choirboys for the extra chairs, and was ready with his beam of ecclesiastical bonhomie for the next arrival. 'Good evening, sir. How nice of you to come. Are you a visitor to Oxford or—?'

'No, I live here.'

The newcomer walked into the hall and sat down at the back, a slightly sour expression on his face. He gave five pence to the pretty pigtailed girl who came up to him and stuck the programme in his pocket. What a day! Almost six hours from Keswick to the Evesham exit: single-line traffic north of Stoke; a multiple pile-

70

up just after Birmingham, with all lanes closed for almost an hour on the south-bound carriageway; flood warnings flashing for the last thirty miles and the juggernaut lorries churning up spray like speed-boats ... And what a so-called holiday! On fine days (he had little doubt) the view from his bedroom at the Swiss Lodore would have been most beautiful; but the mist had driven down from the encircling hills, and it was as much as he could do to spot the grass on the lawn below his window, with its white chairs and tables – all deserted. Some of his fellow-guests had taken to their cars and driven (presumably) in search of some less-bedraggled scenery; but the majority had just sat around and read paperback thrillers, played cards, gone swimming in the heated indoor pool, eaten, drunk, talked intermittently, and generally managed to look rather less miserable than Morse did. He could find no passably attractive women over-anxious to escape their hovering husbands, and the few who sat unattended in the cocktail-lounge were either too plain or too old. In his bedroom Morse found a leaflet on which was printed Robert Southey's 'How the Waters Come Down at Lodore'; but he felt that even a poet laureate had seldom sunk to such banality. And anyway, after three days, Morse knew only too well how the waters came down at Lodore: they came down in bucketfuls, slanting incessantly in sharp lines from a leaden sky.

On Friday (it was 7 April) *The Times* was brought into his room with his early-morning tea; and after looking at the weekend weather forecast he decided to leave immediately after breakfast. It was as he was taking out his chequebook at the reception desk that the folded white leaflet fluttered to the floor: he had pocketed it absent-mindedly from the literature set out on the table at the entrance to St Frideswide's, but it was only now that he read it.

CONCERT

At the Church Hall St Aldates
Friday, April 7th, at 7.30 p.m.

TAP-DANCE TROUPE (Sunday School)
GILBERT & SULLIVAN MEDLEY (Church Choir)
A VICTORIAN MELODRAMA (Drama Group)
Entrance Fee 20p. Programme 5p.

ALL WELCOME
(Proceeds in aid of the Tower Restoration Fund)

It was that last line, pregnant with possibilities, that had monopolized Morse's thoughts as he drove the Lancia south. Were the crenellations really crumbling after all? *Had* they crumbled, when Lawson looked his last over the familiar landmarks of the city? Whenever possible, juries were keen to steer away from 'suicide' verdicts, and if the tower had been at all unsafe the point would have been a crucial one. What Morse really needed was the coroner's report: it would all be there. And it was to the coroner's office that Morse had immediately driven when he finally reached Oxford at 4.30 p.m.

The report, apart from the detailed descriptions of Lawson's multiple mutilations, was vaguer than Morse had hoped, with no mention whatsoever of the parapet from which Lawson had plummeted to earth. Yet there was one section of the report that firmly gripped his interest, and he read it through again. 'Mrs Emily Walsh-Atkins, after giving formal evidence of identification, said that she had remained alone for some minutes in the church after the service. She then waited for about five minutes outside the church, where she had arranged to be picked up by taxi: the service had finished slightly earlier than usual. At about 8.10 a.m. she heard a terrible thud in the churchyard and had looked round to find Lawson's body spread-eagled on the railings. Fortunately two police officers had soon appeared on the scene and Mr Morris' (Morris!) 'had taken her back inside the church to sit down and recover ...' Morse knew that he would have little mental rest until he had seen Mrs W.-A., and it was that lady who was the immediate cause of his attendance at the Church Concert. (Was she the *only* reason, Morse?) He had just missed her at the Home for Ageing Gentlefolk, but they knew where she had gone.

Meiklejohn had finished his long-winded, oily introduction, the lights had been switched off, and now the stage curtains were jerkily wound back to reveal the Tap-Dance Troupe in all its bizarre glory. For Morse the whole thing was embarrassingly amusing; and he was quite unprepared for the wild applause which

73

COLIN DEXTER

greeted the final unsynchronized kneelings of the
eleven little girls, plumed plastic headgear and all,
who for three minutes or so had braved inadequate
rehearsal, innate awkwardness, and the appallingly
incompetent accompaniment of the pianist. To make
matters worse, the troupe had started with a comple-
ment of twelve, but one small child had turned left
instead of right at a crucial point in the choreography,
and had promptly fled to the wings, her face collapsing
in tearful misery. Yet still the audience clapped and
clapped, and was not appeased until the appearance of
the troupe's instructress, alias the piano player, leading
by the hand the unfortunate, but now shyly smiling,
little deserter – the latter greeted by all as if she were a
prima ballerina from the Sadler's Wells.

The Gilbert and Sullivan selections were excellently
sung, and Morse realized that the St Frideswide's choir
contained some first-rate talent. This time, fortunately,
the piano was in the hands of an infinitely more able
executant – Mr Sharpe, no less, former deputy to Mr
Morris (that name again!). Morris . . . the man who had
been on the scene when Josephs was murdered; had
been on the scene, too, when Lawson was – when Lawson
was found. Surely, surely, it shouldn't be at all difficult to
trace him? Or to trace Mrs Brenda Josephs? They must
be somewhere; must be earning some money; must have
insurance numbers; must have a house . . . With clinical
precision the choir cut off the last chord from the finale
of *The Mikado*, and their turn was complete – greeted by
appreciative if comparatively short-lived applause.

It took a good five minutes for the Victorian melo-

74

drama to materialize; minutes during which could be heard the squeaking and bumping of furniture, during which the curtains were twice prematurely half opened, and during which Morse once more looked through the coroner's digest on Lawson's death. There was this fellow Thomas's evidence, for example: 'He had just parked his car in St Giles and was walking down towards Broad Street when he noticed someone on the tower of St Frideswide's. He could not recall seeing anyone standing there before, but it was not unusual to see people looking out over Oxford from St Mary's in the High, or from Carfax tower. He thought that the figure was dressed in black, looking down, his head leaning over the parapet . . .' That was all, really. Only later had he heard of the morning's tragedy and had reluctantly rung up the police – at his wife's suggestion. Not much there, but the man must have been the very last person (Morse supposed) to see Lawson alive. Or was he? He might just have been the first – no, the second – person to see Lawson *dead*. Morse found the key words again: 'looking down, his head leaning over the parapet . . .' How high *were* those parapets? No more than three feet or so, surely. And why bring Lawson's head into it? Why not just 'leaning over the parapet'? And why 'looking down'? Was a man about to leap to his death likely to be all that worried about the place he was going to land? A minister, surely – more than most of his fellow-mortals – might be expected to seek a little consolation from more ethereal realms, whatever the depths of his despair. But if . . . if Lawson had been dead already; if someone had—

The melodrama was under way at last, and in Morse's view a more crudely amateurish production could seldom have merited a public presentation. The play appeared to have been chosen to embrace the largest possible cast, and to allow to all of its participants the briefest possible exposure on the boards, in order to minimize their breathtaking incompetences. The bearded one-armed hero, who at least had learned his lines and spoke them audibly, clumped around in a pair of squeaky army boots, and at one point conducted a crucial telephone conversation by speaking into the ear-piece – of an incongruously modern-looking instrument at that; whilst one of the numerous housemaids was every other line reduced to referring to a copy of her part pasted on the underside of her dustpan. The only feature which prevented the whole thing from degenerating into a farcical shambles was the performance of the heroine herself, a young blonde who acted with a charm and sophistication hopelessly at variance with the pathetically inadequate crew around her. She appeared to know everyone else's part, and covered their lapses and stumbles with impressive aplomb. She even managed, at one stage, to prevent one of the butlers (blind fool! thought Morse) from tripping over an intervening chair as he carried in her ladyship's tea. Mercifully many of the lines (as originally written) must have been extremely amusing, and even voiced by these clowns could elicit a little polite laughter; and when the final curtain drew its veil over the proceedings there seemed to Morse not the slightest sign of embarrassed

relief amongst the audience. Perhaps all church con-
certs were the same.

The Vicar had earlier announced that tea would
be served at the end of the entertainment, and Morse
felt certain that Mrs W.-A. would not be leaving without a cup. All he had to do was find out which one
she was. He looked around in vain for Miss Rawlinson, but it seemed clear that she'd given the evening a
miss – enough of a penance, no doubt, her scrubbing
the pews. But he felt a certain disappointment ...
People were leaving the hall fairly quickly now, but
Morse decided to wait a minute or two. He took out
his programme and looked at it vaguely, but with no
real purpose other than that of seeming not to be
lonely.

'I hope you'll have a cup of tea with us?' Even at this
late stage Meiklejohn was not neglecting his pastoral
duties.

Tea? It had never occurred to Morse that he might
be drinking tea at 9 p.m. 'Yes; thank you. I wonder if
you happen to know a Mrs Walsh-Atkins. I want—'

'Yes, yes. This way. Wonderful concert, wasn't it?'

Morse mumbled inaudibly and followed his guide
into the crowded vestibule where a stout lady was
coaxing a dark-brown liquid from a formidable urn.
Morse took his place in the queue and listened to the
conversation of the two women in front of him.

'You know, it's the fourth time now he's been in one
of them. His dad would have been ever so proud of
him.'

'No one would ever suspect he was blind, would they? Coming on the way he does and all that.'

'It's lots of rehearsal that does it, you know. You have to sort of picture where everything is—'

'Yes. You really must be proud of him, Mrs Kinder.'

'They've asked him to be in the next one, anyway, so he must be all right, mustn't he?'

So the poor devil *had* been blind after all. And learning a part and stepping out on to the stage had probably been about as much of an ordeal as for a sighted person walking through a swamp of crocodiles. Morse suddenly felt very moved, and very humbled. When it came to his turn, he slipped a fifty-pence piece on to the tea-money plate, and hoped that nobody had noticed. He felt oddly out of place there. These were good people, who rejoiced in the simple ties of family and Christian fellowship; who thought of God as a father, and who never in a month of Sabbaths could begin to understand the aberrations of the new theology which thought of Him (if it thought of Him at all) as the present participle of the verb 'to be'. Morse sipped his tea self-consciously, and once more took out his programme and looked for the name of Her Ladyship's butler, whose mother (with what sweet justification!) was feeling so happy and proud. But once again he was interrupted. Meiklejohn was at his shoulder, and with him a diminutive old lady munching a digestive biscuit.

'Mr – er?'

'Morse.'

'You said you wanted to meet Mrs Walsh-Atkins?'

Morse stood above her, acutely conscious of her smallness, and suggested they should sit down back in the hall. He explained who he was, why he was there, and what he wanted to know; and she readily told him of her own part in that dreadful day's events when she'd found Lawson dashed to pieces from the tower, repeating virtually verbatim the words she had used at the inquest.

Nothing! Morse had learned nothing. Yet he thanked her politely and asked if he could fetch her another cup of tea.

'One's enough for me these days, Inspector. But I must have left my umbrella somewhere. If you would be kind enough to . . .'

Morse felt his scalp tingling in the old familiar way. They were seated at a small table at the back of the hall, and there was the umbrella, large as life, lying diagonally across it. There could be little doubt about it: *the old lady must be going blind.*

'Do you mind me asking how old you are, Mrs Walsh-Atkins?'

'Can you keep a secret, Inspector?'

'Yes.'

'So can I,' she whispered.

Whether Morse's decision to patronize the cocktail-lounge of the Randolph was determined by his thirst, or by some wayward wish to find out if Miss Rawlinson might be there, he didn't stop to think. But he recognized no one, left after only one pint, and caught a bus outside the Taylorian. Back home, he poured himself a large neat whisky and put on *Vier Letzte Lieder*. Marvellous. 'Melismatic', as it said on the sleeve ...

It was time for an early night, and he hung up his jacket in the hallway. The programme stuck out of one of the pockets and, third time lucky, he opened it and read it.

'Her Ladyship's Butler – Mr John Kinder.' And then his pulse raced as he looked at the top of the cast: 'Her Ladyship, the Hon. Amelia Barker-Barker – Miss Ruth Rawlinson.'

CHAPTER ELEVEN

MEDIUMS AND CLAIRVOYANTS claim enhanced scope for their talents if they can be physically present in a room where the absent ones – the missing or the plain dead – may have left a few stray emanations behind. Murderers, likewise, have the reputation of nursing an uncontrollable urge to revisit the scene of death, and on Sunday morning Morse found himself wondering whether the murderer of Josephs had ever set foot in St Frideswide's again since the day of his crime. He thought that the answer was probably 'yes', and it was one of the very few positive thoughts he had managed to generate since Friday evening. Somehow his mind had gone completely stale, and on the Saturday he had firmly resolved to abandon all idea of further investigation into a mysterious affair which was none of his business anyway. In the morning he had consulted the Sibyl once more, but had drawn the line at Inverness. In the afternoon he had wasted two idle hours in front of the television set watching the racing from Doncaster. He was restless and bored: there were so many books he could read, so many records he could play – and yet he could summon up no enthusiasm for anything. What *did* he want? His listless mood persisted through to Sunday morning, when not even the few erotic titbits in the *News of the World* could cheer him. He sprawled gloomily in his armchair, his eyes vaguely scanning the multi-coloured spines along the bookshelves. Baudelaire might match his mood, perhaps? What was that line about the prince in 'La Fleurs du Mal'? 'Riche, mais impuissant, jeune et pourtant très vieux . . .' And quite suddenly Morse felt better. Bloody nonsense! He was neither impotent nor senile – far from it! It was time for action.

He rang the number and she answered.

'Hello?'

'Miss Rawlinson?'

'Speaking.'

'You may not remember me. I – I met you in St Frideswide's last Monday.'

'I remember.'

'I was – er – thinking of going to church this morning—'

'Our church, you mean?'

'Yes.'

'You'd better get a move on – it starts at half-past ten.'

'Oh, I see. Well – er – thank you very much.'

'You're very interested in us all of a sudden, Inspector.' There was a suggestion of friendly amusement in her voice, and Morse wanted to keep her on the phone.

'Did you know I came to the social on Friday evening?'

'Of course.' Morse felt a silly juvenile joy about that 'of course'. Keep going, lad!

'I – er – I didn't see you afterwards. In fact I didn't realize that it was you in the play.'

'Amazing what a blonde wig does, isn't it?'

'Who is it?' Someone called behind her voice.

'Pardon?' said Morse.

'It's all right. That was my mother – asking who you are.'

'Oh, I see.'

'Well, as I say, you'd better hurry up if you're going—'

'Are *you* going? Perhaps I could give you—'

'No, not this morning. Mother's had one of her asthma attacks, and I can't leave her.'

'Oh.' Morse hid his disappointment beneath a cheerful farewell, and said 'Bugger it!' as he cradled the phone. *He* was going, though. It wasn't Ruth Rawlinson he wanted to see. He just wanted to get the feel of the place – to pick up a few of those stray emanations. He told himself that it didn't matter two hoots whether the Rawlinson woman was there or not.

Looking back on his first church attendance for a decade, Morse decided that it was quite an experience. St Frideswide's must, he thought, be about as 'spikey' as they come in the Anglican varieties. True, there was no Peter's Pence at the back of the church, no bulletin from the pulpit proclaiming the infallibility of his Holiness; but in other respects there seemed little that separated the church from the Roman fold. There'd been a sermon, all right, devoted to St Paul's humourless denunciation of the lusts of the flesh, but the whole service had really centred round the Mass. It had not started all that well for Morse who, two minutes late, had inadvertently seated himself in the pew reserved for the churchwarden, and this had necessitated an awkward, whispered exchange as the people knelt to confess their wrongdoings. Fortunately, from his vantage-point at the rear, Morse was able to sit and stand and kneel in concert with the rest, although many of the crossings and genuflections proved equally beyond his reflexes as his inclinations. What amazed him more than anything was the number of the cast assembled around the altar, each purposefully pursuing his part: the celebrant, the deacon, the sub-deacon, the incense-swinger and the boat-boy, the two acolytes and the four torch-bearers, and conducting them all a youngish, mournful-faced master of ceremonies, his hands sticking out horizontally before him in a posture of perpetual prayer. It was almost like a floor show, with everyone so well trained: bowing, crossing, kneeling, rising, with a synchronized discipline which (as Morse saw it) could profitably have been emulated by the Tap-Dance Troupe. To these manoeuvres the equally well-disciplined congregation would match its own reactions, suddenly sitting, as suddenly on its feet again, and occasionally giving mouth to mournful responses. The woman seated next to Morse had soon spotted him for the greenhorn that he was, and was continually thrusting the appropriate page of the proceedings under his nose. She herself sang in a shrill soprano, and was so refined in her diction that the long 'o' vowels issued forth as bleating 'ew's: thus, all the 'O Lords' became 'You Lords', and three times at the start of the service, whilst Meiklejohn walked briskly up and down the aisles sprinkling everything in sight with holy water, she had implored the Almighty to wash her from her sins and make her waiter yea waiter than snew. But there was one thing in Morse's favour – he knew most of the hymns; and at one point he thought he almost managed to drown the 'Hewly Hewly Hewly' on his right. And he learned something, too. From Meiklejohn's notices for the week's forthcoming attractions, it was clear that this Mass business was rather more complicated than he'd imagined. There must be three types, it seemed – 'low', 'high' and 'solemn'; and if, as Morse suspected, the low variety wasn't all that posh, if no choir was involved – no organist even? – then what in heaven's name was Morris doing in church when the unhappy Lawson dashed himself to pieces from the tower? People perhaps did sometimes go to church because they wanted to but ... Anyway, it might be worthwhile finding out a bit more about those different masses. And there was something else; something very suggestive indeed. With the exception of Morse himself, all the congregation partook of the blessed bread and the blessed wine, ushered quietly and firmly to the chancel-rails by that same churchwarden who had so nearly lost his seat, and who – doubtless by venerable tradition – *was himself the very last to receive the sacrament.* Josephs had been churchwarden. Josephs must have been the last to kneel at the chancel-rails on the evening of his death. Josephs had drunk some of the communion wine that same night. And Josephs – so the pathologist said – had finished up with some very queer things in his stomach. Was it possible? Was it possible that Josephs had been poisoned at the altar? From his observation of the final part of the ritual, it was clear to Morse that any celebrant with a chalice in his hands could wreak enormous havoc if he had the inclination to do so, for when he'd finished *he could get rid of every scrap of evidence.* Nor did he need any excuse for this, for it was part of the drill: rinse the cup and wipe it clean and stick it in the cupboard till the next time. Yes. It would be tricky, of course, with all those other stage-hands standing around, like they were now; but on the evening of Josephs' murder, the cast must surely have been very much smaller. Again, it was something worth looking into. There was another snag, though, wasn't there? It seemed that the celebrant himself was called upon to drain the dregs that were left in the chalice, and to do it in front of the whole congregation. But couldn't he just pretend to do that? Pour it down the piscina later? Or, again, there might have been nothing left in the chalice at all . . .

There were so very many possibilities . . . and Morse's fancies floated steeple-high as he walked out of the cool church into the sunlit reach of Cornmarket.

CHAPTER TWELVE

IT WAS SOME relief for Morse to recognize the fair countenance of Reason once more, and she greeted him serenely when he woke, clear-headed, on Monday morning, and told him that it would be no bad idea to have a quiet look at the problem itself before galloping off towards a solution. Basically there were only two possibilities: either Lawson had killed Josephs, and thereafter committed suicide in a not surprising mood of remorse; or else some unknown hand had killed Josephs and then compounded his crime by adding Lawson to his list. Of these alternatives, the first was considerably the more probable; especially so if Josephs had in some way been a threat to Lawson, if the dagger found in Josephs' back had belonged to Lawson, and if Lawson himself had betrayed signs of anxiety or distress in the weeks preceding Josephs' death, as well as in the days that followed it. The trouble was that Morse had no one to talk to. Yet someone, he felt sure, knew a very great deal about his three 'ifs', and at 9.45 a.m. he found himself knocking rather hesitantly on the door of number 14 Manning Terrace. Such hesitancy was attributable to two causes: the first, his natural diffidence in seeming on the face of it to be so anxious to seek out the company of the fair Ruth Rawlinson; the second, the factual uncertainty that he was actually knocking on the right door, for there were two of them, side by side; the one to the left marked 14B, the other 14A. Clearly the house had been divided – fairly recently by the look of it – with one of the doors (Morse presumed) leading directly to the upper storey, the other to the ground floor.

'It's open,' shouted a voice behind 14A. 'I can't get any farther.'

For once, Sod's Law had been inoperative, and he had chosen right. Two steps led up to the narrow carpeted passage which served as a hallway (the stair-case was immediately behind the boarded-up wall to the left, and the conversion had left little room for manoeuvre here), and at the top of these steps sat Mrs Alice Rawlinson in her wheelchair, a rubber-tipped walking-stick held firmly across her lap.

'What d'you want?' Her keen eyes looked up at him sharply.

'I'm sorry to bother you – Mrs Rawlinson, isn't it?'

'I said what d'you want, Inspector.'

Morse's face must have betrayed his astonishment, and the old lady read his thoughts for him. 'Ruthie told me all about you.'

'Oh. I just wondered if—'

'No, she's not. Come in!' She worked her chair round in an expertly economical two-point turn. 'Close the door behind you.'

Morse obeyed quietly, and found himself pushed brusquely aside as he tried to help her through the door at the end of the passage. She waved him to an upright armchair in the neatly furnished sitting-room, and finally came to rest herself only about four feet in front of him. The preliminaries were now completed, and she launched into the attack immediately.

'If you want to cart my daughter off for a dirty week-end, you can't! We'd better get that straight from the start.'

'But Mrs Raw—' He was silenced by a dangerously close wave of the stick. (Belligerent old bitch! thought Morse.)

'I disapprove of many aspects of the youth of today – young men like yourself, I mean – especially their intolerable lack of manners. But I think they're quite right about one thing. Do you know what that is?'

'Look, Mrs Raw—' The rubber ferule was no more than three inches from his nose, and his voice broke off in mid-sentence.

'They've got enough sense to have a bit of sex together before they get married. You agree?'

Morse nodded a feeble acquiescence.

'If you're going to live with someone for fifty years—' She shook her head at the prospect. 'Not that I was married for fifty years . . .' The sharp voice had drifted a few degrees towards a more wistful tone, but recovered immediately. 'As I say, though. You can't have her. I need her and she's my daughter. I have the prior call.'

'I do assure you, Mrs Rawlinson, I hadn't the slightest intention of—'

'She's had men before, you know.'

'I'm not sur—'

89

'She was a very lovely girl, was my Ruthie.' The words were more quietly spoken, but the eyes remained shrewd and calculating. 'She's not a spring chicken any more, though.'

Morse decided it was wise to hold his peace. The old girl was going ga-ga.

'You know what her trouble is?' For a distasteful moment Morse thought her mind must be delving into realms of haemorrhoids and body-odour; but she sat there glaring at him, expecting an answer.

Yes, he knew full well what Ruth Rawlinson's trouble was. Too true, he did. Her trouble was that she had to look after this embittered old battle-axe, day in and day out.

'No,' he said. 'You tell me.'

Her lips curled harshly. 'You're lying to me, Inspector. You know her trouble as well as I do.'

Morse nodded. 'You're right. I don't think I could stick you for very long.'

Now her smile was perfectly genuine. 'You know, you're beginning to sound like the man Ruthie said you were.' (Perhaps, thought Morse, she's not so ga-ga after all?)

'You're a bit formidable sometimes, aren't you?'

'All the time.'

'Would Ruth have married – but for you?'

'She's had her chances – though I didn't think much of her choices.'

'Real chances?'

Her face grew more serious. 'Certainly one.'

'Well.' Morse made as if to rise, but got no farther.

'What was *your* mother like?'

'Loving and kind. I often think of her.'

'Ruthie would have made a good mother.'

'Not too old now, is she?'

'Forty-two tomorrow.'

'Hope you'll bake her a cake,' muttered Morse.

'What?' The eyes blazed now. 'You don't understand, either, do you? Bake? Cook? How can I do anything like that? I can't even get to the front door.'

'Do you try?'

'You're getting impertinent, Inspector. It's time you went.' But as Morse rose she relented. 'No, I'm sorry. Please sit down again. I don't get many visitors. Don't deserve 'em, do I?'

'Does your daughter get many visitors?'

'Why do you ask that?' The voice was sharp again.

'Just trying to be pally, that's all.' Morse had had his fill of the old girl, but her answer riveted him to the chair.

'You're thinking of Josephs, aren't you?'

No, he wasn't thinking of Josephs. 'Yes, I was,' he said, as flatly as his excitement would allow.

'He wasn't her sort.'

'And he had a wife.'

She snorted. 'What's that got to do with it? Just because you're a bachelor yourself—'

'You know that?'

'I know a lot of things.'

'Do you know who killed Josephs?'

She shook her head. 'I don't know who killed Lawson, either.'

'I do, Mrs Rawlinson. He killed himself. You'll find the information in the coroner's report. It's just the same as cricket, you know: if the umpire says you're out, you're out, and you can check it up in the papers next morning.'

'I don't like cricket.'

'Did you like Josephs?'

'No. And I didn't like Lawson, either. He was a homosexual, you know.'

'Really? I hadn't heard of any legal conviction.'

'You're surely not as naïve as you sound, Inspector?'

'No,' said Morse, 'I'm not.'

'I hate homosexuals.' The stick lifted menacingly, gripped tight in hands grown strong from long years in a wheelchair. 'I'd willingly strangle the lot of 'em.'

'And I'd willingly add you to the list of suspects, Mrs Rawlinson, but I'm afraid I can't. You see, if someone killed Lawson, as you're suggesting, that someone must have gone up the church tower.'

'Unless Lawson was killed in the church and *someone else* carried him up there.'

It was an idea; and Morse nodded slowly, wondering why he hadn't thought of it himself.

'I'm afraid I shall have to kick you out, Inspector. It's my bridge day, and I always spend the morning brushing up on a few practice hands.' She was winning every trick here, too, and Morse acknowledged the fact.

Ruth was fixing the lock on her bicycle when she looked up to see Morse standing by the door and her mother sitting at the top of the steps behind him.

'Hello,' said Morse. 'I'm sorry I missed you, but I've

had a nice little chat with your mother. I really came to ask if you'd come out with me tomorrow night.' With her pale face and her untidy hair, she suddenly seemed very plain, and Morse found himself wondering why she'd been so much on his mind. 'It's your birthday, isn't it?'

She nodded vaguely, her face puzzled and hesitant.

'It's all right,' said Morse. 'Your mother says it'll do you good. In fact she's very pleased with the idea, aren't you, Mrs Rawlinson?' (One trick to Morse.)

'Well, I – I'd love to but—'

'No buts about it, Ruthie! As the Inspector says, I think it would do you the world of good.'

'I'll pick you up about seven, then,' said Morse.

Ruth gathered up her string shopping bag, and stood beside Morse on the threshold. 'Thank you, Mother. That was kind of you. But' (turning to Morse) 'I'm sorry. I can't accept your invitation. I've already been asked out by – by someone else.'

Life was a strange business. A few seconds ago she'd looked so ordinary; yet now she seemed a prize just snatched from his grasp, and for Morse the day ahead loomed blank and lonely. As it did, if only he had known, for Ruth.

CHAPTER THIRTEEN

'WHAT THE 'ELL do *you* want?' growled Chief Inspector Bell of the City Police. A fortnight in Malaga which had coincided with a strike of Spanish hotel staff had not brought him home in the sweetest of humours; and the jobs he had gladly left behind him had (as ever) not gone away. But he knew Morse well: they were old sparring partners.

'The Spanish brothels still doing a roaring trade?'

'Had the wife with me, didn't I?'

'Tell me something about this Lawson business.'

'Damned if I will. The case is closed – and it's got nothing to do with you.'

'How're the kids?'

'Ungrateful little buggers. Shan't take 'em again.'

'And the Lawson case is closed?'

'Locked and bolted.'

'No harm in just—'

'I've lost the key.'

'All kids are ungrateful.'

'Especially mine.'

'Where's the file?'

'What d'you want to know?'

'Who killed Josephs, for a start.'

94

'Lawson did.'

'Morse blinked in some surprise. 'You mean that?'

Bell nodded. 'The knife that killed Josephs belonged to Lawson. The woman who charred for him had seen it several times on his desk in the vicarage.'

'But Lawson was nowhere near Josephs when—' Morse stopped in his tracks, and Bell continued.

'Josephs was just about dead when he was knifed: acute morphine poisoning, administered, as they say, at the altar of the Lord. What about that, Morse? Josephs was a churchwarden and he was always last at the altar-rail, and he finished up with some pretty queer things in his belly, right? It seems pretty obvious, then, that . . .' It was a strange experience for Morse. *Déjà vu.* He found himself only half-listening to Bell's explanation – no, not Bell's, his own explanation. '. . . rinse the utensils, wipe 'em clean, stick 'em in the cupboard till next time. Easy! Proof, though? No.'

'But how did Lawson—?'

'He's standing in front of the altar, waiting for the last hymn to finish. He knows Josephs is counting up the collection in the vestry as he always does, and Lawson's expecting him to be lying there unconscious; dead, probably, by now. But suddenly Josephs shouts for help, and Lawson comes swooping down the aisle in his batman outfit—'

'Chasuble,' mumbled Morse.

'—and covers him up under his what's-it; he keeps the others – there aren't many of 'em, anyway – away from the vestry, sends for help, and then when he's alone he sticks his knife in Josephs' back – just to make sure.'

95

'I thought the collection was pinched.'

Bell nodded. 'There was one of those down-and-out fellows at the service: Lawson had helped him occasionally – put him up at the vicarage, given him his old suits – that sort of thing. In fact, this fellow had been kneeling next to Josephs at the communion-rail—'

'So *he* could have put the stuff in the wine.'

Bell shook his head. 'You should go to church occasionally Morse. If he had done, Lawson would have been poisoned just like Josephs, because the minister has to finish off what's left of the wine. You know, I reckon your brain's getting addled in your old age.'

'Someone still pinched the collection,' said Morse feebly.

'Oh yes. And I'm sure it was this fellow – Swan, or something like that, his name was. He just saw the money in the vestry and – well, he just nicked it.'

'I thought you said Lawson kept all the others outside.'

'For a start, yes. He had to.'

Morse looked far from convinced, but Bell sailed happily on. 'A reasonably well-educated fellow, by all accounts. We put out a description of him, of course, but . . . They all look much of a muchness, those sort of fellows: none of 'em shave or get their hair cut. Anyway, he'd only be up for petty larceny if we found him. Two or three quid, at the outside – that's all he got. Funny, really. If he'd had a chance to go through Josephs' pockets, he'd have found nearly a hundred.'

Morse whistled softly. 'That means that Lawson couldn't have gone through his pockets, either, doesn't it? They tell me the clergy aren't exactly overpaid these days, and Lawson couldn't exactly have been rolling in—'

Bell smiled. 'Lawson was hellish lucky to get the chance to knife him – let alone go through his pockets. But that's neither here nor there. Lawson *was* rolling in it. Until a few weeks before he died, his deposit account at the bank stood at over £30,000.'

This time Morse's whistle was loud and long. 'Until a few weeks . . .?'

'Yes. Then he took his money out. Almost all of it.'

'Any idea—?'

'Not really.'

'What did the bank manager have to tell you?'

'He wasn't allowed to tell me anything.'

'What *did* he tell you?'

'That Lawson had told him he was going to make an anonymous donation to some charity, and that's why he wanted cash.'

'Some bloody donation!'

'Some people are more generous than others, Morse.'

'Did he take out all this cash before, or after, Josephs was murdered?'

For the first time Bell seemed slightly uneasy. 'Before, actually.'

Morse was silent for a short while. The new pieces of evidence were not fitting at all neatly. 'What was Lawson's motive for killing Josephs?'

'Blackmail, perhaps?'

'Josephs had some hold over him?'

'Something like that.'

'Any ideas?'

'There were a few rumours.'

'Well?'

'I prefer facts.'

'Was Lawson buggering the choirboys?'

'You always did put things so nicely.'

'What facts, then?'

'Lawson had made out a cheque for £250 to Josephs a couple of weeks earlier.'

'I see,' said Morse slowly. 'What else?'

'Nothing.'

'Can I look through the files?'

'Certainly not.'

Morse spent the next hour in Bell's office looking through the files.

Considering the limited number of personnel available, the investigations into the deaths of Josephs and Lawson had been reasonably thorough, although there were a few surprising omissions. It would have been interesting, for example, to read the evidence of every single member of the congregation present when Josephs died, but it seemed that several of them had been only casual visitors – two American tourists amongst them – and Lawson had quite innocently informed them that perhaps they needn't stay. Understandable, no doubt – but very careless and quite improper. Unless . . . unless, thought Morse, Lawson wasn't over-anxious for all of them to tell the police what they'd seen? It was sometimes just those little details, just those little inconsistencies . . . Of the statements that were available, all cleanly set out, all neatly typed, only one arrested Morse's attention: the one, duly signed in the dithery hand of Mrs Emily Walsh-Atkins, attesting to the identification of Lawson.

'Did you interview this old girl?' asked Morse, pushing the statement across the table.

'Not personally, no.'

So far Bell had shown himself a jump or two ahead all round the course, but Morse thought he now saw himself coming through pretty fast on the rails. 'She's as blind as a bloody bat, did you know that? What sort of identification do you think this is? I met her the other night and—'

Bell looked up slowly from the report he'd been reading. 'Are you suggesting that fellow we found draped over the railings *wasn't* Lawson?'

'All I'm suggesting, Bell, is that you must have been pretty hard up for witnesses if you had to rely on her. As I say, she's—'

'She's as blind as a bat – almost your own words, Morse; and, if I remember rightly, exactly the words of my own Sergeant Davies. But don't be too hard on the old dear for wanting to get into the act – it was the most exciting thing that ever happened to her.'

'But that doesn't mean—'

'Hold your horses, Morse! We only needed one identification for the coroner's court, so we only *had* one. Right? But we had another witness all ready, and I don't think *he's* as blind as a bat. If he is, he must have one helluva job when he play the organ in six sharps.'

'Oh, I see.' But Morse didn't see. What was Morris doing at St Frideswide's that morning? Ruth Rawlinson would know, of course. Ruth ... Huh! Her birthday today, and she would be all dolled up for a date with some lecherous lout ...

'Why was Morris at church that morning?'

'It's a free country, Morse. Perhaps he just wanted to go to church.'

'Did you find out if he was playing the organ?'

'As a matter of fact, I did, yes.' Bell was thoroughly enjoying himself again – something he'd seldom experienced in Morse's company before. 'He *was* playing the organ.'

After Morse was gone, Bell stared out of his office window for several minutes. Morse was a clever beggar. One or two questions he'd asked had probed a bit deeper than was comfortable; but most cases had a few ragged ends here and there. He tried to switch his mind over to another channel but he felt hot and sticky; felt he might be sickening for something.

Ruth Rawlinson had lied to Morse – well, not exactly lied. She did have an assignation on the evening of her birthday; but it wouldn't last for long, thank goodness! And then? And then she could meet Morse – if he still wanted to take her out.

At 3 p.m. she nervously flicked through the *m*s in the blue Oxford Area Telephone Directory, and found only one 'Morse' in north Oxford: Morse, E. She didn't know his Christian name, and she vaguely wondered what the 'E' stood for. Irrationally, as she heard the first few rings, she hoped that he wasn't in; and then, as they continued, she prayed that he was.

But there was no answer.

CHAPTER FOURTEEN

FROM THE CITY Police H.Q. Morse walked up past
Christ Church to Cornmarket. To his left he noticed
that the door of Carfax tower stood open, and beside
it a notice inviting tourists to ascend and enjoy a
panoramic view of Oxford. At the top of the tower
he could see four or five people standing against the
skyline and pointing to some of the local landmarks,
and a teenage youth actually sitting on the edge,
with one of his boots wedged against the next parapet. Morse, feeling a twinge of panic somewhere
in his bowels, lowered his eyes and walked on. He
joined the small bus-queue just outside Woolworth,
thinking again of what he'd just been reading: the life-
histories of Josephs and Lawson, the accounts of their
deaths, the subsequent investigations. But for the
moment the filters of his brain could separate out no
new nugget of precious information, and he turned
towards St Giles and looked up at the tower of St
Frideswide's. No one up there, of course ... Just a
minute! Had anyone been up there – recently? Suddenly a curious thought came into his mind – but no,
it must be wrong. There'd been something in Bell's
file about it: 'Each November a group of volunteers go

SERVICE OF ALL THE DEAD

up to sweep the leaves.' It had just been a thought, that's all.

A Banbury Road bus nudged into the queue, and Morse sat upstairs. As they passed St Frideswide's he looked up again at the tower and made a guess at its height: eighty, ninety feet? The trees ahead of him in St Giles had that long-distance look of green about them as the leaves began to open; and the bus, as it pulled into the lay-by outside the Taylorian Institute, was scraping against some of their budded branches, when something clicked in Morse's mind. How tall were the trees here? Forty, fifty feet? Not much more, certainly. So how in the name of gravity did the autumnal leaves ever manage to dance their way to the top of St Frideswide's tower? Wasn't there perhaps a simple answer, though? They *didn't*. The November leaf-sweeping brigade had no need to go up to the main tower at all: they just cleared the lower roofs over the aisle and the Lady Chapel. That must be it. And so the curious thought grew curiouser still: since the time of Lawson's death, when doubtless Bell's minions had sieved every leaf and every fragment of stone, had *anyone* been up to the roof of the tower?

The bell pinged for the bus to stop at the Summertown shops; and simultaneously another bell rang in Morse's mind, and he joined the exodus. In Bell's notes (it was all 'bells' now) there'd been a few tactful mentions of Josephs' weakness for gambling on the horses, and the intelligent early suggestion (before Bell's visit to Josephs' bank manager) that the £100 or so found in the dead man's wallet might have had a fairly simple provenance – the licensed betting-office in Summertown.

Morse pushed open the door and immediately registered some surprise. It was more like a branch of Lloyds Bank than the traditional picture of a bookmaker's premises. A counter faced him along the far wall, with a low grille running the length of it, behind which two young women were taking money and stamping betting-slips. Round the three other walls the racing pages of the daily newspapers were pinned, and in front of them were placed black plastic chairs where clients could sit and study the form guides and consider their own fancies or the tipsters' selections. There were about fifteen people there, all men – sitting or standing about, their minds keenly concentrated on the state of the going, the weights and the jockeys, their ears intent on the loudspeaker which every few minutes brought them the latest news of the betting direct from the courses. Morse sat down and stared vacantly at a page of the *Sporting Chronicle*. To his right, a smartly dressed Chinaman twisted the knob on a small machine affixed to the wall and tore off a betting-slip. And from the corner of his eye Morse could see exactly what he wrote: '3.35 Newmarket – £20 win – The Fiddler'. Phew! Surely most of the punters here had to be satisfied with a modest fifty pence or so each way? He turned his head and watched the Chinaman at the pay-in counter, four crisp fivers fanned out neatly in his right hand; watched the girl behind the grille, as she accepted the latest sacrifice with the bland indifference of a Buddhist deity. Two minutes later the loudspeaker woke up again, and without enthusiasm an impersonal voice announced the 'off'; announced, after a period of silence, the order of the runners at the four-furlong marker; then the winner, the second, the third – The Fiddler not amongst them. To Morse, who as a boy had listened to the frenetically exciting race-commentaries of Raymond Glendenning, the whole thing seemed extraordinarily flat, more like an auctioneer selling a Cézanne at Sotheby's.

The Chinaman resumed his seat beside Morse, and began to tear up his small yellow slip with the exaggerated delicacy of one who practises the art of origami.

'No luck?' ventured Morse.

'No,' said the Chinaman, with a polite oriental inclination of the head.

'You lucky sometimes?'

'Sometime.' Again the half-smile, the gentle inclination of the head.

'Come here often?'

'Often.' And, as if to answer the query on Morse's face, 'Me pretty rich man, you think so?'

Morse took the plunge. 'I used to know a fellow who came in here most days – fellow called Josephs. Used to wear a brown suit. About fifty.'

'Here now?'

'No. He died about six months ago – murdered, poor chap.'

'Ah. You mean Harree. Yes. Poor Harree I know heem. We often talk. He murdered, yes. Me verree sorree.'

'He won quite a bit on the horses, I've heard. Still, some of us are luckier than others.'

'You wrong. Harree verree unluckee man. Always just not there quite.'

'He lost a lot of money, you mean?'

The Chinaman shrugged. 'Perhaps he rich man.' His narrow eyes focused on the 4.00 card at Newmarket, his right hand reaching up automatically for the knob on the wall machine.

Probably Josephs had been losing money pretty consistently, and not the sort of money he could hope to recoup from the unemployment exchange. Yet he'd got money from somewhere, by some means.

Morse considered a little wager of his own on the Chinaman's next selection, but squint as he would he couldn't quite see the name, and he left and walked thoughtfully up the hill. It was a pity. A few minutes after Morse had let himself into his flat, the little Chinaman stood smiling a not particularly inscrutable smile at the pay-out counter. He hadn't really got his English syntax sorted out yet, but perhaps he'd coined as fitting an epitaph for Harry Josephs as any with those five disjointed adverbs: 'Always just not there quite.'

CHAPTER FIFTEEN

'No, I'm sorry, Inspector – he isn't.' It was ten past seven and Mrs Lewis regretted the interruption to *The Archers*: she hoped that Morse would either come in or go away. 'Oxford are playing tonight, and he's gone to watch them.'

The rain had been falling steadily since tea-time, and still pattered the puddles in the Lewises' front drive. 'He must be mad,' said Morse.

'It's working with you, Inspector. Are you coming in?'

Morse shook his head and a raindrop dripped from his bare head on to his chin. 'I'll go and see if I can find him.'

'You must be mad,' muttered Mrs Lewis.

Morse drove carefully through the rain up to Headington, the windscreen-wipers sweeping back and forth in clean arcs across the spattered window. It was these damned holidays that upset him! Earlier this Tuesday evening he had sat in his armchair, once again in the grip of a numbing lethargy that minute by minute grew ever more paralysing. The Playhouse offered him a Joe Orton farce, hailed by the critics as a comedy classic. No. The Moulin Rouge announced that the torrid

Sandra Bergson was leading a sexy, savage, insatiable all-girl gang in *On the Game*: an X trailer, no doubt, advertising a U film. No. Every prospect seemed displeasing, and even women, temporarily, seemed vile. Then he'd suddenly thought of Sergeant Lewis.

It had been no problem parking the Lancia in Sandfield Road, and Morse now pushed through the stiff turnstile into the Manor Road ground. Only a faithful sprinkling of bedraggled spectators standing along the west-side terrace, their umbrellas streaked with rain; but the covered terrace at the London Road end was tightly packed with orange-and-black-scarved youngsters, their staccato 'Ox-ford – clap-clap-clap' intermittently echoing across the ground. One row of brilliant floodlights was suddenly switched on, and the wet grass twinkled in a thousand silvery gleams.

A roar greeted the home team, yellow-shirted, blue-shorted, leaning forward against the slanting rain, and kicking and flicking a series of white footballs across the sodden pitch until they shone like polished billiard balls. Behind him, as Morse turned, was the main stand, under cover and under-populated; and he walked back to the entrance and bought himself a transfer ticket.

By half-time Oxford were two goals down, and in spite of repeated scrutinies of those around him, Morse had still not spotted Lewis. Throughout the first half, when the centre of the pitch and the two goal-mouths had churned up into areas of squelchy morass reminiscent of pictures of Passchendaele, Morse's thoughts had given him little rest. An improbable, illogical, intuitive notion was growing ever firmer in his mind –

a mind now focused almost mesmerically on the tower of St Frideswide's; and the fact that he himself was quite unable to check his forebodings served only to reinforce their probability. He needed Lewis badly – there could be no doubt of that.

Greeted by a cacophony of whistles and catcalls, his black top and shorts shining like a skindiver's suit, the referee came out to inspect the pitch again, and Morse looked at the clock by the giant scoreboard: 8.20 p.m. Was it really worth staying?

A firm hand gripped his shoulder from behind. 'You must be mad, sir.'

Lewis clambered over the back of the seat and sat himself down beside his chief.

Morse felt indescribably happy. 'Listen, Lewis. I want your help. What about it?'

'Any time, sir. You know me. But aren't you on—?'

'*Any* time?'

A veil of slow disappointment clouded Lewis' eyes. 'You don't mean—?' He knew exactly what Morse meant.

'You've lost this one, anyway.'

'Bit unlucky, weren't we, in the first half?'

'What are you like on heights?' asked Morse.

Like the streets around the football ground, St Giles was comparatively empty, and the two cars easily found parking-spaces outside St John's College.

'Fancy a beefburger, Lewis?'

'Not for me, sir. The wife'll have the chips on.'

Morse smiled contentedly. It was good to be back in harness again; good to be reminded of Mrs Lewis' chips. Even the rain had slackened, and Morse lifted his face and breathed deeply, ignoring Lewis' repeated questions about their nocturnal mission.

The large west window of St Frideswide's glowed with a sombre, yellow light, and from inside could be heard the notes of the organ, muted and melancholy.

'We going to church?' asked Lewis; and in reply Morse unlatched the north door and walked inside. Immediately on their left as they entered was a brightly painted statue of the Virgin, illumined by circles of candles, some slim and waning rapidly, some stout and squat, clearly prepared to soldier on throughout the night; and all casting a flickering kaleidoscopic light across the serene features of the Blessed Mother of God.

'Coleridge was very interested in candles,' said Morse. But before he could further enlighten Lewis on such enigmatic subject-matter a tall, shadowy figure emerged from the gloom, swathed in a black cassock.

'I'm afraid the service is over, gentlemen.'

'That's handy,' said Morse. 'We want to go up the tower.'

'I beg your pardon.'

'Who are you?' asked Morse brusquely.

'I am the verger,' said the tall man, 'and I'm afraid there's no possibility whatsoever of your going up to the tower.'

Ten minutes later with the verger's key, and the verger's torch, and the verger's warning that the whole

110

thing was highly irregular, Morse found himself on the first few steps of the ascent – a narrow, steep, scalloped stairway that circled closely upwards to the tower above. With Lewis immediately behind he shone the torch ahead of him, and, increasingly breathless from exertion and apprehension, gritted his teeth and climbed. Fifty-five, fifty-six, fifty-seven . . . On the sixty-third step a narrow window loomed on the left, and Morse shut his eyes, hugging the right-hand wall ever more closely; and ten steps higher, steps still religiously counted, he reached the inexorable conclusion that he would climb one step higher, make an immediate U-turn, descend to the bottom, and take Lewis for a pint in the Randolph. A cold sweat had broken out on his forehead, and the planes registering the vertical and horizontal realities were merging and sliding and slanting into a terrifying tilt. He craved only one thing now: to stand four-square on the solid ground outside this abominable tower and to watch the blessedly terrestrial traffic moving along St Giles. To stand? No, to sit there; to lie there even, the members of his body seeking to embrace at every point the solid, fixed contours of the flat and comforting earth.

'Here you are, Lewis. You take the torch. I'm – I'm right behind you.'

Lewis set off ahead of him, easily, confidently, two steps at a time, upwards into the spiralling blackness; and Morse followed. Above the bell chamber, up and up, another window and another dizzying glimpse of the ground so far below – and Morse with a supreme effort of will thought only of one step upwards at a time, his whole being concentrating itself into the purely physical activity of lifting each leg alternately, like a victim of locomotor ataxia.

'Here we are, then,' said Lewis brightly, shining the torch on a low door just above them. 'This must be the roof, I think.'

The door was not locked and Lewis stepped through it, leaving Morse to sit down on the threshold, breathing heavily, his back tight against the door-jamb and his hands tight against his clammy forehead. When finally he dared to look about him, he saw the tessellated coping of the tower framed against the evening sky and then, almost fatally, he saw the dark clouds hurrying across the pale moon, saw the pale moon hurrying behind the dark clouds, saw the tower itself leaning and drifting against the sky, and his head reeled vertiginously, his gut contracted, and twice he retched emptily – and prayed that Lewis had not heard him.

From the north side of the tower Lewis looked down and across the broad, tree-lined expanse of St Giles. Immediately below him, some eighty or ninety feet, he guessed, he could just make out the spiked railing that surrounded the north porch, and beyond it the moonlit graves in the little churchyard. Nothing much of interest. He shone the torch across the tower itself. Each of the four sides was about ten or twelve yards in length, with a gully running alongside the outer walls, and a flat, narrow walk, about a yard in width, between these walls and the leaded roof which rose from each side in a shallow pyramid, its apex some eight or nine feet high, on which a wooden post supported a slightly crooked weathervane.

He walked back to the door. 'You all right, sir?'

'Yes, fine. Just not so fit as you, that's all.'

'You'll get a touch of the old Farmer Giles sitting there, sir.'

'Find anything?'

Lewis shook his head.

'You looked all round?'

'Not exactly, no. But why don't you tell me what we're supposed to be looking for?' Then, as Morse made no reply: 'You *sure* you're all right, sir?'

'Go and – go and have a look all the way round, will you? I'll – er – I'll be all right in a minute.'

'What's wrong, sir?'

'I'm scared of bloody heights, you stupid sod!' snarled Morse.

Lewis said nothing more. He'd worked with Morse many times before, and treated his outbursts rather as he had once treated the saddeningly bitchy bouts of temper from his own teenage daughters. Nevertheless, it still hurt a bit.

He shone the torch along the southern side of the tower and slowly made his way along. Pigeon-droppings littered the narrow walk, and the gully on this side was blocked somewhere, for two or three inches of water had built up at the south-east corner. Lewis took hold of the outer fabric of the tower as he tried to peer round the east side, but the stonework was friable and insecure. Gingerly he leaned his weight against the slope of the central roofing, and shone the torch round. 'Oh Christ!' he said softly to himself.

There, stretched parallel to the east wall, was the body of a man – although even then Lewis realized that the only evidence for supposing the body to be that of a man was the tattered, sodden suit in which the corpse was dressed, and the hair on the head which was not that of a woman. But the face itself had been picked almost clean to the hideous skull; and it was upon this non-face that Lewis forced himself to shine his torch again. Twice in all – but no more.

CHAPTER SIXTEEN

AT LUNCH-TIME ON the following day, Morse sat alone in the Bulldog, just opposite Christ Church, and scanned an early copy of the *Oxford Mail*. Although the main headline and three full columns of the front page were given over to COMPONENTS STRIKE HITS COWLEY MEN, 'Body Found on Church Tower' had been dramatic enough news to find itself halfway down the left-hand column. But Morse didn't bother to read it. After all, he'd been sitting there in Bell's office a couple of hours previously when one of the *Mail*'s correspondents had rung through and when Bell's replies had been guarded and strictly factual: 'No, we don't know who he is.' 'Yes, I did say a "he".' 'What? Quite a long time, yes. Quite a long time.' 'I can't say at the minute, no. They're holding the post-mortem this afternoon. Good headline for you, eh? P.M. THIS P.M.' 'No, I can't tell you who found him.' 'Could be a link-up, I suppose, yes.' 'No, that's the lot. Ring up tomorrow if you like. I might have a bit more for you then.' At the time Morse had felt that this last suggestion was a bit on the optimistic side, and he still felt so now. He turned to the back page and read the sports headline: UNITED COME UNSTUCK ON PITCH LIKE GLUE. But he didn't read that account, either. The truth was that he felt extremely puzzled, and needed time to think.

Nothing had been found in the dead man's pockets, and the only information imparted by the dark-grey suit, the underclothing, and the light-blue tie was 'Burton', 'St Michael' and 'Munro Spun' respectively. Morse himself had declined to view what Bell had called 'a sticky, putrescent mess', and had envied the perky *sang-froid* of the police surgeon who reported that whoever he was he wasn't quite such a gruesome sight as some of the bodies they used to fish out of the water at Gravesend. One thing was clear. It was going to be a tricky job to identify the corpse: tricky for Bell, that was. And Bell had not been in the best of humours as he'd glared across the table at Morse and reminded him that he *must* have some idea who the fellow was. It was Morse who had taken Lewis to the exact spot, wasn't it? And if he was pretty sure he was going to find a corpse he must have got a jolly good idea whose corpse it was!

But Morse hadn't – it was as simple as that. A peculiar combination of circumstances had concentrated his thoughts on to the tower of St Frideswide's, and all he'd done (whatever Bell suspected) was to obey a compelling instinct which had proved too strong even for his chronic acrophobia. But he'd not expected to find a corpse up there, had he? Or had he? When Lewis had shouted the grim discovery over the roof to him, Morse's mind had immediately jumped to the shadowy figure of the tramp and his miserably thin pickings from the collection-plate. All along he'd felt that it should have been comparatively easy for the police to pick up such a character. People like that had to depend almost entirely on charitable and welfare services of some kind, and were usually well known to the authorities wherever they went. Yet extensive enquiries had led nowhere, and might there not have been a very very simple reason for that?

Morse bought himself another pint and watched the glass as the cloudy sedimentation slowly cleared; and when he sat down again his brain seemed to have cleared a little, too. No; it wasn't the tramp they'd found, Morse felt sure of that. It was the clothes, really – especially that light-blue tie. Light-blue . . . Cambridge . . . graduates . . . teachers . . . Morris . . .

Bell was still in his office.

'What happened to Paul Morris?' asked Morse.

'Buggered off with Josephs' wife, like as not.'

'You don't *know*?'

Bell shook his head. He looked tired and drawn. 'We tried, but—'

'Did you find *her*?'

Again Bell shook his head. 'We didn't push things too far. You know how it is. What with Morris teaching at the same school as his son and—'

'His *what*? You didn't tell me Morris had a son!'

Bell sighed deeply. 'Look, Morse. Whadya want from me? You find me another body last night, and I'm deeply grateful, aren't I? That'll be another half-dozen of my lads out of circulation. And I've just had a call to say somebody's been fished out of the river at Folly Bridge, and we've got more trouble with some squatters down in Jericho.' He took out a handkerchief and sneezed heavily. 'And I'm sickening for the flu, and you want me to go chasing after some fellow who was known to be seein' Josephs' missus pretty regularly long before—'

'Really?' said Morse. 'Why didn't I read that in the report?'

'Come off it!'

'He could have killed Josephs. Jealousy! Best motive of the lot.'

'He was sittin' – playin' the bleedin' organ – when—' Bell sneezed noisily again.

Morse settled back in his chair, for some unfathomable reason looking very pleased with himself. 'You still think it really *was* Lawson you found on the railings?'

'I told you, Morse, we had two identifications.'

'Oh yes. I remember. One from a blind woman and one from the man who ran away with Brenda Josephs, wasn't it?'

'Why don't you go home?'

'You know,' said Morse quietly, 'when you've finished with your squatters, you'd better get a squad of lads to dig up old Lawson's coffin, because I reckon – just reckon, mind – that *you might not find old Lawson in it.*' Morse's face beamed with a mischievous pleasure, and he got up to go.

'That's a bloody fool's thing to say.'

'Is it?'

'Not all that easy, either.' It was Bell who was enjoying himself now.

'No?'

'No. You see, they cremated him.'

The news appeared to occasion little surprise or disappointment on Morse's face. 'I knew a minister once—'

'Well, well!' mumbled Bell.

'—who had one of his feet amputated in the First World War. He got it stuck in a tank, and they had to get him out quick because the thing was on fire. So they left his foot there.'

'Very interesting.'

'He was very old when I knew him,' continued Morse. 'One foot already in the grave.'

Bell pushed his own chair back and got up. 'Tell me about it some other time.'

'He was in a discussion one day about the respective merits of burial and cremation, and the old boy said he didn't mind two hoots what they did with him. He said he'd sort of got a foot in *both* camps.'

Bell shook his head in slow bewilderment. What the hell was *that* supposed to mean?

'By the way,' said Morse. 'What was the name of Paul Morris' son?'

'Peter, I think. Why—?'

'But Morse left without enlightening Bell on the point.

*

P.M. THIS P.M., Bell had said; and as he drove the Lancia up to Carfax the initials kept repeating themselves to his mind: post-mortem, post meridiem, prime minister, Paul McCartney, Post Master, putrifying mess, Perry Mason, Provost Marshal, Peter Morris ... The lights were red at the end of Cornmarket, and as Morse sat waiting there for them to change he looked up yet again at the tower of St Frideswide's looming overhead, and at the great west window which only last night had glowed in the dark when he and Lewis ... On a sudden impulse he pulled round the corner into Beaumont Street and parked his car outside the Randolph. A uniformed young flunkey pounced upon him immediately.

'You can't leave your car here.'

'I can leave the bloody car where I like,' snapped Morse. 'And next time you speak to me, lad, just call me "sir", all right?'

The north porch was locked, with a notice pinned to it: 'Due to several acts of wanton vandalism during the past few months, we regret that the church will now be closed to the public from 11 a.m. to 5 p.m. on weekdays.' Morse felt he would have liked to recast the whole sentence, but he satisfied himself by crossing through 'due' and writing 'owing'.

CHAPTER SEVENTEEN

MORSE RAPPED BRISKLY on the door marked 'Enquiries', put his head round the door, and nodded 'Hello' to a nice-looking school secretary.

'Can I help you, sir?'

'Headmaster in?'

'Is he expecting you?'

'Doubt it,' said Morse. He walked across the narrow office, tapped once on the study door and entered.

Phillipson, headmaster of the Roger Bacon School, was only too pleased to be of help.

Paul Morris, it seemed, had been a music master of the first water. During his short stay at the school he'd been popular both with his teaching colleagues and with his pupils, and his G.C.E. O Level and A Level results had been encouragingly good. Everyone had been mystified – for a start anyway – when he'd left so suddenly, without telling a soul; right in the middle of term, too, on (Phillipson consulted his previous year's diary) 26 October, a Wednesday. He had turned up for school perfectly normally in the morning and presumably gone off, as he often did on Wednesdays, to have lunch at home. And that was the last they'd seen of him. His son, Peter, had left the school just after lessons finished at a quarter to four, and that was the last they'd seen of *him*. The next day several members of staff had pointed out that both of them were absent from school, and no doubt someone would have gone round to the Morris residence if it hadn't been for a call from the Oxford City Police. It seemed that some anonymous neighbour had tipped them off that Morris and his son had left Kidlington and gone off to join a woman ('I suppose you know all about this, Inspector?') – a Mrs Josephs. Inspector Bell had called personally to see Phillipson and told him that a few enquiries had already been made, and that several of Morris' neighbours had seen a car answering the description of Mrs Josephs' Allegro parked somewhere nearby several times during the previous months. In fact, the police had learned from other sources that in all probability Morris and Mrs Josephs had been lovers for some time. Anyway, Bell had asked Phillipson to soft-pedal the whole thing; make up some story about Morris having to be away for the rest of the term – death of one of his parents – anything he liked. Which Phillipson had done. A temporary stand-in had taken over Morris' classes for the remainder of the autumn term, and a new woman appointed from January. The police had visited the house that Morris had rented furnished, and found that most of the personal effects had been taken away, although for some reason a fair number of books and an expensive record-player had been left behind. And that was all, really. Phillipson had heard nothing more from that day to this. To the best of his knowledge no one had received any communication from Morris at all. He had not applied for a reference, and perhaps, in the circumstances, was unlikely to do so.

Not once had Morse interrupted Phillipson, and when finally he did say something it was totally irrelevant. 'Any sherry in that cupboard, Headmaster?'

Ten minutes later Morse left the headmaster's study and leaned over the young secretary's shoulder.

'Making out a cheque for me, miss?'

'"Mrs"; Mrs Clarke.' She wound the yellow cheque from the typewriter carriage, placed it face downwards on her desk, and glared at Morse defiantly. His lack of manners when he'd come in had been bad enough, but—

'You look pretty when you're cross,' said Morse.

Phillipson called her through to his study. 'I've got to go out, Mrs Clarke. Take Chief Inspector Morse along to the first-year-sixth music group, will you? And wash up these glasses when you get back, please.'

Tight-lipped and red-cheeked, Mrs Clarke led the way along the corridors and up to the music-room door. 'In there,' she said.

Morse turned to face her and laid his right hand very gently on her shoulder, his blue eyes looking straight into hers. 'Thank you, Mrs Clarke,' he said quietly. 'I'm awfully sorry if I made you angry. Please forgive me.'

As she walked back down the steps, she felt suddenly and marvellously pleased with life. Why had she been so silly? She found herself wishing that he would call her back about something. And he did.

'When do the staff get their cheques, Mrs Clarke?'

'On the last Friday in the month. I always type them the day before.'

'You weren't typing them just now, then?'

'No. We're breaking up tomorrow, and I was just typing an expenses cheque for Mr Phillipson. He had a meeting in London yesterday.'

'I hope he's not on the fiddle.'

She smiled sweetly. 'No, Inspector. He's a very nice man.'

'You're very nice, too, you know,' said Morse.

She was blushing as she turned away, and Morse felt inordinately envious of Mr Clarke as he watched the secretary's legs disappearing down the stairs. Last Friday in the month, she'd said. That would have been 28 October, and Morris had left two days before his cheque was due. Very strange!

Morse knocked on the music-room door and entered.

Mrs Stewart stood up immediately and made as if to turn off the record-player; but Morse held up his right hand, waved it slightly, and sat down on a chair by the wall. The small class was listening to Fauré's *Requiem*; and with an almost instant ecstasy Morse closed his eyes and listened again to the ethereal sweep of the 'In Paradisum': *aeternam habeas requiem* . . . 'that thou mayest have eternal rest' . . . Too quickly the last notes died away into the silence of the room, and it occurred to Morse that rather too many people had all too recently had a premature dose of that eternal rest thrust forcibly upon them. The score stood at three at the minute; but he had a grim foreboding that soon it might be four.

He introduced himself and his purpose, and was

soon surveying the seven girls and the three boys who were in the first year of their A Level music course. He was making enquiries about Mr Morris; they'd all known Mr Morris; there were various business matters which had to be cleared up, and the police weren't sure where Mr Morris had gone to. Did any of them know anything at all about Mr Morris that might just possibly be of any help? The class shook their heads, and sat silent and unhelpful. So Morse asked them a lot more questions, and still they sat silent and unhelpful. But at least two or three of the girls were decidedly decorative – especially one real honey at the back whose eyes seemed to flash the inner secrets of her soul across the room at him. Morris must have looked at her lustfully just once in a while? Surely so . . .

But he was getting nowhere slowly, that was obvious; and he changed his tactics abruptly. His target was a pallid-looking, long-haired youth in the front row. 'Did you know Mr Morris?'

'Me?' The boy swallowed hard. 'He taught me for two years, sir.'

'What did you call him?'

'Well, I – I called him "Mr Morris".' The rest of the class smirked silently to each other, as if Morse must be a potential idiot.

'Didn't you call him anything else?'

'No.'

'You never called him "sir"?'

'Well, of course. But—'

'You don't seem to realize the seriousness of this

business, lad. So I'll have to ask you again, won't I? What else did you call him?'

'I don't quite see what you mean.'

'Didn't he have a nickname?'

'Well, most of the teachers—'

'What was his?'

It was one of the other boys who came to the rescue. 'Some of us used to call him "Dapper".'

Morse directed his gaze towards the new voice and nodded wisely. 'Yes. So I've heard. Why was it, do you think?'

It was one of the girls now, a serious-looking soul with a large gap between her front teeth. 'He alwayth drethed very nithely, thir.' The other girls tittered and twittered amongst themselves, and nudged each other knowingly.

'Any more contributions?'

It was the third boy who took up the easy theme. 'He always wore a suit, you see, sir, and most of the staff – well' (more sniggering) 'well, you know, most of 'em have beards, the men, I mean' (a great guffaw from the class now) 'and wear jeans and sweaters and all that. But Mr Morris, he always wore a suit and looked – well, smart, like.'

'What sort of suits did he wear?'

'Well' (it was the same boy) 'sort of dark, you know. Party suits, sort of thing. So, well, we called him "Dapper" – like we said.'

The bell rang for the end of the lesson, and several members of the class began to gather their books and file-cases together.

'What about his ties?' persisted Morse. But the psychological moment had passed, and the colour of Morris' ties seemed to have faded from the collective memory.

As he walked up the drive to his car, Morse wondered if he ought to talk to some of the staff; but he hadn't quite enough to go on yet, and decided it would be better to wait for the pathologist's report.

He had just started the engine when a young girl appeared at the driving-window. 'Hello, beautiful,' he said. It was the girl from the back row, the girl with the radar eyes, who leaned forward and spoke. 'You know you were asking about ties? Well, I remember one tie, sir. He often wore it. It was a light-blue tie. It sort of went with the suits he used to wear.'

Morse nodded understandingly. 'That's most helpful. Thank you very much for telling me.' He looked up at her and suddenly realized how tall she was. Strange how all of them looked about the same size when they were sitting down, as if height were determined not so much from the bottom to the shoulder as by the length of the legs – in this case by the length of some very beautiful legs.

'Did you know Mr Morris well?'

'Not really, no.'

'What's your name?'

'Carole – Carole Jones.'

'Well, thank you, Carole. And good luck.'

Carole walked thoughtfully back to the front entrance and made her way to the next lesson. She wondered why she so often felt so attracted to the older men. Men like this inspector fellow; men like Mr Morris . . . Her mind went back to the time they'd sat in the car together; when his hand had lightly touched her breasts, and when her own left hand had gently pushed its way between the buttons of his white shirt – beneath the light-blue tie he'd worn that day; the time when he'd asked her to his house, when he'd answered the door and told her that an unexpected visitor had just arrived and that he'd get in touch with her again – very soon.

But he never had.

CHAPTER EIGHTEEN

MORSE WAS STILL asleep the next morning when his bedside phone rang. It was Superintendent Strange of the Thames Valley Police H.Q.

'I've just had a call from the City Police, Morse. You still in bed?'

'No, no,' said Morse. 'Decorating the lavatory, sir.'

'I thought you were on holiday.'

'A man's got to use his leisure hours profitably—'

'Like clambering over church roofs at the dead of night, you mean.'

'You heard?'

'Heard something else, too, Morse. Bell's got flu. And since you seem to have taken over the case already I just wondered whether you'd like to sort of – take over the case. Officially, I mean.'

Morse shot upright in bed. 'That's good news, sir. When—?'

'From now. It'll be better if you work from St Aldates. All the stuff's there, and you can work from Bell's office.'

'Can I have Lewis?'

'I thought you'd already got him.'

Morse's face beamed with pleasure. 'Thank you, sir. I'll just slip a few clothes on and—'

'Decorating in your pyjamas, Morse?'

'No. You know me, sir. Up with the lark—'

'And to bed with the wren. Yes, I know. And it wouldn't be a bad thing for morale here if you got to the bottom of things, would it? So what about getting out of bed?'

Five minutes later Morse got through to Lewis and reported the good news. 'What are you doing today, old friend?'

'My day off, sir. I'm going to take the wife over to—'

'Were you?' The change of tense was not lost on Lewis, and he listened cheerfully to his instructions. He'd been dreading another visit to his ancient mother-in-law.

The Lancia took only one and a half hours to cover the eighty-odd miles to Stamford in Lincolnshire, where the Lawson clan had lived for several generations. The speedometer had several times exceeded 85 m.p.h. as they drove along, up through Brackley, Silverstone and Towcester, then by-passing Northampton and twisting through Kettering before looking down from the top of Easton Hill on to the town of Stamford, its grey stone buildings matching the spires and towers of its many old churches. *En route* Morse had cheerfully sketched in the background of the St Frideswide's murders; but the sky had grown overcast and leaden, and the sight of thousands of dead elm trees along the Northampton-shire roads seemed a sombre reminder of reality.

'They say those trees commit suicide,' Lewis had

ventured at one point. 'They secrete a sort of fluid to try to—'

'It's not always easy to tell suicide from murder,' muttered Morse.

By late afternoon the two men had uncovered a fairly solid body of information about the late and (it seemed) little-lamented Lionel Lawson. There had been two Lawson brothers, Lionel Peter and Philip Edward, the latter some eighteen months the younger. Both had won scholarships to a public school some ten miles distant, and both had been weekly boarders, spending their Saturday evenings and Sundays during term-time with their parents, who ran a small local business specializing in the restoration of ancient buildings. Academically (it appeared) the two boys were more than competent, with Philip potentially the abler – if also the lazier and less ambitious. After leaving school each of them had spent eighteen months on National Service; and it was during his time in the Army that Lionel, always the more serious-minded of the two, had met a particularly persuasive psalm-singing padre, and been led to the conviction that he was called to the ministry. After demobilization, he had studied hard on his own for a year before gaining acceptance at Cambridge to read theology. During this period Philip had worked for his father for a few years, but seemingly with little enthusiasm; and finally he had drifted away from home, occasionally revisiting his parents, but with no firm purpose in life, no job, and with little prospect of

131

discovering either. Five years ago Mr Lawson senior and his wife had been killed in the Zagreb air crash whilst returning from a holiday in southern Yugoslavia, and the family business had been sold, with each of the two sons inheriting about £50,000 net from the estate.

For most of the day Morse and Lewis had worked separately, each pursuing a different line of enquiry; and it was only on the last visit, to the ex-headmaster of the Lawson boys' public school, that they came together again.

Doctor Meyer's speech was that of an old schoolmaster, deliberate, over-latinized with an apparent dread of imprecision. 'He was a clever boy, young Philip. With a modicum of dedication and perseverance – who knows?'

'You've no idea where he is now?'

The old man shook his head. 'But Lionel, now. He worked like a Trojan – although exactly why the Trojans are proverbially accredited with a reputation for industriousness has always been a mystery to me. His ambition was always to win a scholarship to Oxford, but—' He broke off suddenly as if his memory could take him no farther along that avenue of recollection. But Morse was clearly anxious to push him past a few more trees.

'How long was Lionel in the sixth form?'

'Three years, as I recall it. Yes, that's right. He took his Higher School Certificate at the end of his second year, and got it all right. He took the Oxford entrance examination just after that, in the Michaelmas term, but I had little real hope for him. His mind was not quite – not quite alpha potential. They wrote to me about him, of course. They said they were unable to offer him a place, but the boy's work had not been without merit. They advised him to stay on for a further year in the sixth and then to try again.'

'Was he very disappointed?'

The old man eyed Morse shrewdly and relit his pipe before replying. 'What do you think, Inspector?'

Morse shrugged his shoulders as if the matter were barely of consequence. 'You said he was ambitious, that's all.'

'Yes,' replied the old man slowly.

'So he stayed on another year?'

'Yes.'

Lewis shuffled a little uncomfortably in his chair. At this rate of progress they wouldn't be home before midnight. It was as if Morse and Meyer were at the snooker table, each of them playing his safety shots. Your turn, Morse.

'He took his Higher again?'

Meyer nodded. 'He didn't do quite so well as in the previous year, if I remember rightly. But that is not unusual.'

'You mean he was more worried about preparing for his Oxford entrance?'

'That was probably the reason.'

'But he didn't make it to Oxford?'

'Er – no.'

Something seemed to be puzzling Morse, Lewis could

see that. Was he on to something? But it appeared not. Morse had got to his feet and was pulling on his coat. 'Nothing else you can tell me about him?'

Meyer shook his head and prepared to see his visitors out. He was a short man, and now well over eighty; yet there was still an air of authority in his bearing, and Lewis could well understand (what he'd heard earlier in the day) that Meyer had ruled his school with a rod of iron, and that pupils and staff alike had trembled at his coming.

'Nothing at all?' repeated Morse as they stood at the door.

'There's nothing more I can tell you, no.'

Was there slightly more emphasis on the 'can' than there need have been? Lewis wasn't sure. He was lost as usual anyway.

For the first part of their return journey, Morse seemed rapt in thought; and when he finally did say something Lewis could only wonder what those thoughts had been.

'What was the exact day when Lionel Lawson left school?'

Lewis looked through his notebook. 'November the eighth.'

'Mm.' Morse nodded slowly. 'Tell me when you spot a phone-box.'

When, ten minutes later, Morse got back into the car, Lewis could see that he was very pleased with himself.

'Are you letting me in on this one, sir?'

'Of course!' Morse looked sideways at his sergeant in mild surprise. 'We're partners, aren't we? We do things together, you and me. Or "you and I" as I've no doubt old man Meyer would say. You see, young Lionel Lawson was an ambitious little swot, right? He's not been over-endowed by the Almighty with all that much up top, but he makes up for it by sheer hard work. More than anything else he wants to go up to Oxford. And why not? It's a fine ambition. Let's just recap on Master Lionel, then. He tries once – and he fails. But he's a sticker. He stays on for another year – another year of grind on his set books and the rest of it, and all the time he's being groomed by his masters for his entrance exam. I shouldn't think he's too bothered about not doing so well in his other exams that summer – he's set his sights on higher things. Remember he's already done three years in the sixth form, and he goes back in the autumn term because that's when the entrance exams are always taken. He's all ready for the final furlong – agreed?'

'But he didn't make it.'

'No, you're right. But he didn't *fail* to get in, Lewis – and that's the interesting point. Lawson, L., left school on November the eighth, you tell me. And I'll tell *you* something. That year the entrance papers were sat in the first week of December – I just rang up the Registry at Oxford – *and Lawson, L., didn't sit the examination.*'

'Perhaps he changed his mind.'

'And perhaps somebody changed it for him!'

135

A light flickered dimly in the darkness of Lewis'
mind. 'He was expelled, you mean?'

'That's about it, I reckon. And that's why old man
Meyer was so cagey. He knew a good deal more than
he was prepared to tell us.'

'But we have no real evidence—'

'Evidence? No, we haven't. But you've got to use a
bit of imagination in this job, Lewis, haven't you? So
let's use a bit. Tell me. Why do boys usually get expelled
from public schools?'

'Drugs?'

'They had no drugs in those days.'

'I don't know, sir. I never went to a public school,
did I? There was none of that Greek and Latin stuff for
me. We had enough trouble with the three Rs.'

'It's not the three Rs we're worried about now, Lewis.
It's the three Bs: bullying, beating and buggery! And
Lawson, L., from what we've learned of him, was a
quietly behaved little chap, and I doubt he got expelled
for bullying or beating. What do you think?'

Lewis shook his head sadly: he'd heard this sort of
thing before. 'You can't just – you can't just make up
these things as you go along, sir. It's not fair!'

'As you wish.' Morse shrugged his shoulders, and the
needle on the speedometer touched 90 m.p.h. as the
Lancia skirted Northampton on the eastern bypass.

136

BACK IN OXFORD at about 4.30 p.m. that same afternoon, two men were walking slowly down Queen Street from Carfax. The elder, and slightly the taller of the two, a growth of greyish stubble matting his long vacant face, was dressed in an old blue pin-striped suit which hung loosely on his narrow frame. In his right hand he carried a bull-necked flagon of Woodpecker cider. The younger man, bearded and unkempt, anywhere in age (it seemed) between his mid-forties and mid-fifties, wore a long army-issue greatcoat, buttoned up to the neck, its insignia long since stripped off or lost. He carried nothing.

At Bonn Square they turned into the circle of grass that surrounds the stone cenotaph, and sat down on a green-painted bench beneath one of the great trees girdling the tiny park. Beside the bench was a wire waste-paper basket, from which the younger man pulled out a copy of the previous day's edition of the *Oxford Mail*. The elder man unscrewed the liquor with great deliberation and, having taken a short swig of its contents, wiped the neck of the bottle on his jacket sleeve before passing it over. 'Anything in the paper?'

'Nah.'

Shoppers continuously criss-crossed one another in the pedestrian precinct in front of the park, many of them making their way down the covered arcade between the light-beige brickwork of the Selfridges building and the duller municipal stone of the public library. A few casual glances swept the only two people seated on the park benches – glances without pity, interest or concern. Lights suddenly blazed on in the multi-storeyed blocks around and the evening was ushered in.

'Let's look at it when you've finished,' said the elder man, and immediately, without comment, the paper changed hands. The bottle, too, was passed over, almost rhythmically, between them, neither man drinking more than a mouthful at a time.

'This is what they were talking about at the hostel.' The elder man pointed a thin grubby finger at an article on the front page, but his companion made no comment, staring down at the paving stones.

'They've found some fellow up the top of that tower, you know, just opposite—' But he couldn't quite remember what it was opposite to, and his voice trailed off as he slowly finished the article. 'Poor sod!' he said finally.

'We're all poor sods,' rejoined the other. He was seldom known to communicate his thoughts so fully, and he left it at that, hunching himself down into his greatcoat, taking a tin of shredded tobacco from one of its large pockets and beginning to roll himself a cigarette.

'P'haps you weren't here then, but a fellow got hisself murdered there last – when was it now? – last . . . Augh! Me memory's going. Anyway, a few days later the minister there, he chucks hisself off the bloody tower! Makes you think.'

But it was not apparent that the younger man was given cause to think in any way. He licked the white cigarette-paper from left to right, repeated the process, and stuck the ill-fashioned cylinder between his lips.

'What was his name? Christ! When you get older your memory . . . What was his name?' He wiped the neck of the bottle again and passed it over. 'He knew the minister there . . . I wish I could think of . . . He was some sort of relation or something. Used to stay at the vicarage sometimes. What *was* his name? You don't remember him?'

'Nah. Wasn't 'ere then, was I?'

'He used to go to the services. Huh!' He shook his head as if refusing credence to such strange behaviour. 'You ever go to church?'

'Me? Nah.'

'Not even when you was a lad?'

'Nah.'

A smartly dressed man carrying a briefcase and umbrella walked past them on his way from the railway station.

'Got a coupla bob for a cup o' tea, mister?' It was a long sentence for the younger man, but he could have saved his breath.

'I've not seen him around at all recently,' continued

the other. 'Come to think of it, I've not seen him since the minister chucked hisself ... Were you there when the police came round to the hostel?'

'Nah.'

The elder man coughed violently and from his loose, rattling chest spat out a gob of yellowish phlegm on to the paving. He felt tired and ill, and his mind wandered back to his home, and the hopes of his early years ...

'Gizz the paper 'ere!' said his companion.

Through thin purplish lips the elder man was now whistling softly the tune to 'The Old Folks at Home', lingering long over the melody like a man whose only precious pleasure now is the maudlin stage of drunkenness. 'Wa-a-ay down upon the—' Suddenly he stopped. 'Swan-something. *Swanpole* – that was it! Funny sort of name. I remember we used to call him Swanny. Did you know him?'

'Nah.' The younger man folded the *Oxford Mail* carefully and stuck it through the front of his coat. 'You oughta look after that cough o' yours,' he added, with a rare rush of words, as the elder man coughed up again – revoltingly – and got to his feet.

'I think I'll be getting along. You coming?'

'Nah.' The bottle was now empty, but the man who remained seated on the bench had money in his pockets, and there may have been a glint of mean gratification in his eyes. But those eyes were shielded from public view behind an incongruous pair of dark glasses, and seemed to be looking in the opposite direction as the elder man shuffled unsteadily away.

It was colder now, but the man on the bench was

gradually getting used to that. It was the first thing he'd discovered. After a time you learn to forget how cold you are: you accept it and the very acceptance forms an unexpected insulation. Except for the feet. Yes, except for the feet. He got up and walked across the grass to look at the inscriptions on the stone obelisk. Among the buglers and privates whose deeds were commemorated thereon, he noticed the odd surname of a young soldier killed by the mutineers in Uganda in 1897: the name was Death.

CHAPTER TWENTY

AT 4.30 P.M. ON the Friday of the same week, Ruth Rawlinson wheeled her bicycle through the narrow passageway and propped it against the side of the lawn-mower in the cluttered garden-shed. Really, she must tidy up that shed again soon. She took a white Sainsbury carrier bag from the cycle-basket, and walked back round to the front door. The *Oxford Mail* was in the letter-box, and she quietly withdrew it.

Just a little bit today, but still on page one:

CORPSE STILL UNIDENTIFIED

POLICE still have no positive clue about the identity of the body found on the tower-roof of St Frideswide's Church. Chief Inspector Morse today repeated that the dead man was probably in his late thirties, and revealed that he was wearing a dark-grey suit, white shirt and light-blue tie. Anyone who may have any information is asked to contact the St Aldates Police Station, Oxford 49881. Enquiries have not as yet established any link with the still unsolved murder of Mr Harry Josephs in the same church last year.

Ruth's body gave an involuntary little jerk as she read the article. 'Anyone who may have . . .' Oh God! She had information enough, hadn't she? Too much information; and the knowledge was weighing ever more heavily upon her conscience. And was Morse in charge now?

As she inserted the Yale key, Ruth realized (yet again) how sickeningly predictable would be the dialogue of the next few minutes.

'Is that you, Ruthie dear?'

Who else, you silly old crow? 'Yes, Mother.'

'Is the paper come?'

You know it's come. Your sharp old ears don't miss a scratch, do they? 'Yes, Mother.'

'Bring it with you, dear.'

Ruth put the heavy carrier bag down on the kitchen-table, draped her mackintosh over a chair and walked into the lounge. She bent down to kiss her mother lightly on an icy cheek, placed the newspaper on her lap, and turned up the gas fire. 'You never have this high enough, you know, Mother. It's been a lot colder this week and you've got to keep yourself warm.'

'We've got to be careful with the bills, dear.'

Don't start on that again! Ruth mustered up all her reserves of patience and filial forbearance. 'You finished the book?'

'Yes, dear. *Very* ingenious.' But her attention was fixed on the evening paper. 'Anything more about the murder?'

'I don't know. I didn't know it was a murder anyway.'

'Don't be childish, dear.' Her eyes had pounced

143

upon the article and she appeared to read it with ghoulish satisfaction.

'That man who came here, Ruthie – they've put him in charge.'

'Have they?'

'He knows far more than he's letting on – you mark my words.'

'You think so?'

The old girl nodded wisely in her chair. 'You can still learn a few things from your old mother, you know.'

'Such as what?'

'You remember that tramp fellow who murdered Harry Josephs?'

'Who said he murdered—?'

'No need to get cross, dear. You know you're interested. You still keep all the newspaper clippings, I know that.'

You nosey old bitch! 'Mother, you must *not* go looking through my handbag again. I've told you before. One of these days—'

'I'll find something I shouldn't? Is that it?'

Ruth looked savagely into the curly blue line of flame at the bottom of the gas fire, and counted ten. There were some days now when she could hardly trust herself to speak.

'Well, that's who it is,' said her mother.

'Pardon?'

'The man up the tower, dear. It's the tramp.'

'Bit elegantly dressed for a tramp, wouldn't you say, Mother? White shirt and a—'

'I thought you said you hadn't seen the paper, dear.' The charge was levelled with a silky tongue.

Ruth took a deep breath. 'I just thought you'd like to find it for yourself, that's all.'

'You're beginning to tell me quite a few little lies, Ruthie, and you've got to stop it.'

Ruth looked up sharply. What was that supposed to mean? Surely her mother couldn't know about . . .? 'You're taking nonsense, Mother.'

'So you don't think it *is* the tramp?'

'A tramp wouldn't be wearing clothes like that.'

'People can change clothes, can't they?'

'You've been reading too many detective stories.'

'You could kill someone and then change his clothes.'

'Of course you couldn't.' Again Ruth was watching her mother carefully. 'Not just like that anyway. You make it sound like dressing up a doll or something.'

'It would be difficult, dear, I know that. But, then, life is full of difficulties, isn't it? It's not impossible, that's all I'm saying.'

'I've got two nice little steaks from Sainsbury's. I thought we'd have a few chips with them.'

'You could always change a man's clothes *before* you killed him.'

'What? Don't be so silly! You don't identify a body by the clothes. It's the face and things like that. You can't change—'

'What if there's nothing left of his face, dear?' asked Mrs Rawlinson sweetly, as if reporting that she'd eaten the last piece of Cheddar from the pantry.

Ruth walked over to the window, anxious to bring the conversation to a close. It was distasteful and, yes, worrying. And perhaps her mother wasn't getting quite so senile after all . . . In her mind's eye Ruth still had a clear picture of the 'tramp' her mother had been talking of, the man she'd known (though she'd never actually been told) to be Lionel Lawson's brother, the man who had usually looked exactly what he was – a worthless, feckless parasite, reeking of alcohol, dirty and degraded. Not quite always, though. There had been two occasions when she'd seen him looking more than presentable: hair neatly groomed, face shaven freshly, finger-nails clean, and a decently respectable suit on his back. On those occasions the family resemblance between the two brothers had been quite remarkable . . .

'. . . if they ask me, which doubtless they won't—' Mrs Rawlinson had been chattering non-stop throughout, and her words at last drifted through to Ruth's consciousness.

'What would you tell them?'

'I've *told* you. Haven't you been listening to me, dear? Is there something wrong?'

Yes, there's a lot wrong. You, for a start. And if you're not careful, mother dear, I'll strangle you one of these days, dress you up in someone else's clothes, carry your skinny little body up to the top of the tower, and let the birds have a second helping! 'Wrong? Of course there isn't. I'll go and get tea.'

Rotten, black blotches appeared under the skin of the first potato she was peeling, and she took another

146

from the bag she had just bought – a bag marked with the words 'Buy British' under a large Union Jack. Red, white and blue ... And she thought of Paul Morris seated on the organ-bench, with his red hood, white shirt and blue tie; Paul Morris, who (as everyone believed) had run off with Brenda Josephs. But he hadn't, had he? Someone had made very, very sure that he hadn't; someone who was sitting somewhere – even now! – planning, gloating, profiting, in some way, from the whole dreadful business. The trouble was that there weren't many people left. In fact, if you counted the heads of those that *were* left, there was really only one who could conceivably ... Surely not, though. Surely Brenda Josephs could have nothing to do with it, could she?

Ruth shook her head with conviction, and peeled the next potato.

CHAPTER TWENTY-ONE

ALTHOUGH HER HUSBAND (unbeknown to her) had borrowed on the mortgage of their house in Wolvercote, Mrs Brenda Josephs was now comfortably placed financially, and the nurses' hostel in the General Hospital on the outskirts of Shrewsbury provided more than adequate accommodation. On Paul's specific instructions, she had not written to him once, and she had received only that one letter from him, religiously guarded under the lining of her handbag, much of which she knew by heart: '... and above all don't be impatient, my darling. It will take time, perhaps quite a lot of time, and whatever happens we must be careful. As far as I can see there is nothing to worry us, and we must keep it that way. Just be patient and all will be well. I long to see you again and to feel your beautiful body next to mine. I love you, Brenda – you know that, and soon we shall be able to start a completely new life together. Be discreet always, and do nothing until you hear from me again. Burn this letter – now!'

Brenda had been working since 7.30 a.m. on the women's surgical ward, and it was now 4.15 p.m. Her

Friday evening and the whole of Saturday were free, and she leaned back in one of the armchairs in the nurses' common room and lit a cigarette. Since leaving Oxford her life (albeit without Paul) had been fuller and freer than she could ever have hoped or imagined. She had made new friends and taken up new interests. She had been made aware, too, happily aware, of how attractive she remained to the opposite sex. Only a week after her appointment (she had given, as her referee, the name of the matron for whom she had worked prior to her nursing at the Radcliffe) one of the young married doctors had said to her, 'Would you like to come to bed with me, Brenda?' Just like that! She smiled now as she recollected the incident, and an unworthy thought, not for the first time, strayed across the threshold of her mind. Did she *really* want Paul all that badly now? With that son of his, Peter? He was a nice enough young boy, but ... She stubbed out her cigarette and reached for the *Guardian.* There was an hour and a half to wait before the evening meal, and she settled down to a leisurely perusal of the day's news. Inflation figures seemed mildly encouraging for a change; but the unemployment figures were not, and she knew only too well what unemployment could do to a man's soul. Middle East peace talks were still taking place, but civil wars in various parts of Africa seemed to be threatening the delicate balance between the superpowers. In the Home News, at the bottom of page three, there was a brief item on the discovery of a body on the tower of an Oxford church; but Brenda didn't reach it. The young doctor sat down beside her, unnecessarily but not distressingly close.

'Hello, beautiful! What about us doing the crossword together?'

He took the paper from her, folded it over to the crossword, and unclipped a biro from the top pocket of his white coat.

'I'm not much good at crosswords,' said Brenda.

'I bet you're good in bed, though.'

'If you're going to—'

'One across. Six letters. "Girl takes gun to district attorney." What's that, do you think?'

'No idea.'

'Just a minute! What about BRENDA? Fits, doesn't it? Gun – "bren"; district attorney – "D.A." Voilà!'

Brenda snatched the paper and looked at the clue: 'Girl in bed – censored.' 'You're making it up,' she laughed.

'Lovely word "bed", isn't it?' He printed the letters of 'Brenda' on the margin of the paper, and then neatly ringed the three letters 'b', 'e', 'd' in sequence. 'Any hope for me yet?'

'You're a married man.'

'And you ran away.' He underlined the three remaining letters 'r', 'a', 'n', and turned impishly towards her. 'No one'll know. We'll just nip up to your room and—'

'Don't be silly!'

'I'm not silly. I can't help it, can I, if I lust after you every time I see you in your uniform?' His tone was light and playful, but he suddenly became more serious as the door opened and two young nurses came in. He spoke softly now. 'Don't get cross with me if I keep trying, will you? Promise?'

'Promise,' whispered Brenda.

He wrote BANNED into the squares for 1 Across, and read out the clue for 1 Down. But Brenda wasn't listening. She didn't wish to be seen sitting so closely to the young doctor as this, and soon made up an excuse to go to her room, where she lay back on her single bed and stared long and hard at the ceiling. The door was locked behind her, and no one would have known, would they? Just as he'd said. If only ... She could hardly bring herself to read her own thoughts. If only he'd just walk up the stairs, knock on the door and ask her again in his simple, hopeful, uncomplicated way, she knew that she would invite him in, and lie down – just as she lay there now – gladly unresistant as he unfastened the white buttons down the front of her uniform.

She felt tired, and the room was excessively stuffy – the radiator too hot to touch. Gradually she dozed off, and when she awoke her mouth was very dry. Something had woken her; and now she heard the gently reiterated knock-knock at the door. How long had she slept for? Her watch told her it was 5.45 p.m. She fluffed her hair, straightened her uniform, lightly smeared on a little lipstick and, with a little flutter of excitement in her tummy, walked across to the door of her room, newly painted in dazzling white gloss.

It was lying by the same door that a member of the cleaning staff found her the next morning. Somehow she had managed to crawl across from the centre of the small room; and it was clear that her fingers had groped in vain for the handle of the door, for the lower panels were smeared with the blood coughed up from her throat. No one seemed to know exactly where she came from, but the letter the police found beneath the lining of her handbag suggested strongly that she was, or had been, on the most intimate terms with a man called 'Paul', who had given his address only as 'Kidlington', and who had urged the recipient to burn the evidence immediately.

CHAPTER TWENTY-TWO

IT WAS ON Saturday morning, and in the middle of page two of the long-delayed post-mortem report on the corpse found on the tower, that Morse came to the conclusion he might just as well be reading the *Chinese People's Daily*. He appreciated, of course, the need for some technical jargon, but there was no chance whatsoever for a non-medical man to unjumble such a farrago of physiological labellings. The first paragraph had been fairly plain sailing, though, and Morse handed the report over to Lewis:

> The body is that of an adult Caucasian male, brachycephalic. Height: 5 ft 8½ in. Age: not easy to assess with accuracy, but most likely between 35 and 40. Hair: light brown, probably cut a week or so before death. Eyes: colouring impossible to determine. Teeth: remarkably good, strongly enamelled, with only one filling (posterior left six). Physical peculiarities: none observable, although it cannot be assumed that there were no such peculiarities, since the largest patch of skin, taken from the lower instep (left), measures only . . .

Lewis passed the report back, for he had little wish to be reminded too vividly of the sight picked out so recently by the narrow beam of the verger's torch. Moreover, his next job promised to be quite gruesome enough for one morning, and for the next half-hour he sifted through the half-dozen transparent plastic bags containing the remnants of the dead man's clothes. Morse himself declined to assist in the un-savoury operation and expressed only mild interest when he heard a subdued whistle of triumph from his subordinate.

'Let me guess, Lewis. You've found a label with his name and telephone number.'

'As good as, sir.' In a pair of tweezers, he held up a small rectangular bus-ticket. 'It was in the breast-pocket of the jacket – 30p fare on 26 October. I reckon the fare from Kidlington to Oxford's about 30p—'

'Probably gone up by now,' muttered Morse.

'—and surely' (Lewis' eyes suddenly sparkled with excitement) 'that was the day when Paul Morris disap-peared, wasn't it?'

'Never my strong point – dates,' said Morse.

For the moment, however, nothing was going to dampen Lewis' enthusiasm. 'Pity his teeth were so good, sir. He's probably not been near a dentist for years. Still, we ought to be able to—'

'You're taking an awful lot for granted, you know. We neither of us have the slightest proof about who the fellow is, agreed? And until—'

'No, we haven't. But there's not much sense in closing our eyes to the obvious.'

154

'Which is?'

'That the man we found is Paul Morris,' replied Lewis with firm confidence.

'Just because a young girl in one of his classes says he used to wear a dark suit—'

'And a blue tie.'

'—and a blue tie, all right, that makes him Paul Morris, you say? Lewis! You're getting as bad as I am.'

'Do you think I'm wrong?'

'No, no. I wouldn't say that. I'm just a little more cautious than you, shall we say?'

This was ridiculous. Morse, as Lewis knew only too well, was a man prepared to take the most prodigious leaps into the dark; and yet here he was now – utterly blind to the few simple facts that lay staring him in the face in broad daylight. Forget it, though!

It took Lewis no more than ten minutes to discover that Paul Morris had been a patient at the Kidlington Health Centre, and after a little quiet but urgent pressure the senior partner of that consortium was reading through the details on his medical card.

'Well?' asked Morse, as Lewis cradled the receiver.

'Fits pretty well. Thirty-eight years old, five feet nine inches, light-brown hair—'

'Fits a lot of people. Medium height, medium colouring, medium—'

'Don't you *want* to find out who he is?' Lewis stood up and looked down at Morse with unwonted exasperation in his voice. 'I'm sorry if all this doesn't fit in with any clever little theory you've thought up, but we've got to make some sort of start, haven't we?'

Morse said nothing for a few moments, and when he did speak his quiet words made Lewis feel ashamed of the tetchiness which had marked his own.

'Surely you can understand, can't you, Lewis, why I'm hoping that rotting corpse isn't Paul Morris? You see, if it is, I'm afraid we'd better start looking round pretty quickly, hadn't we? We'd better start looking round for yet another corpse, my old friend – a corpse aged about twelve.'

Like Bell, the landlord of 3 Home Close, Kidlington, had flu, but he gave Morse a sneezy blessing to look over the property, rented out (since Morris left) to a young married couple with one baby daughter. But no one answered Lewis' repeated knockings. 'Probably shopping,' he said as he sat down again next to Morse in the front of the police car.

Morse nodded and looked vaguely around him. The small crescent had been built some time in the early 1930s – a dozen or so red-brick, semi-detached properties, now beginning to look their age, with the supports of their slatted wooden fences virtually sopped and sapped away. 'Tell me, Lewis,' he said suddenly. 'Who do *you* think murdered Josephs?'

'I know it's not a very original idea, sir, but I should think it must have been this down-and-out fellow. Like as not he decided to pinch the collection-money, and Josephs got in his way, and he knifed him. Another possibility—'

'But why didn't Josephs yell the place down?'

'He did try to shout for help, sir, if you remember. Couldn't make himself heard above the organ, perhaps.'

'You could be right, you know,' said Morse, almost earnestly, as if he'd suddenly woken up to the fact that the obvious way of looking at things wasn't necessarily the wrong one. 'What about Lawson? Who killed him?'

'You know better than I do, sir, that the majority of murderers either give themselves up or commit suicide. There's surely not much doubt that Lawson committed suicide.'

'But Lawson didn't kill Josephs, did he? You just said—'

'I was going on to say, sir, that there was another possibility. I don't think Lawson himself actually killed Josephs, but I think he may have been *responsible* for killing him.'

'You do?' Morse looked across at his subordinate with genuine interest. 'I think you'd better take it a bit more slowly, Lewis. You're leaving me a long way behind, I'm afraid.'

Lewis allowed himself a mild grin of modest gratification. It wasn't often that Morse was the back-marker – just the opposite in fact: he was usually about three or four jumps ahead of his stable-companion. 'I think there's more than a possibility, sir, that Lawson got this down-and-out fellow to kill Josephs – probably by giving him money.'

'But why should Lawson want to kill Josephs?'

'Josephs must have had some hold over him.'

'And Lawson must have had some hold on this down-and-out fellow.'

'How right you are, sir!'

'Am I?' Morse looked across in a semi-bewildered way at his sergeant. He remembered how when he was taking his eleven-plus examination he was seated next to a boy renowned for his vacuous imbecility, and how this same boy had solved the tenth anagram whilst Morse himself was still puzzling over the third.

'As I see it,' continued Lewis, 'Lawson must have been looking after him all ways: meals, clothes, bed, everything.'

'He must have been like a sort of brother to him, you mean?'

Lewis looked at Morse curiously. 'Bit more than that, wasn't he, sir?'

'Pardon?'

'I said it was a bit more than being like a brother to him. He *was* a brother, surely.'

'You mustn't believe every piece of gossip you hear.'

'And you mustn't automatically disbelieve it, either.'

'If only we had a bit more to go on, Lewis!' And then the truth hit him, as it usually did, with a flash of blinding simplicity. Any corroboration he'd wanted had been lying under his nose since his visit with Lewis to Stamford, and a shiver of excitement ran along his scalp as at last he spotted it. 'Swanpole' had appeared several times in Bell's files as the probable name of the man who had been befriended by the Reverend Lionel

Lawson, the man who had so strangely disappeared after the murder of Josephs. But, if all the rumours were right, that man's real name was Philip Edward Lawson, and whether you were a rather timid little fellow trying your eleven-plus question-paper, or whether you were a souring middle-aged detective sitting in a panda-car, *Swanpole was an anagram of P. E. Lawson.*

'I reckon this'll be mother and infant,' said Lewis under his breath. And indeed the heavily pregnant, dowdily dressed young woman dragging a two-year-old child along the pavement duly announced that she herself was the present occupier of 3 Home Close and that this was her daughter, Eve. Yes, she said, since the landlord had no objections, they could come in and have a look round the house. With pleasure.

Morse declined the offer of a cup of tea, and went out into the back garden. Clearly someone had been very busy, for the whole plot showed every evidence of a systematic and recent digging-over; and in the small garden-shed the tines of the fork and the bottom half of the spade were polished to a silvery smoothness.

'I see your husband's keen on growing his own veg,' said Morse lightly, as he wiped his shoes on the mat by the back door.

She nodded. 'It was all grass before we came, but, you know, with the price of things these days—'

'Looks as if he's been doing a bit of double-digging.'

'That's it. Took him ages, but he says it's the only way.'

COLIN DEXTER

Morse, who hardly knew a sweet pea from a broad bean, nodded wisely, and gratefully decided he could forget about the garden.

'Mind if we have a quick look upstairs?'

'No. Go ahead. We only use two of the bedrooms – like the people who was here before us did. But – well, you never know . . .' Morse glanced down at her swollen belly and wondered how many bedrooms she might need before her carrying days were over.

Young Eve's bower, the smallest of the bedrooms, was redolent of urine, and Morse screwed up his nose in distaste as he cursorily bent down over the uncarpeted floorboards. A dozen Donald Ducks on the newly decorated walls seemed to mock his aimless investigations, and he quickly left the room and closed the door behind him.

'Nothing in either of the other rooms, sir,' said Lewis, joining Morse on the narrow landing, where the walls had been painted in a light Portland beige, with the woodwork cleanly finished off in white gloss. Morse, thinking the colours a good match, looked up at the ceiling – and whistled softly. Immediately above his head was a small rectangular trap-door, some 3 feet by $2\frac{1}{2}$ feet, painted as lovingly as the rest of the woodwork.

'You got a step-ladder?' Morse shouted downstairs.

Two minutes later Lewis was poking his head over the dusty beams and shining a torch around the rafters. Here and there a little of the early afternoon light filtered through ill-fitting joints in the tiles, yet the surprisingly large roof-space seemed dismal and darkly silent as Lewis took his weight on his wrists, gently levered himself up into the loft, and warily trod from beam to beam. A large trunk occupied the space between the trap-door and the chimney-stack, and as Lewis opened the lid and shone his torch on the slightly mildewed covers of the books inside a black, fat-bellied spider scurried its way out of reach. But Lewis was no arachnophobe, and quickly satisfying himself that the trunk was packed only with books he prodded around amid the rest of the débris: a furled Union Jack on a long blue pole, its colours faded now and forlorn; an old camp-bed probably dating from the Baden-Powell era; a brand-new lavatory-pan, patched (for some unfathomable purpose) with strips of gummed brown paper; an antiquated carpet-sweeper; two rolls of yellow insulation material; and a large roll of something else – surely? – pushed up tight between the beams and the roof-angle. Bending forward as low as he could, and groping in front of him, Lewis managed to reach the bundle, where his finger-tips prodded something soft and where his torch-light shone on to a black shoe sticking out of one end, the toe-cap filmed with a layer of grey dust.

'Anything there?' Lewis heard the quiet urgent voice from below, but said nothing. The string tying the bundle together broke as he tugged at it, and there unrolled before him a collection of good-quality clothes: trousers, shirts, underclothes, socks, shoes and half a dozen ties – one of them a light Cambridge blue.

Lewis' grim face appeared suddenly framed in the darkened rectangle. 'You'd better come up and have a look, sir.'

161

They found another roll of clothes then, containing very much the same sort of items as the first. But the trousers were smaller, as indeed were all the other garments, and the two pairs of shoes looked as if they might have fitted a boy of about eleven or twelve. There was a tie, too. Just the one. A brand-new tie, with alternate stripes of red and grey: the tie worn by the pupils of the Roger Bacon Comprehensive School.

CHAPTER TWENTY-THREE

A GOOD MANY of the gradually swelling congregation were acid-faced spinsters of some fifty or sixty summers, several of whom glanced round curiously at the two strangers who sat on the back row of the central pews, next to the empty seat now clearly marked CHURCH-WARDEN. Lewis both looked and felt extraordinarily uncomfortable, whilst Morse appeared to gaze round him with bland assurance.

'We do what everybody else does, understand?' whispered Morse, as the five-minute bell ceased its monotonous melancholy toll, and the choir set out in procession from the vestry and down the main aisle, followed by the incense-swinger and the boat-boy, the acolytes and torch-bearers, the master of ceremonies, and three eminent personages, similarly but not identically dressed, the last wearing, amongst other things, alb, biretta and chasuble – the ABC of ecclesiastical rig as far as Morse as yet had mastered it. In the chancel, the dramatis personae dispersed to their appropriate stations with practised alacrity, and suddenly all was order once more. Ruth Rawlinson, in a black, square choir-hat, took her place just beneath a stone-carved angel and the assembled choir now launched into the

163

Mass. During this time the churchwarden had slipped noiselessly into his seat, and handed Morse a little scrap of paper: 'Setting, *Iste Confessor* – Palestrina'; at which Morse nodded wisely before passing it on to Lewis.

At half-time, one of the eminent personages temporarily doffed his chasuble and ascended the circular steps of the pulpit to admonish his flock against the dangers and follies of fornication. But Morse sat throughout as one to whom the admonition was not immediately applicable. Once or twice earlier his eyes had caught Ruth's, but all the female members of the choir were now sheltered from view behind a stout octagonal pillar, and he leaned back and contemplated the lozenge-shaped panes of stained glass – deepest ruby, smoky blue and brightest emerald – his mind drifting back to his own childhood, when he had sung in the choir himself . . .

Lewis, too, though for different reasons, very soon lost all interest in fornication. Being, in any case, the sort of man who had seldom cast any lascivious glances over his neighbour's wife, he let his mind wander quietly over the case instead, and asked himself once more whether Morse had been right in his insistence that another visit to a church service would be certain to spark off a few flashes of association, 'to give the hooked atoms a shake', as Morse had put it – whatever that might mean . . .

It took some twenty minutes for the preacher to exhaust his anti-carnal exhortations; after which he descended from the pulpit, disappeared from view through a screen in the side of the Lady Chapel, before re-emerging, chasuble redonned, at the top of the main chancel. This was the cue for the other two members of the triumvirate to rise and to march in step towards the altar where they joined their brother. The choir had already picked up their Palestrina scores once more, and amid much genuflexion, crossing and embracing the Mass was approaching its climactic moment. 'Take, eat, this is my body,' said the celebrant, and his two assistants suddenly bowed towards the altar with a perfect synchronization of movement and gesture – just as if the two were one. Yes, just as if the two were one ... And there drifted into Morse's memory that occasion when as a young boy he'd been taken to a music-hall show with his parents. One of the acts had featured a woman dancing in front of a huge mirror, and for the first few minutes he had been unable to fathom it out at all. She wasn't a particularly nimble-bodied thing, and yet the audience had seemed enthralled by her performance. Then his mind had clicked: the dancer wasn't in front of a mirror at all! The apparent reflection was in reality another woman; dancing precisely the same steps, making precisely the same gestures, dressed in precisely the same costume. There were two women – not one. So? So, if there had been two dancers, could there not have been two priests on the night when Josephs was murdered?

The kittiwake was soaring once again ...

Five minutes after the final benediction, the church was empty. A cassocked youth had finally snuffed out the last candle in the galaxy, and even the zealous Mrs Walsh-Atkins had departed. *Missa est ecclesia.*

Morse stood up, slid the slim red *Order of Service* into his raincoat pocket, and strolled with Lewis into the Lady Chapel, where he stood reading a brass plaque affixed to the south wall.

> In the vaults beneath are interred the terrestrial remains of Jn. Baldwin Esq., honourable benefactor and faithful servant of this parish. Died 1732. Aged 68 yrs. Requiescat in pace.

Meiklejohn smiled without joy as he approached them, surplice over his left arm. 'Anything else we can do for you, gentlemen?'

'We want a spare set of keys,' said Morse.

'Well, there *is* a spare set,' said Meiklejohn, frowning slightly. 'Can you tell me why—?'

'It's just that we'd like to get in when the church is locked, that's all.'

'Yes, I see.' He shook his head sadly. 'We've had a lot of senseless vandalism recently – mostly school-children, I'm afraid. I sometimes wonder . . .'

'We shall only need 'em for a few days.'

Meiklejohn led them into the vestry, climbed on to a chair, and lifted a bunch of keys from a hook underneath the top of the curtain. 'Let me have them back as soon as you can, please. There are only four sets now, and someone's always wanting them – for bell-ringing, that sort of thing.'

Morse looked at the keys before pocketing them: old-fashioned keys, one large, three much smaller, all of them curiously and finely wrought.

'Shall we lock the door behind us?' asked Morse. It was meant to be lightly jocular, but succeeded only in sounding facetious and irreverent.

'No, thank you,' replied the minister quietly. 'We get quite a lot of visitors on Sundays, and they like to come here and be quiet, and to think about life – even to pray, perhaps.'

Neither Morse nor Lewis had been on his knees throughout the service; and Lewis, at least, left the church feeling just a little guilty, just a little humbled: it was as if he had turned his back on a holy offering.

'C'm on,' said Morse, 'we're wasting good drinking time.'

At 12.25 p.m. the same day, a call from the Shrewsbury Constabulary came through to the Thames Valley Police H.Q. in Kidlington, where the acting desk sergeant took down the message carefully. He didn't *think* the name rang any bells, but he'd put the message through the appropriate channels. It was only after he'd put the phone down that he realized he hadn't the faintest idea what 'the appropriate channels' were.

CHAPTER TWENTY-FOUR

MORSE WAS LINGERING longer than usual, and it was Lewis who drained his glass first.

'You feeling well, sir?'

Morse put the *Order of Service* back in his pocket, and finished his beer in three or four gargantuan gulps. 'Never better, Lewis. Fill 'em up.'

'Your round, I think, sir.'

'Oh.'

Morse leaned his elbows beside the replenished pints and continued. 'Who murdered Harry Josephs? That's the key question really, isn't it?'

Lewis nodded. 'I had a bit of an idea during the service—'

'No more ideas, please! I've got far too many already. Listen! The prime suspect's got to be the fellow Bell tried to trace. Agreed? The fellow who'd stayed several times at Lawson's vicarage, who was at the church when Josephs was murdered, and who disappeared afterwards. Agreed? We're not *quite* certain about it, but there's every chance that this fellow was Lionel Lawson's brother, Philip Lawson. He's hard up and he's a wino. He sees some ready cash on the collection-plate and he decides to pinch it. Josephs tries to stop him, and gets a knife in the back for his trouble. Any problems?'

'How did Philip Lawson come to have the knife?'

'He'd seen it lying around the vicarage, and he decided to pocket it.'

'Just on the off chance?'

'That's it,' said Morse, as he turned unblinking towards Lewis.

'But there were only a dozen or so people at the service, and the collection wouldn't have come to more than a couple of quid.'

'That's it.'

'Why not wait till one of the Sunday-morning services? Then he'd have the chance of fifty-odd quid.'

'Yes. That's true.'

'Why didn't he, then?'

'I dunno.'

'But no one actually *saw* him in the vestry.'

'He skipped it as soon as he'd knifed Josephs.'

'Surely someone would have seen him – or heard him?'

'Perhaps he just hid in the vestry – behind the curtain.'

'Impossible!'

'Behind the door to the tower, then,' suggested Morse. 'Perhaps he went up to the tower – hid in the bell-chamber – hid on the roof – I dunno.'

'But that door was locked when the police arrived – so it says in the report.'

'Easy. He locked it from the inside.'

'You mean he had – he had the key?'

'You say you read the report, Lewis. Well? You must have seen the inventory of what they found in Josephs' pockets.'

The light slowly dawned in Lewis' mind, and he could see Morse watching him, a hint of mild amusement in the inspector's pale-blue eyes.

'You mean – they didn't find any keys,' he said at last.

'No keys.'

'You think he took them out of Josephs' pocket?'

'Nothing to stop him.'

'But – but if he looked through Josephs' pockets, why didn't he find the money? The hundred quid?'

'Aren't you assuming,' asked Morse quietly, 'that that was all there was to find. What if, say, there'd been a *thousand*?'

'You mean—?' But Lewis wasn't sure what he meant.

'I mean that everyone, *almost* everyone, Lewis, is going to think what you did: that the murderer didn't search through Josephs' pockets. It puts everyone on the wrong scent, doesn't it? Makes it look as if it's petty crime – as you say, a few pennies off the collection-plate. You see, perhaps our murderer wasn't really much worried about *how* he was going to commit the crime – he thought he could get away with that. What he didn't want was anyone looking too closely at the *motive*.'

Lewis was growing increasingly perplexed. 'Just a minute, sir. You say he wasn't much worried about how he murdered Josephs. But how *did* he? Josephs was poisoned as well as stabbed.'

'Perhaps he just gave him a swig of booze – doctored booze.'

Again Lewis felt the disconcerting conviction that Morse was playing a game with him. One or two of the points the chief had just made were more like those flashes of insight he'd learned to expect. But surely Morse could do better than this? He could do better himself.

'Josephs could have been poisoned when he took communion, sir.'

'You think so?' Morse's eyes were smiling again. 'How do you figure that out?'

'I reckon the churchwarden is usually the last person to take communion—'

'Like this morning, yes.'

'—and so this tramp fellow is kneeling there next to him and he slips something into the wine.'

'How did he carry the poison?'

'He could have had it in one of those rings. You just unscrew the top—'

'You watch too much television,' said Morse.

'—and sprinkle it in the wine.'

'It would be a whitish powder, Lewis, and it wouldn't dissolve immediately. So the Rev. Lionel would see it floating on top. Is that what you're saying?'

'Perhaps he had his eyes closed. There's a lot of praying and all that sort of thing when—'

'And Josephs himself? Was he doing a lot of praying and all that sort of thing?'

'Could have been.'

'Why wasn't Lawson poisoned, then? It's the minister's

171

job to finish off any wine that's left and, as you say, Josephs was pretty certainly the last customer.'

'Perhaps Josephs swigged the lot,' suggested Lewis hopefully; and then his eyes irradiated a sudden excitement. 'Or perhaps, sir – or perhaps the two of them, the two Lawson brothers, were in it together. That would answer quite a lot of questions, wouldn't it?'

Morse smiled contentedly at his colleague. 'You know, Lewis, you get brighter all the time. I think it must be my company that does it.'

He pushed his glass across the table 'Your turn, isn't it?'

He looked around him as Lewis waited patiently to be served: it was half past one and Sunday lunch-time trade was at its peak. A man with a rough beard, dressed in a long ex-army coat, had just shuffled through the entrance and was standing apprehensively by the bar; a man in latish middle age, it seemed, wearing that incongruous pair of sunglasses, and grasping an empty flagon of cider in his hand. Morse left his seat and walked over to him.

'We met before, remember?'

The man looked slowly at Morse and shook his head. 'Sorry, mate.'

'Life not treating you so good?'

'Nah.'

'Been roughing it long?'

'Last back-end.'

'You ever know a fellow called Swanpole?'

'Nah. Sorry, mate.'

'Doesn't matter. I used to know him, that's all.'

'I knew somebody who did,' said the tramp quietly. 'Somebody who knew the fellah you was just talking about.'

'Yes?' Morse fumbled in his pockets and pushed a fifty-pence piece into the man's hand.

'The old boy I used to go round with – 'e mentioned that name recently. "Swanny" – that's what they called 'im, but 'e's not round these parts any more.'

'What about the old boy? Is he still around?'

'Nah. 'E's dead. Died o' pneumonia – yesterday.'

'Oh.'

Morse walked back thoughtfully to the table, and a few minutes later watched a little sadly as the landlord showed the tramp the way to the exit. Clearly there was no welcome for the poor fellow's custom here, and no cider slowly to be sipped on one of the city's benches that Sunday afternoon; not from this pub anyway.

'One of your pals?' grinned Lewis, as he placed two more pints on the table.

'I don't think he's got any pals.'

'Perhaps if Lawson were still alive—'

'He's just the man we've got to talk about, Lewis – suspect number two. Agreed?'

'You mean he suddenly disappeared from in front of the altar, murdered Josephs, and then came back and carried on with the service?'

'Something like that.'

The beer was good, and Lewis leaned back, quite happy to listen.

'Come on, sir. I know you're dying to tell me.'

'First, let's just follow up your idea about the

poisoned chalice. There are too many improbabilities in the way you looked at it. But what if the Rev. Lionel himself put the morphine in the wine? What then? After his brother's had a swig, he can pretend that the chalice is empty, turn round to the altar, slip in the powder, pour in a drop more wine, give it a quick stir – no problem! Or else he could have had two chalices – one of 'em already doctored – and just put the one down and pick up the other. Easier still! Mark my words, Lewis. If it was either of the two brothers who poisoned Josephs, I reckon the odds are pretty heavily on the Rev. Lionel.'

'Let me get it straight, sir. According to you, Lionel Lawson tried to kill Josephs, only to find that someone had done a far neater job a few minutes later – with a knife. Right?' Lewis shook his head. 'Not on, sir, is it?'

'Why not? The Rev. Lionel knows that Josephs'll go straight to the vestry, and that in a few minutes he's going to be very dead. There's one helluva dose of morphine in the communion wine and the strong probability is that Josephs is going to die all nice and peaceful like, because morphine poisoning isn't a painful death – just the opposite. In which case, Josephs' death may well pose a few problems; but no one's going to be able to pin the murder on the Rev. Lionel. The chalice has been carefully washed out and dried, in strict accord with ecclesiastical etiquette – a wonderful example of a criminal actually being encouraged to destroy the evidence of his crime. Beautiful idea! But then things began to go askew. Josephs must have guessed that something was desperately wrong with him, and before he collapsed in the vestry he just managed to drag himself to the curtains and shout for help – a shout that all the congregation heard. But someone, *someone*, Lewis, was watching that vestry like a hawk – the Rev. Lionel himself. And as soon as he saw Josephs there he was off down the aisle like an avenging Fury; and he was down there in the vestry before anyone else had the nous or the guts to move; and once inside he stabbed Josephs viciously in the back, turned to face the congregation, and told 'em all that Josephs was lying there – murdered.' (Morse mentally congratulated himself on an account that was rather more colourful and dramatic than Bell's prosaic reconstruction of exactly the same events.)

'He'd have got blood all over him,' protested Lewis.

'Wouldn't have mattered much if he'd been wearing the sort of outfit they were wearing this morning.'

Lewis thought back to the morning service and those deep-crimson vestments – the colour of dark-red blood ... 'But why finish Josephs off with a knife? He'd be almost dead by then.'

'Lionel was frightened that Josephs would accuse him of doing the poisoning. Almost certainly Josephs would have guessed what had happened.'

'Probably everyone else would, too.'

'Ah! But if you stabbed Josephs in the back as well, people are going to ask who did *that*, aren't they?'

'Yes. And they're going to think that was Lawson, too. After all, it was Lawson's knife.'

'No one knew that at the time,' said Morse defensively.

175

'Did Bell think that's how it happened?'

Morse nodded. 'Yes, he did.'

'And do *you*, sir?'

Morse seemed to be weighing the odds in the mental balance. 'No,' he said finally.

Lewis leaned back in his chair. 'You know, when you come to think of it, it's a bit improbable that a minister's going to murder one of his own congregation, isn't it? That sort of thing doesn't happen in real life.'

'I rather hope it does,' said Morse quietly.

'Pardon, sir?'

'I said I rather hope it *does* happen. You asked me if Lionel Lawson killed Josephs in a particular way, and I said I didn't think so. But I reckon it *was* Lionel Lawson who killed Josephs, though in a rather more simple way. He just walked down to the vestry, knifed poor old Harry Josephs—'

'And then he walked back!'

'You've got it!'

Lewis' eyes rolled towards the tobacco-stained ceiling and he began to wonder if the beer had not robbed the inspector of his wits.

'With all the congregation watching him, I suppose.'

'Oh, no. They didn't see him.'

'They didn't?'

'No. The service at which Josephs was killed was held in the Lady Chapel. Now, if you remember, there's an archway in the screen separating this chapel from the central chancel, and I reckon that after the bread and wine had been dished out Lawson took a few of the

176

utensils across from the altar in the Lady Chapel to the main altar – they're always doing that sort of thing, these priests.' (Lewis was hardly listening any more, and the landlord was wiping the tables, collecting glasses and emptying the ashtrays.) 'You want to know how he performed this remarkable feat, Lewis? Well, as I see it, the Rev. Lionel and his brother had got everything worked out, and that night the pair of 'em were all dressed up in identical ecclesiastical clobber. Now, when the Rev. Lionel walked out of the Lady Chapel for a few seconds, it wasn't the Rev. Lionel who walked back! There are only a few prayerful old souls in the congregation, and for that vital period the man standing in front of the altar, kneeling there, praying there, *but never actually facing the congregation*, is brother Philip! What do you think, Lewis? You think anyone looking up could have suspected the truth?'

'Perhaps Philip Lawson was bald.'

'Doubt it. Whether you go bald depends on your grandfather.'

'If you say so, sir.' Lewis was growing increasingly sceptical about all this jiggery-pokery with duplicate chalices and chasubles; and, anyway, he was anxious to be off home. He stood up and took his leave.

Morse remained where he was, the forefinger of his left hand marrying little droplets of spilt beer on the table-top. Like Lewis, he was far from happy about his possible reconstructions of Josephs' murder. But one idea was growing even firmer in his mind: there must have been some collaboration somewhere. And, like as not, that collaboration had involved the two brothers.

But how? For several minutes Morse's thoughts were chasing round after their own tails. For the thousandth time he asked himself where he ought to start, and for the thousandth time he told himself that he had to decide who had killed Harry Josephs. All right! Assume it was the Rev. Lionel – on the grounds that *something* must have driven him to suicide. But what if it wasn't Lionel who had thrown himself from the tower? What if it was Philip who had *been* thrown? Yes, that would have been very neat ... But there was a virtually insuperable objection to such a theory. The Rev. Lionel would have to dress up his brother's body in his own clothes, his own black clerical front, his dog-collar – everything. And that, in such a short space of time after the morning service, was plain physically impossible! But what if...? Yes! What if Lionel had somehow managed to persuade his brother to change clothes? Was it possible? Phew! Of course it was! It wasn't just possible – it was eminently probable. And why? *Because Philip Lawson had already done it before.* He'd agreed to dress up in his brother's vestments so that he could stand at the altar whilst Josephs was being murdered! Doubtless he'd been wonderfully well rewarded for his troubles on that occasion. So why not agree to a second little charade? Of course he would have agreed – little thinking he'd be dressing up for his own funeral. But with one seemingly insuperable problem out of the way another one had taken its place: two people had positively identified the body that had fallen from the tower. Was that a real problem, though? Had Mrs Walsh-Atkins really had the stomach to look all that carefully at a face that was as smashed and bleeding as the rest of that mutilated body? Had her presence outside the church just been an accidental fluke? Because someone else had been there, had he not? Someone all ready to testify to the identity – the false identity – of the corpse: Paul Morris. And Paul Morris had subsequently been murdered because he knew too much: knew, specifically, that the Reverend Lionel Lawson was not only still in the land of the living, but was also a murderer, to boot! A double-murderer. A triple-murderer...

'Do you mind drinking up, sir?' said the landlord. 'We often get the police round here on Sunday mornings.'

CHAPTER TWENTY-FIVE

ON THE SAME day, just after eight o'clock in the evening, a middle-aged man, his white shirt open at the neck, sat waiting in a brightly lit, well-furnished room. He was lounging back on a deep sofa, its chintz covers printed in a russet-and-white floral design, from which, smoking a king-sized Benson & Hedges cigarette, he vaguely watched the television. She was a little late tonight; but he had no doubts that she would come, for she needed him just as much as he needed her. Sometimes, he suspected, even more so. A bottle of claret, already opened, and two wineglasses stood on the coffee-table beside him, and through the half-opened bedroom door he could see the hypotenuse of white sheet drawn back from the pillows.

Come on, girl!

It was eight-ten when the key (she had a key – of course she did!) scraped gently in the Yale lock and she entered. Although a steady drizzle persisted outside, her pale-blue mackintosh seemed completely dry as she slipped it from her shoulders, folded it neatly across its waist, and put it over the back of an armchair. The white cotton blouse she wore was drawn tight across her breasts, and the close-fitting black skirt clung to the curve of her thighs. She said nothing for a while; merely looked at him, her eyes reflecting no affection and no joy – just a simmering animal sensuality. She walked across the room and stood in front of him – provocatively.

'You told me you were going to stop smoking.'

'Sit down and stop moaning, woman. Christ! You make me feel sexy in that outfit.'

The woman did exactly as she was told, almost as if she would do anything he asked without demur; almost as if she thrived on the brusque crudity of his commands, There were no tender words of preliminary love-play on either side, yet she sat close to him as he poured two full glasses of wine, and he felt the pressure of her black-stockinged leg (good girl – she'd remembered!) against his own. In token of some vestigial respect they clinked their glasses together, and she leaned back against the sofa.

'Been watching the telly all night?' Her question was commonplace, uninterested.

'I didn't get back till half past six.'

She turned to look at him for the first time. 'You're a fool going out like that. Especially on Sundays. Don't you realize—?'

'Calm down, woman! I'm not a fool, and you know it. Nobody's seen me slipping out of here yet. And what if they did? Nobody's going to recognize me now.' He leaned across her and his fingers deftly unfastened the top button of her blouse. And then the next button.

As always with this man, the woman experienced that curious admixture of revulsion and attraction –

COLIN DEXTER

compulsive combination! Until so very recently a virgin,
she was newly aware of herself as a physical object,
newly conscious of the power of her body. She lay back
passively as he fondled her far beyond the point which
a few months previously would have been either pleasing or permissible; and she seemed almost mesmerized
as he pulled her up from the sofa and led the way
through to the bedroom.

Their coitus was not exceptionally memorable –
certainly not ecstatic; but it was satisfactory and satisfying. It usually was. As usual, too, the woman now lay
between the sheets silently, feeling cheap and humiliated. It was not only her body that was naked, but her
soul, too; and instinctively she drew the top of the sheet
up to her neck and prayed that for a little while at least
he would keep his hands and eyes away from her. How
she despised him! Yet not one half, not one quarter as
much as she had learned to despise herself.

It had got to stop. She hated the man and the power
he had come to wield over her – yet she needed him,
needed the firm virility of his body. He had kept himself
wonderfully fit ... but, then, that wasn't ... wasn't
surprising ... not really ... not really ...

Briefly she fell asleep.

He spoke to her as she stood by the door, the mackintosh loosely over her shoulders. 'Same time on
Wednesday?'

Once more the humiliation of it all settled heavily
upon her, and her lip was shaking as she replied.

'It's got to stop! You know it has!'

'Stop?' His mouth was set in a conceited sneer. 'You couldn't stop. You know that as well as I do.'

'I can stop seeing you whenever I like, and there's nothing you or anybody else—'

'Isn't there? You're in this as deeply as I am – don't you ever forget that!'

She shook her head, almost wildly. 'You said you'd be going away. You promised!'

'And I shall be. I'll be going very soon now, my girl, and that's the truth. But until I do go I keep seeing you – understand? I see you when I want, as often as I want. And don't tell me you don't enjoy it, because you do! And you know you do.'

Yes, she knew it, and she felt her eyes prickling with hurt at his cruel words. How could she do this? How could she hate a man so much – and yet allow him to make love to her? No! it just couldn't go on like this! And the solution to all her troubles was so childishly simple: she just had to go and see Morse, that was all; tell him everything and face the consequences, whatever they were. She still had a bit of courage left, didn't she?

The man was watching her carefully, half-guessing what was going through her mind. He was used to taking swift decisions – he always had been; and he saw his next moves as clearly as if he were a grandmaster playing chess with a novice. He had known all along that he would have to deal with her sooner or later; and, although he had hoped it would be later, he realized now that the game must be finished quickly.

For him, sex had always come – would always come – a poor second to power.

He walked over to her, and his face for once seemed kind and understanding as he placed his hands so very lightly on her shoulders, his eyes looking searchingly into hers.

'All right, Ruth,' he said quietly. 'I'll not be a nuisance to you any more. Come and sit down a minute. I want to talk to you.' Gently he took her arm and led her unresisting to the sofa. 'I won't make any more demands on you, Ruth – I promise I won't. We'll stop seeing each other, if that's what you really want. I can't bear to see you unhappy like this.'

It had been many weeks since he had spoken to her in such a way, and for a while, in the context of her wider grief, she felt infinitely grateful for his words.

'As I say, I'll be going away soon and then you can forget me, and we can both try to forget what we've done. The wrong we've done – because it *was* wrong, wasn't it? Not about us going to bed together – I don't mean that. That was something lovely for me – something I shall never regret – and I'd hoped . . . I'd hoped it was lovely for you, too. But never mind that. Just promise me one thing, Ruth, will you? If you ever want to come to me – while I'm here, I mean – please come! Please! You know I'll be wanting you – and waiting.'

She nodded, and the tears trickled down her cheeks at the bitter-sweet joy of his words as he cradled her head against his shoulder and held her firmly to him.

She stayed there for what seemed to her a long, long time; yet for him it was little more than a functional interspace, his cold eyes staring over her shoulder at the hateful wallpaper behind the television. He would have to kill her, of course: that decision had been taken long ago anyway. What he was quite unable to understand was the delay. Surely the police were not so stupid as they seemed? Nothing so far – *why*? – about the Shrewsbury murder. Nothing definite about the body on the tower; Nothing at all about the boy . . .

'Your mother all right?' He asked it almost tenderly.

She nodded and sniffed. It was time she was back home with that mother of hers.

'Still cleaning the church?'

She nodded again, continued her sniffing, and finally broke away from him.

'Mondays, Wednesdays and Fridays?'

'Just Mondays and Wednesdays now. I'm getting a bit slack in my old age.'

'Still in the mornings?'

'Mm. I usually go about ten. And I've been going for a drink in the Randolph when I've finished, I'm afraid.' She laughed nervously, and blew her nose loudly into her sopping handkerchief. 'I could do with a quick drink now if—'

'Of course.' He fetched a bottle of Teacher's whisky from the sideboard and poured a good measure into her wineglass. 'Here you are. You'll feel better soon. You feel better *now*, don't you?'

'Yes, I do.' She took a sip of the whisky. 'You – you remember when I asked you whether you knew anything about – about what they found up on the church tower?'

185

'I remember.'

'You said you hadn't any idea at all—'

'And I hadn't – haven't. Not the faintest idea. But I expect the police will find out.'

'They just say they're – they're making enquiries.'

'They've not been bothering you again, have they?'

She breathed deeply and stood up. 'No. Not that I could tell them anything about *that.*'

For a moment she thought of Morse with his piercing eyes. Sad eyes, though, as if they were always looking for something and never quite finding it. A clever man, as she realized, and a nice man, too. Why, oh why, hadn't someone like Morse found her many years ago?

'What are you thinking about?' His voice was almost brusque again.

'Me? Oh, just thinking how nice you can be when you want. That's all.'

She wanted to get away from him now. It was as if freedom beckoned her from behind the locked door, but he was close behind her and his hands were once again fondling her body; and soon he had forced her to the floor where, within a few inches of the door; he penetrated her once again, snorting as he did so like some animal, whilst she for her part stared joylessly at a hair-line crack upon the ceiling.

CHAPTER TWENTY-SIX

'THEY TELL ME you can start a fibroblast from the commercial banger,' said Morse, rubbing his hands delightedly over the crowded plate of sausages, eggs and chips which Mrs Lewis had placed before him. It was half past eight on the same Sunday evening.

'What's a fibroblast?' asked Lewis.

'Something to do with taking a bit of tissue and keeping it alive. Frightening really. Perhaps you could keep a bit of somebody alive – well, indefinitely, I suppose. Sort of immortality of the body.' He broke the surface of one of his eggs and dipped a golden-brown chip into the pale-yellow yolk.

'You won't mind if I have the telly on?' Mrs Lewis sat down with a cup of tea, and the set was clicked on. 'I don't really care what they do to me when I'm gone, Inspector, just as long as they make absolutely certain that I'm dead, that's all.'

It was an old fear – a fear that had prompted some of the wealthier Victorians to arrange all sorts of elaborate contraptions inside their coffins so that any corpse, revivified contrary to the expectations of the physicians, could signal from its subterranean interment immediate intelligence of any return to consciousness. It was a fear, too, that had driven Poe to write about such things with so grisly a fascination; and Morse refrained from mentioning the fact that those whose most pressing anxiety was they might be lowered living into their graves could have their minds set at rest: the disturbing medical truth was they quite certainly *would* be so lowered.

'What's on?' mumbled Morse, his mouth full of food.

But Mrs Lewis didn't hear him. Already, Svengali-like, the television held her in its holy trance.

Ten minutes later Lewis sat checking his football pools from the *Sunday Express*, and Morse leaned back on the sofa and closed his eyes, his mind preoccupied with death and people being lowered ... lowered into their graves ...

Where – where was he?

Morse's head and shoulders jerked backwards, and he blinked himself awake. Lewis was still engrossed in the back page of the *Sunday Express*, and on the television screen a head butler was walking sedately down some stairs to a wine-cellar.

That was it! Silently Morse cursed himself for his own stupidity. The answer had stared him in the face that very same morning: 'In the vaults beneath are interred the terrestrial remains ...' A wave of excitement set his senses tingling as he stood up and drew back the edge of the curtain from the window. It was dark now, and the pane was spattered with fine drizzle.

Things could wait, surely? What on earth was going to be gained by another nocturnal visit to a dark, deserted church that couldn't wait until the light of the morning? But inevitably Morse knew that he couldn't wait and wouldn't wait.

'Sorry about this, Mrs Lewis, but I shall have to take the old man away again, I'm afraid. We shouldn't be long, though; and thanks again for the meal.'

Mrs Lewis said nothing, and fetched her husband's shoes from the kitchen. Lewis himself said nothing, either, but folded the newspaper away and resigned himself to the fact that his Lit-plan permutations had once more failed to land him a fortune. It was the 'bankers' that always let him down, those virtual certainties round which the plan had to be constructed. Like this case, he thought, as he pulled on his shoes: no real certainties at all. Not in his own mind anyway; and from what Morse had said at lunch-time no real certainties in *his* mind, either. And where the Dickens, he wondered, were they off to now?

As it happened, the church was neither dark nor deserted, and the main door at the north porch creaked open to reveal a suffused light over the quiet interior.

'Do you think the murderer's here, sir – confessing his sins?'

'I reckon somebody's confessing something,' muttered Morse.

His ears had caught the faintest murmurings and he pointed to the closed curtains of the confessional, set into the north wall.

Almost immediately an attractive young woman emerged, her sins presumably forgiven, and with eyes averted from the two detectives click-clacked her way out of the church.

'Nice-looking girl, sir.'

'Mm. She may have what you want, Lewis; but do you want what she's got?'

'Pardon, sir?'

The Reverend Canon Meiklejohn was walking silently towards them on his rubber-soled shoes, removing a long, green-embroidered stole from round his neck.

'Which of you wants to be first, gentlemen?'

'I'm afraid I've not been sinning much today,' said Morse. 'In fact there's many a day when I hardly get through any sinning at all.'

'We're all sinners, you know that,' said Meiklejohn seriously. 'Sin, alas, is the natural state of our unregenerate humanity—'

'Is there a crypt under the church?' asked Morse.

Meiklejohn's eyes narrowed slightly. 'Well, yes, there is, but – er – no one goes down there. Not as far as I know anyway. In fact I'm told that no one's been down there for ten years or so. The steps look as if they've rotted away and—'

Again Morse interrupted him. 'How can we get down there?'

Meiklejohn was not in the habit of being spoken to

so sharply, and a look of slight annoyance crossed his face. 'I'm afraid you can't, gentlemen. Not now anyway. I'm due at Pusey House in about—' He looked down at his wristwatch.

'You don't really need me to remind you what we're here for, do you, sir? And it's not to inspect your Norman font, is it? We're investigating a murder – a series of murders – and as police officers we've every right to expect a bit of co-operation from the public. And for the minute *you're* the public. All right? Now. How do we get down there?'

Meiklejohn breathed deeply. It had been a long day and he was beginning to feel very tired. 'Do you really have to talk to me as if I were a naughty child, Inspector? I'll just get my coat, if you don't mind.'

He walked off to the vestry, and when he returned Morse noticed the shabbiness of the thick, dark overcoat; the shabbiness, too, of the wrinkled black shoes.

'We shall need this,' said Meiklejohn, pointing to a twenty-foot ladder against the south porch.

With a marked lack of professionalism, Morse and Lewis manœuvred the long ladder awkwardly out of the south door, through the narrow gate immediately opposite, and into the churchyard, where they followed Meiklejohn over the wet grass along the south side of the outer church wall. A street lamp threw a thin light on to the irregular rows of gravestones to their right, but the wall itself was in the deepest gloom.

'Here we are,' said Meiklejohn. He stood darkly over a horizontal iron grille, about six feet by three feet, which rested on the stone sides of a rectangular shaft cut into the ground. Through the grille-bars, originally painted black but now brown-flaked with rust, the torch-light picked out the bottom of the cavity, about twelve feet below, littered with the débris of paper bags and cigarette-packets. To the side of the shaft furthest from the church wall was affixed a rickety-looking wooden ladder, and parallel to it an iron hand-rail ran steeply down. Set just beneath the church wall was a small door: the entrance to the vaults.

For a minute or so the three men looked down at the black hole, similar thoughts passing through the mind of each of them. Why not wait until the sane and wholesome light of morning – a light that would dissipate all notions of grinning skulls and gruesome skeletons? But no. Morse put his hands beneath the bars of the grille and lifted it aside easily and lightly.

'Are you sure no one's been down here for ten years?' he asked.

Lewis bent down in the darkness and felt the rungs of the ladder.

'Feels pretty firm, sir.'

'Let's play it safe, Lewis. We don't really want any more corpses if we can help it.'

Meiklejohn watched as they eased down the ladder, and when it was resting firmly on its fellow Lewis took the torch and slowly and carefully made his way down.

'I reckon someone's been down here fairly recently, sir. One of the steps near the bottom here's broken, and it doesn't look as if it happened all that long ago.'

'Some of these hooligans, I expect,' said Meiklejohn to Morse. 'Some of them would do anything for what they call a "kick". But look, Inspector, I really must be going. I'm sorry if I – er . . .'

'Forget it,' said Morse. 'We'll let you know if we find anything.'

'Are you – are you expecting to find something?'

Was he? In all honesty the answer was 'yes' – he was expecting to find the body of a young boy called Peter Morris. 'Not really, sir. We just have to check out every possibility, though.'

Lewis' voice sounded once more from the black hollow. 'The door's locked, sir. Can you—?'

Morse dropped his set of keys down. 'See if one of these fits.'

'If it doesn't,' said Meiklejohn, 'I'm afraid you really will have to wait until the morning. My set of keys is just the same as yours and—'

'We're in, Meredith,' shouted Lewis from the depths.

'You get off, then, sir,' said Morse to Meiklejohn. 'As I say, we'll let you know if – er – if . . .'

'Thank you. Let's just pray you don't, Inspector. This is all such a terrible business already that—'

'Goodnight, sir.'

With infinite pains and circumspection Morse eased himself on to the ladder, and with nervously iterated entreaties that Lewis make sure he was holding 'the bloody thing' firmly he gradually descended into the shaft with the slow-motion movements of a trainee tight-rope walker. He noted, as Lewis had just done, that the third rung from the bottom of the original wooden ladder had been snapped roughly in the middle, the left-hand half of it drooping at an angle of some forty-five degrees. And, judging from the yellowish-looking splintering at the jagged fracture, someone's foot had gone through the rung comparatively recently. Someone fairly heavy; or someone not so heavy, perhaps – with an extra weight upon his shoulder.

'Do you think there are any rats down here?' asked Morse.

'Shouldn't think so. Nothing to feed on, is there?'

'Bodies, perhaps?' Morse thought yet again of leaving the grim mission until the morning, and experienced a little shudder of fear as he looked up at the rectangle of faint light above his head, half-expecting some ghoulish figure to appear in the aperture, grinning horridly down on him. He breathed deeply.

'In we go, Lewis.'

The door creaked whiningly on its rusted hinges as inch by inch Lewis pushed it open, and Morse played his torch nervously to one side and then to the other. It was immediately clear that the main supporting pillars of the upper structure of the church extended down to the vaults, forming a series of stone recesses and dividing the subterranean area into cellar-like rooms that seemed (at least to Lewis) far from weird or spooky. In fact the second alcove on the left could hardly have been less conducive to thoughts of some skeletal spectre haunting these nether regions. For within its walls, dry-surfaced and secure, was no more than a large heap of coke (doubtless for the church's earlier heating system) with a long-handled spatulate instrument laid across it.

'Want a bit of free coke, sir?' Lewis was leading the way, and now took the torch from Morse and shone it gaily around the surprisingly dry interior. But as they progressed deeper into the darkness it became increasingly difficult to form any coherent pattern of the layout of the vaults, and Morse was already hanging back a little as Lewis shone the torch upon a stack of coffins, one piled on top of another, their lids warped and loose over the shrunken, concave sides.

'Plenty of corpses here,' said Lewis.

But Morse had turned his back and was staring sombrely into the darkness. 'I think it'll be sensible to come back in the morning, Lewis. Pretty daft trying to find anything at this time of night.' He experienced a deeper shudder of fear as he grew aware of something almost tangibly oppressive in the dry air. As a young boy he'd always been afraid of the dark, and now, again, the quaking hand of terror touched him lightly on the shoulder.

They retraced their way towards the entrance, and soon Morse stood again at the entrance to the vaults, his forehead damp with cold sweat. He breathed several times very deeply, and the prospect of climbing the solid ladder to the ground above loomed like a glorious release from the panic that threatened to engulf him. Yet it was a mark of Morse's genius that he could take hold of his weaknesses and almost miraculously transform them into his strengths. If anyone were going to hide a body in these vaults, he would feel something (surely!), at least *something*, of this same irrational fear of the dark, of the dead, of the deep-seated terror that forever haunted the subconscious mind? No one, surely, would venture too far, alone and under the cover of night, into these cavernous, echoing vaults? His foot kicked a cigarette-packet as he walked past the heap of coke, and he picked it up and asked Lewis to shine the torch on it. It was a golden-coloured empty packet of Benson & Hedges, along the side of which he read: 'Government health warning. Cigarettes can seriously damage your health. Middle tar.' When had the Government decided to stipulate such a solemn warning to cigarette addicts? Three, four, five years ago? Certainly not – what had Meiklejohn said? – ten years!

'Have a look under the coke, will you?' said Morse quietly.

Five minutes later Lewis found him. He was a young boy, aged about eleven or twelve, well preserved, just over five feet in height, and dressed in school uniform. Round his neck was a school tie, a tie tightened so viciously that it had dug deep into the flesh around the throat; a tie striped alternately in the regulation red and grey of the Roger Bacon School, Kidlington.

In the Pending file of the duty-sergeant's tray at Thames Valley H.Q., there still lay the handwritten message taken down from Shrewsbury.

CHAPTER TWENTY-SEVEN

LEWIS REACHED BELL'S office at 9.15 a.m. the following morning, but Morse had beaten him to it and was sitting behind the desk shouting into the phone with a livid fury.

'Well, get the stupid bugger, then. Yes! *Now.*' He motioned Lewis to take a seat, the fingers of his left hand drumming the desk-top in fretful impatience.

'You?' he bellowed into the mouthpiece at last. 'What the hell do you think you're playing at? It's been sitting under your bloody nose since yesterday lunch-time! And all you can do is to sit on that great fat arse of yours and say you're sorry. You'll be sorry, my lad – you can be sure of that. Now, just listen to me carefully. You'll go along to the Super's office as soon as I give you permission to put that phone down, and you tell him exactly what you've done and exactly what you've *not* done. Is that understood?'

The unfortunate voice at the other end of the line could only have mumbled something less than propitiatory, and Lewis sat almost fearfully through the next barrage of abuse.

'What are you going to tell him? I'll tell you what you're going to tell him, my lad. First, you tell him you

197

deserve the bloody V.C. All right? Second, you tell him it's about time they made you chief constable of Oxfordshire. He'll understand. Third, you tell him you're guilty of the blindest bloody stupidity ever witnessed in the history of the force. That's what you tell him!' He banged down the phone and sat for a minute or so still seething with rage.

Sensibly Lewis sat silent, and it was Morse who finally spoke. 'Mrs Josephs was murdered. Last Friday, in a nurses' hostel in Shrewsbury.'

Lewis looked down at the threadbare carpet at his feet and shook his head sadly. 'How many more, sir?'

Morse breathed deeply and seemed suddenly quite calm again.

'I dunno.'

'Next stop Shrewsbury, sir?'

Morse gestured almost hopelessly. 'I dunno.'

'You think it's the same fellow?'

'I dunno.' Morse brooded in silence and stared blankly at the desk in front of him. 'Get the file out again.'

Lewis walked across to one of the steel cabinets. 'Who was on the other end of the rocket, sir?'

Morse's face broke into a reluctant grin. 'That bloody fool, Dickson. He was sitting in as duty-sergeant yesterday. I shouldn't have got so cross with him really.'

'Why did you, then?' asked Lewis, as he put the file down on the desk.

'I suppose because I ought to have guessed, really – guessed that she'd be next on the list, I mean. Perhaps I was just cross with myself, I dunno. But I know one thing, Lewis: I know that this case is getting out of hand. Christ knows where we are; I don't.'

The time seemed to Lewis about right now. Morse's anger had evaporated and only an irritable frustration remained to cloud his worried features. Perhaps he would welcome a little bit of help.

'Sir, I was thinking when I got home last night about what you'd been saying in the Bulldog. Remember? You said that Lawson, the Reverend Lawson, that is, might just have walked straight down—'

'For God's sake, Lewis, come off it! We're finding corpses right, left and centre, are we not? We're in the biggest bloody muddle since God knows when, and all you can do is to—'

'It was you who said it – not me.'

'I *know* – yes. But leave me alone, man! Can't you see I'm trying to think? *Somebody's* got to think around here.'

'I was only—'

'Look, Lewis. Just forget what I said and start thinking about some of the *facts* in the bloody case. All right?' He thumped the file in front of him viciously. 'The facts are all in here. Josephs gets murdered, agreed? All right. Josephs gets murdered. The Reverend Lionel Lawson jumps off the bloody tower. Right? He jumps off the bloody tower. Morris senior gets murdered and gets carted off to the same bloody tower. Right? Exit Morris senior. Morris junior gets strangled and gets carted off down the crypt. Right? Why not just accept these facts, Lewis? Why fart around with all that piddling nonsense about – Augh! Forget it!'

Lewis walked out, making sure to slam the door hard behind him. He'd had just about enough, and for two pins he'd resign from the force on the spot if it meant getting away from this sort of mindless ingratitude. He walked into the canteen and ordered a coffee. If Morse wanted to sit in peace – well, let the miserable blighter! He wouldn't be interrupted this side of lunch-time. Not by Lewis anyway. He read the *Daily Mirror* and had a second cup of coffee. He read the *Sun* and had a third. And then he decided to drive up to Kidlington.

There were patches of blue in the sky now, and the overnight rain had almost dried upon the pavements. He drove along the Banbury Road, past Linton Road, past Belbroughton Road, and the cherry- and the almond trees blossomed in pink and white, and the daffodils and the hyacinths bloomed in the borders of the well-tended lawns. North Oxford was a lovely place in the early spring; and by the time he reached Kidlington Lewis was feeling slightly happier with life.

Dickson, likely as not, would be in the canteen. Dickson was almost always in the canteen.

'I hear you got a bit of a bollocking this morning,' ventured Lewis.

'Christ, ah! You should have heard him.'

'I did,' admitted Lewis.

'And I was only standing in, too. We're so short here that they asked me to take over on the phone. And then this happens! How the hell was I supposed to know who she was? She'd changed her name anyway, and she only *might* have lived in Kidlington, they said. Huh! Life's very unfair sometimes, Sarge.'

'He can be a real sod, can't he?'

'Pardon?'

'Morse. I said he can be a real—'

'No, not really.' Dickson looked far from down-hearted as he lovingly took a great bite from a jam doughnut.

'You've not been in to the Super yet?'

'He didn't mean that.'

'Look, Dickson. You're in the force, you know that – not in a play-school. If Morse says—'

'He didn't. He rang me back half an hour later. Just said he was sorry. Just said forget it.'

'He didn't!'

'He bloody did, Sarge. We had quite a pally little chat in the end, really. I asked him if I could do anything to help, and d'you know what he said? Said he just wanted me to find out from Shrewsbury C.I.D. whether the woman was killed on Friday. That's all. Said he didn't give a monkey's whether she'd been knifed or throttled or anything, just so long as she was killed on Friday. Funny chap, ain't he? Always asking odd sort of questions – never the questions you'd think he'd ask. Clever, though. Christ, ah!'

Lewis stood up to go.

'It wasn't a sex murder, Sarge.'

'Oh?'

'Nice-looker, they said. Getting on a little bit, but it seems quite a few of the doctors had tried to get off with her. Still, I've always thought those black stockings are sexy – haven't you, Sarge?'

'Was she wearing black stockings?'

201

Dickson swallowed the last of his doughnut and wiped his fingers on his black trousers. 'Don't they all wear—?'

But Lewis left him to it. Once more he felt belittled and angry. Who was supposed to be helping Morse anyway? Himself or Dickson? Aurrgh!

It was 11.45 a.m. when Lewis re-entered St Aldates Police Station and walked into Bell's office. Morse still sat in his chair, but his head was now resting on the desk, pillowed in the crook of his left arm. He was sound asleep.

CHAPTER TWENTY-EIGHT

MRS RAWLINSON WAS getting more than a little anxious when Ruth had still not arrived home at five minutes to one. She suspected – knew, really – that Ruth's visits to the Randolph were establishing themselves into a regular lunch-time pattern, and it was high time she reminded her daughter of her filial responsibilities. For the moment, however, it was the primitive maternal instinct that was paramount; and increasingly so as the radio news finished at ten past one with still no sign of her daughter. At a quarter past one the phone rang, shattering the silence of the room with a shrill, abrupt urgency, and Mrs Rawlinson reached across for the receiver with a shaking hand, incipient panic welling up within her as the caller identified himself.

'Mrs Rawlinson? Chief Inspector Morse here.'

Oh my God! 'What is it?' she blurted out. 'What's happened?'

'Are you all right, Mrs Rawlinson?'

'Yes. Oh, yes. I – I just thought for a moment . . .'

'I assure you there's nothing to worry about.' (But didn't *his* voice sound a little worried?) 'I just wanted a quick word with your daughter, please.'

'She's – she's not in at the moment, I'm afraid. She—' And then Mrs Rawlinson heard the key scratching in the front door. 'Just a minute, Inspector.'

Ruth appeared, smiling and fresh-faced, round the door.

'Here! It's for you,' said her mother as she pushed the receiver into Ruth's hand, and then leaned back in her wheelchair, luxuriating in a beautifully relieved anger.

'Hello?'

'Miss Rawlinson? Morse here. Just routine, really. One of those little loose ends we're trying to tie up. I want you to try to remember, if you can, whether the Reverend Lawson wore spectacles.'

'Yes, he did. Why—?'

'Did he wear them just for reading or did he wear them all the time?'

'He always wore them. Always when I saw him anyway. Gold-rimmed, they were.'

'That's very interesting. Do you – er – do you happen to remember that tramp fellow? You know, the one who sometimes used to go to your church?'

'Yes, I remember him,' replied Ruth slowly.

'Did he wear spectacles?'

'No-o, I don't think he did.'

'Just as I thought. Good. Well, that's about all, I think. Er – how are you, by the way?'

'Oh, fine; fine, thanks.'

'You still engaged on your – er – your good works? In the church, I mean?'

'Yes.'

'Mondays and Wednesdays, isn't it?'

'Ye-es.' It was the second occasion she'd been asked the same question within a very short time. And now (she knew) he was going to ask her what time she usually went there. It was just like hearing a repeat on the radio.

'Usually about ten o'clock, isn't it?'

'Yes, that's right. Why do you ask?' And why did she suddenly feel so frightened?

'No reason, really. I just – er – I just thought, you know, I might see you again there one day.'

'Yes. Perhaps so.'

'Look after yourself, then.'

Why couldn't *he* look after her? 'Yes I will,' she heard herself say.

'Goodbye,' said Morse. He cradled the phone and for many seconds stared abstractedly through the window on to the tarmacadamed surface of the inner yard. Why was she always so tight with him? Why couldn't she metaphorically open her legs for him once in a while?

'You ask some very odd questions,' said Lewis.

'Some very important ones, too,' replied Morse rather pompously. 'You see, Lawson's specs were in his coat pocket when they found him – a pair of gold-rimmed specs. It's all here.' He tapped the file on the death of the Reverend Lionel Lawson which lay on the desk in front of him. 'And Miss Rawlinson said that he always wore them. Interesting, eh?'

'You mean – you mean it wasn't Lionel Lawson who—'

'I mean exactly the opposite, Lewis. I mean it *was* Lionel Lawson who chucked himself off the tower. I'm absolutely sure of it.'

'I just don't understand.'

'Don't you? Well, it's like this. Short-sighted jumpers invariably remove their specs and put 'em in one of their pockets before jumping. So any traces of glass in a suicide's face are a sure tip-off that it wasn't suicide but murder.'

'But how do you know Lawson was short-sighted. He may have been—'

'Short-sighted, long-sighted – doesn't matter! It's all the same difference.'

'You serious about all this?'

'Never more so. It's like people turning their hearing-aids off before they have a bath or taking their false teeth out when they go to bed.'

'But the wife never takes hers out when she goes to bed, sir.'

'What's your wife got to do with it?'

Lewis was about to remonstrate against the injustice of such juvenile logic, but he saw that Morse was smiling at him. 'How do you come to know all this stuff about suicides anyway?'

Morse looked thoughtful for a few seconds. 'I can't remember. I think I read it on the back of a match-box.'

'And that's enough to go on?'

'It's something, isn't it? We're up against a very clever fellow, Lewis. But I just can't see him murdering

Lawson, and then very carefully taking off his specs and putting 'em back in their case. Can you?'

No, Lewis couldn't see that; couldn't see much at all. 'Are we making any progress in this case, sir?'

'Good question,' said Morse. 'And, as one of my old schoolmasters used to say, "Having looked that problem squarely in the face, let us now pass on." Time we had a bit o' lunch, isn't it?'

The two men walked out of the long three-storey stone building that forms the headquarters of the Oxford Constabulary, up past Christ Church, across Carfax, and turned into the Golden Cross, where Morse decided that, for himself at least, a modicum of liquid refreshment was all that would be required. He had always believed that his mind functioned better after a few beers, and today he once again acted on his customary assumption. He should, he realized, be off to Shrewsbury immediately; but the prospect of interviewing hospital porters and nurses and doctors about times and places and movements and motives filled him with distaste. Anyway, there was a great deal of routine work to be done in Oxford.

Lewis left after only one pint, and Morse himself sat back to think. The flashing shuttles wove their patterns on the loom of his brain, patterns that materialized in different shapes and forms, but patterns always finally discarded. After his third pint, there was nothing to show for his cerebrations except the unpalatable truth that his fanciful theories, all of them, were futile, his thinking sterile, his progress nil. Somewhere, though, if only he could think where, he felt convinced that he had missed something – something that would present him with the key to the labyrinth. Yes, that's what he needed: the key to the— He had the key to the *church*, though. Was it there, in the church itself, that he had overlooked some simple, obvious fact that even at this very second lay waiting to be discovered?

CHAPTER TWENTY-NINE

MORSE RELOCKED THE door in the north porch after him, conscious that he must try to look upon the interior of the church somehow differently. Previously he had gazed vaguely across the pews, his mind wafted away to loftier things by the pervasive sickly sweet smell of the incense and the gloomy grandeur of the stained-glass windows. Not so now. He fingered through half a dozen devotional tracts, neatly stacked side by side on a wall-ledge just inside the door to the left; he examined a sheaf of leaflets to be filled in by those who wished to be added to the electoral roll; he drew back a curtain just behind the font and noticed a bucket, a scrubbing-brush and two sweeping-brushes. This was much better – he felt it in his bones! He examined postcards (6p each), which carried exterior views of the church taken from several angles, large close-ups of the famous font (much admired, it seemed, by all save Morse), and full frontal photographs of one of the grinning gargoyles on the tower (how on earth had anyone taken those?); then he turned his attention to a stack of Guides to St Frideswide's (10p each), and another stack of Parish Notes (2p each) in which details of the current month's activities were fully listed; then, beside the west wall, he noted again the heaps of prayer books with their dull-red covers and the heaps of hymn-books with their— He suddenly stopped, experiencing the strange conviction that he had already overlooked the vital clue that he'd been looking for. Was it something he'd just seen? Something he'd just heard? Something he'd just smelt? He went back to the door, retraced his few steps around the porchway, and then duplicated as far as he could his exact actions since entering the church. But it was no use. Whatever it was – if it was anything – was still eluding his grasp. Maddeningly. Slowly he paced his way up the central aisle and there stood still. The hymns from the previous evening's service were there, white cards with their red numbers, slotted into a pair of hymn-boards, one on either side of him. Odd! Why hadn't they been taken down? Was that one of Ruth Rawlinson's jobs? The bucket and the scrubbing-brush looked as if they had been used very recently, almost certainly by Ruth herself that very morning. Had she forgotten the hymn-boards? Or was that the job of the Vicar? Or one of the choir? Or one of the supernumerary assistants? For someone had to look after such matters. Come to think of it, someone had to decide the hymns, the psalms, the collects, epistles and gospels and the rest. Morse knew nothing about it, but he presumed that it was all laid down in some great holy book available for the guidance of the clergy. Must be. Like all those saints' days and other religious festivals. No one could carry all that stuff around in his head. What was more, someone would have to keep some sort of record of all the services every week – surely so! – especially when you had as many services as—*That* was it! He walked quickly back to the north porch and picked up a copy of the Parish Notes, and stared with curious excitement at the front page:

CHURCH OF ST FRIDESWIDE, OXFORD

SERVICES

Sundays Mass and Holy Communion 8 a.m.
10.30 a.m. (High) and 5.30 p.m.
Evening Service 6 p.m.
Weekdays Mass on Tuesdays and Fridays 7.30 a.m.
On Feast Days 7.30 a.m. and 7.30 p.m.
(Solemn)

CONFESSIONS

Tuesdays, Fridays and Saturdays, all at midday.
Or by arrangement with the clergy.

CLERGY

The Revd Canon K. D. Meiklejohn (Vicar),
St Frideswide's Vicarage.
The Revd Neil Armitage (Curate),
19 Port Meadow Lane.

APRIL

1st   In Octave of Easter
2nd   LOW SUNDAY. Preacher at 10.30 a.m.
The Bishop of Brighton. Annual Parish
Meeting 6.15 p.m.
3rd   ST RICHARD OF CHICHESTER
Mass at 8 a.m. and 7.30 p.m.

4th	Holy Hour 11 a.m.
5th	Mothers' Union 2.45 p.m.
6th	Deanery Synod 7.45 p.m.
8th	Holy Hour 5 to 6 p.m.
9th	EASTER II ...

So it went on, through the whole month, with one major Feast Day (Morse noted) in two of the other three weeks. But so what? Was there anything here that was of the slightest interest or value? The name 'Armitage' was new to Morse, and he suspected that the Curate was probably a fairly recent acquisition, and had almost certainly been one of the three wise men in the purple vestments. Still, with all those services on the programme, there'd be need of a helping hand, wouldn't there? It would be a pretty hefty assignment for one poor fellow, who presumably was entrusted, in addition, with the pastoral responsibilities of visiting the lame and the sick and the halt and the blind. My goodness, yes! Meiklejohn would certainly need a co-labourer in such an extensive vineyard. And then a little question posed itself to Morse's mind, and for a second or two the blood seemed to freeze in his cheeks. *Did Lawson have a curate?* It should be easy enough to find out, and Morse had a peculiar notion that the answer might be important, though exactly *how* important he had, at this point, no real idea at all.

He pocketed the Parish Notes, and turned back into the church. A long tasselled rope barred access to the altar in the Lady Chapel, but Morse stepped irreverently over it and stood before the heavily embossed and embroidered altar-cloth. To his immediate left was the arched opening to the main altar, and slowly he walked through it. In a niche to the left of the archway was an Early English piscina, and Morse stopped to look at it carefully, nodding slowly as he did so. He then turned left, made his way along the high carved screen which separated the Lady Chapel from the main nave, skipped lightly across the entrance to the Lady Chapel, and came to a halt outside the vestry. For some reason he looked quite pleased with himself and nodded his head again several times with a semi-satisfied smile.

He stood where he was for several minutes looking around him once more; and, indeed, had he but realized it, he was now within a few yards of the clue that would smash some of his previous hypotheses into a thousand pieces; but for the moment the Fates were not smiling upon him. The north door was opened and Meiklejohn entered, carrying a carton of electric light-bulbs, in the company of a young man balancing an extending ladder on his shoulder.

'Hello, Inspector,' said Meiklejohn. 'Discovered anything more yet?'

Morse grunted non-commitally, and decided that the investigation of the vestry could, without any cosmic ill-consequence, be temporarily postponed.

'We're just going to change the bulbs,' continued Meiklejohn. 'Have to do it, you know, every three or four months. Quite a few have gone already, I'm afraid.'

Morse's eyes travelled slowly up to the tops of the walls where, about forty feet above the floor he could see a series of twin electric-light bulbs, each pair set about twenty feet apart. Meanwhile the ladder had been propped up beneath the nearest lights, and in a progressively more precarious stutter of elongations the two men were pushing the ladder even higher until the slimly converging top of the third extension now rested about two or three feet below the first pair of bulbs.

'I'm afraid,' said Morse, 'that I just haven't got the stomach to stop and witness this little operation any further.'

'Oh, it's not so bad, Inspector, as long as you're careful. But I must admit I'm always glad when it's over.'

'He's a better man than I am,' said Morse, pointing to the young man standing (rather nervously?) on the second rung and gently manœuvring the ladder on to a more firmly based vertical.

Meiklejohn grinned and turned to Morse quietly. 'He's about as bad as you are – if not worse. I'm afraid I have to do the job myself.'

And may the good Lord be with you, thought Morse, as he made his rapid exit, completely forgetting that he was debtor to church funds to the sum of 2p; forgetting, too, that there was a most important question he had yet to put to the daredevil incumbent of St Frideswide's.

In all there were twenty bulbs to change, and as always the job was taking an unconscionably long time to complete. To any observer of the scene, it would have appeared that the young man who stood dutifully with his foot placed firmly on the bottom rung of the ladder seemed quite incapable of raising his eyes above the strict horizontal as Meiklejohn repeatedly ascended to the dizzy heights above him where, standing on the antepenultimate rung, he would place his left hand for support against the bare wall, stretch up to twist out one of the old bulbs, place it carefully in his coat pocket, and then insert one of the new bulbs with an upward thrust of his right arm which virtually lifted his body into unsupported space. With the merest moment of carelessness, with the slightest onset of giddiness, the good vicar would have lost his precarious balance and plunged to his death on the floor so far below; but mercifully the task was now almost complete, and the ladder was in place below the last pair of bulbs when the door (which had remained unlocked) creaked open to admit a strange-looking man whose beard was unkempt, who was dressed in a long, shabby greatcoat, and who wore an incongruous pair of sunglasses. For a moment or two he looked about him, unaware of the presence of the other two men. The afternoon had grown dull and the electricity had been turned off whilst the bulbs were being changed.

'Can I help you?' asked Meiklejohn.

'What?' The man started nervously. 'Cor, you frightened me, guv.'

'Please do have a look around. You're most welcome.'

'Sorright. I just – I just wanted to – er . . .'

'I can show you around myself in a minute if you can—'

'Nah. Sorright, guv.' He shuffled out, and Meikle-john raised his eyebrows to the young man. The ladder was ready again now and he put his right hand up to the rung just above his head – and then stopped.

'You remember my predecessor here – poor Mr Lawson? He had a way with these down-and-outs, they tell me. Often used to have one or two of them staying with him for a few days. You probably know that anyway. Perhaps I should make more of an effort than I do. Still, we're all different, Thomas. Just as the good Lord made us.' He smiled, rather sadly, and began to climb. 'Perhaps poor Mr Lawson wasn't very good at changing light-bulbs, eh?'

Thomas managed a ghostly-weak smile in response and took up his guardian rôle on the bottom rung, his eyes once more averted from the fast-disappearing soles of the vicar's black shoes. Funny, really! He'd joined St Frideswide's church just over a year ago (he was an undergraduate at Hertford College) and he remem-bered the previous vicar very well indeed. He thought he remembered other things, too. For example, he thought he remembered the tramp who'd just walked in. Hadn't he seen him in church once or twice?

CHAPTER THIRTY

THE DECISION TO travel to Shrewsbury was taken, momentarily and arbitrarily, when Morse had walked out of the church on his way back to St Aldates; and as Lewis drove the police car round the Woodstock Road roundabout and headed out on to the A34 both men were mentally calculating the possible time schedule. It was already 4.20 p.m. Two hours, say, to get there – if the traffic was reasonable; two hours actually there; another two hours back. So, with a bit of luck, they could be back in Oxford by about 10.30 p.m.

Morse, as was his wont, spoke little in the car, and Lewis was quite happy to give his whole attention to the motoring. They had started in time to miss the diurnal mass exodus from Oxford which begins at about a quarter to five and continues its semi-paralytic progress for almost another hour. It was good fun, too, driving in a conspicuously marked POLICE car. As always other road-users immediately became punctilious about speed restrictions as they spied the pale-blue and white car in their mirrors, and ostentatiously shunned the slightest suspicion of sub-standard driving, behaving with a courtesy and care that were wildly at variance with their customary frenetic aggression.

So it was now.

Lewis turned left off the A34 through Chipping Norton, up through Bourton-on-the-Hill, through Moreton-in-Marsh, and then, with the Vale of Evesham opening out in a vast panorama before them, down the long, steep hill into Broadway, its houses of mellowed Cotswold stone gleaming a warm yellow in the late afternoon sun. At Evesham, Morse insisted that they took the road to Pershore, in which town he enthused lovingly over the red-brick houses with their white-painted window-frames; and at Worcester he directed Lewis along the Bromyard Road.

'I've always thought,' said Morse, as they turned north from Leominster on to the A49, 'that this is one of the prettiest roads in England.'

Lewis sat silent. It was also a pretty long way round, and at this rate it would be about seven before they reached Shrewsbury. Yet as they drove past Church Stretton it seemed to Lewis that Morse was perhaps right; and even more so as they left the Long Mynd behind them, when the sun, still hovering over the Welsh hills far off on the western horizon, suffused the early evening sky with a fiery glow and turned the white clouds to the softest shade of purple.

It was half past seven when finally the two Oxford detectives were seated in the Superintendent's office at the Salop Police H.Q.; and it was half past eight when they emerged. Morse had said little, and Lewis less, and neither man felt that the meeting was of more than routine value. There were no grounds for suspecting anyone, and not the slightest whisper of a likely motive.

The dead woman had been quietly popular with her fellow-nurses, slightly less quietly popular with the surgeons and housemen, and it was difficult to believe that even Florence Nightingale herself could have found too many faults with her efficient and experienced nursing. One of the doctors had spoken to her the previous evening, had sat in the nurses' common room with her doing a crossword puzzle; but, although he was probably the last person (apart from the murderer) to see her alive, there was no reason whatsoever to suspect that he'd had anything to do with her death. But somebody had. Somebody had strangled her brutally with her own belt and left her for dead on the floor by the side of her bed, from where she had later managed to crawl to the door of her room to try desperately to call for help. But no one had heard her, and no one had come.

'I suppose we'd better see her?' said Morse dubiously, as they all trooped out of the Superintendent's office.

In the cream-tiled police morgue, a constable pulled out a sliding container from a stainless-steel structure, and turned back the sheet from the face – white, waxy-textured and washed, the lolling bloodshot eyes bearing their chilling witness to the agony of her death. At the base of her neck and running up to her right ear was the hideous groove left by the belt.

'Probably left-handed,' muttered Lewis, 'if he strangled her from the front, that is.' He turned towards Morse as he spoke, and noticed that the great man had his eyes shut.

Five minutes later Morse was looking immeasurably happier as he sat in the anteroom surveying the contents of the murdered woman's pockets and handbag.

'We should be able to check the handwriting easily enough,' said Lewis, as he saw Morse studying the letter from Kidlington.

'We hardly need to, do we?' said Morse, putting it to one side and turning to the other contents of the handbag. There were two pocket diaries, a lady's handkerchief, a leather purse, three luncheon vouchers, and the usual bric-à-brac of feminine toiletry: perfume, nail-file, comb, hand-mirror, eye-shadow, lipstick and tissues.

'Was she wearing much make-up when you found her?' asked Morse.

The Superintendent frowned slightly and looked less than comfortable. 'I think she was wearing some, but – er . . .'

'I thought you said she'd just come off duty. They don't let 'em slink round the wards all tarted up, surely?'

'You think she might have been expecting somebody?'

Morse shrugged his shoulders. 'Possibility, isn't it?'

'Mm.' The Superintendent nodded thoughtfully, and wondered why he hadn't thought of that himself; but Morse had brushed aside the cosmetics as if whatever interest they might momentarily have exercised over him was now a thing of the past.

The purse contained six one-pound notes, about fifty pence in small change, and a local bus timetable. 'No driving licence' was Morse's only comment, and the

Superintendent confirmed that as far as they knew she'd had no car since coming to work at the hospital.

'She was pretty anxious to cover up her tracks, Super. Perhaps,' he added quietly, 'perhaps she was frightened that somebody would find her.' But again he seemed to lose interest in the line of thought upon which he had embarked, and proceeded to turn his attention to the two slim diaries, one for the current, one for the previous year.

'She wasn't exactly a Samuel Pepys, I'm afraid,' said the Superintendent. 'The odd jotting here and there, but not much to go on as far as I can see.'

Mrs Brenda Josephs had certainly started off the two years with admirable intentions, and the first few days of each of the two Januarys were fairly fully documented. But, even then, such *aide-mémoire* entries as her 'Six fish fingers' or '8.30 Nurses' Social' seemed hardly likely to lead the Salop or the Oxon constabulary very much nearer to the apprehension of her murderer. The expression on Morse's face was mildly sour as he flicked rather aimlessly through the pages, and in truth he found little to hold his attention. On the day of Brenda's death he noticed the single entry 'Periods due'; rather pathetic, but of little consequence.

Lewis, who hitherto had felt his contribution to the visit to have been less than positively constructive, picked up the diary for the previous year and examined it with his usual exaggerated care. The writing was neatly and clearly charactered, but for the most part so small that he found himself holding the diary at arm's length and squinting at it lop-sidedly. Against virtually every Sunday throughout the year up to mid-September were the letters 'SF', and these same letters were repeated at irregular intervals and on irregular week-days throughout the the same period. 'SF'? The only thing he could think of was Science Fiction, but that was obviously wrong. There was something else, though. From July up until late September there was a series of 'P's, written (almost imperceptibly) in pencil in the ruled blue lines which separated the days of the month from each other. And the day was always a Wednesday.

'What does "SF" stand for, sir?'

'Saint Frideswide's,' said Morse without a moment's thought.

Yes. That must be it. Harry Josephs (as Lewis now recalled) had been disqualified from driving, and it was his wife's duty to take him down to the church in her own car. That fitted all right. Sunday mornings for the big service of the week, and then, at intermittent intervals, the mid-week days whenever some prestigious saint or other held an anniversary. That was it. No doubt about it.

'What does "P" stand for, sir?'

Morse reeled them off with the fluency of a man who had devoted too many hours of his life to the solving of crosswords: 'soft', 'president', 'prince', 'page', 'participle'.

'Nothing else?'

'Phosphorus?'

Lewis shook his head. 'Probably the initial of some-one's name. It's a capital "P".'

'Let's have a look, Lewis.'

'Could be "Paul", sir? Paul Morris?'

'Or Peter Morris – if she's a paedophile.'

'Pardon?'

'Nothing.'

'Always on Wednesdays, though, sir. Perhaps she suddenly decided she wanted to see him more often—'

'And her old man was in the way and so she bumped him off?'

'I've heard of odder things. She said she'd nipped off to the pictures that night, didn't she?'

'Mm.' Morse's interest appeared to be engaged at last. 'How much does it cost to go to the pictures these days?'

'Dunno, sir. A quid? One-fifty?'

'Expensive for her, wasn't it? She couldn't have been there much more than an hour, at the most.'

'*If* she went, sir. I mean, she mightn't have gone to the pictures at all. She might have just crept quietly back into the church and—'

Morse nodded. 'You're quite right. She probably had the best motive of the lot of 'em. But you're forgetting something. The door creaks like hell.'

'Only the north door.'

'Really?' But Morse had clearly lost all interest in creaking doors, and Lewis found himself once more wondering why they'd bothered to come all this way. Nothing had been learned. No progress had been made.

'There's another "P", isn't there?' said Morse suddenly. 'We've forgotten Philip Lawson.'

Yes, Lewis had forgotten Philip Lawson; but where on earth was *he* supposed to fit into this particular picture?

The constable packed up Brenda Josephs' possessions, replaced them in their plastic bags, and redeposited the bags in a labelled cabinet. Morse thanked the Superintendent for his co-operation, shook hands with him, and got into the car beside Lewis.

It was on the Kidderminster road about six or seven miles south of Shrewsbury that a wave of chilling excitement, starting from the bottom of the back, gradually crept up to the nape of Morse's neck. He tried to conceal the agitation of his mind as he questioned Lewis. 'Did you say that Brenda Josephs marked off the days when she took her husband to church?'

'Looked like it, sir. And quite a few times apart from Sundays.'

'"SF", you said. She put "SF"?'

'That's about it, sir. As you said, it's "St Frideswide's". Not much doubt about that.' He turned suddenly and glanced at Morse, who was staring with extraordinary intensity into the outer darkness of the night. 'Unless, of course, you think it stands for something else?'

'No, no. It doesn't stand for anything else.' And then, very quietly, he said, 'Turn round, please. We're going back.'

The luminous dial on the fascia board showed half past ten, just gone, and things were running way behind even the most pessimistic schedule. But Lewis turned round at the earliest possible opportunity. He also was a man under authority.

The constable in the police mortuary reopened the cabinet and shook out the contents of the plastic bags once more. They were always a funny lot – these fellows from other forces.

Morse managed to keep his hand from shaking as he picked up the earlier of the two diaries and turned to the one specific page. And as he looked at the page the blood seemed to congeal in his jowls, and a slow smile of joyous satisfaction formed about his mouth.

'Thank you very much, Constable. Thank you very much. You don't think I could take this diary?'

'I don't know about that, sir. The Super's gone off now and—'

Morse held up his right hand like a priest delivering the benediction. 'Forget it! Doesn't matter!' He turned quickly to Lewis. 'See that?' He pointed to the space for Monday, 26 September, the day on which Harry Josephs had been murdered; and Lewis' forehead creased into a frown as he looked at it, and then looked at it again. The space was completely blank.

'You remember your Sherlock Holmes, Lewis?' But whether or not Lewis was familiar with the works of that great man was not immediately apparent, for clearly Morse himself had a good many passages of Holmesian dialogue by heart, and before Lewis could reply he proceeded to recite one:

' "Is there any point to which you would wish to draw my attention?"

' "To the curious incident of the dog in the night-time."

' "The dog did nothing in the night-time."

225

COLIN DEXTER

'"That was the curious incident."'

'I see,' said Lewis, seeing not.

'How fast will she go?' asked Morse as he clambered into the police car once more.

'About ninety – bit more – on the straight.'

'Well, put the flasher on and start the siren up. We must get back to Oxford quickly, all right?'

The car sped through the darkened countryside, down through Bridgnorth and Kidderminster, along the old Worcester Road to Evesham, and then in an almost incredibly short time back to Oxford. An hour and a half – almost to the minute.

'Back to the station, is it?' asked Lewis as he turned into the Northern Ring Road.

'No. Take me straight home, Lewis. I'm tired out.'

'But I thought you said—'

'Not tonight, Lewis. I'm dead beat.' He winked at Lewis and slammed the door of the Ford behind him. 'Good fun, wasn't it? Sleep tight! We've got work to do in the morning.'

Lewis himself drove off home happily. His honest soul had very few vices – but fast driving was certainly one of them.

CHAPTER THIRTY-ONE

PERHAPS THE EVENTS of the past few days had disturbed the Reverend Keith Meiklejohn rather less than they should have done; and being an honest man the realization of this was worrying to him. It was true that, inducted as he had been only in the previous November, he had not known the Morris family personally, and could not therefore be expected to react too keenly to the tragic discoveries of what (if rumour were to be believed) were the bodies of father and son. Yet as he sat in his study at 9.30 a.m. on Tuesday morning he knew that his compassion should have been engaged more deeply, and he wondered about himself; wondered about his church, too.

Meiklejohn was a robust, well-built man, forty-one years of age and happily unmarried. His childhood had been spent in a family household brimming with evangelical piety, and one forever frequented by inveterate god-botherers and born-again Baptists. From his earliest years the promises of eternal life and the terrors of the lake that burneth with fire and brimstone had been as real to him as liquorice allsorts and the landscape of his Dorset home. In his early youth, whilst his classmates discussed the prospects of their favourite football teams

or the merits of their new racing bikes, young Keith
had grown zealous over matters ecclesiastical and theological and by the age of sixteen the way ahead was
quite clear: he was destined to take holy orders. As a
young curate he had at first been moderately low-
church in his views on the liturgy and the sacraments;
but gradually he had been more and more attracted
towards the doctrines of the Oxford Movement, and at
one point he had come within a communion wafer of
conversion to the Roman Church. But all that was in
the past. With a new-found balance, he discovered he
could tread the tight-rope of High Anglicanism with
security and confidence, and it was pleasing to him that
his congregation appeared to think well of him for
doing so. His predecessor, Lionel Lawson, had not (it
seemed) found universal favour with an ecclesiastical
stance that was decidedly more middle-and-leg than
middle-and-off. In fact, when Lawson's curate, some
five years earlier, had been promoted to a parish of his
own there had been no request to the Bishop for a
replacement, and Lawson himself had coped single-
handed with the manifold duties of St Frideswide's
parish. Inevitably, of course, there had been cuts in
services, and it was Meiklejohn's resolve to restore as
soon as possible the daily masses at 11.15 a.m. and 6.15
p.m. which were a wholly necessary feature (as he saw
things) of a church that was dedicated to the glory of
God.

Yet, as he sat at the ancient roll-top desk, the page
over which his pen had been poised for several minutes
remained blank. It was high time he preached again on

transubstantiation: a tricky issue, of course, but one that was vital for the spiritual health of the brethren. But could that sermon wait, perhaps? His limp-leather copy of the Holy Writ lay open before him at the book of Hosea. A marvellous and memorable piece of writing! It was almost as if the Almighty himself had not really known what to do with his people when their goodness and mercy were as evanescent as the mists or the early dews that melted away in the morning sun. Was the Church in danger of losing its love? For without love the worship of God and the care of the brethren was little more than sounding brass and tinkling cymbals . . . Yes, a possible sermon was just beginning to shape itself nicely. Not too forcefully expressed: nothing to smack too strongly of the stamping pulpit-thumper. But then another verse caught his eye from an earlier chapter of the same prophecy: 'Ephraim is joined to idols; let him alone.' Another striking verse! Idolaters were, after all, those within the Church – not those outside it. Those who worshipped, but who worshipped a false representation of God. And not just the golden calf, either. There was always a danger that other representations could get in the way of true worship: yes – he had to admit it! – things like incense and candles and holy water and crossings and genuflections, and all the sheer apparatus of ceremonial which could perhaps clog up the cleansing power of the Holy Spirit. It was possible, too – only too easy, in fact – to be blinded to the spiritual health of the Church by the arithmetical aggregation of its membership, especially when he considered (as he did with pride) the undoubted increase in the numbers attending divine worship since his own arrival. The records showed that there had been times under Lawson's régime when attendance had been just a little disappointing; and indeed some occasions in mid-week when it had been difficult to muster much of a congregation at all! But God didn't just count heads – or so Meiklejohn told himself; and he pondered again the central problem that had dominated his earlier thinking: should he not be more concerned than he was about the spiritual health of his church?

He was still undecided about the text of his next sermon, the page still blank beneath his pen, the disturbing words of the prophet Hosea still lying before him, when the door-bell rang.

Had it been the will of Providence that he had been pondering the state of St Frideswide's soul? At the very least, it was an uncanny coincidence that his visitor was soon asking him the very same questions he had been asking himself; asking them pretty bluntly, too.

'You had a big congregation last Sunday, sir.'

'About usual, Inspector.'

'I've heard that you get even more people than Lawson did.'

'Perhaps so. Certainly in the week, I think.'

'The crowds are flocking back, so to speak?'

'You make it sound like a football match.'

'Bit more interesting than the last football match I saw, I hope.'

'And one doesn't have to queue up at the turnstiles, Inspector.'

'You keep a fairly accurate record of the congregations, though?'

Meiklejohn nodded. 'I've continued my predecessor's practice in that respect.'

'Not in all respects?'

Meiklejohn was aware of the Inspector's blue eyes upon him. 'What are you trying to say?'

'Was Lawson lower-church in his views than you are?'

'I didn't know him.'

'But he was?'

'He had views, I believe, which were – er . . .'

'Lower-church?'

'Er – that might be a way of putting it, yes.'

'I noticed you had three priests in church on Sunday morning, sir.'

'You've still got quite a lot to learn about us, Inspector. There were myself and my curate. The sub-deacon need not be in holy orders.'

'Three's a bit more than the usual ration, though, isn't it?'

'There are no ration-books when it comes to divine worship.'

'Did Lawson have a curate?'

'For the first part of his time here, he did. The parish is a large one, and in my view should always have a curate.'

'Lawson was on his own, then – for the last few years?'

'He was.'

'Did you ever hear, sir, that Lawson might have been a fraction too fond of the choirboys?'

'I – I think it quite improper for you or for me to—'

'I met his former headmaster recently,' interrupted Morse, a new note of authority in his voice. 'I felt he was concealing something, and I guessed what it was: the fact that Lionel Lawson had been expelled from school.'

'You're sure of that?'

Morse nodded. 'I rang the old boy up today and put it to him. He told me I was right.'

'Expelled for homosexuality, you say?'

'He refused to confirm that,' said Morse slowly. 'He also refused to deny it, I'm afraid, and I'll leave you to draw your own conclusions. Look, sir. I want to assure you that whatever you may have to tell me will be treated in the strictest confidence. But it's my duty as a police officer to ask you once again. Have you heard any rumours that Lawson was at all inclined to that sort of thing?'

Meiklejohn looked down at his feet and picked his words with uneasy care. 'I've heard one or two rumours, yes. But I don't myself think that Lawson was an active homosexual.'

'Just a passive one, you mean.'

Meiklejohn looked up, and spoke with quiet conviction: 'It is my view that the Reverend Mr Lawson was not a homosexual. I am, of course, sometimes wrong, Inspector. But in this case I think I am right.'

'Thank you,' said Morse, in the tone of a man who says 'Thank you for nothing'. He looked round the room at the bookshelves, lined with rows of theological works, the spines of most of them either dark-blue or brown. It was in this dark and sombre room that Lawson himself would have sat, probably for several hours each day, during his ten-year ministry at St Frideswide's. What had *really* gone wrong here? What strange tales of the human heart and the deep abyss of human consciousness could these walls and these books tell, if only they had tongues to speak to him? Could Meiklejohn tell him any more? Oh, yes, he could. There was just that one final question, the most vital question he would ask in the whole case. It was the question which had suddenly sprung to life in his mind the previous evening on the road just a few miles south of Shrewsbury.

He took from his pocket the now-crumpled Parish Notes for April.

'You print one of these every month?'

'Yes.'

'Do you' – this was it, and his mouth seemed suddenly to grow dry as he asked it – 'do you keep copies of them from previous years?'

'Of course. It's a great help in compiling the Parish Notes to have the previous year's copy. Not so much with the Easter period, of course, but—'

'Can I look at last year's Notes, please, sir?'

Meiklejohn walked over to one of the bookshelves and took out a loose-leafed folder. 'Which month's copy do you want?' His eyes reflected a shrewd intelligence. 'September, perhaps?'

'September,' said Morse.

'Here we are, yes. July, August . . .' He stopped and looked a little puzzled. 'October, November . . .' He turned back to January and went very carefully through the issues once more. 'It's not here, Inspector,' he said slowly. 'It's not here. I wonder . . .'

Morse was wondering, too. But – please! – it wouldn't be too difficult to find a copy somewhere, would it? They must have printed a few hundred – whoever 'they' were.

'Who prints these for you, sir?'

'Some little man in George Street.'

'He'd surely keep the originals, wouldn't he?'

'I'd have thought so.'

'Can you find out for me – straight away?'

'Is it that urgent?' asked Meiklejohn quietly.

'I think it is.'

'You could always check up from the church register, Inspector.'

'The *what*?'

'We keep a register in the vestry. Every service – I think it *is* a service you're looking for? – every service is recorded there. The time, the type of service, the minister officiating, the offertory – even the number of the congregation, although I must admit that's a bit of a rough guess sometimes.'

Morse allowed himself an exultant grin. His hunch had been right, then! The clue for which he'd been searching was where he'd always thought it would be – under his very nose inside the church itself. The next time he had a hunch, he decided, he would pursue it with a damned sight more resolution than he had done this one. For the moment, however, he said nothing. He was there – almost there anyway – and he felt the thrill of a man who knows that he has seven draws up on the football pools and is just going out to buy a sports paper to discover the result of the eighth match.

The two men walked down the wide staircase and into the hallway, where Meiklejohn took his coat from the clothes-stand, stained dark brown like almost every other item of furniture in the large, echoing vicarage.

'A lot of room here,' said Morse they stepped out into the street.

Again the Vicar's eyes flashed with intelligence. 'What you mean to say is that I ought to turn it into a hostel, is that it?'

'Yes, I do,' replied Morse bluntly. 'I understand your predecessor used to take in a few waifs and strays now and then.'

'I believe he did, Inspector. I believe he did.'

They parted at George Street, and Morse, in a state of suppressed excitement, and already fingering the heavy church-keys in his raincoat pocket, walked on down Cornmarket to St Frideswide's.

CHAPTER THIRTY-TWO

JUST AS MEIKLEJOHN had said, the bulky, leather-bound register stood on its shelf in the vestry, and Morse felt the same amalgam of anxiety and expectation with which as a schoolboy he had opened the envelopes containing his examination results: any second – and he would know. The pages of the register were marked in faded blue lines, about a third of an inch apart, with each line, stretched across the double page, quite sufficient to accommodate the necessary information. On the left-hand page were written the day, the date, and the time of the service, followed by some brief specification of the particular saint's day, feast day, et cetera; on the right-hand page the record was continued with details of the type of service celebrated, the number present in the congregation, the amount taken at the offertory, and lastly the name (almost always the signature) of the minister, or ministers, officiating. Doubtless in a church permeated by a more fervent evangelicalism, there would have been the biblical reference of the text which the preacher had sought to propound; but Morse was more than delighted with the information he found in front of him. The register had fallen open at the current month and he noted the last entry: 'Monday, 3rd April. 7.30 p.m. St Richard of Chichester. Low Mass. 19. £5.35. Keith Meiklejohn M.A. (Vicar).' Then he turned back a thickish wedge of the book's heavy pages. A little too far, though: July, the previous year. On through August, and his heart suddenly seemed to sink within him as the thought flashed into his mind that someone might well have torn out the page he was seeking. But no! There it was now, staring him in the face: 'Monday, 26th Sept. 7.30 p.m. The Conversion of St Augustine. Solemn Mass. 13. – . Lionel Lawson M A. (Vicar).' For several minutes Morse stared at the entry with a blank fixity. Had he been wrong after all? For there it was, all printed out in Lawson's own hand – the precise details of the service at which Josephs had been murdered: the date and time, the occasion, the type of service (which, of course, accounted for Paul Morris' presence); the number in the congregation, the offertory (the sum quite naturally unknown and unrecorded, except perhaps for a few brief seconds in Josephs' brain before he met his death), and then Lawson's signature. All there. All in order. What had Morse hoped to find there? Surely he had not expected the amount of the offertory to be recorded? That would have been an elementary mistake of such monumental stupidity on Lawson's part that if repeated in other aspects of his crime would have led to an arrest within a few hours by any even moderately competent detective. No. Morse had not been looking for any such mistake. The simple truth of the matter was that *he'd expected there to be no entry at all.*

The door at the north porch creaked open, and Morse felt a sudden brief surge of primitive fear as he stood alone in the silent church. Somewhere, perhaps somewhere very near, there was a murderer still at large, watching every latest development with a vicious, calculating mind; watching even now, perhaps, and sensing that the police might be hovering perilously close to the truth. Morse walked on tiptoe to the heavy red curtain which cloaked the entrance to the vestry and cautiously peered through.

It was Meiklejohn.

'This is what you want, Inspector,' he said breezily. 'You must excuse me, if you will. We've got a service here at eleven.'

He handed to Morse a single sheet of paper, printed on both sides in faded black ink, with rows of asterisks dividing up the Parish Notes for the previous September into a series of closely typed paragraphs, of which the first, in double columns, gave full details of that month's forthcoming (and, in one case, fatal) functions. Morse sat down in the back pew and looked down intently at the sheet.

He was still looking down at the sheet several minutes later when Mrs Walsh-Atkins made her careful way down the central aisle, passing her left hand from pew-head to pew-head as she progressed, until finally settling herself in her accustomed seat where she knelt down, her forehead resting on the crook of her left arm, for a further protracted audience with the Almighty. A few other faithful souls had come in, all of them women, but Morse had not heard their entrances, and it was clear to him that the hinges on the door at the south porch had received a more recent oiling than those of its fellow at the north porch. He registered the point, as if it might be of some importance.

Morse sat through the devotional service – literally 'sat'. He made no pretence to emulate the gestures and movements of the sprinkling of ageing ladies; but a neutral observer would have marked a look of faintly smiling contentment on his features long before Meiklejohn's solemn voice at last, at very long last, intoned the benediction.

'It *was* what you wanted, I hope, Inspector?' Meiklejohn was leaning forward over the low table in the vestry, writing down the details of the service in the register with his right hand, his left unfastening the long row of buttons down his cassock.

'Yes, it was, and I'm most grateful to you. There's just one more thing, sir. Can you tell me anything about St Augustine?'

Meiklejohn blinked and looked round. 'St Augustine? Which St Augustine?'

'You tell me.'

'There were two St Augustines. St Augustine of Hippo, who lived about A.D. 400 or thereabouts. He's chiefly famous for his *Confessions* – as you'll know, Inspector. The other one is St Augustine of Canterbury, who lived a couple of hundred years or so later. He's the one who brought Christianity to Britain. I've got several books you could borrow if—'

'Do you know when either of 'em was converted?'

'Converted? Er – no, I'm afraid I don't. In fact I

wasn't aware that there was any such biographical data – certainly not about our own St Augustine anyway. But as I say—'

'Which one of 'em do you celebrate here, sir?' Upon Meiklejohn's answer, as Morse now knew, hung all the law and prophets, and the light-blue eyes that fixed the Vicar were almost hostile in their unblinking anticipation.

'We've never celebrated either of them,' said Meiklejohn simply. 'Perhaps we should. But we can't have an unlimited succession of special days. If we did, none of them would be "special", if you follow me. "When everyone is somebody, then no one's anybody."'

Phew!

After Meiklejohn had left, Morse hurriedly checked the three previous years' entries for September in the register, and almost purred with pleasure. The institution of any celebration to mark the conversion of one or other of the great Augustines had only begun – if it had begun at all – in the September of the previous year. Under the Reverend Lionel Lawson!

As Morse was about to leave the church, he saw that Mrs Walsh-Atkins had finally risen from her knees, and he walked back to help her.

'You're a faithful old soul, aren't you?' he said gently.

'I come to all the services I can, Inspector.'

Morse nodded. 'You know, it's surprising really that you weren't here the night when Mr Josephs was murdered.'

The old lady smiled rather sadly. 'I suppose I must have forgotten to look at the Parish Notes that week.

That's one of the troubles of growing old, I'm afraid – your memory just seems to go.'

Morse escorted her to the door and watched her as she walked away up to the Martyrs' Memorial. Had he wished, he could have told her not to worry too much about forgetting things. At the very least there had been no error of memory on her part over the Parish Notes for the previous September. For in those same notes, the notes which Meiklejohn had just found for him, *there was not a single word about the service at which Josephs would be murdered.*

CHAPTER THIRTY-THREE

LEWIS HAD SPENT a busy morning. He had co-ordinated arrangements with the Coroner's Sergeant for the forthcoming inquests on the Morrises, *père et fils*; he had written a full report on the Shrewsbury trip; and he had just come back from acquainting a rapidly recovering Bell with the latest developments in the case when Morse himself returned from St Frideswide's, looking tense yet elated.

'What time does the *Oxford Mail* go to press, Lewis?'

'First edition about now, I should think.'

'Get me the editor on the blower, will you? Quick! I've got some news for him.'

Morse very hastily scribbled a few notes, and when Lewis handed him the phone he was ready.

'I want this in tonight's *Mail*, is that clear? Absolutely vital. And what's more it's got to go on the front page somewhere. Got your pencil ready? Here goes. Headline: ARREST IMMINENT IN ST FRIDESWIDE'S MURDER HUNT. Got that? Good. Now, here's your copy. Exactly as I tell you. I don't want any sub-editor buggering about with so much as a comma. "The Oxford police today reported that their long investigation into the murder last September of Mr Harry Josephs is now

virtually complete stop The further deaths at St Frideswide's reported in these columns last week are now
known to be connected with the earlier murder comma
and the bodies discovered comma one on the tower
and one in the crypt of the church comma have been
positively identified as those of Mr Paul Morris comma
formerly music-master of the Roger Bacon School
Kidlington comma and of his son Peter Morris comma
former pupil of the same school and a member of the
church choir stop The police confirmed also that a
woman found murdered last week in a nurses' genitive
plural hostel in Shrewsbury was Mrs Brenda Josephs
comma wife of Mr Harry Josephs stop Chief Inspector
Morse capital M-o-r-s-e of the Thames Valley Constabulary told reporters today that public response to earlier
appeals for information had been extremely encouraging comma and that evidence is now almost complete."
No. Change that last bit: "and that only one more key
witness remains to come forward before the evidence is
complete stop In any case an arrest is confidently
expected within the next forty hyphen eight hours
stop" End of copy. You got all that? Front page, mind,
and give it a good big headline – about the same size
type you use when Oxford United win.'

'When did that last happen?' asked the editor.

Morse put down the phone and turned to Lewis.
'And here's a little printing job for you. Get it typed
and stick it on the outside of the south door at St
Frideswide's.'

Lewis looked down at what Morse had written:
'Because of imminent danger from falling masonry

243

immediately above the inside of the porch, this door must on no account be opened until further notice'.

'Come back as soon as you've done that, Lewis. There are a few things I've got to tell you.'

Lewis stood up and tapped the note with his fingers. 'Why don't we just lock the door, sir?'

'Because there's only one lock on it, that's why.'

For once Lewis refused to rise to the bait, put a clean white sheet of paper into the typewriter carriage, and turned the ribbon to 'red'.

The hump-backed surgeon put his head round the door of Bell's office just after 3 p.m., and found Morse and Lewis in earnest conversation.

'Won't interrupt you, Morse. Just thought you ought to know we're not much forrader with that fellow you found up the tower. I dunno as we're ever going to be certain, you know.'

Morse seemed neither surprised nor overmuch interested. 'Perhaps you're getting too old for the job.'

'Not surprising, Morse, old son. We're all ageing at the standard rate of twenty-four hours *per diem*, as you know.'

Before Morse could reply, he was gone, and Lewis felt glad that the interruption was so brief. For once in the case he knew exactly (well, almost exactly) where they were and why they were there.

*

It was just after half past four when one of the paper-boys from the Summertown Newsagents turned into Manning Terrace on his racing-bicycle, the drop handlebars (in one of the stranger perversions of fashion) turned upward. Without dismounting he took a copy of the *Oxford Mail* from the canvas bag thrown over his shoulder, folded it expertly in one hand, rode up to the door of number 7, and stuck it through the letter-box. Four doors in a row next, all on the right-hand side, starting with number 14A, where Ruth Rawlinson was just inserting her Yale key after an afternoon's shopping in Oxford.

She took the paper from the boy, put it under her right arm, and carried the two fully laden shopping bags into the house.

'Is that you, Ruthie dear?'

'Yes, Mother.'

'Is the paper come?'

'Yes, Mother.'

'Bring it with you, dear.'

Ruth put her carrier bags down on the kitchen table, draped her mackintosh over a chair, walked into the lounge, bent down to kiss her mother lightly on the cheek, placed the newspaper on her lap, turned up the gas fire, almost commented on the weather, wondered why she hadn't already gone mad, realized that to-morrow was Wednesday – oh God! How much longer would she be able to stand all this – her mother, and him? Especially *him*. There was little enough she could do about her mother, but she could do something about him. She just wouldn't go – it was as simple as that.

'Ruth! Come and read this!' said her mother.

Ruth read through the front-page article. Oh my God!

The man seated on the deep sofa, its chintz covers designed in the russet-and-white floral pattern, was not surprised by the factual material reported in the front-page article, but he was deeply worried by its implications. He read the article through many, many times and always would his eyes linger on the same lines: 'only one more key witness remains to come forward before evidence is complete. In any case an arrest is confidently expected within the next forty-eight hours.' It was the piece about the 'key witness' which he found the more disturbing. Himself he could look after without help from anyone, but . . . In a flash, as always, the decision was taken. Yes, it had to be tomorrow – tomorrow morning. It *would* be tomorrow morning.

It was not only Ruth Rawlinson, therefore, who had decided to miss the regular Wednesday-evening rendez-vous. Someone else had now made exactly the same decision for her.

CHAPTER THIRTY-FOUR

AT FIVE MINUTES past ten the next morning, Ruth Rawlinson was not so wholly preoccupied with other things that she failed to notice and to admire the baskets of daffodils that bedecked the lamp-standards all the way along St Giles. But, if the morning was bright and sunny, her own mood was full of dark foreboding, for affairs were getting terrifyingly out of hand. Having been informed of the identities of the two bodies found at St Frideswide's, having learned of the death of Brenda Josephs, and knowing in any case far more than the police could know, her thoughts were in constant and grievous agitation. What was to stop her, at this very second, from cycling straight on through Cornmarket and down St Aldates to the Oxford City Police H.Q.? In any case, it was her duty to do so. It had always been her moral duty, but it was something more than that now: it was a personal cry for help as the walls began to close in around her. Five minutes earlier, when she had left Manning Terrace, her firm resolve had been to go to see Morse immediately and tell him the whole tragic tale. But that resolution was now crumbling, and she told herself that she needed a chance to think things out a little more clearly; a chance to brace herself emotionally, before plunging her own life, and thereby her mother's life, too, into utter ruin and desolation. Yes. She needed time – just a little more time. She propped her bicycle against the wall of the south porch, fastened the lock through the rear wheel, and then saw the notice on the door, pinned rather too high and typed in red capitals. Registering no particular surprise, Ruth Rawlinson walked round to the door at the north porch. It was open.

From the sub-manager's office on the top floor of the large store almost opposite, Lewis followed Ruth's progress with his binoculars – just as he had followed the progress of the others who had entered the church since 8.45 a.m., when the door at the north porch had first been unlocked. But they had been few, and his task had been far easier than he could have imagined. A flamboyantly dressed group of what looked from above like American tourists had gone in at 9.10 a.m.: ten of them. And at 9.22 a.m. ten of them had emerged into the sunlight and drifted off towards Radcliffe Square. At 9.35 a.m. a solitary white-haired lady had gone in, and had come out, her morning devotions completed, about ten minutes later. During the same time, a tall, bearded youth, carrying an extraordinarily large transistor radio, had gone in, only to make his exit some twenty seconds later, doubtless (as it appeared to Lewis) having mistaken the place for somewhere else. That was all – until Lewis recognized

Ruth Rawlinson. He'd accepted the offer of a cup of coffee five minutes after she'd gone in, but had kept his binoculars trained on the north entrance, even refusing to turn round to express his thanks. This, if Morse were right (and Lewis thought he was), could be the vital time. Yet half an hour later it hardly seemed as if it were going to be so. There had been no further visitors, if one discounted, that is, an innocent-looking white-haired terrier which had urinated against the west wall.

Some of the daffodils on the sides of the altar steps were now well past their prime, and Ruth picked them out, neatly rearranging the remainder, and mentally deciding to buy some more. She then walked boustrophedon along the pews on either side of the main aisle, replacing on their hooks whatever loose hassocks had been left on the floor, flicking the pew-ledges with a yellow duster, and at the same time collecting a few stray hymn-books and prayer-books. At one point she peered curiously up at the stonework above the south porch, but was unable to identify any visible signs of impending collapse.

Morse watched her with mixed emotions. He watched her large eyes and her full sensitive lips, and he realized once again how attractive she could have been to him. Even her little mannerisms were potentially endearing: the way she would blow a stray wisp of hair away from her face; the way she would stand, her hands on her waist, with something approaching pride on her face after completing one of her humble tasks. And yet, at the same time, he was conscious that she was in far more imminent danger than the masonry above the south porch was ever likely to be. If he was right (which after 10.20 a.m. he was beginning to doubt somewhat), Ruth Rawlinson was not likely to die in her nightdress, but in the very church in which he was now sitting, carefully concealed behind the dull-red curtain of the confessional. His intermittent fears that she would decide to spring-clean his own observation-post had hitherto proved groundless; but now, arms akimbo, she was looking searchingly around her. Did it matter all that much, though, if she did find him? He could explain as best he could – even take her over to the Randolph for a drink, perhaps. Yet he was glad when he heard the tell-tale clatterings and the drumming of cold water into the bottom of the scrubbing-bucket.

Several members of the public had entered the church during this time, and at each clinking of the latch and creaking of the door Morse felt the tension rise within him – only to fall again as the visitors stared rather vacantly around them, fumbled through the church literature, and without exception departed again within ten minutes of their arrival. Lewis had seen them go in; seen them leave, too – the coffee long since cold at his elbow. But Morse's own vigilance was becoming progressively less keen, and he began to feel just a little bored. The only book within arm's reach was a stiff-backed bible, whose pages he now turned desultorily, thinking back as he did so to his youth. Something had gone sadly wrong somewhere with his own spiritual development, for he had almost completely lost his early ebullient faith and he now had to confess that when faced with the overwhelming difficulties of forming any coherent philosophy of life and death he had come to regard the teachings of the Church as so much gobbledegook. He could be wrong, of course. Probably *was* wrong – just as he was probably wrong about this morning. Yet it had seemed such a logical time – certainly the time *he* would have chosen had he found himself in the murderer's shoes.

At some point in his musings, he thought he had heard a twanging metallic noise, but only now did it register fully. Could it have been the north door being locked? If so, it must surely have been locked from the outside. Yes. Blast it! He'd forgotten that notice about the recent vandalism, and someone must have come and locked the place up. But surely that someone would have looked into the church first? There was Ruth in there, for a start, although she probably had a key herself. *Did* she have a set of keys? What about any others who were in the church? If Ruth hadn't got a key, they'd all be shut up in there, wouldn't they?

Morse was only too conscious how woolly and confused his thinking was becoming – when he suddenly froze in his seat. He heard a man's voice, very close to him. It said, 'Hello, Ruth!' That was all. Quite a pleasant voice by the sound of it, but it seemed to turn Morse's blood to ice. Someone must have locked the door all right. *From the inside.*

CHAPTER THIRTY-FIVE

'WHAT ARE YOU doing in here?' she asked sharply. 'I didn't hear you come in.'

'No, you wouldn't would you? I've been here a long time. Up on the tower. It's cold up there; but you get a wonderful view, and I like looking down on things — and people.'

(Oh, Lewis! If only your eyes had not been focused quite so closely on the door!)

'But you must go! You can't stay here! You shouldn't be out at all!'

'You *worry* too much.' He laid a hand on her shoulder as they stood together in the central aisle, and pulled her towards him.

'Don't be silly!' she whispered harshly. 'I've told you – we agreed—'

'The door's locked, my beauty, have no fear. I locked it myself, you see. There's only the two of us here, so why don't we sit down for a little while?'

She pushed his hand from her. 'I've told you. It's got to finish.' Her lips were quivering with emotion, and she was very close to tears. 'I can't take any more of this. I just can't! You've got to go away from here. You've got to!'

'Of course I have. That's exactly what I've come to see you for – can't you understand that? Just sit down, that's all. Not too much to ask, is it, Ruth?' His voice was silkily persuasive.

She sat down and the man sat next to her, no more than ten feet or so from the confessional. (The man's heavy brown shoes, as Morse could now see, were of good quality, but appeared not to have been cleaned for many weeks.) For some time neither of them spoke as the man's left arm rested across the back of the pew, the hand lightly gripping her shoulder. (The finger-nails, as Morse could now see, were clean and well manicured, reminding him of a clergyman's nails.)

'You read the article,' she said flatly. It was not a question.

'We both read the article.'

'You must tell me the truth – I don't care what you say, but you must tell me the truth. Did you – ' (her voice was faltering now) ' – did you have anything to do with all that?'

'Me? You must be joking! You can't honestly believe that – surely you can't, Ruth!' (The man, as Morse could now see, wore a pair of dingy grey flannels, and above them a large khaki-green jumper, with leather shoulder-patches, reaching up to the neck in such a way that it was not clear whether or not he wore a tie.)

Ruth was leaning forward, her elbows on the top edge of the pew in front of her, her head in her hands. From the look of her she might well be praying, and Morse guessed that she probably was. 'You're not telling me the truth. You're *not*. It was *you* who killed them! All of them! I *know* you did.' She was a lost soul now, uncaring in the bitter depths of her misery as she buried her head in her hands. Morse, as he watched her, felt a profound and anguished compassion welling up within him; yet he knew that he must wait. The previous day he had guessed at the truth behind the grim succession of tragedies, and here and now that very same truth was working itself out, not more than a few yards away from him.

The man made no denial of the charges spoken against him, but his right hand seemed to be working round his throat, his face momentarily turned away. (The face, as Morse had already noticed, was that of a man in his late forties – or early fifties perhaps, for both the long, unkempt, blackish hair and the beard which covered his face were heavily streaked with white and grey.)

Here it all was, then – in front of him. It was all so very simple, too – so childishly simple that Morse's mind, as always, had refused to believe it and had insisted instead on trying to find (and, indeed, almost finding) the weirdest, most complex solutions. Why, oh, why, just for once in a while was he not willing to accept and come to terms with the plain, incontrovertible facts of any case – the facts that stared him point-blank in the face and simply shrieked out for a bit of bread-and-butter common sense and application? The man sitting here now, next to Ruth Rawlinson? Well, Morse? Of course it was! It was Lionel Lawson's brother – *Philip Lawson*; the man so despised in the stories of clever detection, the man so despised by Morse himself; the man who committed a not-very-clever crime for the very meanest of rewards; the layabout, the sponger and the parasite, who had bedevilled his long-suffering brother's life from their earliest schooldays together; the cleverer boy, the more popular boy, the favourite – the boy who had grown up without a thread of moral fibre in his being, the boy who had wasted his considerable substance on riotous living, and who had come back to prey once more upon his wretched brother Lionel; come back, with a complete knowledge of his brother's life and his brother's weaknesses; come back with threats of betrayal and public exposure – threats which Lionel had paid off with help and kindness and compassion and, doubtless, with money, too. And then – yes, and then came the time when Lionel himself, for once in his life, had desperately needed the help of his worthless brother, and was more than prepared to pay for it; the time when the two brothers had planned the execution and arranged the subsequent cover-up of Harry Josephs' murder, a murder planned meticulously at the very moment when Paul Morris had just opened the diapason stop on the organ, and was doubtless drowning the church with the last verse of 'Praise to the Holiest in the Height' or something.*fff*.

These were the thoughts that flashed across Morse's mind in that instant, with the multiple murderer sitting there just in front of him, his left arm still resting along the back of the pew, his right hand still fumbling with something round his neck; and Ruth still bending forward in her posture of semi-supplication, still so pathetically vulnerable.

Then, even as he watched, Morse felt his every muscle tense in readiness as the adrenalin coursed through his body. The fingers of the man's left hand were holding the narrower end of a tie; a dark navy-blue tie with broad diagonal scarlet stripes bordered by very much thinner ones of green and yellow; and as Morse watched the scene being enacted immediately before his eyes his mind came to a dead stop in its tracks, seemed to turn a reverse somersault and to land in a state of complete stupefaction.

But the time for thought was past; already the man's left hand had looped the tie round the woman's neck; already the right hand was moving to meet it – and Morse acted. It was ill luck that the low door of the confessional opened inwards, for he had to clamber awkwardly in the narrow space and by the time he was out the element of surprise was gone; and as the tourniquet was already tightening about Ruth's throat she cried a terrible cry.

'Keep your distance!' snarled the man, springing to his feet and dragging Ruth up with him, the tie cutting cruelly into her neck. 'You heard me! Keep it there! Not a step farther or else.'

Morse hardly heard him. He lunged desperately at the pair of them, and Ruth fell heavily in the central aisle as Morse seized the man's right arm and tried with all his considerable strength to twist it behind his back. But with almost ridiculous ease his adversary shook himself clear and stood there, a vicious hatred blazing in his eyes.

'I know you,' said Morse, panting heavily. 'And you know who I am, don't you?'

'Yes, I know you, you bastard!'

'There's no sense in trying anything – I've got my men all round the church—' (the words were coming out in a series of breathless snatches) 'there's no way for you to get out of here – no way at all – now – now please be sensible – I'm going to take you from here – there's nothing to worry about.'

For a while the man stood quite motionless, only his eyes roving about in their sockets as if weighing the situation with a frenetic logicality, as if searching for some desperate remedy. Then something seemed to snap in the man, as if the glaze that suddenly dilated the eyes had effaced the very last vestiges of any rational thought. He turned swiftly, almost athletically, on his heel, and with his descending peal of maniacal laughter echoing under the vaulted roof he ran to the back of the church and disappeared behind the curtains of the vestry.

At that point (as Lewis later protested) Morse could have chosen several more logical courses of action than the one which he in fact pursued. He could have gone to the door at the north porch and signalled Lewis immediately; he could have led Ruth from the church and locked the door behind him, with his quarry cornered and powerless; he could have sent Ruth, if sufficiently recovered, to get help, and himself stayed where he was, performing no more than a watchdog brief until that help arrived. But Morse did none of these things. He felt that strangely compelling and primitive instinct of the hunter for the hunted, and he walked almost boldly to the vestry where in a sudden flurry he flung the curtains aside on their rollers. No one was there. The only other doorway from the vestry led to the tower, and Morse walked across the parquet floor and tried the door. Locked. He took out his keys, selected the right one first time, unlocked the door and, standing cautiously to one side, pulled it open. On the lowest of the circular stone steps, he saw a man's greatcoat, long, shabby and dirty; and, placed neatly on top of it, a pair of dark sunglasses.

CHAPTER THIRTY-SIX

TRACERIES OF BLACKENED cobwebs lined the under-lintels of the stone steps above his head as step by step Morse ascended the circular stairway. He was conscious of no fear: it was as if his paranoiac acrophobia was temporarily suspended, subsumed by the saner, more immediate danger from the man somewhere above him. Up and up he climbed, the door to the bell-chamber just appearing on his right when he heard the voice from high above him.

'Keep going, Mr Morse. Lovely view from the top.'

'I want to talk to you,' shouted Morse. He put his hands out to the walls on either side of him and looked upwards towards the tower. For a second his balance threatened to desert him as he caught sight, through the small low window to his left, of the shoppers walking along Cornmarket, far, far below him. But a raucous laugh from above served only to restore his equilibrium.

'I only want to talk to you,' repeated Morse, and climbed another six steps. 'I only want to *talk* to you. As I told you, my men are outside. Be sensible, man. For Christ's sake, be sensible!'

But there was no reply.

Another window, again to his left, and the angle

down on to the stream of shoppers was now virtually vertical. Strangely, however, Morse realized that he could now look down without that wave of incipient panic. What for the life of him he was unable to do was to look across at the store almost opposite, where he knew that the faithful Lewis would still be watching the door at the north porch with his wonted, unwavering vigilance.

Another six steps. And another six steps.

'The door's open, Mr Morse. Not much farther.' Then again the almost insane laugh, but softer this time – and more menacing.

On the second step from the top of the tower and with the door (as the man had asserted) wide open, Morse stopped.

'Can you hear me?' he asked. He was breathing heavily, and he realized sadly how ill-conditioned he had allowed his body to become.

Again, there was no reply.

'It must have been heavy work carting a body up here.'

'I've always kept fit, Mr Morse.'

'Pity the ladder collapsed, though. You could have hidden 'em both in the crypt then, couldn't you?'

'Well, well! How observant we are!'

'Why did you have to kill the boy?' asked Morse. But if there was a reply a sudden tugging gust of wind cut across the words and whipped them away.

It was clear to Morse that the man was not concealed behind the tower door and after taking one further step he could now see him, standing facing him at the northern wall of the tower, about thirty feet away, on the narrow gully that divided the sides of the tower from the shallow central eminence. With a peculiarly detached inconsequentiality, Morse noticed how very large the weather-vane was, and for a second or two he wondered whether he would soon be waking from a terrifying dream.

'Come down. We can't talk here. Come on.' Morse's tone was gentle and persuasive. He knew the whole truth at last, and his one remaining duty was to get this man down safely. 'Come on. Come down. We can talk then.' Morse climbed the final stop, and felt the wind pulling at his thinning hair.

'We'll talk now, Mr Morse, or we won't talk at all. Do you understand what I mean?' The man hitched himself up and sat on the coping between two of the crenellations, his feet dangling loosely above the tower floor.

'Don't do anything stupid!' shouted Morse, his voice betraying a sudden panic. 'That solves nothing. That's no way out for you. Whatever else you are, you're not a coward.'

The last word seemed to strike a chord which could still vibrate with something of its former attunement, for the man jumped lightly down and his voice was steady now. 'You're right, Mr Morse. Dangerous sitting there like that, especially in the wind.'

'Come on!' Morse's mind was racing now. This was the time when it mattered so desperately that he said and did exactly the right things. He felt sure that there must be some suitable phrases in the psychiatrist's hand-book that would soothe the raging of a maddened

261

lion; but his own brain was quite incapable of formu-
lating any such irenic incantations. 'Come on,' he said
again; then, as a minor variant, 'Come along.' And, in
spite of the bankruptcy of these banal exhortations,
Morse felt that he was adopting the right sort of
approach, for there now seemed some hesitation in the
other's manner, some indication of a slightly saner
attitude.

'Come along,' repeated Morse, and took one slow
step towards the man. Then another step. Then
another. And still the man stood motionless, his back
to the north wall of the tower. Only five or six yards
now separated them, and Morse took yet a further step
towards him. 'Come along.' He held out his hand as if
to lend support to one who has passed the dangers of a
long walk along a tight-rope, and now is only a few feet
from final safety.

With a snarl on his bearded lips, the man launched
himself at Morse and pinned him round the shoulders
with a vicious vice-like power. 'No one's ever called me
a coward,' he hissed. 'No one!'

Morse managed to grab hold of the man's beard
with both hands and to force his head back inch by
inch until they both lost their balance and fell heavily
against the leaded slope of the central roofing. Morse
felt himself pinned beneath the other man's body, his
legs and shoulders utterly powerless. He felt strong
hands at his throat, the thumbs digging deep into the
flesh; and his own hands were now frantically gripping
the man's wrists, temporarily staying the irresistible
thrust, his lips stretched to their widest extremity over

his gritted teeth, his eyes closed with a desperate tight-
ness, as though somehow this might lend him a few
extra seconds of time, an extra ounce of strength. The
blood thudded in his ears like someone pounding
against a heavy door that would admit no entrance, and
from somewhere he heard what sounded like the tinkling crash of a broken milk bottle; and the noise registered coolly and clinically in his brain, as if his mind
was now outside himself, contemplating events with an
objective detachment that was wholly devoid of panic
or fear. He saw the scene with such clearly focused
clarity. He was driving through the night along the fast,
straight, narrow stretch of road from Oxford to Bicester, a long stream of cars coming towards him, ever
coming towards him, their twin headlights staggered
slightly in a continuous double line of yellow circles,
ever approaching – and then flashing past him. And
now there was another vehicle coming straight towards
him, coming on the wrong side of the road, its offside
blinker flashing as it closed upon him. Yet (amazingly!)
his hands remained firm and steady on the driving-
wheel ... Perhaps that was one of death's most
guarded secrets? Perhaps the fear of dying, perhaps
even death itself, was nothing but a great deception
after all ... The headlights turned to spinning yellow
circles in his brain, and then as he opened his eyes he
could see only the dull sky above him. His knees were
drawn up under the man's stomach: but so oppressive
was the weight upon him that he could gain no leverage
at all. If only he could find the strength to co-ordinate
his arms and his knees, there might just be the chance

of unbalancing the man and turning him sideways, and thus for a few seconds relieving the overpowering pressure of the hands at his throat. But his strength was almost gone, and he knew that his body, any second now, would almost gladly capitulate as the aching muscles in his arms screamed out for rest. He was relaxing already, his head resting almost comfortably now against the cold surface of the central roofing. That weather-vane really was enormous! How on earth could anyone have carried such a weight up here, up the circling staircase, up and up and up, with such a great weight upon his shoulder?

The full realization of his situation registered for the last time, and for a few seconds longer his grip on the man's wrists held firm as he dredged up the very last drop of his energy. But he had nothing more to offer. His grip on the steering-wheel slowly relaxed and as he closed his eyes the lights from the oncoming cars were dazzlingly bright. He thought of the final words of Richard Strauss's last song: 'Ist dies etwa der Tod?'

CHAPTER THIRTY-SEVEN

MORSE REALIZED THAT something miraculous had occurred. The body so inexorably pressing down upon him had become, in the self-same moment of time, both heavier and lighter; the grip at his throat both tighter and looser. The man groaned as if in some intolerable agony, and as he did so Morse's knees thrust him away, almost lightly and easily. The man reeled away towards the side of the tower where he frantically reached out to the nearest crenellation to stay himself. But his impetus was too great. The stonework crumbled away as his right hand jarred into it for support; and head first the man plunged over the parapet. Then was to be heard the diminuendo of a terrifying 'Yaooh' as the man's body fell somersaulting to the ground far below, and finally a deadly thump followed by the terrified shrieks of those passing by at the foot of the tower.

Lewis stood there still clutching the top end of a long brass candlestick. 'You all right, sir?'

Morse remained where he was, blissfully breathing in the heady air in mighty gulps. The pain in his arms was like raging toothache, and he spread them out beside him, lying there on the gently sloping roof like a man who is crucified.

'Are you all right?' It was another voice now, a gentler, softer voice, and slim, cool fingers pressed themselves against his wet forehead.

Morse nodded, and looked up at her face. He saw that there was a slight down of very fair hair upon her cheeks and light-brown freckles on either side of her nose. She was kneeling beside him, her large eyes brimming with happy tears. She held his head in her arms and pressed him closely to her for what to Morse seemed many days and many hours.

They said nothing to each other. When they slowly descended from the tower, she leading but only so little a way in front that their hands could remain firmly clasped, they still said nothing. When a few minutes later Lewis saw them they were sitting in the back pew of the Lady Chapel, her tear-stained face resting happily on his shoulder. And still they said nothing.

Lewis had seen the two men on the tower, had almost broken his own neck clambering down the five flights of stairs, had knocked several young ladies out of the way as he had run through the ground-floor cosmetic department, and finally, like some frustrated Fury, had hammered and hammered with his fists against the north door. The woman was still in there, he knew that, but it occurred to him that something might have happened to her; and in desperation he had hurled a large stone through the lowest and most convenient window with the dual purpose of making himself heard and of creating a possible means of entry. And the

266

woman had heard him. The door was unlocked and, grabbing a candlestick from the shrine of the Blessed Virgin, he had taken the tower staircase three steps at a time and once on the roof he had smashed the candlestick with all his force across the middle of the back of Morse's bearded assailant.

Two duty-policemen were already on the scene when Lewis emerged. A ring of people, standing some four or five yards off, surrounded the dead body, and an ambulance, already summoned, was whining its way down St Giles from the Radcliffe Infirmary. Lewis had plucked a cassock from one of the hooks in the vestry, and now draped it over the dead man.

'Do you know who he is?' asked one of the policemen.

'I think so,' said Lewis.

'You all right?' The hump-backed police surgeon was the third person to have asked the same question.

'Fine. Few weeks on the Riviera and I'll be fine. Nothing serious.'

'Huh! That's what they all say. Whenever I ask my patients what their parents died of, they all say the same – "Oh, nothing serious".'

'I'd tell you if I wasn't all right.'

'You know, Morse, don't you, that every single person ever born has at least one serious illness in life – the last one?'

Mm. It was a thought.

Lewis came back into the church: things were almost ready outside. 'You all right, sir?'

'Oh, for Christ's sake!' said Morse.

Ruth Rawlinson still sat on the rear pew of the Lady Chapel, her eyes staring blankly ahead of her – composed, silent and passive.

'I'll see her home,' said Lewis quietly. 'You just—'

But Morse interrupted him. 'She can't go home, I'm afraid. You'll have to take her down to the station.' He breathed heavily and looked away from her. 'She's under arrest, and I want you personally to take her statement.' He turned to Lewis with inexplicable anger in his voice. 'Is that clear? You! Personally!'

Unspeaking and unresisting Ruth was led away to a police car by one of the constables; and after she was gone Morse, Lewis and the police surgeon followed.

The crowd outside, now standing three or four deep around the covered body, watched their emergence with deep interest, as if the principal protagonists in a drama had just walked on to the stage: the hump-backed, rather elderly man, who looked (had he been around in 1555) as if he might have viewed unmoved the sight of Ridley and Latimer as they had burned to death in front of Balliol, only a few hundred yards away; next, the placid-looking, rather thick-set man, who earlier had seemed to be in charge of all the operations but who now appeared to fade a little into the background as if he were in the presence of his superiors; and finally a slimmer, balding, pale-faced man with piercing eyes, in whose sombre mien – if in any of the trio's – lay the look of a natural authority.

They stood there, these three, over the covered body.

'You want to look at him, Morse?' asked the police surgeon.

'I've seen enough of him,' muttered Morse.

'His face is all right – if you're feeling squeamish.'

The surgeon pulled back the top of the cassock from the dead man's face, and Lewis looked down at it with great interest and intensity.

'So that's what he looked like, sir.'

'Pardon?' said Morse.

'Lawson's brother, sir. I was just saying that—'

'That's not Lawson's brother,' said Morse quietly; so quietly in fact that neither of the other men seemed to hear him.

The Book of Ruth

CHAPTER THIRTY-EIGHT

Statement given by Miss Ruth Rawlinson, 14A Manning Terrace, Oxford, dictated by Miss Rawlinson, signed by the same, and witnessed by Sergeant Lewis, Thames Valley Police (C.I.D.)

Perhaps it is easier to start twenty years ago. I was then in the first-year sixth at Oxford High School studying for my A Levels in English and History and Economics. The headmistress came into the class one morning and called me outside. She told me that I must be a brave girl because she had some very sad news for me. My father who worked as a printer with Oxford University Press had suffered a massive coronary thrombosis and had died within an hour of being admitted to the Radcliffe Infirmary. I remember a feeling of numbness more than anything and little real grief. In fact for the next few days I felt almost a sense of pride as the mistresses and the other girls treated me with a kindness I had never really known before. It was just as if I were a heroine who had suffered much misfortune with great fortitude. But that wasn't the case at all really. I didn't dislike my father but we had never been close to each other. A perfunctory kiss when I went up to bed or a pound note sometimes when I'd done well in examinations but he had shown little real interest and no real love. Perhaps it wasn't his fault. My mother had been struck down with multiple sclerosis and although at that time she was still reasonably mobile my father's first and every thought was for her welfare and happiness. He must have loved her very dearly and his death was a terrible blow to her. Almost from that day onwards she seemed to change. It was as if the woman she had been could never come to terms with such bereavement and therefore had to become a different person. Something happened to me too. I suddenly began to lose all pride in my school work and I began to lose all love for my mother. I suspected that she exaggerated her physical handicaps and all the cooking and washing and cleaning and shopping I did for her were accepted with less and less gratitude. I stayed on at school and took my A Levels the next year but I didn't apply for a university place although oddly enough my mother wanted me to. Instead I took a year's course at the Marlborough Secretarial College in the High and soon found that I had a real aptitude for the work. Even before I left the college I had been offered three posts and I finally accepted a very good offer from Oxford University Press as a personal and confidential secretary to a man who had known my father slightly. He was a very kind boss and a very clever man and the five years I spent with him were the happiest of my life. He was a bachelor and a year or so after starting with him he began to ask me out for an occasional meal or a visit to the Playhouse and I accepted. He never tried to take the slightest advantage of me and only when he used to take my arm through his as we walked to the car was there the slightest physical contact between us. Yet I fell in love with him – quite hopelessly as I thought. Then two things happened almost within a few days of each other. My boss asked me if I would marry him and there was a sudden sharp deterioration in my mother's condition. Whether these two things were connected it is impossible for me to say. I had told her about the proposal of marriage and she had told me what she thought about it in typically forthright terms. He was just a dirty old man looking for a bit of regular sex and look at the huge difference in our ages. Ridiculous! I should find myself some nice young man about my own age – that is if I had finally decided to leave her to rot away in some lonely home for chronic invalids. She worked herself up into a most distraught state and I realize that I am perhaps being less than fair in doubting her genuine shock at the news I had brought her. Anyway her G.P. told me that she was very poorly indeed and would have to go into hospital immediately. Then two more things happened almost at once. My mother returned home now needing a great deal of daily attention and I told my boss that I couldn't accept his proposal and that in the circumstances it would be better for me to leave. I remember the look of childlike sadness and disappointment in his eyes. When I left three weeks later he took me out for a marvellous meal at the Elizabeth and he talked quite happily all the evening. When he took me home and we sat in the car trying to say our very awkward farewells I turned to him and kissed him freely and lovingly on the mouth. From that day I grew my own shell round me just as my mother had grown hers. Doubtless I am much more like my mother than I would want to believe. Anyway mother had probably been quite right. When I left work I was twenty-four and my boss was forty-nine. I met him once or twice after that just casually in the street. We asked the usual polite questions and went our ways. He never married. Two years afterwards he died of a brain haemorrhage and I went to his funeral. Looking back on it I feel no deep regrets that we didn't marry but I shall always regret that I never offered to become his mistress. These facts may seem irrelevant but I mention them only in the hope that someone may be able to understand why things began to go wrong and not in order to exonerate myself in any degree for my own part in the terrible business that was to come.

I must now talk about money. With my own quite handsome little salary now cut off, our financial situation had to be considered carefully and my mother thought that my own C-grade pass in A Level Economics was a sure guarantee of prudence and wizardry in monetary matters. Soon therefore I came to have a very full knowledge of all our financial affairs and it wasn't long before my mother gladly handed over all the responsibility to me. There was no problem with the house since my father had taken out a combined mortgage and life-insurance policy on it. It was far too big for the two of us but its market value was now about ten times greater than when my father had bought it twenty-five years earlier and with his death it was ours. At that time too my mother had realizable assets of about £2,000 in various stock-market equities and my own deposit account with Lloyds stood at over £800. In addition my

mother had a small widow's pension accruing from a
policy my father had taken out with the Press and from
this time I also began to claim a dependency allowance
from the Department of Social Security. For the next ten
years or so I took on quite a lot of typing duties at home
– mostly theses for doctorates and manuscripts for
hopeful authors and that sort of thing. So we lived with
a reasonable degree of comfort and security. And then
two years ago came the stock-market slump and I was
persuaded to realize my mother's stock capital for less
than £500. If only I had held on for another six months
all would have been well or at least not half so disastrous
but there were great fears at the time of a complete
collapse in the market. As the shares plummeted even
lower in the weeks that followed it seemed that I had
been wise to act as I had done but the truth was that I
had been badly advised and that I had acted disastrously. I kept all this from my mother as best I could and
this was not difficult. She had no real knowledge about
financial affairs. Whilst my father was alive he had
managed his small resources with a shrewd compe-
tence and would never let my mother worry about such
things or enquire too closely into them. Since his death
the burden of responsibility had fallen on my own
slimmer shoulders and my mother fully expected that all
was still well. I was too ashamed of my own incompet-
ence to let her think otherwise. I decided then (and
remember this was only two years ago) to put all our
remaining assets into my one idea of a sound investment. I've already mentioned that our house was far too
big for the two of us and I had my plans for it. We would

divide the house into two with mother and myself living on tho ground floor and another family on the first floor. My idea was to partition the front hall so that the stairs to the upper floor led directly to a completely self-contained residence. The bathroom and toilet were already on that floor anyway and the only major reconstruction necessary was a kitchen sink upstairs and a small bathroom downstairs with a second front door so that there need be no sharing of keys or door-bells and no postal complications. A friend from St Frideswide's (yes I shall be coming to that soon) drew up some neat little plans for me and after finding out that no planning permission was required I asked for estimates. They all seemed to me surprisingly high but I decided we could just manage the lowest estimate of £1,500. So I went ahead and the work began a few months later with heaps of sand and piles of bricks and builders' planks appearing in the front driveway. Everything was going well until a year last February when my mother received a letter from an old friend of hers who had heard of a marvellous clinic in Switzerland which specialized in the treatment and care of multiple sclerosis. No magical cures were promised but there were glowing reports from satisfied clients and the brochure included with the letter gave full details of the three-week course together with technicolour pictures of the clinic itself overlooking Lake Thun with the snowy summits of the Alps behind and the foothills alive with saxifrage and eidelweiss. The cost was £630 which included the return air fare from Heathrow to Basel and transport to and from the clinic. Never before this time had I fully understood the terrible tyranny of money. If I had it my mother could go. If I didn't she couldn't go. There were no gradations of merit or need. I was rather sceptical about any treatment for my mother's illness but the clinic was obviously a reputable one and I knew that a period abroad would do my mother some good. She had not stirred out of the house for more than eighteen months and often couldn't even be bothered to get out of bed and into her wheelchair. But now for the first time in years she had taken a firm decision herself. She wanted to go and was excited at the prospect. She went. Although I spent the three weeks of her absence working as hard and as long as I could as a temporary typist by day and as a waitress in the evenings I found the time exhilarating and I once more discovered some of the joy of living. But things were not working out at all well. The builders were finding unexpected snags and I received a letter from the head of the firm saying that if the work was to be properly carried out the estimate would have to be increased by £350. My mother's return did nothing to help of course and when it was discovered that the waste pipes on the ground floor would quite definitely have to be replaced I was compelled to ask the builders to lay off work for a few weeks since I was unable to meet the next monthly instalment. By the middle of the summer I was at my wits' end. It was then I went to see the Reverend Lionel Lawson.

CHAPTER THIRTY-NINE

Statement given by Miss Ruth Rawlinson (continued)

The first time I had been in St Frideswide's was as a
girl in the High School choir when we had sung the
Stainer Crucifixion with the Oxford augmented choirs.
Several of us sang there again especially when the choir
was short of sopranos and contraltos for the Palestrina
masses. So I got to know some of the people there and
began to feel quite at home. Soon I became a regular
member of the choir not because I had any deep
conviction about High Anglicanism but because I
enjoyed having a different ambit of action and acquaintances. There was an old woman there who cleaned the
church every morning of the week – a woman so
crippled with arthritis that the carrying of mops and
buckets was in itself a positive affirmation of her faith
and will. I got to know her well and one day I asked her
about herself and she said ever so simply and happily
that she hoped God would one day reward her for what
she was doing but that if He decided she was not
worthy then she still wished to praise and glorify Him
for the blessings he had given her. Instead of feeling
surprised or cynical about this I felt myself most profoundly moved and when she died I vowed that I would
try to take upon myself at least some part of her good
works. And so I found myself scrubbing and polishing

and the rest and discovering just a little bit of the fulfilment in life that the old woman had experienced. In the course of this self-imposed pennance I naturally got to know Lionel Lawson quite well and as I say it was to him that I went for help and advice when I could no longer cope with our financial crisis. I had one of the great surprises of my life when he told me that if all I was worrying about was money I could and should forget my worries immediately. He asked me what I needed and when I told him he sat down at his desk (where I noticed a paper-knife in the form of a crucifix) and wrote out a cheque for £500. It was just like a miracle and when I told him that I had no idea of when I could repay him or how I could thank him enough he just said that he might be in trouble himself one day and if he was he'd like to know that I would try to help him in any way I could. Of course I promised that I would do absolutely anything for him, and I remember clearly how at the time I hoped and prayed that I would one day be able to do some really big favour for him in return. As I was leaving the vicarage that day I saw a man coming out of the kitchen downstairs. For a moment I didn't recognize him although his face looked familiar. He was rather shabbily dressed but he was freshly shaven and his hair had been recently trimmed. I knew that Lionel had a few of the men from the Church Army Hostel to stay with him for a day or two and sometimes he would persuade them to come along to church services. Then I recognized him. He was much the same age and build as Lionel but the last time I'd seen him he'd had a week or so's growth of stubble on his face and his hair had been long and dirty. It was only later that I learned that this man was Lionel's brother Philip.

It was shortly after this time that Harry Josephs came into my life. One way and another tensions were growing between various members of the church at the end of last summer. It was then that I first heard a nasty rumour about Lionel possibly liking the company of choirboys rather more than he should but I couldn't bring myself to believe it. Even now I am quite convinced that if Lionel was in some way homosexually inclined his weakness was a very gentle and a completely passive one. But there was another rumour almost everyone seemed to have heard about to the effect that Paul Morris the church organist was very much too fond of Harry Josephs' wife Brenda who almost always brought Harry to the services. Harry himself had been disqualified from driving for some reason. Brenda was often seen talking to Paul although she herself would rarely stay in the church for a service and one of the women in the congregation told me she had once seen them holding hands. I must admit that although I had no direct evidence to go on I began to suspect more and more that this second rumour might be true. And then I knew it was true because Harry Josephs told me so. The first time he had called at my home there were the three of us because mother happened to be up that day and he was very pleasant and polite and he stayed for about two hours. After that he called quite regularly always in the morning and we took to sitting together in the lounge when mother was in bed. In some ways he reminded me a bit of my old boss because he made no attempt at all to take the slightest advantage of me. Not then anyway. But he couldn't hide the fact that he was a lonely and disappointed man and before long he told me that he knew all about his wife's affair with Paul Morris. At first I think he must have come to see me just to find a little sympathy because he never once asked my opinion of what he should do. But then one day as we walked to the front door he just turned to me and told me that he found me attractive and that he would love to go to bed with me. Of course I felt a little bit flattered and certainly I had no moral scruples about the situation. We had been drinking sherry together and I was feeling rather more vivacious and daring than I normally do. What was I to say? I was still a virgin. I was forty-one. I had turned down the only man I had so far fallen in love with. I knew that life was passing me by and that if I didn't get to know something about sex fairly soon I never would. Not that I said any of this to Harry. In other circumstances I think I would have reminded him that he was married and that I liked and respected his wife too much to think of anything between us. As it was I think I just smiled and told him not to be so silly. He didn't say anything else but he looked so dejected and humiliated as he stood at the front door that I suddenly felt terribly sorry for him. Immediately to our right was the newly installed door to 14B which had just been painted Cambridge blue. I had the key in my pocket and I asked him if he'd like to have a look at the flat. He made love to me on the mattress of the unmade

283

bed in the back room. It wasn't a particularly happy initiation for me but I experienced little regret. In fact I almost felt a sense of satisfaction and for the next few months we made love together once a week. As I became a little more practised in the physical side of it all I found myself enjoying the act of sex itself more and more. But I knew that something was sadly wrong because I felt so shoddy and cheap after it was over and I began to hate myself for wanting sex at all. I tried to stop it but looking back I think my try was half-hearted. The man seemed to have some power over me and I began living more and more on my nerves. I started worrying about my mother finding out although she seemed to suspect nothing. I started worrying about the neighbours too but goodness knows why because the houses on either side of us were multi-occupied with an ever-changing stream of temporary tenants or under-graduates. Above all I was worried about myself. The truth was that I now needed Harry more than he needed me and he knew this. Whatever agonies of self-reproach I suffered after he was gone I knew that I would be thinking all the time about our next meeting. I began to hate him as well as myself. He was like a drug to which I was fast becoming an addict.

It is perhaps important for you to know all this if you are to understand what happened to me later.

CHAPTER FORTY

Statement given by Miss Ruth Rawlinson (continued)

One Wednesday morning in early September my mother had a bad attack and I decided I had to put off my cleaning visit from the Wednesday morning to the Wednesday evening. But I had keys to the church and could get in whenever I wanted to so a break in my regular routine didn't matter. I locked the door behind me (I almost always used the south door because I could leave my bicycle in the porch there) and I was cleaning the confessional when I heard the north door being unlocked. Paul Morris and Lionel Lawson's brother (as I now knew) Philip came in. For some reason I felt frightened and I sat quietly where I was. I couldn't hear anything they said but it was clear to me that Paul was being blackmailed and that he couldn't and wouldn't pay up very much longer. I didn't understand too much of what was going on and I felt confused and worried. I just kept sitting where I was and I'm not sure exactly what happened next. But a few minutes later it was clear to me that Paul must have gone and that Lionel himself had come into the church because I could now hear the two brothers talking to one another. Again I didn't catch too much of what they were saying but the little I managed to pick up hit me like a thunderbolt. They were talking about murdering Harry Josephs. I was so astounded that the scrubbing-brush I was holding fell clattering to the floor – and they found me. Philip Lawson left almost immediately and then Lionel talked to me for a long long time. I am not prepared even now to disclose everything he told me then but the simple fact is that he begged me for my co-operation. He reminded me of course of my earlier promise to him and he offered to write me a cheque for £5,000 immediately (£5,000!) if I would do as he asked. He said that this payment was for me to keep the upstairs flat free so that his brother Philip could live there for what was likely to be no more than a month at the outside. I felt completely dumbfounded and could hardly begin to realize the implications of all this. At home things were going from bad to worse. The £500 loan from Lionel had all gone and although the flat was now virtually ready our own part of the house was living on borrowed time. According to the builders the whole of the ground floor badly needed rewiring and the water tank was corroded and likely to burst any day. To cap it all the gas central-heating had broken down completely only that very week after a few days of fitful functioning. I had not taken into account either the decoration of the con-verted kitchen upstairs and the only estimate I'd had on that was a horrifying £200. Just imagine my feelings then! But there was something else. I should have mentioned it much earlier but since it is the one thing in the whole case which inescapably incriminates me you will perhaps understand my reluctance – my refusal almost – to mention it. Lionel explained to me that I could now discharge my obligation to him and that this would involve me in the telling of one lie. No. Even now I am not being quite truthful. He made me swear on my most solemn honour I would tell this one lie. He emphasized repeatedly that it would only be one lie – it would involve me in nothing more than that and he insisted that it would be perfectly simple for me to carry out. I didn't care! I was desperately glad to be able to help him and I agreed without a second's hesitation. My mind was in a complete whirl as I left the church that evening. Of Harry Josephs I tried not to think at all. I suppose I almost managed to persuade myself that I had misheard the whole thing. But of course I hadn't. I knew that for some reason or other Harry Josephs was going to die and that my own commitment to tell one simple lie was quite certainly going to be associated with that (for me) not unwelcome event. Where did Philip Lawson fit in? I couldn't then be sure but if money was involved with me surely it would be involved with him too. The conviction gradually grew in my mind that Lionel had hired his brother to murder Harry Josephs and if this was the case my own part in the business – my own lie – would have something to do with being with a certain person at a certain time. An alibi. Yes. I began to feel convinced that such was the case – and again I didn't care! During this time I felt no burden of conscience. It was money now that played the tyrant. Sex was no longer the dominating force and even if it had been I had plenty of opportunity. Several times I had met a man in the Randolph cocktail-bar who showed he was obviously attracted towards me. He was a sales consultant for some prestigious firm and I had little doubt that the room he had in the Randolph would leave little to ask for in terms of physical comfort. I suspect he had taken up with another woman but it was me that he really wanted. At this time too I was becoming increasingly mean with money. Now I had far more than ever before in my whole life I found myself not even offering to pay for any drinks and accepting expensive meals and generally being an utterly selfish parasite. I bought no new clothes no perfume no special tit-bits for meals. As I grew mean with money I grew mean in other ways too. The same week I rang Harry Josephs and told him that our weekly date was off because my mother was very ill again. Lying like that was ridiculously easy for me now. Good practice! At home the boiler they said could just about be repaired and so I refused to buy a new one. I regarded the first rewiring estimate as ridiculously high so I got a local odd-job man in to do it for half the price. Not that he made a wonderful success of it. I decided to redecorate the upstairs kitchen myself and I found I thoroughly enjoyed doing it. For years I had put 50p in the collection-plate each Sunday morning. Now I put in 20p. But I still cleaned the church. It was my one pennance and I seemed to take more pride than ever in my self-imposed duties. You will think all of this very strange yet it is exactly how I felt and acted. From the way I have just been talking I am conscious that I have made it sound as if it all took place over a long time. But of course it didn't. It was only just over three weeks until the 26th September.

On that day the five of us met at 7 p.m. at St Frideswide's: Brenda Josephs and Paul Morris and

Lionel Lawson and Philip Lawson and myself. The doors were locked and I received my instructions. The candles were to be lit in the Lady Chapel and prayer books set out as if for thirteen members of a congregation – including the churchwarden's pew! I think that last thing was the worst of all really. Paul was playing something on the organ and he seemed to me to look more strained than any of us. Brenda was standing by the font dressed in a smart two-piece green suit and looking quite expressionless. Lionel was busying himself with what appeared to be the usual preparations for a mass – his face quite normal as far as I could tell. Lionel's brother was just as spruce as when I had last seen him and was sitting in the vestry drinking from a bottle which Lionel had no doubt provided for him. At about 7.15 Lionel asked Brenda and myself to go and stand up at the altar in the Lady Chapel and to stay there until he told us. Almost immediately we heard the key being fitted into the north door and Harry Josephs walked in carrying a fairly large brown-paper parcel under his arm. He looked flushed and excited and it was obvious that he had been drinking quite heavily. He saw the pair of us and nodded – but whether to me or to Brenda I couldn't tell. We sat down on the steps of the altar and I think that both of us were trembling. Then the organ suddenly stopped and Paul came through and pressed his hand lightly on Brenda's shoulder before walking up towards the vestry. For several minutes we could hear the men's mumbled voices and then there was a scuffling of feet followed by a dull low sort of moan. When Lionel fetched us he was dressed in surplice and cope. He was breathing heavily and looked very shaken. He said that when the police came I was to tell them that there had been about a dozen or more in the congregation mostly American visitors and that I had heard Harry cry out for help from the vestry during the playing of the last hymn. Whether Brenda was still with me I can't remember. I just walked slowly down to the vestry in a daze. I could see him clearly. He lay there quite still in his brown suit and the cassock he always wore in church with Lionel Lawson's paper-knife stuck deep in his back.

Of the other deaths in this nightmarish business I know nothing at all. But I am convinced that Lionel himself committed suicide unable to face what he had done. I am only too glad that at least he cannot be accused of the murders of Brenda Josephs and the Morrises. As I now finish this long statement my thoughts are with my mother and I beg of you to look after her for me and to tell her − but I can't think what you can tell her. I suppose it will have to be the truth.

Signed: RUTH RAWLINSON

'Well?'

Morse put down the statement and looked at Lewis with some distaste. He had been away from the station for more than six hours and had left word of his whereabouts to no one. It was now 8 p.m., and he looked tired.

'Whoever typed that isn't very fond of commas, is she?'

'She's a jolly good girl, sir. Wish we had her up at Kidlington.'

'She can't spell "penance".'

'She can take about 130 words a minute, though.'

'Did Miss Rawlinson speak as fast as that?'

'Pretty fast, yes.'

'Strange,' said Morse.

Lewis looked at his chief with an air of weary puzzlement. 'Clears the air a bit, doesn't it, sir?'

'That?' Morse picked up the statement again, separated the last few sheets, tore them across the middle, and deposited them in the wastepaper basket.

'But you can't just tear—'

'What the hell? The factual content of those pages isn't worth a sheet of lavatory paper! If she's decided to persist in her perjury, she'll get twice as long! Surely you can see that, man?'

Lewis saw very little. He'd been pleased with his day's work – still was; but he, too, felt very tired now and shook his head without bitterness. 'I reckon I could do with a bit of rest, sir.'

'Rest? What the hell are you talking about? You save my life for me and all you want to do is indulge in a bit of Egyptian P.T. Rubbish! We're going to celebrate, you and me.'

'I think I'd rather—'

'But don't you want to hear what I've been up to, old friend?' He looked slyly for a minute at Lewis, and then smiled – a smile which but for a slight hint of sadness could have been called wholly triumphant.

The Book of Revelation

CHAPTER FORTY-ONE

THE FRIAR BACON stands a little way back from the A40 Northern Ring Road, its name commemorating the great thirteenth-century scientist and philosopher, and its beer pleasing to the critical palate of Chief Inspector Morse. The sign outside this public house depicts a stout, jolly-looking man in Franciscan habit, pouring out what appears at first glance to be a glass of Guinness, but what on closer scrutiny proves to be a quantity of some chemical liquid being poured from one glass phial to another. Well, that's what Morse said. Inside they ordered beer and sat down. And then Morse spoke as follows.

'There are some extremely odd points in this case, Lewis – or rather there were – each of them in itself suggestive but also puzzling. They puzzled all of us, and perhaps still do to some extent, because by the time we'd finished we'd got no less than five bodies on our hands and we were never in a position to learn what any of the five could have told us. So, if first of all we look for motive, it's likely to be little more than intelligent guesswork, although we've got some little bits of evidence here and there to help us on our way. Let's start with Harry Josephs. He's getting desperately short of money, and what little he manages to get hold of he promptly donates to his bookmaker. Unbeknown to his wife he borrows money from his insurance company against his house – and he's soon through that, too. Then – as I strongly suspect, Lewis – he starts embezzling church funds, of which there are temptingly large sums and to which he has easy access. Then – I'm guessing again – Lionel Lawson must have found out about this; and if he reports the matter we've got the humiliating prospect of a highly respected ex-officer caught pilfering from the till. It would surely be the last straw for a man who's already lost his job and his money, and who's in real danger of losing his wife as well. Then take Lionel Lawson. Rumours are beginning to spread about him – nasty rumours about his relations with the choirboys, and someone soon made him very much aware of them – pretty certainly Paul Morris, whose son Peter was actually in the choir. Again we've got the prospect of public humiliation: a highly respected minister of the C. of E. caught interfering with the choirboys. Then there's Paul Morris himself. He's having what he hopes is a discreet affair with Harry Josephs' wife, but rumours are beginning to spread about that, too, and it's not very long before Harry gets to know what's going on. Next we come to Ruth Rawlinson. She's got her eyes and ears open more than most, and very soon she gets to know a great deal – in fact a great deal more than is good for her. But she's got a good many problems herself, and it's directly because of them that she becomes caught up in the case. Last, there's Lawson's brother, Philip, who as far as I can see only comes permanently on to the Oxford scene last summer. He's been an idle beggar all his life, and he still was then – absolutely on his uppers and looking yet again to his brother for help. Lionel has him to stay at the vicarage, and it isn't long before the old tensions begin to mount again. By the way, Lewis, I'm not making that last bit up, but I'll come back to it later. What have we got then? We've got enough miscellaneous motives here for a multitude of murders. Each of those involved has some cause to fear at least one of the others, and at the same time some hope he might profit from it all. There's enough potential blackmail and hatred to boil up into a very, very ugly situation. The only thing needed to set the whole reaction off is a catalyst, and we know who that catalyst was – the Reverend Lionel Lawson. It's he who's got the one priceless asset in the case – money: about forty thousand pounds of it. What's more, this money means very little to him personally. He's perfectly happy to struggle along on the miserable little stipend he's allowed by the mean-minded Church Commissioners, because whatever weaknesses he may have the love of money is not among 'em. So, he carefully tests the ice, and after a few tentative steps he finds that the ice on the pond is thick enough to hold all of 'em. What does he offer? To his brother Philip – money, and the chance to perpetuate his dissolute life-style for a few more years to come. To Josephs – money, and the chance to clear up his financial affairs and get away to start a new life somewhere else, minus his wife. To Morris – again, doubtless, money, if that's what Morris wanted; but he can also probably ensure that Morris gets Brenda Josephs as well, and the chance for both of 'em to get away and start a new life together, with a healthy bank balance into the bargain. To Ruth Rawlinson – money, and the chance to settle once and for all her chronic anxiety over her domestic problems. So Lionel Lawson sets up his scheme, with the others as his willing accomplices. He fixes up a bogus service to celebrate some non-existent feast – and then the deed is done. The witnesses happily perjure themselves and at the same time vouch for one another's alibis. Lionel is standing at the altar, Paul Morris is playing the organ, Ruth Rawlinson is sitting in the congregation, and Brenda Josephs is across the road at the cinema. If they all stick to their stories, they're all in the clear. All the suspicion, of course, is going to fall on brother Philip; but Lionel has told him – and probably told everyone else – that everything has been most carefully arranged for him: within a few minutes of the murder, he will have caught a train from Oxford station and will be on his way to some pre-arranged hotel booking, with several thousand pounds in his pocket for his troubles. And for all that a little suspicion is a cheap price to pay, wouldn't you say?'

Morse finished his beer and Lewis, who for once had beaten him to it, walked up to the bar. It was quite clear to him, as Morse had said, that there was a whole host of motives in the case interlocking and (if Morse were right) mutually complementary and beneficial. But where did all this *hatred* against Harry Josephs spring from? All right, the lot of them were getting into

298

a terrible mess, but (again, if Morse were right) money seemed to be coping quite adequately with all their problems. And why, oh, why, all this peculiar palaver in the church? It all seemed a ridiculously complicated and quite unnecessary charade. Why not just kill Josephs and dump his body somewhere? Between them that would have been infinitely simpler, surely? And what about the actual murder itself? Morphine poisoning *and* a knife in the back. No. It didn't really add up.

He paid for the beer and walked circumspectly back to their table. He wouldn't be thanked if he slopped as much as a cubic millimetre on to the carpet.

Morse took a mighty swallow from his beer and continued. 'We've now got to ask ourselves the key question: how can we account for enough hatred – on somebody's part – against Harry Josephs? Because unless we can answer that question we're still groping about in the dark. And closely connected with it we've got to ask ourselves why there was all this clumsy kerfuffle at the phoney service, and also why Josephs was killed twice over. Well, let's deal with the last question first. I'm sure you've heard of those firing squads when you get, say, four men with rifles, all quite happy to shoot the poor fellow tied to the post, but three of 'em have blanks up the barrel and only one has a live bullet. The idea is that none of 'em will ever know which one actually fired the fatal shot. Well, I thought that something of the sort may have happened here. There were three of 'em, remember, and let's say none of 'em is too keen on being solely responsible for the killing. Now, if Josephs, as well as being poisoned and stabbed, had also been bashed on the head, I reckon the evidence would have pointed strongly to my being right. But we learned from the post-mortem that there were two causes of death, and not three. Somebody gives Josephs morphine in some red wine; and then somebody, either the same somebody or somebody else, stabs him in the back. Why bother to kill him twice over? Well, it may well be that two of 'em *were* involved in the actual murder; a division of labour could have been agreed for the reason I've just mentioned. But there was a far more important reason than that. Are you ready for a bit of a shock, Lewis?'

'Ready for anything, sir.'

Morse drained his glass. 'By Jove, the beer's good here!'

'It's your turn, sir.'

'Is it?'

The landlord had come through into the lounge-bar, and for a few minutes Lewis could hear him discussing with Morse the crass stupidity of the selectors of the England football team.

'These are on the house,' said Morse, planting the two pints carefully on the Morrells' beer-mats. (For a man proposing to treat his junior officer for services rendered, he seemed to Lewis to be getting away with things extremely lightly.) 'Where was I now? Ah, yes. You didn't ask me where I'd been today, did you? Well, I've been up to Rutland again.'

'Leicestershire, sir.'

Morse appeared not to hear. 'I made one bad blunder in this case, Lewis. Only one. I listened too much to rumour, and rumour's a terrible thing. If I tell everybody that you're having an affair with that comma-less typist of yours, you'd suddenly find yourself trying like hell to prove you weren't – even though there was absolutely no truth in it. Like they say, you throw enough mud and some of it'll stick. Well, I reckon that's what happened with Lionel Lawson. If he was a homo-sexual, he must have been one of the very mildest variety, I think. But once the charge had been sug-gested he found himself in the middle of a good deal of suspicion, and I was one of those prepared to think the worst of him. I even managed to convince myself, without the slightest shred of evidence, that when he was expelled from school it must have been because he was buggering about with some of the younger lads there. But suddenly I began to wonder. What if I'd been quite wrong? What if Lionel Lawson's old headmaster wasn't too unhappy about letting me believe what I did – *because the truth of the matter was far worse?* I thought I knew what this truth was, and I was right. Today I met Meyer again, as well as Lionel's old housemaster. You see, the Lawson brothers were an extremely odd mixture. There was Lionel the elder brother, a hard-working, studious swot, not too gifted academically, struggling along and doing his best, bespectacled even then, lacking in any confidence – in short, Lewis, a bit of a bore all round. And then there was Philip, a clever little beggar, with all the natural gifts any boy could ask for – a fine brain, good at games, popular, good-looking, and yet always idle and selfish. And the parents dote on – guess who? – young, glamour-pants

Philip. It doesn't require much imagination to see the situation from Lionel's point of view, does it? He's jealous of his brother – increasingly and, finally, furiously jealous. From what I've been able to learn there was a young girl mixed up in it all, when Lionel was eighteen and Philip a year or so younger. She wasn't a brilliant looker by all accounts – but she was Lionel's girl. Until, that is, Philip decided to step in; and probably for no other reason than to spite his brother he took her away from him. It was from that point that the whole of the tragedy dates. At home, one weekend, *Lionel Lawson tried to kill his brother.* He tried to use the kitchen-knife, and in fact he wounded him quite seriously – *in the back.* Things were hushed up as far as possible and the police were quite happy to leave the situation in the hands of the school and the parents. Some arrangement was worked out, with both the boys being taken away from the school. No charge was brought, and things, so it seemed, settled down. But the records couldn't be altered, could they, Lewis? The fact was that at the age of eighteen Lionel Lawson had tried unsuccessfully to murder his brother. So if, as I said, we're looking for any festering, insatiable hatred in this case, then we've found it: the hatred that existed between Lionel Lawson and his younger brother.'

It was all very interesting and suggestive, Lewis could see that; but he couldn't really see how it affected many of the problems in the present case. Morse was going on, though, and the shock he'd spoken of was imminent.

'At first I thought that Lionel Lawson had killed

302

Harry Josephs and had then faked his own suicide by dressing up his brother in clerical get-up and chucking him from the top of the tower. What could be neater? All you'd want was someone who would agree to a wrong identification of the body, and such a person was readily available in Paul Morris, a man who would have profited twofold from the murder of Josephs: first, by pocketing a considerable sum of money; and, second, by having Josephs' wife for himself. But you made the point to me yourself, Lewis, and you were absolutely right: it's one helluva job to dress up a dead man in someone else's clothes. But it's not an *impossible* job, is it? Not if you're all prepared for the difficulties and if you've got plenty of time. But in this particular instance you were right, I'm convinced of that. It was Lionel Lawson, not his brother Philip, who fell from the tower last October. In his own conscience Lionel must have realized that he'd done something so terrible and so unforgivable that he just couldn't live with it any longer. So he took his spectacles off, put them in their case – and jumped. And while we're on this identification business, Lewis, I must confess I had my fair share of doubts about whether the body we found on the tower really was Paul Morris. If it wasn't, the possibilities were staggeringly interesting. But, although we've no satisfactory identification as yet, you can take my word for it that it *was* Paul Morris. Yes, indeed. And so at long last I began to shelve all these fanciful theories, and I just looked at the simple possibility that all of us had completely ignored from the very beginning. Ruth Rawlinson herself came very near to telling the truth and giving the game away in that ridiculous statement of hers when she said that she was prepared to tell one lie – *one lie.* She told us, as you'll remember, that this lie was about the service in St Frideswide's that never took place, and about her silence in the plotting of Harry Josephs' murder. But listen, Lewis! That wasn't the real lie at all. The real lie was about something else: she lied about the identification of the body lying dead in St Frideswide's vestry that night in September! *That* was her one big lie. Because, you see, the body found murdered that night was not the body of Harry Josephs at all! *It was the body of Lionel Lawson's brother – Philip Lawson.*'

CHAPTER FORTY-TWO

Extract from the transcript of proceedings held on 4 July at Oxford Crown Court against Miss Ruth Isabel Rawlinson on the charges of perjury and conspiracy, Mr Gilbert Marshall, Q.C., prosecuting for the Crown, Mr Anthony Johns, Q.C., acting for the defence.

Marshall: Let us turn, if we can, away from these rather nebulous areas of motive, and come to the events of last September, specifically to the evening of Monday the twenty-sixth of that month. The Court will be glad, I know, to hear your own explanation of the events which took place that unholy night.

Morse: It is my view, sir, that a conspiracy had been formed to murder Mr Philip Lawson, and that this conspiracy involved the Reverend Lionel Lawson, Mr Paul Morris and Mr Harry Josephs. I am quite sure in my own mind that the statement made by the defendant about the events of that evening is substantially correct. Correct, that is, as far as it goes, since I am convinced that Miss Rawlinson was not in a position to know the detailed sequence of events, being neither an active party in, nor an actual witness to, the murder itself.

Marshall: Try to confine yourself to the question, Inspector, will you? It is for the Court to determine the degree of the defendant's involvement in this crime — not for you. Please continue.

Morse: If I were to guess the sequence of events that night, sir, it would have to be something like this. Lionel Lawson was able somehow to persuade his brother Philip that it would be greatly to his advantage to be in the church at a certain time that evening. It would have been no great problem to persuade him to drink a glass of red wine whilst they waited there – wine that had already been doctored with morphine. The fact that the man found dead at the church that night could have died, or certainly would have died, of morphine poisoning was clearly established by the post-mortem findings; but the provenance of the morphine itself was never discovered, in spite of extensive police enquiries. However, there was one of the three men who had earlier had direct and daily access to a complete pharmacopoeia, a man who had worked for eighteen months as a chemist's assistant in Oxford. That man, sir, was Harry Josephs. And it was Josephs who, in my view, not only suggested but actually administered the lethal dose of morphine in the wine.

Marshall: Can you tell us why, if the man was already dead, it was necessary to stab him into the bargain?

Morse: I don't think he was already dead, sir, although I agree he would have been unconscious fairly soon after drinking the wine. Whatever happened, though, he had to be dead when the police arrived, because there might always be the outside chance of his recovering and telling the police what he knew. Hence the knife. And so if I may say so, sir, the key question is not why he was stabbed in the back – but why he was given morphine. And in my considered view the reason was this: it was absolutely vital from Lionel Lawson's point of view that his brother's clothes should be changed, and you can't stab a man in the back and then change his clothes without removing the knife and stabbing him again. By arrangement, Josephs had changed from the brown suit which by all accounts he always wore and brought it with him to the church that night. Without any doubt, I should think, the suit was wrapped up in the brown-paper parcel which Miss Rawlinson mentions in her statement. The police would obviously examine the dead man's clothes in the minutest detail, and an actual change of clothes would be the one certain way of making the deception appear absolutely authentic. And so, when Philip Lawson had slumped unconscious in the vestry, his own clothes were removed and Josephs' clothes put on him – a difficult and lengthy job, I should imagine, but there were three of them to do it and time was very much on their side. Then they dressed him in Josephs' cassock and the moment of truth had now arrived for Lionel Lawson. I suspect that he asked the other two to leave him, and then he completed a task which he had attempted once before and in which he had failed so disastrously. He looked down on the brother he had hated for so long, and he stabbed him in the back with his paper-knife. As I say, I don't myself think that Philip Lawson was dead at that point, and the defendant's statement tends to confirm this view, since what she heard must almost certainly have been the dying man's final groans. The police were summoned immediately, the body wrongly identified, both by the defendant and by Paul Morris, and I think you know the rest, sir.

Marshall: Doesn't all this seem to you an extraordinarily complicated business, Inspector? To me, at least, it seems quite ludicrously so. Why didn't the Reverend Lionel Lawson just murder his brother himself?

Judge: It is my duty to remind prosecuting counsel that it is not the Reverend Mr Lawson who is on trial in this court, and it is improper for the witness to answer the question in the form in which it has been phrased.

Marshall: Thank you, m'lord. Will the witness please explain to the Court why, in his view, the Reverend Mr Lawson, supposing him to have been responsible for his brother's death, did not proceed in this matter in a significantly more simple manner?

Morse: In my opinion, sir, two things were absolutely imperative for the Reverend Lawson. First that his brother should die – a matter which, as you suggest, he could perhaps have coped with single-handedly all right if he'd tried. But the second imperative need was far trickier, and one which he could never have coped with by himself, however hard he tried. He had to have someone who was willing to be identified as the dead man and who was also prepared to disappear immediately from the Oxford scene. Let me explain, sir, why I think this was so. Philip Lawson had let it be known to several people, including the defendant, for example, that he was Lionel Lawson's brother. So if he had been murdered and identified as the man who had often been seen at the vicarage, in the church, and so on, it would only have been a matter of time before the police discovered his true identity. And once that was known other facts would have been swift to follow. An attempt had already been made upon the man's life once before – with a knife – by his elder brother. Police enquiries would very quickly have been channelled in the right direction and virtually certain suspicion would have centred on the Reverend Lawson. As I say, sir, it was absolutely vital not only that Philip Lawson should die but also that he should be wrongly identified. As the Court now knows, he was indeed wrongly identified – as Harry Josephs; and Harry Josephs himself disappeared from the scene, although as it happens he didn't disappear very far. That same night he moved into the upstairs flat at 14B Manning Terrace, and he lived there until he died. He'd taken Philip Lawson's clothes from the church and no doubt the idea was that he should destroy them. But for various reasons Josephs grew restless—

Marshall: Before you go on with your evidence, Inspector, I must ask you if it is your view that the defendant's relations with Mr Josephs had ever been in any way more – shall we say? – more intimate than merely providing him with the daily necessities of living?

Morse: No.

Marshall: You are aware, no doubt, of the evidence before the Court from an earlier witness of several visits by Mr Josephs to Manning Terrace during the course of last summer?

Morse: I am, sir.

COLIN DEXTER

Marshall: And it is your view that these visits were of a purely – er – purely social nature?

Morse: It is, sir.

Marshall: Please continue, Inspector.

Morse: I think the idea must have been for Josephs to stay where he was until the dust had settled and then to get right away from Oxford somewhere. But that again has to be guesswork. What is certain is that he very soon learned that the Reverend Lionel Lawson had committed suicide and—

Marshall: I'm sorry to interrupt you again, but is it your view that in that death, at least, the late Mr Josephs could have had no hand whatsoever?

Morse: It is, sir. News of Lawson's death, as I say, would have been a big shock to Josephs. He must have wondered what on earth had gone wrong. Specifically he must have wondered many times whether Lawson had left a note and, if so, whether the note in any way incriminated himself and the others. Quite apart from that, though, Josephs had been dependent on Lawson. It was Lawson who had arranged his present hide-out and it was Lawson who was arranging his impending departure from Oxford. But now he was on his own, and he must have felt increasingly isolated. But again that's guesswork. What is clear is that he started going out into Oxford during the early winter months. He wore Philip Lawson's old clothes, with the long dirty great-coat buttoned up to the neck; he wore a pair of dark glasses; he grew a beard; and he found that he could merge quite anonymously into the Oxford background. It was about this time, too, I think, that he must have realized that there was now only one other person who knew exactly what had taken place in the vestry that September evening; and that person was Paul Morris, a man who had robbed him of his wife, a man who was probably going to live with her after the end of the school term, and a man who had done very nicely out of the whole thing, without actually doing very much at all himself. It is my own view, by the way, sir, that Paul Morris may not have been quite so eager to get away with Mrs Josephs as he had been. But Josephs himself could have no inkling of that, and his hatred of Morris grew, as did his sense of power and his rediscovered capacity for the sort of action he had once known as a captain in the Royal Marine Commandos. On some pretext or other Josephs was able to arrange a meeting with Paul Morris at St Frideswide's, where he killed him and hid his body – though probably not, at that point, on the roof of the tower. Remember that no keys had been found in the clothing of the man murdered in the vestry; and it is clear that Josephs kept them for himself, and was therefore able to use the church for the murders of Paul Morris and his son Peter. Not only that, though. He was compelled to use the church. He was disqualified from driving, and without a licence, of course, he couldn't even hire a car. If he'd had a car, he would probably have tried to dispose of the bodies elsewhere; but in this respect, at least, he was a victim of circumstance. Later the same day – at tea-time in fact – he also arranged to meet Peter Morris, and there can be little doubt that the young boy was also murdered in St Frideswide's. I'm pretty sure his first idea was to hide both bodies in the crypt, and as soon as it was dark he put the boy in a sack and opened the door at the south porch. Everything must have seemed safe enough and he got to the grilled entrance to the crypt in the south churchyard all right – it's only about fifteen yards or so from the door. But then something happened. As he was carrying the body down, the ladder snapped and Josephs must have had an awkward fall. He decided that he couldn't or daren't repeat the process with a much bigger and heavier body; so he changed his plans and carried Paul Morris' body up to the tower roof.

Marshall: And then he decided to murder his wife?

Morse: Yes, sir. Whether at this point he knew exactly where she was; whether he had actually been in touch with her; whether he was able to find out anything from Paul Morris – I just don't know. But once the bodies – or just one of them – were found, he was going to make absolutely sure that *she* didn't talk, either; and, in any case, with Paul Morris now out of the way, his jealous hatred was directing itself ever more insanely against his wife. For the moment, however, he had a dangerous job on his hands. He had to get to the Morrises' house in Kidlington and try to make everything there look as if they'd both left in a reasonably normal manner. It was no problem getting into the house. No keys were found on either of the Morrises, although each of them must have had a latch-key. Once inside—

Marshall: Yes, yes. Thank you, Inspector. Could you now tell the Court exactly where the defendant fits into your scheme of things?

Morse: I felt reasonably certain, sir, that Miss Rawlinson would be safe only so long as she herself had no knowledge of the identities of the bodies found in St Frideswide's.

Marshall: But as soon as she did – tell me if I am wrong, Inspector – Josephs decided that he would also murder the defendant?

Morse: That is so, sir. As you know, I was an eyewitness to the attempted murder of Miss Rawlinson, and it was only at that point that I was convinced of the true identity of the murderer – when I recognized the tie he tried to strangle her with: the tie of the Royal Marine Commandos.

Marshall: Yes, very interesting, Inspector. But surely the defendant was always just as much of a threat to the murderer as Brenda Josephs was? Don't you think so? And, if she was, why do you think he treated the two women so differently?

Morse: I believe that Josephs had grown to hate his wife, sir. I made the point earlier in my evidence.

Marshall: But he didn't feel the same hatred towards the defendant – is that it?

Morse: I don't know, sir.

Marshall: You still wish to maintain that there was no special relationship between the defendant and Mr Josephs?

Morse: I have nothing to add to my earlier answer, sir.

Marshall: Very well. Go on, Inspector.

Morse: As I say, sir, I felt convinced that Josephs would attempt to kill Miss Rawlinson almost immediately, since it must have been clear to him that things were beginning to move very fast indeed, and since Miss Rawlinson was the only person left, apart from himself, who knew something of the truth – far too much of it, he must have felt. So my colleague, Sergeant Lewis, and myself decided we would try to bring the murderer out into the open. We allowed a slightly inaccurate report on the case to appear prominently in the *Oxford Mail* with the sole purpose of making him suspect that the net was already beginning to close on him. I thought that wherever he was – and remember that I had no idea whatsoever that he was living in the same house as Miss Rawlinson – he was almost certain to use the church once more. He would know exactly the times when Miss Rawlinson would be cleaning there, and he had his plans all ready. In fact, he got to church very early that morning, and managed to ruin the precautions which we had so carefully taken.

Marshall: But fortunately things worked out all right, Inspector.

Morse: I suppose you could say that. Thanks to Sergeant Lewis.

Marshall: I have no more questions.

Johns: I understand, Inspector, that you heard the conversation between my client and Mr Josephs before the attempt to strangle her was made.

Morse: I did.

Johns: In that conversation, did you hear anything which might be considered by the Court to be mitigating evidence in the case against my client?

Morse: Yes. I heard Miss Rawlinson say that she—

Judge: Will the witness please speak up for the Court?

Morse: I heard Miss Rawlinson say that she had decided to go to the police and make a full statement of all she knew.

Johns: Thank you. No further questions.

Judge: You may stand down, Inspector.

CHAPTER FORTY-THREE

'WHAT BEATS ME,' said Bell, 'is how many crooks there are around – in a church, too! I always thought those sort of people walked straight down the middle of the paths of righteousness.'

'Perhaps most of them do,' said Lewis quietly.

They were sitting in Bell's office just after the verdict and sentence had been passed on Miss Ruth Rawlinson. Guilty; eighteen months' imprisonment.

'It still beats me,' said Bell.

Morse was sitting there, too, silently smoking a cigarette. He either smoked addictively or not at all, and had given up the habit for ever on innumerable occasions. He had listened vaguely to the mumbled conversation, and he knew exactly what Bell had meant, but ... His favourite Gibbon quotation flashed across his mind, the one concerning the fifteenth-century Pope John XXIII, which had so impressed him as a boy and which he had committed to memory those many years ago: 'The most scandalous charges were suppressed; the vicar of Christ was only accused of piracy, murder, rape, sodomy, and incest.' It was no new thing to realize that the Christian church had a great deal to answer for, with so much blood on the hands of its temporal administrators, and so much hatred and bitterness in the hearts of its spiritual lords. But behind it all, as Morse knew – and transcending it all – stood the simple, historical unpalatable figure of its founder – an enigma with which Morse's mind had wrestled so earnestly as a youth, and which even now troubled his pervasive scepticism. He remembered his first visit to a service at St Frideswide's, and the woman singing next to him: 'Wash me, and I shall be whiter than snow.' Wonderful possibility! The Almighty, as it were, wiping the slate clean and not just forgiving, but forgetting, too. And it was forgetting that was the really hard thing. Morse could find it even in his own cynical soul to forgive – but not to forget. How could he forget? For a few blissful moments on that day in St Frideswide's he had felt such a precious affinity with a woman as he had felt only once before; but their orbits, his and hers, had crossed too late in the day, and she, like all other lost souls, like the Lawsons and Josephs and Morris, had erred and strayed from the ways of acceptable human behaviour. But how could his mind not be haunted by the revelations she had made? Should he go to see her now, as she had asked? If he *was* to see her, it would have to be very soon.

Dimly and uninterestedly his mind caught up with the conversation once more: 'Doesn't reflect very well on me, does it, Sergeant? I'm in charge of the case for months, and then Morse here comes along and solves it in a fortnight. Made me look a proper Charley, if you ask me.' He shook his head slowly. 'Clever bugger!'

Lewis tried to say something but he couldn't find the right words. Morse, he knew, had the maddeningly brilliant facility for seeing his way through the dark labyrinths of human motive and human behaviour, and he was proud to be associated with him; proud when Morse had mentioned his name in court that day. But such matters weren't Lewis' forte; he knew that, too. And it was almost a relief – after Morse – to get back to his usual pedestrian and perfunctory duties.

Morse heard his own name mentioned again and realized that Bell was talking to him.

'You know, I still don't understand—'

'Nor do I,' interrupted Morse. Throughout the case he had made so many guesses that he could find no mental reserve to fabricate more. The words of St Paul to the Corinthians were writ large in his brain: 'There is a manifestation and there is a mystery'; and he felt sure that whatever might be puzzling Bell was not likely to be one of the greater mysteries of life. Wasn't one of the real mysteries the source of that poison which had slowly but inexorably dripped and dripped into Lionel Lawson's soul? And that was almost as old as the seed of Adam himself, when Cain and Abel had presented their offerings before the Lord . . .

'Pardon?'

'I said the pubs'll soon be open, sir.'

'Not tonight for me, Lewis. I – er – I don't feel much like it.'

He got up and walked out of the office without a further word, Lewis staring after him in some bewilderment.

'Odd bugger!' said Bell; and for the second time

within a few minutes Lewis felt he had to agree with him.

Obviously Ruth had been crying, but she was now recovered, her voice dull and resigned. 'I just wanted to thank you, Inspector, that's all. You've been – you've been so kind to me, and – and I think if anyone could ever understand me it might have been you.'

'Perhaps so,' said Morse. It was not one of his more memorable utterances.

'And then—' She sighed deeply and a film of tears enveloped her lovely eyes. 'I just wanted to say that when you asked me out that time – do you remember? – and when I said – when I—' Her face betrayed her feelings completely now, and Morse nodded and looked away.

'Don't worry about it. I know what you're going to say. It's all right. I understand.'

She forced herself to speak through her tears. 'But I *want* to say it to you, Inspector. I want you to know that—' Again, she was unable to go on; and Morse touched her shoulder lightly, just as Paul Morris had touched Brenda Josephs lightly on the shoulder on the night of Philip Lawson's murder. Then he got up and made his way quickly out along the corridor. Yes, he understood – and he forgave her, too. But, unlike the Almighty, he was unable to forget.

*

319

Mrs Emily Walsh-Atkins had been called upon to identify the battered corpse of Harry Josephs. (It was Morse's idea.) She had done so willingly, of course. What an exciting time this last year had been! And the goldfish flashed its tail almost merrily in her mind as she recalled her own part in the tragic events which had centred upon her chosen church. Her name had appeared once more in the *Oxford Mail* – in the *Oxford Times*, too – and she had cut out the paragraphs carefully, just as Ruth Rawlinson before her, and kept them in her handbag with the others. One Sunday morning during the hot summer which followed these events, she prayed earnestly for forgiveness for her sins of pride, and the Reverend Keith Meiklejohn, standing benignly beside the north porch, was kept waiting even longer than usual until she finally emerged into the bright sunshine.

Mrs Alice Rawlinson had been taken to the Old People's Home in Cowley immediately after her daughter's arrest. When Ruth was freed, after serving only eleven of her eighteen months' sentence, the old lady returned to 14A Manning Terrace, still going strong and looking good for several years to come. As she was helped into the ambulance on her way home, one of the young housemen was heard to murmur that anyone who predicted how long a patient had got to live was nothing but a bloody fool.

*

A few books had been found in Harry Josephs' upstairs flat at 14B Manning Terrace; and after the case was over these had been given to Oxfam, and were slowly sold, at ridiculously low prices, at the second-hand charity bookshop in north Oxford. A seventeen-year-old boy (by some curious coincidence, a boy named Peter Morris) bought one of them for five pence in the early summer. He had always been interested in crime, and the large, fat, glossy volume entitled *Murder Ink* had immediately attracted his attention. That same night whilst browsing through the assorted articles, he came to a piece about suicides on page 349, heavily underlined in red biro: *Myopic jumpers invariably remove their eyeglasses and put them in a pocket before jumping.*

CHAPTER FORTY-FOUR

MORSE TOOK HIS holidays later the following year and decided, again, to go to the Greek islands. Yet somehow his passport remained unrenewed in its drawer, and one sunny morning in mid-June the chief inspector caught a bus down from north Oxford into the city. For an hour he wandered contentedly around the Ashmolean where amongst other delights he stood for many minutes in front of the Giorgione and the Tiepolo. Just before midday he walked across to the cocktail-bar at the Randolph and bought a pint of beer, for he would never lend his lips to anything less than that measure. Then another pint. He left at half past twelve, crossed Cornmarket, and walked into St Frideswide's. The north door creaked no longer, but inside the only sign of life was the flickering candles that burned around the statue of the Virgin. The woman he was seeking was not there. As once before, he decided to walk up to north Oxford, although this time he witnessed no accident at the Marston Ferry crossroads. Reaching the Summertown shops, he called into the Dew Drop, drank two further pints of beer, and continued on his way. The carpet-shop, from which Brenda Josephs had once observed her husband, had now been taken over by an insurance firm, but otherwise little seemed to have changed. When he came to Manning Terrace, Morse turned into it, paused at one point for a second or two, and then continued along it. At number 14A he stopped, knocked briskly on the door, and stood there waiting.

'You!'

'I heard you'd come home.'

'Well! Come in! Come in! You're the first visitor I've had.'

'No, I won't do that. I just called by to tell you that I've been thinking a lot about you since you've been – er – away, and you'd blush if I told you what happened in my dreams.'

'Of course I wouldn't!'

'Don't take any notice of me – I've had too much beer.'

'*Please* come in.'

'Your mother's there.'

'Why don't you take me to bed?'

Her large eyes held his, and in that moment a sparkling mutual joy was born.

'Can I use your "gents"?'

'There's one upstairs – it's a "ladies", too.'

'Upstairs?'

'Just a minute!'

She was back almost immediately with a Yale key labelled 14B in her hand.

'Hadn't you better tell your mother—?'

'I don't think so,' she said, and a slow smile spread across her lips as she closed the door of 14A quietly behind her and inserted the key into 14B.

Morse's eyes followed her slim ankles as she climbed the carpeted stairs ahead of him.

'Bedroom or lounge?'

'Let's go into the lounge a few minutes first,' said Morse.

'There's some whisky here. Do you want a drink?'

'I want you.'

'And you can have me. You know that, don't you?'

Morse took her in his arms as they stood there, and kissed her tenderly on her sweet, full lips. Then, as if the moment were too unbearably blissful to be prolonged, he pressed her body tightly to him and laid his cheek against hers.

'I dreamed about you, too,' she whispered in his ear.

'Did I behave myself?'

'I'm afraid so. But you're not going to behave yourself now, are you?'

'Certainly not.'

'What's your Christian name?' she asked.

'I'll tell you afterwards,' said Morse quietly, as his fingers lingered lightly on the zip at the back of her brightly patterned summer dress.